FOR ALWAYS
and
THE SEARCH FOR LOVE

Claire Lorrimer was born in Sussex, where she also spent her early school years. Her life is mainly centred around her work but her other interests include reading, travel and entertaining. She comes from an artistic family, numbering musicians, writers and painters among them – her mother was the famous romantic novelist Denise Robins.

FOR ALWAYS
and
THE SEARCH
FOR LOVE

Claire Lorrimer

PAN BOOKS

For Always first published 2001 by Severn House Publishers Ltd
The Search For Love first published 2000 by Severn House Publishers Ltd

This omnibus edition published 2002 by Pan Books
an imprint of Pan Macmillan Ltd
Pan Macmillan, 20 New Wharf Road, London N1 9RR
Basingstoke and Oxford
Associated companies throughout the world
www.panmacmillan.com

ISBN 1 405 00442 8

A CIP catalogue record for this book is available from
the British Library.

Printed and bound in Great Britain by
Mackays of Chatham plc, Chatham, Kent

FOR ALWAYS

FOR ALWAYS

One

1954

"You're a lot thinner, Lindsey!" remarked her friend Marie-Louise as she settled herself more comfortably in the armchair beside the fireplace.

"Am I? Yes, I suppose I have lost a bit of weight!"

Lindsey Carter's mind was not on herself. Ever since Marie-Louise had turned up unexpectedly and knocked on her front door ten minutes ago, she had been striving to discover the real reason for her visit. It could have been caused by so many reasons . . . pure friendliness, for she had known Marie-Louise as an intimate friend since they met at school at the age of ten; it could be because Marie-Louise wished to express in person her sympathy at the loss of Lindsey's husband three months ago; or she could have come as a kind of ambassadress for Glynn, her brother.

"I would have come ages ago," Marie-Louise was saying with obvious sincerity, "but your aunt told me you had asked her to let all your friends know that you would prefer to be left alone for a while. You . . . you got my letter, Lindsey?"

Lindsey averted her face; the newly discovered guilt she was feeling she knew must show on her face. Marie-Louise had written a sweet letter, expressing her concern for Lindsey and the boys, telling her not to hesitate to ask if there were any kind of help she could give, offering them a home for a while until she made up her mind what she was going to do. But of course, Lindsey and Marie-Louise both knew

1

that she would not go to Woodley Manor . . . because of Glynn.

Glynn, thirty-four, and five years senior to his sister and Lindsey, had been in love with her since she was seventeen. It had seemed so right then . . . that she should love and be loved by the brother of her dearest friend and constant companion. Glynn had been at Oxford and it had been first love for both of them. There had never been an engagement, but all their friends and both families took it for granted that when Glynn came down and settled in his father's paper firm, he and Lindsey would be married.

It had all been too perfect, Lindsey thought. They were too much the "ideal" couple. Even their looks complemented one another. Glynn, like Marie-Louise, was dark-eyed and had dark curly hair, each having assumed the physical and temperamental characteristics of their Spanish grandmother. Lindsey had auburn hair and green eyes and her temperament was as reserved as Glynn's was the opposite. She was the introvert, he the extrovert. He acted impulsively, Lindsey never without thought and caution. Yet their interests, their ideals, their dreams had been identical. What had gone wrong? What had broken up such a promising affair? Thinking back, Lindsey thought that they had been too much in love, too intense, too demanding. Love such as theirs knew no compromise and they had both been so young. When Lindsey discovered that Glynn had a girlfriend up at Oxford, her pride had been wounded beyond recovery. In her youthful idealism, she had been unable to understand how he could have held another girl in his arms. She had wanted no one near her but Glynn.

Marie-Louise had tried hard to bring them together again. But it had served no purpose. Lindsey had felt she hated Glynn for the hurt he had inflicted on her and she had refused to so much as see him again.

Three years later she had met and married Elvin Carter. She had been twenty, Elvin thirty. She had believed herself in love with him . . . not in the same way she had loved Glynn . . .

2

nothing would ever be the same as that first love; but she had respected and admired him. At thirty he had been very much a man of the world: suave, accomplished, socially immensely popular and very, very sure of himself. It had taken her a little under six months of marriage to discover that she had no love and very little respect for him at all.

Lindsey had never told anyone how she felt . . . not even her understanding aunt. Maybe Mrs Melbourne had guessed, but she had always respected Lindsey's right to keep her innermost feelings to herself, and she had not questioned her. No one but Lindsey knew that she had been contemplating divorce when she discovered Richard was on the way. She had had to decide then whether she wished to leave Elvin and try to bring up the child alone, or make the best of her mistake and stay with her husband.

She had no doubt that she had grounds for divorce. Elvin had what her aunt would have called a "kept woman" . . . an actress of very inferior ability whom he had installed, long before he met Lindsey, in a flat in town. It was typical of Lindsey that she never told Elvin she knew about the other woman in his life until she had made up her mind what she was going to do about it. Elvin had been thoroughly disconcerted and quite weaponless when she told him calmly that she was pregnant, that she knew about the woman he kept in London, and that if he did not wish her to divorce him, he must pay the woman off and give her his word never to see her again.

Elvin had done both. In the following year, Lindsey had busied herself with her new baby son and kept her husband from her room. In fairness to him, she had had to admit that he had kept his word to her, at least as far as she knew, and was the best of husbands and fathers. In fact he was a devoted father and his young son seemed to mean everything in the world to him. Lindsey tried to rediscover her love for him, but either because it had never really existed, or because she could not bring herself to trust any man with her heart again, she had been unable to find anything more than affection for

3

him. Because she felt it her duty, she had let herself become a wife to him in the full sense of the word and Simon was born nine months later. Now her two sons were eight and seven and Elvin was dead.

He had been killed out riding. Messages of sympathy had poured in from all their friends, and each one had left Lindsey with an even deeper feeling of guilt. For everyone had taken it for granted that they were a happily married and devoted couple and that she must be broken-hearted. Instead, she had felt nothing at all . . . not even regret. As the shock wore off, she had even known relief . . . relief that she no longer had to give her body to a man she did not love; that she need no longer pretend to Elvin and to anyone they knew an affection she had long ceased to have. It was because she felt unable to pretend any longer that she had refused to see anyone after the funeral except the lawyers.

Then she had had a further shock. They must have been living up to the limit of Elvin's income. She had never bothered very much about money matters since Elvin had told her there was no need. They owned a large country house, three servants, two cars; Elvin had his hunter and the boys their ponies. Twice a year they went on holiday, once by themselves winter-sporting in Switzerland or Austria, once with the children to Cornwall in the summer. Elvin had given her a generous personal allowance and she had never been in need.

Now she learned that Elvin's capital was exactly two hundred and fifty-two pounds. Apart from this, he had left her only what she would realize from the sale of their possessions. He had not even had a life insurance policy.

Lindsey did not mind for herself. But she had minded terribly for her two little sons. Both were at an expensive prep school in Surrey, which they loved, and both were down for one of the big public schools. She could not bear to relinquish the idea of giving them the education she had planned for them.

In her calm, practical way, she had worked everything out.

For Always

The big house where they had lived for nine years was sold
and realized six thousand pounds. She spent a little of this
money on having the lodge at the drive gates modernized.
It had been the gardener's cottage and had a kitchen, two
tiny bedrooms and one living-room. One of the bedrooms
she had had converted into a bathroom, the other done up as
a ship's cabin for the boys. The living-room she had furnished
cleverly with one or two of the smaller and nicest pieces from
the house, with a divan where she herself would sleep when the
boys were on holiday. The three servants were given notice,
the horses and one of the cars sold. The old Austin she kept
because she knew that if she were to take a job of any kind
she must have transport to her work, and the nearest bus route
or railway station were four miles away.

When the remainder of the furniture was sold, Lindsey found
herself with ten thousand pounds. She immediately took the
money to her bank and opened a special account for the boys'
education. It would cost her about two thousand five hundred
pounds to keep the boys at prep school for another five years,
with at least five hundred pounds for their clothes and extras.
Another five thousand would be needed for their public school.
The two thousand which remained she would need to draw
on until she found work . . . for in the meanwhile she must
keep herself and the boys in the holidays. It was not going to
be easy.

It was her aunt who suggested she should start writing again.
She had had a number of short stories published before she was
married . . . light romantic stories which had sold surprisingly
easily. If she could turn them out in sufficient quantities, or
even attempt a novel, she could begin to make a name for
herself and earn a living. Moreover, she could cram the
maximum amount of work into the term time and leave
herself free for Simon and Richard in the holidays.

Marie-Louise was asking her now about her work.

"Your aunt told me you'd taken up writing again, Lindsey.
How is it going?"

Lindsey put down the coffee she had been making in the kitchen, and told her friend about the literary agent she had found and the few successes she had had with the work she had done so far. Marie-Louise listened sympathetically and before long Lindsey was telling her the true state of her finances. Marie-Louise was shocked. All Lindsey's friends knew she had sold the big house and gone to live in the gardener's cottage, but they had taken it for granted that The Lodge was large and that Lindsey had spent a lot of money "doing it up", and was merely exchanging a large house for a smaller. None had known just how badly off she was, although Marie-Louise had been surprised when Lindsey showed her the extent of her little home.

Impulsively, she said:

"I think you're wonderfully brave, Lindsey. All the same, I wish you'd come to me. You know I'd have lent you something to tide you over. I simply don't understand Elvin . . . I mean, how could he have left so little money? We all thought you were rich folk!"

Lindsey smiled.

"I suppose it was because we lived like 'rich folk' that I find myself in this position now. But don't worry, Marie-Louise. We'll manage."

"Perhaps you won't have to manage for long," Marie-Louise said slowly. "You're still very young, darling, and lovelier than ever. You'll marry again."

Her last remark was a half question. She saw the colour flare into Lindsey's pale cheeks and recede, leaving her whiter than before.

"Never, never!" she said violently.

Misunderstanding, Marie-Louise said gently:

"My dear, I know now it must seem impossible. I know how devoted you were to Elvin. But . . . well, one does somehow get over these things in time . . . and then you'll fall in love with someone else."

"I didn't love Elvin."

It was one of the rare occasions when Lindsey spoke

impulsively. The words seemed to be dragged from deep down within her where they had lain secret for so many years. It was only a little while before she found herself telling Marie-Louise the whole story of her married life.

"So you see, I'll never take another risk," Lindsey ended quietly. "I loved Glynn once . . . and he betrayed that love. Then I thought I loved Elvin, only to find out he was worse! Oh, I know he was a good husband to me later. That's one of the reasons I feel so guilty now. He tried so hard to make me love him . . . and he was very generous to me. Above all, he was a good father to Simon and Richard. But he knew I couldn't love him . . . and we were neither of us happy. I should have tried harder . . . but I never knew—"

"Don't reproach yourself, Lindsey. I'm sure Elvin wasn't unhappy, and you did your best. You forgave him when you could have left him. The trouble with you, my friend, is that you are so much of an idealist. You always expect everything to be perfect. Human beings aren't perfect. I've found that out for myself. And forgive me for saying this, darling, but you are a very hard judge. You know, all those years ago, you condemned Glynn without giving him a chance to explain. You wouldn't even let me explain for him."

"How could you explain?" Lindsey said helplessly. "Glynn couldn't deny it when I asked him to tell me if it were true. I didn't want to hear the details. I don't now."

"Lindsey, Glynn still loves you! He's never married because of you, and he never will."

Lindsey bit her lip.

"Did he ask you to come and tell me that?"

Marie-Louise was too truthful by nature to lie, even for Glynn's sake. She nodded her head.

"He believed, as I did, that you loved Elvin. I think if he had known the truth he would have come himself. But he imagined you would be grieving and all he wanted was for me to tell you that he still cared . . . and always would. Lindsey, he wants to marry you. I know you don't love him, but you

surely have some fondness left for him. He's very well off and
he could give you and the boys a home. He'd make a good
father, too . . . he's always been fond of children. Couldn't
you think about it?"

"I'm sorry!" Lindsey said gently, because, after all, Glynn
was Marie-Louise's brother. "I wouldn't marry anyone for
what they could give me . . . knowing I could give nothing
in return."

"Then you really hate Glynn?"

Lindsey hesitated, seeking in her heart for the truth. She
couldn't deny that when her marriage had first started to go
wrong she had sometimes thought of Glynn . . . sometimes
remembered the sweetness and innocence and wonder of that
first love. But always she remembered his betrayal and she
had hated him even more violently than she had hated Elvin
when she had discovered the same weakness in him. Because
she had never loved Elvin as she had loved Glynn, never given
her heart completely into his keeping as Glynn had once held
it in his hands to do with as he wished, she had not felt the
same depth of pain and disillusion. Even now, nearly twelve
years later, she could feel again the torture of her emotions
when she had told Glynn she never wanted to see him again.
She had nursed her resentment against him; never hating him
more than on those long silent nights when she had lain alone
in her big double bed, Elvin's wife, and longed for Glynn with
all the remembered ardour of their passionate desire for each
other. In her own way, she had been as unfaithful to Elvin in
her mind as he had been to her. She hated Glynn for having
had this power over her and now, when her longing for him
was long since dead, only the hate remained and the feeling
of guilt towards Elvin.

"I never want to see him again, Marie-Louise. I'm sorry . . .
and I'm truly sorry if he still thinks himself in love with me. I
believe that he only thinks it, if he really does, because I threw
him over . . . the only one, probably, who did not succumb to
his charms."

"How bitter you are!" Marie-Louise said thoughtfully. "One wonders why!"

Lindsey swung round, her face tortured.

"It's easy for you, Marie-Louise . . . or should I say difficult for you to understand? You fell in love and married a decent man who loves you. You're still as much in love with him as the day you met him and he with you. How can you understand what it means to have that love trampled on? Can you not imagine your feelings if Mike behaved as Glynn did?"

"My dear, Glynn did next to nothing. If that was all Mike ever did to hurt me, I should forgive him a thousand times over. Loving means forgiving. Glynn only—"

"Please don't let's talk about him," Lindsey broke in. "It's all over and forgotten. There's no use in harping back on what happened; and anyway, it isn't right to be talking like this when it's only a few months since Elvin was killed. I'm not hypocritical enough to pretend about my feelings for him, but I feel I do owe him some respect. He's Simon's and Richard's father, and I'll never forget that. They adored him."

"How are they?" Marie-Louise asked, dropping the subject which seemed so painful to her friend.

Lindsey's face lit up as it always did when she spoke of the children. Marie-Louise was godmother to Simon, and she was nearly as devoted to him as his mother! For a while they talked about the children.

"Won't you come and stay a week with us during the Easter holidays?" Marie-Louise asked. Guessing the reason for Lindsey's hesitation, she added: "Glynn won't be there . . . he's going abroad with some friends. Do come, Lindsey! Mike will enjoy the boys' company, and they can all go riding together."

"The boys don't ride any more," Lindsey said. "I'd rather they didn't have even the odd ride. I explained to them that we couldn't afford it now and that they would have to give up luxuries if they wanted to stay at school. They both chose school without hesitation."

"You mean, you let them choose?" Marie-Louise asked surprised.

Lindsey smiled.

"Yes! They're quite old enough to understand if you explain to them simply. I don't believe children should be treated as shuttlecocks to be batted around at their parents' wishes. They've got minds and brains and a certain amount of intelligence. I showed them on paper how much money we had, roughly what it would cost to keep them at school, how little we would have over for the holidays. I told them the advantages of the school life, more especially as they have no father at home to teach and train them ... how they might benefit later. I dare say there was a lot they didn't understand, but they knew I thought it best and they trust me. So when I left them to decide and told them I would act on their wishes, they talked it over and decided on school."

"Aged eight and seven years!" Marie-Louise gasped.

Lindsey laughed.

"Well, children are very logical. If you'd heard their discussion, you'd understand. It went something like this: Simon, 'I want to go on riding!' Richard, 'Well, there's a swimming-pool at school ... and shooting and boxing and soccer!' 'But we mightn't be able to go to the circus at Christmas.' 'Well, we've seen a circus once.' 'Well, I'd jolly well hate to leave school. And school's longer than holiday time ...' So, you see, they weighed up the advantages quite coolly and made their choice," Lindsey ended.

"Their minds are uncluttered," Marie-Louise said thoughtfully. "I sometimes wish we could all be at school again and able to decide things so easily."

"Yes!" said Lindsey. "So do I!"

When Marie-Louise left late that afternoon, Lindsey went back to her desk and pulled out her typewriter. Because of the wasted day, she was five hundred words behind schedule. But then, the day hadn't really been wasted. She had renewed her friendship with Marie-Louise and it had only now made her realize how lonely and alone she had been in spirit. Maybe this was not such a good thing after all. She could not settle down to work and sat motionless at her desk for a long while, thinking over the day's conversation and remembering . . . remembering . . .

"I will not live in the past!" she said suddenly aloud. "I will live for the future . . . for the boys and for my work. My life will be full and I shall get used to being alone."

Nonetheless, her eyes strayed to the calendar and she saw with relief that it was only two weeks to Easter, when Simon and Richard would be home.

Two

Lindsey sat in the typists' office feeling strangely nervous. She was glad that she had dressed with such care and looked her best because it helped to give her confidence. She had never been in quite this position before . . . a working woman hoping to impress her employer with her capabilities and by doing so get an increase in her pay!

Not that Paris Rogers was an employer exactly. He was her literary agent and she had not as yet met him, although much correspondence had passed between them. She remembered the mixed feelings with which she had opened and read his last letter.

> *Dear Mrs Carter,*
>
> *We are glad to be able to tell you that Merrifield and Co. have accepted your novel* Until the End *and have offered an outright payment of £50. While I think it is better to have royalties, however small, I am afraid I have been unable to secure these for you in the contract they offer on this book. You will appreciate that it is a first novel and under the circumstances, £50 is not unreasonable.*
>
> *I would suggest that you agree to this sum on a "goodwill" basis and let me press for better terms for the next book.*
>
> *Perhaps if you are likely to be in town in the near future, you would drop in to talk this matter over.*
>
> *Yours sincerely,*
>
> *Paris Rogers*

Her first thought had been of pure pleasure. Her very first book was going to be published! It was thrilling and very rewarding after the days and weeks of hard work. But then, as she began to calm down a little, she realized that it was not after all so rewarding. Fifty pounds went nowhere. It was all she was to receive for two months' solid work of eight hours a day! She remembered how her back had ached after hours at her typewriter; how her eyes had become red-rimmed and sore from looking at the small print; how deadly tired and drained she had felt as she neared the last of the eighty thousand words. Then when the last word had been written, she had had to go through it all again making careful corrections; and finally the worst job of all – retype it on good paper with extra care. For all this, she was to receive fifty pounds. Better, surely, to stick to short-story writing. A short story would bring in ten pounds for about four thousand words. If she had spent the time that had been taken to write her novel, writing instead twenty short stories, she would have had two hundred pounds for her trouble.

Feeling that there must be something wrong, Lindsey decided to pay a visit to her agent as he had suggested. Maybe he could advise her. Thrilling as it was to know you were having a first novel published, she could not forget that she was now the breadwinner and her ambitions must always be governed by the amount of money she could make.

So here she was, a little apprehensive and yet at the same time determined to be hard and businesslike so that this Paris Rogers (where had he come by that extraordinary first name?) did not consider her someone to be treated casually.

The young typist who had disappeared to tell Mr Rogers that Mrs Carter wished to see him, reappeared to tell Lindsey she could go into Mr Rogers' office. The girl cast a shy smile at Lindsey, whom she considered to be wonderfully attractive and smart. It was all very well to be young and pretty, thought the girl, who was both. But an older woman in her thirties had something else – something more . . . or this one did. A chic maturity . . . a poise . . . a finished look . . . one of these, or was it all three? There was nothing very unusual about the black suit or the black-and-white silk scarf knotted at her neck, and yet she looked perfectly turned out.

Unaware of the admiration she had evoked, Lindsey followed the girl along a dark passage and then a door opened and she heard a voice say:

"Do come in, Mrs Carter. I've been looking forward to meeting you."

Lindsey was not quite sure what kind of man she had expected her agent to be . . . certainly much older than the man who was offering her a cigarette and telling her to sit down opposite him and make herself comfortable. Certainly not so rugged and, yes, handsome. No one could deny that Paris Rogers was handsome. He looked all wrong behind an office desk. He belonged out of doors, on a horse, with a tennis racket in his hand, or sailing his own yacht! He looked, in short, like one of the many advertisements of sunburnt, healthy sportsmen to be found in glossy magazines. His voice, however, was not quite so easy to place. It had a faint accent . . . almost unnoticeable and yet just sufficient to make a listener wonder if he were English.

Paris Rogers was, in fact, only half English. His mother was French and had met and married his father in France, where he had a publishing firm. Paris had been brought up in the city after which he was named and was bilingual. At the outbreak of war he had left with many other young Frenchmen for England and joined the Commandos. When at last the war was over, he had learned that both his mother and father had been killed by the Germans for harbouring escaped prisoners of war and the publishing firm which was to have been his future no longer existed.

By this time, Paris' love of his second native country had become very real and he had decided to start life again in

England. With another man, he had begun this literary agency and in a very short while had begun to make money and to do very well. He had numerous contacts in France, where he sold foreign rights of the work he handled in England, and enjoyed his occasional trips over there – part business and part pleasure. There was a young French girl of nineteen, the daughter of friends of his parents, whom he was seriously considering marrying. He was not really in love with her, but his French upbringing was such that he was quite in favour of arranged marriages, and Monique Ferreaux was extremely well off. She would bring him a handsome dowry and make him a pretty, charming wife into the bargain.

Now, as he looked into the green eyes of the young woman facing him across his desk, he forgot Monique Ferreaux' very existence. He felt as if he had been hit hard in the midriff. No one had warned him that Mrs Carter, who had written a novel he had not himself troubled to read, was like this! As he spoke calmly and impersonally about the weather and her journey here, he was trying to fathom what made this woman . . . really only a girl still . . . so incredibly and instantly attractive to him. Was it the combination of green eyes and auburn hair? Yet she was not nearly as pretty as other women he had known. The mouth was a trifle too large, the nose a little too long and thin. Yet when she smiled, a little shyly . . . nervous perhaps . . . he knew that she was going to mean something – something very big – in his life.

"Let me see, Mrs Carter!" he said, pulling himself together and glancing down at the carbon copy of his last letter to her. "We sent you the contract for your novel?"

"Yes, I have it here!" Lindsey said, searching in her handbag. "It's really why I came to see you, Mr Rogers. I . . . I'm naturally very pleased that it's going to be published . . . my book . . . and don't think I'm ungrateful for the trouble you may have had to get it accepted. But . . . well, the truth is, I am a little shaken by the terms offered to me . . . I worked so hard . . . it . . . it hardly seems worth all the trouble."

Surreptitiously, the man glanced at the expensive suit and smart little feathered hat . . . the shoes and gloves and bag. As a Frenchman, he knew good clothes when he saw them. Surely she was not in need of money? And yet who could not do with more however well off they were?

"Well, we might be able to do better for your next book," he said, smiling into her eyes. "In fact, I'm sure we shall be able to do so."

Lindsey bit her lip, a little-girl gesture he found charming.

"I'm not sure I shall write another one," she said slowly. "You see, it pays me so much better to write short stories. For the same number of hours' work as I spent on this book, I could have earned two hundred pounds."

He was momentarily a little puzzled. Surely with that soft, dreamy look she could not underneath be hard-boiled and mercenary. It did not fit into the character he read in her face.

As if suddenly aware of his puzzlement, and not wanting him to think her mercenary, she said on impulse:

"I have two young sons, Mr Rogers . . . and as my husband died recently, I have to do everything I can to support them as he . . . he and I had . . . had planned. I need every penny I can make. I really came today to ask your advice about it."

Paris Rogers leant back in his chair and gave himself a few moments to digest this interesting information while he lit a cigarette. So she was a widow . . . with two young sons.

"I see your point, Mrs Carter," he said at last. "As a matter of fact, I still recommend that you continue to write novels. I'll be quite frank with you . . . I haven't as yet read your first one. Until I do, I am not really able to advise you. But if, as I imagine, it is of the light romantic vein, then I am sure it will pay you better to continue writing books rather than stories. You see, as you continue writing, you will become better known, asked for by the libraries, and we can get you a bigger advance. On the next book you will have royalties. Then there are foreign rights to be sold and, if you are lucky, serial rights. In a little while you should be able to make at least five hundred pounds on every book you write."

He spoke so confidently that Lindsey found herself relaxing and giving him an answering smile. She liked him. There was something very attractive about his voice and in the half smile that seemed to haunt his mouth. There was, too, a certain expression in his eyes that confused and yet pleased her. She was not too inexperienced to realize that he found her attractive, and even while his opinion meant nothing to her personally, no woman is averse to being made to feel she is attractive.

"Look, Mrs Carter, it is almost lunch-time. Would you do me the pleasure of lunching with me and we can continue our discussion over some good wine?"

For a moment she hesitated. It was true that she had no plans for lunch . . . that she would enjoy eating out after having cooked so many dull little meals for herself. There was no reason why she should not go . . . no reason why she should not let her agent take her out to lunch if he wished. Yet some inner instinct told her that this was not to be altogether a business lunch.

She shook her shoulders as if to shake off her last doubts and, smiling back at him, thanked him very much.

Paris Rogers did not very often take his authors out to lunch. Sometimes he lunched with a colleague or male author, but for the most part his female novelists bored and irritated him. But when Lindsey Carter accepted his invitation, he felt nothing but triumph and elation. He was not really surprised, for he knew, without undue conceit, that he had never had to exert much effort to get any girl or woman to do as he wished. In fact, he had discovered quite early in life that there was not much fun for him in the opposite sex. They were too ready and willing to come when he called. He enjoyed their company, but to him they were playthings, or pretty decorations; secretly he despised them a little even while they amused him.

This attitude was not really his fault, since women had

always run after him and denied him the excitement and thrill of winning their affections. There was, of course, always the early thrill when he was not quite sure if they would respond . . . just as he had been for a moment uncertain if Lindsey Carter would agree to lunch with him a moment ago. But he knew, too, that it was never very long before he had only to lift his finger to bring them to his feet.

He took Lindsey to a little French restaurant where the furnishings were rather drab and dreary, but where the food was exquisite, and the wine perfect. Like all Frenchmen, he knew exactly how to look after a woman . . . that she liked to have her meal ordered for her on occasions, what might appeal to her palate, and how to make her feel at ease in his company.

Lindsey, at first a little shy and uncertain of herself, thawed out quickly. She was amused by her escort's absorption in his food while he ate and complimented him on his choices. He told her then a little of his upbringing and discovering he was half French explained a lot to Lindsey that had puzzled her and made her feel more at ease.

"I hope you will come to town more often!" the man said as they drank their black coffee. "I'd like to be able to take you out to lunch again."

"I've enjoyed it very much!" Lindsey said truthfully. "But I don't expect I'll be up for quite a while. My children come home from school the day after tomorrow."

He had forgotten the two little boys. He asked her about them, and as she talked of them he knew that here was a really devoted mother . . . one who would always put her children before herself. He knew, too, that he would have to go carefully . . . to make the children like him if he was to have any kind of part in Lindsey's life. And he knew quite definitely that this was what he intended to do. No woman he had ever met had attracted him quite the way Lindsey did. There was some strange combination of childishness and maturity which he found irresistible. She sat opposite him, very much a mature woman of the world, talking intelligently on any subject he brought up, and then, suddenly, she would give that shy smile, or blush a faint pink or twist her hands together unconsciously in her lap just as a little girl might do. He found her utterly charming and had no intention of letting her go out of his life.

"Perhaps, then, we could all have lunch together?" he suggested to her surprise. "Surely you will come to London with your boys for some treat . . . the Zoo, perhaps? I would be glad then to escort you all!"

"That's really very kind of you!" Lindsey said. "I . . . I really don't know what to say. The boys . . . well, they're very young still. They can be good, but they can be the opposite. Maybe you . . ." Her voice trailed away uncertainly.

"But I am extremely fond of children!" Paris said quickly. "Please say that I may meet them?"

Lindsey hesitated. She had told the boys quite clearly that they were to expect no treats this holiday. She could not afford them . . . it was as simple as that. Picnics, swimming in the nearby lake . . . that kind of thing, yes. But trips to London with expensive fares and tickets . . . no!

Almost by telepathy he seemed to guess the reason for her hesitation. He said easily:

"I seldom have the chance to drive my car . . . I have an Aston Martin, you know. I would so much enjoy a drive to the country. Maybe I could run down one weekend and drive you all up to town for the day?"

Lindsey knew the children would be thrilled. She wanted to accept for them and yet, curiously enough, she did not want to accept herself. She could not have said why, for she liked Paris Rogers as far as she knew him and had greatly enjoyed lunching with him.

As she still did not speak, the man said:

"I will give you a ring, if I may, in a few weeks' time? By then the children will be home and you will know better your plans. Would that be all right?"

Lindsey agreed that it would. She could, after all, refuse his invitation far more easily on the telephone! And yet, did she want to refuse? If so, why? Was it that this man seemed a little too sure of himself . . . and of her? This was, supposedly, a business lunch. Taking the boys to the Zoo would be a personal affair. Did she want to make a personal friend of her agent?

Going home in the train, she pondered the question anxiously. Why should she not have friends . . . men friends? Was it wrong because Elvin had died such a short while ago? And yet, she had not loved him and it was hypocritical to pretend that she was still in mourning for him. She had the children to think of. It was not good for them to have only female company all the time.

So she argued with herself, knowing somewhere deep down inside her heart that Paris Rogers was not a man for casual friendships . . . that it could never remain for long a platonic one; that she found him attractive and yet at the same time feared what he could offer her.

"How silly I am being!" she thought. "What have I to be afraid of? If I don't like him, I can always refuse to see him."

The difficulty was, of course, that he was her agent. It was wrong to mix business with pleasure. Suppose she did refuse this invitation? Would it affect his efforts to do his best for her as an agent? But no! That would hardly be fair and he had seemed a straightforward enough character. In any case, if the worst happened, she could always find another agent. She was free . . . free to do as she wished. If she could only be sure what it was she did wish.

Then she forgot him as her thoughts turned to the children, and she remembered with a warm heart that she would have them back soon.

Three

W hen some two weeks later Paris Rogers telephoned his invitation to her, Lindsey thanked him, but made some excuse. It must have been clear to him that her excuses were not genuine and Lindsey hoped very much that he would let the matter drop. It was not that she had changed her mind about him. In fact for twenty-four hours after her luncheon with him she had realized that she had been very much attracted to him and liked him very much. But then the children came home and she was utterly absorbed in them, and Paris Rogers faded into the background of her mind; only to be recalled once or twice with the thought that it would really be best to keep their acquaintance a purely business one.

When she replaced the receiver, she felt a moment's regret for the finality of her refusal. Perhaps it was stupid of her . . . and then Simon called to her and she forgot Paris again. She had no time for work . . . for her writing. Each morning was filled with the domestic duties she now had to fulfil herself . . . bed-making, breakfast, housework, shopping, lunch, all to be done as speedily as possible so that she would have the afternoon quite free for the children. Fortunately, the days were warm and sunny and they were all surprisingly happy. In the evenings she washed and ironed after the boys were in bed and soon afterwards, exhausted, she, too, would go to bed in the sitting-room and sleep soundly and dreamlessly.

Lindsey was surprised at her own feelings of contentment. She had been so afraid that the boys would miss their old home, their father, their ponies, the outings. Instead, they made no mention of their previous holidays, nor of their father, and accepted each day on its merits, enjoying the small chores she allotted to them and delighted with their tiny "cabin" room and the simple, isolated life they led. A new intimacy had grown between the three of them and Lindsey realized that she had never really made companions of her two young sons before. They had been her children, she their mother. Now they were all three the best of friends.

She was only occasionally a little worried . . . and then about money. The account came in for the autumn term and she saw with horror that the fees had gone up . . . only ten pounds a term per boy, but that meant a further twenty pounds she could ill afford and which she could not allow for from her capital. And both the boys had grown . . . inches it seemed, since last term. Simon needed a new coat, Richard football boots; both needed socks, handkerchiefs, underwear, ties. She hoped desperately that a windfall would arrive before the end of the holidays. Maybe Paris Rogers would be able to sell her novel as a serial to one of the women's magazines. He had promised to try while explaining that it was not always easy to break in when you were unknown. Or some foreign rights . . . she wondered fleetingly if he had yet taken time to read the book and decided probably he had. She had not thought it good herself and felt that his failure to write to her about it must mean he held the same opinion!

In fact, Paris had read her book and come to the conclusion that it was no better and no worse than most of that kind of light romantic stuff they handled. He rather doubted his ability to sell either serial or foreign rights. He had, in fact, given a great deal of thought to the question of Lindsey's writing. He knew she needed money and he wanted very much to be able to help her. His interest in her as a person rather than as a writer had doubled since she had refused his second invitation. He had known, as she supposed, that she would find some other excuse if he asked her again, and his vanity was piqued. He had been so sure she *would* come, especially as he had allowed two weeks

22

to elapse before getting in touch with her . . . ample time to let her believe he was not interested.

Paris had little doubt as to the moves in the game played so often between men and women. The rules varied, but the moves all ran to pattern. You met an attractive woman and asked her out . . . aroused her interest and then, when she was reasonably certain you would find some way to see her again, you stayed away. Just when she was on the verge of getting in touch herself, thinking of some excuse for doing so, you made your second move. After that, it was so easy . . . too easy. As to the rules, well, they varied according to the men and women who played the game . . . or did not "play the game", Paris told himself wryly. Some men took any advantage they could . . . just as did some women. Others played along as far as they were welcome . . . and that had been his own rule. He had never forced himself upon any woman. For that matter, he'd never had to. Monique, of course, was a little different. For one thing she was a French girl of good family, and even in these post-war days one did not play that particular game with girls like her. Here the rules were quite different. You courted her family . . . and were content with encouraging smiles from the girl and perhaps, occasionally, a stolen kiss. With Monique, Paris invariably felt himself back in his extreme youth . . . and it irked him a little, even while it had amused him . . . to be behaving like a nineteen-year-old himself . . . he, a man of thirty-five!

Paris Rogers was strangely put out by Lindsey's disinterest. For his part, he had thought of little else but his meeting with her and how soon he could reasonably contrive a second. Now there was to be no second . . . But surely he would not allow himself to give in so easily? There must be a way . . . some way, of seeing her again. Work, perhaps? But what had he to tell her about her book? She had signed the contract at the end of her luncheon; the next stage – proofs to be sent for her correction – would not arise for many months owing to the bottle-neck at most publishers . . .

unless, of course, the book were by Winston Churchill or of that calibre. Lindsey Carter was only a moderately good writer . . . and unknown as yet.

It was then the letter came to his office and only quite by chance that he happened to glance through the firm's reply to it and discover this new way to Lindsey Carter. It was almost time for him to leave the office when his secretary brought in some letters for signature.

"Mr Bates has gone home, Mr Rogers. Could you sign these for him?"

He was scrawling his name to the typed pages without reading them when Lindsey's name stood out suddenly and he lifted the sheet away from the others to read it. It was in answer to a letter from a Miss June Helmer who worked at Merrifield and Co. in the Art department. She had been asked to do a book jacket for *Until the End*, by Lindsey Carter. Could Miss Carter's agent possibly let her know if this could be the pseudonym or married name of Lindsey Herrod, with whom she had been very friendly at school and not seen since?

The reply, written by his partner, Tim Bates, was a masterpiece of tact. Assuming that Mrs Carter might not wish to make contact with this erstwhile school friend . . . supposing that Mrs Carter had been Miss Herrod . . . he wrote:

I am today forwarding your letter to Mrs Lindsey
Carter who, I have no doubt, will get in touch with you
if, as you believe, she is an old friend of yours . . .

"Is the enclosure there for Mrs Carter's letter?" Paris asked the secretary, who was watching him curiously.

She nodded and, leafing through the letters he had already signed, she handed it to him.

Paris read it briefly, and then said:

"I'll have a word with Mr Bates tomorrow about both these

24

letters. Meanwhile, you can get these others posted. This is not urgent, so it won't matter."

The secretary left without hesitating, for Mr Rogers was the senior partner and could hold up Mr Bates' letters if he chose. She was anxious only to be off before the worst of the rush hour.

Paris sat down at his desk and thought. He could rewrite Tim's letter and sign it himself with some personal remark added to it. But she could ignore his remark if she wished, and he somehow felt she would. Her reply could be:

> *Dear Mr Rogers,*
> *Thank you for your letter. I am getting in touch with Miss Helmer who is, in fact, an old friend of mine.*

or alternatively:

> *I have not written to Miss Helmer, but perhaps you would let her know that I was not at school with her.*

In either event, he would be no nearer seeing her.

He could, of course, find some way of making friends with the unknown quantity, Miss June Helmer. Having done so, he could then write to Lindsey saying he had met an old friend of hers who wished very much to see her again. Could they make up a foursome and dine together one evening? This had distinct possibilities but it meant getting to know Miss Helmer, who might in turn not be an old school chum of Lindsey's.

Paris shrugged his shoulders. His own uncertain feelings surprised him. Why bother at all? Why was it so important that he should see Lindsey again . . . and soon? What was she to him . . . just another attractive woman? Why didn't he ring up some other girl now and ask her out to dinner and dance somewhere and forget all about those green eyes and that amazing auburn hair; that wide, shy mouth and the soft voice?

"Hell!" he said violently, and standing up too quickly, he spilled a bottle of ink over his desk. He swore again and then, more calmly, he rang the buzzer. One of the typists appeared and mopped up the mess. She was a fuzzy blonde of about seventeen, who adored him. Tonight she did not annoy him quite as much as usual.

"Look, Betty, be a dear and get Merrifields on the phone for me . . . see if you can contact a Miss Helmer, will you? Art department."

A few minutes later he was speaking to Miss Helmer and, as he had hoped, persuaded her, by nothing more than his charming voice, to look in on her way home to discuss the question of Miss Carter's identity.

The office was empty but for himself when June Helmer arrived . . . a pretty enough, fair girl – a little plump, perhaps, but pleasant. Oddly enough, as he summed her up, Paris thought it quite possible that she and Lindsey could have been friends. They discussed the matter for a few moments and then Paris said casually:

"My word, I'd no idea it was so late. How about coming round to my Club with me for a drink? We could finish this discussion much more easily and more comfortably there."

She knew, of course, that it wasn't necessary but, like practically every other woman he knew, she was sufficiently attracted by him to accept his invitation. She had passed thirty and was still unmarried – her Australian fiancé having been killed in the war, as she told him later over dinner.

Now she was quite resigned to a career instead of marriage. Paris laughed at the suggestion, but was not sure that she wasn't right . . . unless she got out of the habit of thinking that way, he told her. Men didn't marry career girls . . . at least, unless they couldn't help it! (Had he been thinking of Lindsey?)

"Oh, nonsense!" June Helmer laughed. "Nowadays most

men are jolly glad to have a helping hand with the family exchequer!"

Paris said suddenly:

"Do you really think Mrs Carter is your school friend?"

"Yes, I'm almost sure," June said, recovering her surprise. "I'm almost certain I saw the announcement of her marriage in the paper years ago, to a man called Carter. I remember it because there was another girl at school we both knew with that surname and I wondered if it were a relative . . . brother or something. I often wondered what happened to Lindsey. She was such a sweet girl, with dreamy eyes and slightly reddish hair."

Paris drew in his breath sharply.

"That does sound like . . . like Mrs Carter!" He realized how quickly and unjustifiably he had come to think of her as Lindsey!

"Hopelessly idealistic. We none of us thought she'd ever meet anyone who came up to scratch!" June said reminiscently. "There was another friend we had . . . Marie-Louise someone or other. We all used to go around together and swore eternal vows of friendship! And we meant it at the time, too."

"And still do mean it!" Paris encouraged. "After all, that's really why you are here, isn't it, to find her again? I think she is almost certainly your friend. I'll give her a ring and tell her I've met you, and if she is the one, we'll arrange a grand reunion."

Paris lost no time in carrying out his promise. At ten thirty the next morning, he put through a call to Lindsey. She sounded surprised and a little breathless when he gave his name.

"Just a minute . . . I'll turn off the washing machine . . . Simon, do be quiet, darling . . ." ——

Then a child's voice said:

"Ho ho ho and a bottle of rum . . ." but before it could complete the doggerel, he heard her voice again saying:

"Richard, put that phone down!" There was a sharp click and Paris knew he had been cut off. Grinning, he put the call through again and this time she was very apologetic.

"I'm frightfully sorry!" she said. "Richard took me literally!"

27

"So I gathered. Look, Mrs Carter, I've just run into someone I think is an old friend of yours. I didn't give her your home address in case you didn't wish to be bothered by her. Her name is June Helmer."

"June Helmer . . . June! Why, of course I know her, though I haven't seen her for years and years!" Her voice was young and enthusiastic. "Do please tell me where to get hold of her."

He didn't want to do quite that. He said quickly:

"She was almost certain it was you and we thought . . . at least, the idea was that if you were doing nothing much tomorrow, I'd run her down to your cottage. It's Saturday, so she won't be working."

During the ensuing silence, he felt his heart thumping in his chest and knew himself for a complete fool. If not a fool, then for a man in love . . . and surely the two were the same? To let so much personal feeling hang on her reply . . .

"Why, yes! I . . . I think that would be all right. It . . . wouldn't it be a bit . . . well, dull for you? We're sure to be gossiping like a couple of . . . of long-lost friends!" She laughed awkwardly. He knew that she would prefer him not to be going, too, but he would not allow her to escape now. He said:

"Oh, I'll keep busy minding the children while you talk . . . that is, if you really think you can put up with us?"

As quickly as he could, he put a call through to June Helmer's department, thanking himself for having had the presence of mind to get her telephone extension last night.

"Miss Helmer, I've just been speaking to Lindsey Carter on the phone . . . she is your friend and she's very anxious indeed to see you again. She doesn't come up to town much because of her two small boys and I offered to drive you down tomorrow when I go!"

"Why, that's awfully kind of you!" June said. "As a matter of fact, I had arranged to go home this weekend . . . to my people in Torquay, but I could postpone it till next weekend. Yes, I'll do that . . . thanks again, Mr Rogers!"

So far so good! thought Paris. The next step was to get to know Miss Helmer sufficiently well to be calling her June by the time they arrived at Lindsey's cottage. He had let both girls believe he was more friendly than he was with the other.

For the rest of the day he felt triumphant that his plans had succeeded, but by evening he had begun to lose a little of his customary self-confidence. He began to question himself again as to why he was going to this extraordinary amount of trouble to see a girl . . . a woman . . . who had little if any interest in him. No doubt tomorrow she would ignore him completely and he would have wasted his day!

Fool! he told himself again, and then, suddenly calm and oddly satisfied, he relaxed and said quietly, "No, not a fool . . . just desperately in love . . . for the first time in my life!"

The thought sobered him. He knew himself to be frightened by the peculiar way he was behaving . . . peculiar compared with his normal standards . . . that he, Paris Rogers, should actually have to go to such lengths to see an attractive woman! Lindsey would be flattered if she knew the truth.

As it happened, she suspected him of using June Helmer as an excuse to see her again and far from being flattered was merely perturbed. In a moment of complete honesty, she knew that her relationship with this man could never be calm, steady, mediocre. He was not made of that kind of material . . . and she correctly sensed his strange power over women. She was equally determined that he should not have a chance to wield any power over her; she had neither the time nor the desire for an emotional upheaval in her life. That, she told herself, was finished for ever, for always. Glynn, the young lover; Elvin, the husband . . . two men in her life and she wished no more. Now she was mother and breadwinner, and the sooner Paris Rogers understood it, the better.

So she told herself, and was more than a little annoyed to find that the following morning, against every conscious effort, she was listening for the sound of a car.

June Helmer liked Paris. She had decided this in the hour's

29

Claire Lorrimer
drive into the country during which time he had been a lively
and entertaining companion. There was no denying she found
him extremely attractive, but then, she told herself, so would
any woman. He had so much about him to charm . . . and he
knew so well how to do so! Yet even while she realized that
he was trying to make her like him, she could not feel annoyed,
for she had no delusions that he was interested in *her*. It was
quite obvious that he was desperately keen on Lindsey!

She managed to get some enlightenment on the years that
had passed since she last saw Lindsey, learned that she was
widowed only a few months ago and that she had two boys
aged seven and eight. She heard, through Paris' description,
that Lindsey was to him, anyway, a very attractive woman.
She wondered if she, too, would think her so and decided
that probably she would, since Lindsey had been attractive
even as a schoolgirl. She had never seemed to go through
that gawky stage and there had been a kind of mature poise
about her at seventeen which might well have foretold the
present woman of nearly thirty. Paris explained also how he
had met Lindsey and confessed disarmingly that he hoped to
get to know her better . . . and as a friend . . . not merely as
her literary agent.

"Isn't it a mistake to mix business and pleasure?" June
unconsciously echoed Lindsey's sentiments.

Paris laughed . . . a deep-toned masculine sound that fitted
his large well-built frame.

"Well, if it must come eventually to a choice between the
two I will willingly resign as her agent. I don't think that
I should be very much the loser. Lindsey as a writer has
imagination and originality, but not great talent. Her work
will sell on a small but steady level, and I would not expect
to make very much money either for or from her. I don't of
course say this to her, for she is at the start of her career and
I understand it is very important to her."

"Naturally!" June agreed, thinking in terms of prestige rather
than finance. "I started to read the manuscript last night. It is

30

at present in my keeping, since I'm to do the jacket for it. Frankly, I agree with your summing up, although I speak of course only as one of her possible public . . . without your specific knowledge. Of course, she may improve and write a phenomenal bestseller!"

Paris did not think so, but he forbore to say so. He changed the subject and asked June to tell him more about herself.

"Oh, my life has been very dull!" she said with a sigh. "I was in the Wrens during the war and those years were definitely the most exciting of my life. I loved my work and . . . and for a time I was very happy. Then my fiancé was killed and life seemed pretty grim for a while. One gets over such things . . . at least, up to a point. I've never wished to marry anyone else and I don't think I ever will."

"Then you believe that the big . . . the one true love . . . happens only once in a lifetime?" Paris asked curiously.

June was silent for a moment. Then she said:

"Yes, I think I do. Maybe for some people it is otherwise . . . I don't know. But I think for everyone there is one person . . . one before all others . . . and if you have the misfortune to lose them . . . then they seem irreplaceable. Anything else is second best. I suppose if you are an idealist, as I am, you consider that second best is no good."

"I am not an idealist!" Paris said. "Yet I think I subscribe to your views. I have seen too much of life . . . and with present company excluded, of course, of your sex . . . to be left with many illusions or ideals. I think I am foremost a realist."

"But not entirely, since you believe there is such a thing at all as 'love'," June remarked astutely. "If you were truly disillusioned, you would be telling me that there is only attraction, emotion, biological responses . . . which give a temporary impression of love."

"We are getting very profound for eleven in the morning!" Paris said, laughing again. "I think you and I will be very good friends. Just occasionally I think this is possible between men and women, don't you?"

31

"Yes, I think so . . . sometimes!" June said, smiling. She herself had many men friends, but she could believe that Paris did not often keep women as friends . . . they would want to mean something different to him before long.

June Helmer, sensible, ordinary girl that she was, neither outstandingly pretty nor plain, neither very clever nor stupid, with no particular vices or talents, was nonetheless an extremely likable person. She was popular, too, with both sexes and had many invitations to a variety of different entertainments. Her very averageness made her adaptable and a good mixer and she had, consequently, seen quite a bit of life . . . mostly other people's experience of it . . . during her thirty years. She knew quite a lot, therefore, about people and Paris presented no great problem to her. He fitted into her category of "charming cad" . . . by which she meant the type of man who took everything his good looks, or money, or both, offered him and gave very little back in the way of real affection, loyalty or friendship. That he was thoroughly spoilt, and probably always had been, she had no doubt. Only one thing puzzled her with a faint nagging bewilderment . . . that she should like him . . . feel a kind of inner sympathy towards him . . . whereas in the past she had always disliked this particular type of male.

Then she laughed at her own thoughts, for she knew so little of this man, met only the day before yesterday, that she felt herself being unfair in summing him up so quickly and pushing him into one of her "categories for people". No doubt Lindsey would explain him in due course and tell her what he meant in her life. With a man like Paris, June could not believe that he could mean nothing. Apart from people like herself who were more or less immune, women must always either love or hate him. Which did Lindsey do? She wondered and wondered again if she and her once well-loved school friend could find a way to renew their confidence in each other after all these years.

Four

For Lindsey, the day did not start well. The morning post, always late, had brought a letter from Glynn. Busy as she was trying to get the cottage tidy and a cold lunch prepared before Paris Rogers and June Helmer arrived, she could not prevent herself stopping to open and read it. The handwriting, remembered after all these years, had given her heart a nasty jolt.

Dearest Lindsey,

Marie Louise has told me that a letter from me would not be welcome and that you still prefer not to see me again. Yet I must write. Have you no heart, Lindsey? For thirteen years I have loved you . . . and only you. Does this mean nothing to you? Have I not proved with the years that I never was unfaithful to you in my heart? I have been constant in my affection for you since the day I met you. I will not bore you with details of the childish affair in Oxford which you persisted in misunderstanding . . . or even allowing me to explain. I ask you only to believe that I never stopped loving you.

I dare to write in this vein only because Marie-Louise told me that you are not grieving for your husband. I forced this and other information from her so do not blame her for betraying confidences . . . I gave her no peace. Just as you give me no peace, Lindsey. Have pity for me in your heart and even while I dare not hope that you can ever find it in your heart to love me again, surely it is not necessary for us to continue without even friendship? Your refusal to see me makes it impossible for you to come to my home and this distresses Marie-Louise as much as it does me. If you wish it, I will promise on my honour never to mention the word love to you . . . nor will I pester you with affection or references to the past. Let us be friends, Lindsey . . . that is all I ask even while I cannot forbear to go on hoping that one day in the future you will come to me of your own accord.

Always and forever, your devoted and lonely,

Glynn

Lindsey was as much surprised as shocked to read such a letter from Glynn after all these years. Marie-Louise had often tried to tell her that Glynn still cared, but Lindsey had had no idea that Glynn felt so deeply. Maybe he had not allowed himself to do so while Elvin was alive and only now, when he knew her to be free, had he come into the open.

Somehow, his letter brought him back to her mind as vividly as if she had seen him only the day before. The warm impulsiveness of his phrases so exactly portrayed Glynn's nature. It disturbed her brutally from her former dormant emotions. She had loved him so terribly once. Now, what could he mean to her? A memory of past love . . . no more? A shadow of remembered passion and a silhouette of her lost youth? Or could it be more? Could this queer trembling in her limbs, the uncertainty, the fast beating heart mean that the past could come alive again and be re-lived?

Then Simon and Richard came running into the room talking in their high, excited voices and she knew that she was not the same girl who had once loved Glynn. He might not have changed, but life had changed her. Better, surely, to let the past remain so and to look forward to a future which she herself could control. Glynn should not imprison her heart and mind again.

"I won't see him!" she told herself, putting the letter in the pocket of her slacks. "I don't want to see him and I won't. I'll write and tell him so."

"It's the car . . . a super new black one!" Simon penetrated her thoughts. And from Richard:

"It is an Aston Martin, Mum! Do you think Mr Rogers will give us a ride?"

"Heavens, have they come?" Lindsey cried, her hands going to her disordered hair and her mind conscious only of the fact that she had not changed into the freshly ironed cotton frock or remade up her face. "Darlings, run out and try to keep them talking for a few moments while I change. Will you do that?"

Obediently, they chased out of the front door, and Lindsey flew upstairs and feverishly changed her clothes, thanking goodness that the weather was warm enough to permit the minimum – no stockings, white sandals and the gingham cotton frock.

The speed with which she changed brought colour to her cheeks and when she finally went downstairs to greet her guests, Paris stared at her and thought with surprise that she was even lovelier than he remembered.

"I refuse to believe that those big schoolboys can be your children!" he told her flatteringly. "You look seventeen."

"Indeed you do, Lindsey!" June cried, flinging her arms round Lindsey and giving her a brief friendly hug. "You are just exactly as I remember you!"

The awkwardness that Paris' compliment had made her feel passed in the reunion with June . . . plumper than Lindsey remembered from school days, but undoubtedly the same girl.

"Take Mr Rogers and Aunty June into the garden," she told the children, "while I make some coffee."

"Please," said Paris quickly, "could I not be Uncle Paris?"

"What a funny name!" Simon said, with a grin that turned to a grimace as he caught his mother's disapproving glance.

But Paris only laughed and agreed that it was funny, promptly endearing himself to the child.

Turning the percolator on for coffee, Lindsey was glad of the brief respite to her nervous system. Had she been leading such a solitary life that the arrival of two guests could seem so disturbing? she wondered wryly. Maybe she should get out and about a bit more if she were going to tremble so violently for no known reason at all.

I wish he hadn't come! she thought, as she put coffee cups on a tray and added milk and sugar. I wish it had been just June and the children and myself! There was something about this man which made her acutely self-conscious and awkward and she did not like the feeling. She did not like him, in fact.

Later, when Paris was taking the boys for a run in his car, she said as much to June.

"But, Lindsey, why ever not?" June asked curiously. "I find him charming. Of course, women have spoilt him terribly and I think he knows he's attractive, but one likes him in spite of that . . . or at least, I do!"

"Well, I don't!" Lindsey said too emphatically. "He frightens me . . . the way I might feel in a cage with a lion!"

June laughed delightedly.

"Oh, my dear, I'm sure he would be flattered to have made that impression! If he makes you feel that way, then I'd say 'Beware your heart, my girl!'"

"Oh, don't let's talk about him!" Lindsey said nervously. "I wish he hadn't come today. I'm sure he used you as an excuse to come. I refused his last invitation, but I wanted to see you and couldn't be so rude as to say I'd rather you came on your own!"

"At least give him credit, then, for ingenuity!" June smiled.

Lindsey relaxed a little and nodded her head.

"He has his uses, I suppose . . . getting Simon and Richard out of the way while we gossip."

"Very thoughtful and tactful!" June agreed. "It is nice to see you again, Lindsey!"

"It's almost as if we'd never not been meeting, isn't it?" Lindsey said warmly. "We always did pick up our friendship after the holidays as if those months apart hadn't been. I shall be grateful to Paris for this reunion, anyway."

The first name slipped out without thought and she found herself blushing and quickly averted her face from June. But June had noticed and began to wonder what would be the outcome of this affair between Paris Rogers and her old friend. Something made her feel that Paris would be the winner for all Lindsey vowed she didn't like him. It seemed to the astute, observant June that Lindsey was really afraid of Paris . . . not in the physical sense of course, but afraid of what he might mean to her. Was she, in fact, afraid of love?

In the half hour that Paris was away with the boys the two girls exchanged confidences eagerly. Lindsey did not go so far as to admit she had years ago ceased to love Elvin, and felt no grief for his passing, but she did tell June briefly that her marriage had not been a success and that now she was going to devote her life to the children and her new career.

June, in turn, told Lindsey of the man she had loved who had been killed and while she, too, was intending to devote her future to her career in the commercial art world, she could not believe that anyone with Lindsey's sensitive, emotional temperament could lead that kind of life for very long. She was so obviously made to be wife, lover as well as mother. She attracted love and needed it. Her nature was wholly feminine and while she was independent in her mind, her heart must always depend on others for affection.

They talked of the children for a while and then June asked after Marie-Louise. In a sudden rush of confidences, Lindsey told June how recently she had seen their mutual friend, told her, too, what Marie-Louise had said about Glynn and her own teenage adoration for him. Then she finally showed June Glynn's letter and asked for her advice about her reply.

June was surprised. She had thought of Lindsey only in connection with Paris and now here was another man, not in her life exactly, but wanting to come back into it! Lindsey might well wish to withdraw herself from the matrimonial field, but it did not look as if the men she knew would let her do so for long. And June could well understand why. There was something completely captivating about her friend. Not just the interesting combination of colouring, the wide green eyes and beautiful reddish hair; but there was something in the expression of those eyes which must always provoke men to wish to discover what lay behind that soft wistful expression . . . something in the rather large curved mouth that was unconsciously provocative and promising of hidden passions.

"I don't think I can advise you!" she said at last. "I don't know how you feel about this man, Glynn. I think his letter is absolutely sincere, and if, as you say, you haven't met in all these years, then he is certainly offering proof of constancy. But it isn't easy to revive past love and if you really hated him, then maybe it would be kindest not to see him again and to let him know that quite finally. But do you hate him, Lindsey? Hate and love can be akin!"

"I don't know what I feel!" Lindsey said with a sigh. "I don't hate him . . . not now. I just feel indifferent towards him. I don't want to be bothered and I feel sure he would be a bother! I don't want to fall in love or have anyone in love with me. I wish he hadn't written!"

"Then why not throw his letter into the nearest waste-paper basket and forget he ever did?" June suggested, amused.

"Is that what you would do?" Lindsey asked.

June laughed again.

"No! But then, I am not you. Personally, I would be far too flattered at the thought of being loved for so long. I should also be far too curious to see him again . . . at least once, just so that I could be really sure I didn't want him back in my life. I agree that's selfish in a way, but it could apply both ways. He might find he no longer cared for me . . . only thought he had."

"How silly I am being to get so worked up about it!" Lindsey said, laughing now. "I think I'm too much on my own here; little things become too important when you've no one to talk to about them. Will you come down often, June? I've purposely lost touch with all the mutual friends that Elvin and I acquired. They are mostly very rich and I don't want always to be trying to keep up to a level I cannot possibly emulate. It's bad for the boys, too."

The sound of the car returning interrupted their conversation and Lindsey soon found herself smothered by two flushed, excited little boys.

"Uncle Paris let me toot the horn and do the indicators!" Simon breathed in her face.

"And we went over sixty miles an hour!" said Richard. "Do you know, Mum, Uncle Paris can fly an aeroplane? And he was a commando in the war. Once he had to bale out in a parachute, and it was in France where the Germans were, but he hid and got back to England!"

There was no question that Paris was already a hero to her two small sons, and Lindsey wasn't quite sure whether she was annoyed or merely amused. June thought that Paris hadn't been wasting his time! The children were nearest to Lindsey's heart, and Paris, in attracting them, was taking a step nearer to their mother.

After lunch, the children went to lie down on a rug beneath the oak tree at the end of the lawn for their rest. June felt she owed it to Paris to leave him a brief time alone with Lindsey. He had, after all, brought them together again and had driven her down today, however selfish his motive may have been for doing so!

She knew that Lindsey was looking at her hard, trying to communicate to her that she did not wish to be left alone with Paris, but she went nevertheless, saying she would really enjoy a short walk to work off the excellent lunch Lindsey had given her.

"We'll come with you, shall we?" Lindsey said wildly to Paris, but he remained in his deck chair, saying easily:

"Oh no, Mrs Carter, please let's relax here. As a matter of

fact, there are one or two little matters of business I'd like to talk over with you!"

Lindsey had no alternative but to sit down again and watch June wander off. She turned back to the man beside her and saw that he was smiling directly into her eyes. The colour stole into her cheeks and she felt furious with him.

"Please don't be cross!" he said disarmingly, just as Simon or Richard might have done. "I didn't mean to make a nuisance of myself, but I honestly have some news for you. I've sold the French book and serial rights of your novel!"

Lindsey looked surprised and delighted.

"Oh, that's wonderful!" she cried. "How clever of you!"

"You should get about a hundred and fifty pounds for the two!" Paris said easily. "At the present rate of exchange. I thought you would be glad."

"What paper will the serial appear in?" Lindsey asked.

"Oh, I forget the name for the moment . . . one of the weekly women's magazines. They don't send us copies, of course, but I'll try to get hold of them for you in due course when I'm over in France. By the way, I meant to tell you that if you would like the money immediately, we are quite willing to advance it."

Lindsey thought for a moment. She could do with some money . . . at least before the end of the holidays. She would need it badly, in fact. But she did not want to borrow.

"I'd really rather not borrow!" she said frankly.

"It is hardly that!" Paris said. "Many of our authors do it . . . there is such a gap between their presenting the finished work and its being published. We merely advance the money that will come in due course. As long as the contract is signed, there is no risk to us and we are quite willing to do this to help our authors. The novel will probably not appear till the autumn, perhaps not even until after Christmas if there are any hold-ups – a long time to wait for payment for a book you wrote in the spring."

"In that case," Lindsey said, "I'd be very glad of a cheque."

Then Paris began to speak about the boys and to compliment her on their beautiful manners, which had greatly impressed him.

Lindsey no longer found it difficult to talk. She explained that the boys went to an excellent prep school and that she could not really take credit herself. He asked her to tell him about the English system of education, and was obviously surprised to learn how much money she needed to give a child the best schooling these days.

"Fortunately I have sufficient capital to see them both through their public schools," Lindsey said simply. "But if they wish to go on to university they will have to win scholarships!"

"That is not a bad system!" Paris agreed. "If they have real academic talent, then they will win their prizes, and if not, then it is really a waste to send them to university. It depends, no doubt, on what careers they wish to take up!"

"Well, at present, Richard wants to be a tram conductor and Simon a vet! Of the two, I think only Simon's wish is likely to endure! He's amazingly fond of and interested in animals and has a curious way of being able to deal with even the most difficult ones. I once found him in a shop patting a bull terrier on a lead with an amazed owner watching him who told me that the dog usually bit anyone but his master and hated children!"

"Have they pets of their own?" Paris asked.

"No, I'm afraid not. We . . . I sold their ponies of course and, frankly, I don't feel we can afford a dog."

This piece of information confirmed Paris' opinion that she was, indeed, having to go very carefully financially. She had said as much in his office the day they had met, but people had such different standards as to what constituted being "poor". If she were having to watch the five or six shillings a week it would need to buy dog meat, then he had no doubt that she had nothing but her earnings to live on. He wondered whether she was right to be using her capital to send the two small boys to

41

such expensive schools. In a way it seemed crazy, and yet he admired her for doing so. It was obvious that she adored them and that they had become the mainspring of her life. He would not forget that.

Watching her as she lay back in her deck chair, her eyes closed and her face turned upwards to the warm rays of the sun, he knew that he was really in love with her . . . that he had not just imagined his state of mind. He wanted, for the first time in his life, her interests before his own. He wanted to make her happy . . . to see her smile . . . to relieve her of worry and care and make her life a heaven. For himself he wished nothing more than to be able to do this for her. Oddly enough, the physical attraction for her was in temporary obeyance . . . his thoughts on a higher plane. And yet he could not deny the attraction as he sat there watching her. It flared into the foreground as she opened her eyes suddenly and they widened and the pupils dilated as she saw his eyes on her. He held her gaze for a long moment and then she said breathlessly:

"Why do you stare at me?"

"Because I have never met anyone quite like you in my whole life!" Paris said truthfully. "I have known many women, some perhaps prettier, but none with your . . . your charm!"

Lindsey bit her lip, her heart thumping in her throat, or so it seemed, as she took in his compliment. She could find no reply and remained silent, her hands twisting together in her lap in a gesture he remembered from their last meeting.

"Lindsey . . . please let me call you by such a pretty name, and please will you call me Paris? I am hoping so much that we can be friends . . . not just business acquaintances. Do you not agree we should make good companions?"

"I . . . I don't know!" Lindsey said stupidly, out of her depth now the conversation had taken such a personal note.

"But I am sure of it!" Paris said quickly. "I think you are a little afraid of me, Lindsey, but you have no need to be. You can trust me implicitly, I assure you."

Again Lindsey could find nothing to say.

"Will you not look at me again?"

In moments of extreme emotion, Paris became a little more French in his speech and mannerisms, and she noticed it in his phrasing as much as in the expressive hands. She felt hopelessly undirected and almost as if she were hypnotized. Slowly, she raised her eyes and looked at him again and drew in her breath sharply. Then he said softly:

"Give me your hand to hold! It is cold, Lindsey. I shall fetch your coat!"

But he did not move or release her hand, and gradually she felt herself relax and her mind became a kind of blank; she no longer seemed to be part of herself, but a ghost standing behind her own chair, observing these two people sitting in the warm sun holding hands and wondering about their feelings for one another.

Then Paris said:

"Why would you not come to London again? Your refusal forced me to force myself upon you today in a most unfair way! I would much prefer that you invited me and that I should not have had to invite myself!"

Lindsey became part of herself and felt a new warmth go through her. She actually smiled.

"Since you are being honest, I will be too. I was not at all sure that I wished to see you again!"

"But you are sure now?"

Lindsey hesitated, but only for a moment. Then she said:

"Yes, yes, I think so!"

"Then we shall have that day at the Zoo together? All four of us? Next week, perhaps?"

"All right!" Lindsey agreed. "I know the boys would love it!"

"And so shall I," Paris said. "Now I must let go your hand for I see your friend coming back through the trees."

As she followed his direction, Lindsey's glance took in the children, chattering quietly beneath the dappled shadows of the big tree, of the sun and the bees busy about the lavender bush, of June's sturdy figure growing larger as it walked slowly towards them. It seemed to her that she was seeing everything in a new, rosy, sun-drenched light . . . as if she had been a long way away and come back.

I'm happy! she thought. And, generously, she turned her head and smiled at Paris, silently admitting him to her world and a little closer to her heart.

Five

M arie-Louise gave Glynn's hair a sisterly ruffling. The gesture was full of affection, for she dearly loved this only brother of hers, and there had always been great friendship and understanding between them both. Fortunately Glynn and her husband, Michael, were also great friends, and brother and sister continued to see a great deal of each other even after Marie-Louise's marriage.

"So she's really coming!" Marie-Louise said again, happy for Glynn in his happiness. "Frankly, I never believed she would, but I hoped for your sake your letter might just touch some remembered chord and turn the tide in your favour."

The man put down his untouched glass and stood up, stretching himself . . . not slowly and lazily like some men, but nervously, restlessly, as were most of his movements. Of only medium height and build, but perfectly proportioned, he was an attractive man. The dark eyes were nearly always on fire with some impulsive idea or enthusiasm and the generous mouth mobile and expressive. There was nothing calm or placid about Glynn, as his sister knew well, and tonight he was even more "alight", as she termed it, than usual. Lindsey, of course, was the reason. She was glad for Glynn's sake that Lindsey had agreed to spend next weekend with them at Woodley Manor, the home she and Mike and Glynn shared. At the same time she was apprehensive. Glynn was setting so much store by this social visit and yet it might mean no more than that to Lindsey.

In fact, Lindsey had clearly stated in her letter to Glynn that *as a friend* of his and Marie-Louise's, she would be glad to accept his kind invitation to spend the weekend with them.

Glynn had confided in his sister the tone of his first letter to Lindsey, the one in which he had told her he still loved her. He had shown Marie-Louise Lindsey's reply.

> *Dear Glynn,*
>
> *Your letter came as a surprise and while it was nice to hear from you again after all these years, I was not very happy to hear of the sentiments you expressed in it. Somehow I cannot but feel that you only imagine you still care about me in the old way . . . that you are being sentimental and reviving an emotion that died many years ago. It did for me anyway, and only on that understanding could it be possible for us to renew our friendship.*
>
> *I would, of course, love to see Marie-Louise, and I am ashamed to say that I have only once met Michael, chiefly because I have so often refused her invitations to stay because you were there. I realize that this rather childish behaviour has made things difficult for all of us and if you think we could be just friends, then there is nothing I should like better.*
>
> *Perhaps you would write to me again.*
>
> > *As ever,*
> >
> > *Lindsey*

How much of that letter was the truth about his feelings? Glynn had wondered. Was he being sentimental? Was he trying unconsciously to revive old memories and sentiments? Could you go on loving a girl you hadn't seen for ten years? She could not be the same person he had loved all that time ago. Yet he had never wanted to marry anyone else; never quite got over the shock and bitterness of their broken engagement. It was true, of course, that he had taken out that girl in Oxford all those years ago, kissed her, made love to her that evening on the river. But dash it all, he told himself with well-remembered indignation, he and Lindsey were not actually engaged, at least, not officially, and they were both very young. Moreover, Lindsey was extremely strait-laced, and he had felt it necessary to restrict the ardour of his feelings when he kissed her out of respect for her extreme youth and innocence. And a chap was only human. The other girl had been there . . . offered him anything he chose to take, and he had been weak enough to take it! Was he to be punished indefinitely for that one lapse? At first he had been sure that Lindsey would come round in time. But as the weeks and then months passed, he began to lose hope. His last desperate hopes were finally dashed when Lindsey announced her engagement to Elvin Carter. It had been the blackest day in his life. On the day following, he joined the army in a fit of mixed anger, pique, bitterness and despair. But, foolhardy though he had been in the risks he had incurred, his life seemed charmed and he had come through unscathed.

There had, of course, been other girls in his life since that first passionate love . . . but none who meant much to him, and returning to civilian life again after the army, he knew he would never marry. Then came the news of Elvin Carter's sudden death and the past flooded his memories and all the old hopes renewed themselves. They doubled when Marie-Louise told him that, far from being grief-stricken, Lindsey seemed almost relieved to find herself a widow.

Only to Glynn, whom she loved with Michael best in the world, would Marie-Louise have betrayed her friend's confidence. Now she did not regret it, for there seemed at least as if there were another chance for Glynn. Lindsey professed that she wanted only friendship from Glynn, but time could alter that, and if Glynn were not in too much of a hurry, he might, in time, win Lindsey's affections. The Glynn of thirty-three was a much more attractive man than the boy of twenty Lindsey had once loved. He still had the same boyish eagerness about everything he undertook, the

47

same impulsive nature and enthusiasm for life. Yet there was a certain wistfulness about the eyes that was very attractive and he had not had that in the old days. Marie-Louise could not believe that Lindsey would find Glynn changed much or for the worse.

She added her own postscript to Glynn's second letter, an invitation to bring the children for a weekend. And now, to her surprise, Lindsey had said she would come.

Lindsey, herself, was as surprised as Marie-Louise. Now that there were only two days between her and meeting Glynn again, she was regretting the hurried written acceptance to their invitation. What had made her say she would go? she asked herself for the hundredth time since doing so. Was it just curiosity, as June had professed she would feel? Was it just because she was lonely? Or had it something to do with Paris Rogers? Was it that, having agreed to see him again with all that it implied . . . and she had no illusions now as to his interest in her . . . she felt the need of other friends and interests to counter-balance the new element in her life? Was it because something about Paris frightened her even while it attracted her and she felt the need of a more solid background? When he had left in his sports car that Saturday, holding her hand in farewell just a moment longer than necessary, he had taken with him that strange, almost hypnotic spell he seemed by his presence to have been able to cast on her all day. He had made it quite clear that he found her attractive . . . that he wanted to see her again and had contrived that meeting against her wishes in order to do so. He had been perfectly honest with her, but she didn't trust him. As June had said, he had so much charm that one couldn't help but like him even while suspecting the inner conceit! For Lindsey, there was a challenge in that conceit . . . a wish to show him that he could not lift his little finger to get what he wanted; to show him that all women were not the easy game he supposed them to be; that he was not as attractive to the opposite sex as he believed.

The trouble was he *was* attractive. Lindsey was sufficiently honest with herself to know that he had unsettled her in his way as much as Glynn's letter and all the memories it evoked had unsettled her in another. Well, at least she was not afraid to face up to these fresh challenges to her peace of mind. She would meet Paris as she had promised, but first she was going back to the past . . . to Glynn.

But Fate decreed otherwise. On the Friday morning Simon started coughing, and by evening, what she had suspected to be merely a cold became measles! The doctor, who had no doubt about the matter, left instructions for Simon to remain in bed until his temperature dropped.

"Not serious," he said, "but catching. I expect the other boy will get it, too, eh, Richard?"

Lindsey was disappointed now that she had no need for further anxiety about Simon. The boys had had most of the other childhood complaints and the sooner they got this one over and done with, the better. It was just that, contrariwise, now that she could not go away, she desperately wanted to! She wired an explanation to Marie-Louise and tried not to feel too depressed by the anti-climax. She could even be amused at her own contrary emotions and share a laugh at herself with June, who happened to telephone her that night for a friendly chat.

"I'd come down and cheer you up!" June said. "But I simply must go and see Mother and Dad. I'm off at the crack of dawn tomorrow and I can't put it off again. As you know, I should have gone last weekend."

When she did not forget her own thoughts in trying to keep Simon quiet and Richard occupied, Lindsey found herself listening through the whole of Saturday for the telephone. For surely Glynn would ring her? But when the phone did ring late on Saturday night, it was not Glynn but Paris Rogers' voice speaking to her.

"Oh, it's you!" she said, and then blushed as he replied quickly:

"Did you think I was someone else? I'm sorry if I am a disappointment to you!"

Suddenly Lindsey laughed. She was, after all, glad to talk to anyone. She explained briefly about her weekend plans that had had to be cancelled because of Simon.

"I'm so sorry!" Paris' voice came to her with a note of genuine regret. "He's not too ill with it, I hope?"

"No, not really!" Lindsey said. "Just a bit demanding. Richard, of course, is bursting with health and irritable because I'm tied to the sick room and he has no one to play with."

"Suppose I run down in the car tomorrow and take Richard off your hands for the day?"

Lindsey's first instinct was to refuse. It was only a week since he had last been here. Then, thinking of the child, she paused and finally capitulated.

"Well, if you really would care to, I'm sure Richard would be thrilled!" she said hesitantly.

"I'd love it," Paris said again.

"I'm afraid I shall probably be tied here," Lindsey said pointedly.

"And I am not to expect the pleasure of your company!" This time his voice was definitely amused. "Do not worry, Lindsey. I shall never make the mistake of competing with your sons for your affections!"

"I don't think you very often make mistakes," Lindsey said, surprised at her own reply.

"Sometimes, perhaps, but no one is infallible. You know, you have not yet called me by name. Is my first name so ludicrous that you cannot bring yourself to use it?"

"No!" Lindsey said, her smile audible in her tone of voice. "Merely a little unusual. Here is Richard in his pyjamas. Perhaps you would like to tell him yourself what you have in store for him."

"I would rather tell you what I have in store for you!" Paris said lightly. "Nonetheless, I would enjoy a word with Richard."

Lindsey listened, amused, while Richard made breathless replies . . . "OOOh, Uncle Paris . . . how scrummy! . . . Yes, please, Uncle Paris . . . Oooo, yes, I would!"

Then the boy put down the receiver. Lindsey felt a little put out and asked Richard why he had not given the phone back to her.

"Uncle Paris said he'd see you tomorrow!" Richard said with surprise. "I didn't know you wanted to say something, Mummy!"

"I didn't!" Lindsey said, but all the same, she was again left with the feeling of incompleteness. Maybe this was just what Paris had intended.

"He's going to take me to Marlow, on the river!" Richard told her as she shooed him up the stairs to bed. "We're going to have a picnic lunch in a basket, and he's going to fill it with all the things I like. And he's bringing his fishing-rod in case I want to fish. I say, Mum, isn't he jolly nice?"

"He's very kind to you!" Lindsey said. Nice seemed hardly the word to describe this unusual man and the effect he had on her and the family. Of course, it was only natural that the boys should enjoy a man's company. However much she tried, a woman could not make herself father and mother to a child . . . fishing, for instance. She couldn't teach the boys. All the same, it was thoughtful of Paris to remember the picnic lunch to save her the trouble. In spite of herself, she rather wished she were going too! Had Paris intended her to feel that way?

"How silly I am being, attributing all these odd motives to his behaviour!" Lindsey told herself crossly as she settled down to her typewriter. "He's just amusing himself . . . nothing more. He probably has no current girlfriend and is filling in time flirting with me!"

She resolved to guard against the children growing to expect him as a regular visitor. She would not want them disappointed when he found someone more interesting to fill his Sunday afternoons!

*   *   *

Paris was surprising himself. Not only had he suggested of his own volition that he take out an eight-year-old boy for the whole of Sunday, but when it came to the point, he actually enjoyed doing so! The boy was excellent company and extremely intelligent, and Paris soon forgot that he was trying to charm Lindsey's son and began to treat the child as an individual. They became the greatest friends. As they congratulated each other on the minute roach they had managed to land in the boat between them, Paris felt himself back in his own childhood, almost forgotten so long was it since he had troubled to remember. He knew, suddenly, why men married and begot sons. For the first time, he seriously considered the advantages of marriage . . . not of convenience, which meant mostly for business reasons such as marriage with Monique would mean; but a union between a man and a woman who shared common interests, who loved one another and who had children, like this boy, to brighten their lives and enlarge their outlook. He was surprised at the amount he had learned in a few hours from Lindsey's son.

"It's been a spiffing day!" Richard sighed his pleasure as they at last made their way back to the cottage. "I wish we could do it again."

"We will, or something better!" Paris promised sincerely. "I've enjoyed it, too."

"We're rather muddy!" Richard said, uniting them on a common level. "Mum'll be cross if we don't wash before tea!"

Paris glanced down at himself and burst out laughing. The immaculate light grey trousers and white silk shirt in which he had begun the day were spattered with river mud. And if his face was anything like Richard's, Lindsey would indeed not allow them to the tea table.

It was nearly five o'clock when they reached home. Knowing how exacting Richard could be, and guessing that Paris was not exactly used to children, Lindsey had been expecting them back most of the afternoon. At four she began to worry and when at last the car stopped at the gate, she was relieved and a little angry with Paris. Hadn't he realized she had spent the last hour imagining Richard at the bottom of the river?

Apparently not. Looking a good deal larger, but very little older, than the grubby eight-year-old beside him, Paris waved and climbed out of the car, his face one big smile.

"We've had a wonderful day. Look what we caught!"

Lindsey's anger ebbed away as she saw the three tiny fish hanging on a string being so proudly exhibited. She began to laugh, and the next moment a flushed, sunburnt, muddy little boy was falling all over her as he recounted the day's delights. Over the top of his curly head, Lindsey's eyes met those of the man who had given the boy so much pleasure, and she was grateful.

"Don't thank me!" Paris said quietly. "It's for me to thank you for lending him to me."

To cover her surprise, Lindsey said abruptly:

"Tea has been ready for ages. Richard, show Uncle Paris where he can wash off some of that river mud."

As he passed her, he said in a voice inaudible to the boy running ahead:

"Now you have spoken my name and the day is made perfect!"

And surprising her again, he left her standing in the sunlight, holding the three small fish in her hand.

Simon, whose temperature had been normal all day, was allowed to come down in his dressing-gown after tea so that he should not miss "all the fun". His face was by now a mass of spots, but his bright eyes and freckles shone through in spite of them.

"Lucky devil!" he said as Richard recounted his adventures for the third time.

"Simon!" his mother said automatically.

"Well, he is a lucky devil!" Simon said. "Wish I could have gone."

"I've got something else up my sleeve for you . . . a surprise to make up for the measles!" Paris said.

"What is it?" both boys cried.

"A surprise!" Paris said again. "And not even your mother knows, so it is no use asking her. It will come tomorrow . . . or if not tomorrow, then Tuesday at the very latest. You will just have to be patient until then."

Later, when the boys were in bed and they were sitting once more on the terrace in the fading light, the birds chattering and calling to one another in a sudden rush of noise before they went to roost, Lindsey turned to her companion and said:

"Tell me what you have in store for Simon, Paris."

He smiled at her.

"Certainly not! Then it would cease to be a surprise. I hope you will not be cross with me about it."

"I'm sure I won't be!" Lindsey said with genuine warmth. "You are very kind to the boys, and I'm only afraid you will spoil them."

"I shall try not to do so. Can I hope that you intend to give me the chance nevertheless?"

"What do you mean?" Lindsey asked, her voice uncertain now that his held that intimate note.

"That you will permit me to see them . . . and you, often enough to risk my spoiling all of you!" Paris said simply.

Why do I automatically try to resist every suggestion he makes? Lindsey asked herself as she pondered his question. She knew, of course, that what he really asked her meant something else, too. He was asking for the right to become her friend . . . and perhaps more. At least she could feel sure now about the first . . . Paris had already proved himself a friend and, after all, in spite of her earlier thoughts to the contrary, she enjoyed this new friendship. It had already brought new interest and colour and, yes! excitement to her life. Why should she refuse what was offered her? Why go on trying to fight against circumstances? There were no commitments attached to Paris' friendship. She could, of her own free will, end it when she chose or when it started to go beyond the level she wished.

The man was studying her face closely while she sat so

quietly and deeply immersed in her own thoughts. She seemed to have this curious knack of being able to withdraw herself spiritually from him even while her physical presence remained so near that he could touch her if he chose.

Idly, he reached out a hand and touched her fingertips. Immediately, her startled green eyes turned to his and he saw the faint colour rush to her cheeks and was content. Whatever she might say, he knew for certain that she was not indifferent to him. But for the first time in his life, it was not a woman's physical response that he wished for. He wanted her to like him . . . to be completely honest, to love him. Dare he hope now that he might one day make her his wife? Was this what he really wanted? To have her beside him always to love and cherish? And, of course, the boys, too, he knew now. They were, after all, part of Lindsey and he loved them for what they held of her as much as he had grown to like young Richard today for himself. And the boys liked him. Not that that meant a great deal. Boys could be fickle and if they began to realize that they might have him as a rival for Lindsey's love, they might change their ideas about him!

No, even if Lindsey should by some magic learn to care for him, the path would not be easy. Yet he had no doubt that he would continue fighting for her. This was the most important thing that had ever happened to him and he knew better than to let it slip through his fingers.

Lindsey said suddenly:

"Do you think it is possible for men and women to be friends, Paris?"

He gave his rather mischievous smile.

"It depends, no doubt, on the man and the woman. Even allowing that sex will sooner or later rear its ugly head, I do not see why this should prevent two people being excellent companions. But I do not really mean that. For one thing, I don't in my heart believe that sex is ugly . . . not if it is accompanied by true affection."

"Yet you who have been brought up in France, must believe

in marriages of convenience?" Lindsey asked curiously.

"I'm not sure!" Paris said truthfully. "I did believe they very often were the happiest marriages. Now I am not sure. I think to be happy . . . really happy . . . one must desire another's happiness before one's own. That is true love, is it not?"

She found herself surprised at his comments. Somehow she had not thought that he would touch below the surface of easy emotions . . . that he should be so profound. And he sounded quite sincere.

"You surprise me!" she told him. "You're not a bit as I thought you were the first time I met you."

"I don't think I am!" Paris agreed with a smile. "I think you have an excellent influence on me. You should see much more of me for the good of my soul! You are shivering . . . are you cold, Lindsey? I think we should go in. And it is time I returned to town!"

It had grown nearly dark while they had sat talking and Lindsey did feel cold although she had not known it. She stood up and said:

"Would you like some coffee before you go? I'm sorry I can't offer you a drink."

"Coffee would be fine!" Paris said, standing up, too. But as she moved away from him, he reached out his arms and before she was fully aware of what was happening, she was imprisoned in his embrace. For one brief moment she resisted him . . . trying to pull free, but then his mouth came down to hers, gently at first and then with sudden fierce passion, and she knew herself lost.

This is why I feared him! she thought wildly before she quite lost her head in the magic of that first kiss. I am afraid of the power he has over me. Paris . . . Paris . . . And then her face looked up to his, offering him her lips to kiss again and again.

When at last Paris released her, his breath coming unevenly and his face very white in the darkness, Lindsey knew that he was, after all, not to be feared. He could so easily have swept

56

her away in the strong tide of passion that had engulfed them both. Such was the element of his kisses . . . a strange mixture of tenderness, possessiveness, even skill, that it had been only a matter of moments before she felt his desire for possession to equal her own. She had not felt this basic human need, this urgent demand of all her senses, since those days, so long ago, when she had been in Glynn's arms. Glynn! She had forgotten him . . . just as surely as she had forgotten Elvin . . . the children . . . everything but the touch of the man beside her.

"I think I should leave you now!" Paris said very softly. "I could not trust myself to stay. You are not angry with me, Lindsey?"

"No!" she whispered back. "No!"

Deeply disturbed, amazed at herself, uncertain, she was a little frightened, but not angry. She knew that she could have drawn back had she wished. He had not forced his kisses on her. She had wanted them every bit as much as she had wanted to return them.

"Good night, *chérie!*" he said, his voice very gentle as were his arms as they went around her once more. He touched her lips with a featherweight kiss, and then, as she stood there in the darkness, he turned away from her and left her alone.

It was the same as it had been after his last visit. As soon as his car had disappeared into the now starry night, she began to recover her whirling senses. She had the curious feeling once again as if she had been in some odd kind of hypnotic trance; made to feel and behave in a way that was quite foreign to her. She could think logically and coolly and as she went round the house automatically setting things straight and tidying up the scattered toys, emptying ashtrays, she pondered the enigma of her emotions. Was it true, after all, to say that she behaved in a way foreign to her? Had she not, deep within her, always been a passionate, emotional creature? Was it not just that she had trained herself to be otherwise . . . beginning when Glynn had forced her to feel so cheap, and deliberately changing herself to be emotionally independent when her husband proved himself even less worthy of her love than Glynn? Was she about to make a fool of herself for the third time in her life? She felt that Paris was exactly the kind of man to make her do so! Even June, who was not in any way personally involved, had thought him "a charming cad". Paris undoubtedly wanted something from her, but she could not believe that it was love . . . nor that he was offering love. He wanted an affair, she told herself with distaste. And he would be justified in thinking himself encouraged after her behaviour tonight!

She had wanted Paris as a lover just as surely as she had known in every fibre of her being that they belonged together in this physical sense. Romantic and idealistic as she still was in spite of the way life had treated her, Lindsey was appalled at her own betraying emotions. That Paris might have fallen in love with her never crossed her mind. She had had preconceived ideas about him which, as it happened, were not untrue concerning his life up to the time he had met her! Now she could find no reason to change them. Nor was love or marriage predominant in her own mind. She had, on the contrary, firmly made up her mind that she would do without both for the rest of her life. What she did not realize was that she had made no allowance for the fact that she was still a young and very beautiful woman. That deep within her, and brought to the surface tonight, the normal feelings of a woman still existed; even while her mind rejected them. So she was hopelessly confused and sleep did not come to her until the very early hours of the succeeding dawn.

Six

Monday afternoon's post brought an enormous box full of roses for Lindsey and a guinea pig for Simon. She knew that it would fall on her to look after the little animal while Simon was at school, but his pleasure was so enormous that she could not be cross. In any event, the pale yellow roses were so beautiful that she could not feel anything but kindly disposed towards the man who had sent them.

The morning post had brought a letter from Glynn, saying how sorry he was that they had not been able to come and that, if she would allow them, he could pay her a visit with Marie-Louise the following Saturday. If, on the other hand, Simon was well enough to travel, would she come to them?

Lindsey felt no wish to go. Somehow in the bright morning sunshine, the hours of yesterday no longer seemed frightening or distasteful and she felt in a strange way resigned. She would not try to fight against Paris and anything he might mean, but would wait and see what happened. She knew this to be weakness, but she could not bring herself to mind. It was so much easier to let things rest as they were than to write telling him she never wanted to see him again. In any event, this was not true as she knew deep down inside herself. One could not ignore Paris . . . only face up to the challenge he presented. But she felt emotionally too tired on this new, bright day to face up to Glynn, too. Here at least she could write making some excuse not to meet.

But she had still not written a reply when the following

morning she received a long letter from Marie-Louise. After expressing her sympathy about Simon, she wrote on:

I think you would have been touched, for want of a better word, to see Glynn's face when your telegram came. He was fearfully disappointed, Lindsey, and it was all I could do to prevent him jumping into the car and driving down to see you at once. I had to explain that he would probably receive a very poor welcome since you were undoubtedly cluttered up for the time being with doctors and thermometers and the usual sick-room activities.

I am worried about Glynn, Lindsey. He is setting such store by this meeting with you. I am sure that in his heart of hearts he is hoping you will still be a little in love with him. I know this must seem mad to you after all these years and I sometimes wonder how Glynn can be so sure he is still in love with you! You know how dearly I love my brother and I don't want him hurt. At the same time, I can see that the only way for him to straighten out his life is for you two to meet again. Either it will all come right or, which I suppose is far more likely, it will all go wrong and you'll both find you mean nothing to each other. At least then Glynn will be free of the memory of you which still haunts him. He is the kind of man who needs to be married. It's strange really because I used not to think that, but ever since the army he seems to have drifted without any real purpose. I think a wife and family would give him that purpose.

I hope this will not embarrass you when you eventually come face to face with him. I've no doubt that you will carry off the awkwardness of the first few moments with your usual poise and calm and, of course, the children will help. I gather Glynn is hoping you'll come next weekend, measly Simon as well!

> *With love, darling,*
> *Marie-Louise*

Not only was Lindsey embarrassed, but now she felt she could no longer put off the weekend as she had intended. She even felt annoyed that she had not written yesterday before Marie-Louise made her plea for Glynn.

She could, of course, say that Simon was not well enough either to travel or have visitors, or that she was too busy nursing him to entertain. But this would only postpone matters, for she realized that sooner or later she must meet Glynn again and lay the ghost of their adolescent love affair once and for all. Curious how with Elvin's death it seemed to have become resurrected! Of course, it was ridiculous of Glynn to imagine that he still loved her after all this time. How could he know what manner of person she had become? As Marie-Louise suggested, it was simply that he was clinging to a sentimental memory. She had for a long time had to fight against that memory herself. Perhaps, for all their sakes, she could face up to the weekend and however awkward it might turn out to be, finally write "*finis*" to the whole thing.

Since they would be travelling in Lindsey's old Austin and there was therefore no risk of Simon spreading the infection to other children, the doctor saw no reason why he should not go away. There were no children in Marie-Louise's house, and Richard was in quarantine, anyway. On Saturday morning they packed the car with their few belongings which included Pop, the guinea pig, despite Lindsey's objections.

"He needn't come indoors. Aunt Marie can't mind if I leave him out!" Simon cajoled. "*Please*, Mummy!"

So Pop, so called because he was ginger-coloured, was going too. The boys were restless and excited for they had known Marie-Louise, Simon's godmother, ever since either of them could remember, and yet they had never been to her house before . . . a fact they accepted without question as children do accept the normal run of things. This visit was by no means normal and they were both fidgety, trying Lindsey's nerves, on the hour's drive. At least it gave her little time for thought and she was actually relieved when at last they turned into Woodley Manor's drive.

The house was, as Lindsey remembered so well, a beautiful example of Georgian architecture. It belonged to Marie-Louise's and Glynn's parents who were living in South America, and it was here that Lindsey had come to stay as a young girl; here she had first met Glynn, first fallen so madly in love with him! And the place, red bricks glowing on a breathless sunny spring day, seemed not to have grown a second older since she had last been here.

The air coming in through the car windows was heady with the smell of newly cut grass, and Simon had already noticed "a man driving a lawn mower . . . can I do it, too, Mummy?"

As she switched off the ignition key and the boys reached for the door handle, Lindsey remained where she was, her heart beating with sudden nervousness. Was the past ever really dead? How could it be when time could stand still and everything remain so completely unchanged as Woodley Manor? Even the great thick branches of wistaria twisting up the wall and round the window frames appeared to be in the same position.

It was all so beautiful . . . so exactly as she remembered it. And why not, since the family had plenty of money to keep the place up to its pre-war standards? Even the manservant who opened the door to them was the same.

"It's James, isn't it?" she said, holding out her hand.

"Why, Miss Herrod! I never realized . . . Madam said a Mrs Carter was coming . . . Welcome back, miss."

His pleasure in seeing her again was touching, and reminded Lindsey that James had often been the one to cook bacon and eggs for herself and Glynn at one or two a.m. when they returned from a late party.

"These are my two boys, Simon and Richard!" she said, and was proud of them when they held out their hands as she had done. James might be a butler, but he was also a good friend, or had been, to her and Glynn.

"Madam and the Master and Mr Glynn are on the croquet lawn!" James told her. "Would you care to go to your rooms before joining them, Miss . . . I mean, Madam?"

"If you'll take the suitcases, I think we'll go straight out and find them!" Lindsey said, afraid that any longer delay would only make her more nervous than she was.

"Of course, you know the way!" James said. "Nothing has changed here, Madam . . . even the garden-door still squeaks!"

A faint smile crossed Lindsey's lips. How often had she and Glynn tried to open that door without a sound when they came in from a moon-drenched garden hoping his parents would not know they had been so long in the summer-house making love!

Glynn, who had always been James' favourite since he was a small boy, had been able to twist the manservant round his little finger. He had quite brazenly suggested that James oil the door, but somehow oiling had never done the trick and James had said he thought it was the way the house was built and nothing would alter it!

She passed the beautiful curved staircase and paused for a moment to watch James go slowly up the steps with their luggage. How slow he was . . . they had used to jump them two or three at a time . . . but then, James must be getting old. Even at seventeen she had thought him so. This was nearly half her lifetime later . . .

"Oh, do come on, Mummy!" Richard clamoured. "You look as if you've seen a ghost."

"Perhaps I have!" Lindsey said, smiling at him. "I used to stay here quite often when I was a young girl."

"As young as me?" Simon asked.

"As young as I . . ." Lindsey corrected automatically. "No, darling . . . I suppose I was nearly grown up."

"Then you are *old* now?" Simon asked, puzzled.

"Yes . . . yes, I suppose I am!" Lindsey said with another smile.

"You aren't going to die, are you?" Simon asked anxiously.

"But of course not!" Lindsey reassured him. "Come on, darlings . . . let's go into the garden."

Would Glynn, too, think her old? Would he find her so much changed? Would he have changed so that she might not recognize him?

Then, from across the lawn, she heard Marie-Louise's voice calling to her, and beyond her, saw the two men, one dark, the other, Marie-Louise's husband, fair.

All three came across the lawn in a group. The children ran forward to greet Marie-Louise and Lindsey forced herself to move slowly in their direction. She knew she was trembling and knew, too, a purely feminine wish that she had taken time to go upstairs and freshen her make-up, tidy her hair.

Then Glynn's hand was reaching out for hers and she looked up into the dark glowing eager eyes and the years rolled slowly and inexorably backwards as he spoke her name.

"Lindsey!" he said again. "How wonderful that you are really here at last!"

Then Marie-Louise came between them, holding the two small boys one by each hand and presented them to Glynn. He looked at them both for a long moment and said:

"They both have a look of you, Lindsey!"

Then Michael was suggesting a drink on the terrace, and the first moment of meeting was already in the past.

"We've been amazingly lucky with the weather . . ." – Michael's voice.

"So I called him Pop because he's ginger, Aunt Marie . . ." – Simon.

"And he's got forty-eight spots. I counted them . . ." – Richard.

Glynn's laugh . . .

Then she found her own voice and heard herself speaking

perfectly normally of the car and how well it had driven the distance despite its age.

"Marie-Louise tells me you've started writing . . . books and things!" Glynn addressed her as they reached the terrace and settled down in deck chairs. "Do tell me about it, Lindsey!"

But she didn't want to talk on that subject . . . a subject which must automatically include Paris.

"I'm one of those shy authors!" she said lightly. "I don't like to talk about my work. Tell me about you, Glynn. It's so many years since—" She broke off, but Glynn filled in the sentence without embarrassment.

"Since we last had a chin-wag . . . yes, it is a long while . . . far too long. It really is lovely to have you here again, Lindsey. You know, you really haven't changed a bit . . . perhaps a little thinner in the face . . . but otherwise not at all."

"I want some beauty hints from you, Lindsey!" Marie-Louise broke in. "I know I don't look seventeen!"

"It's only this dress!" Lindsey said, suddenly shy. "I lead such a quiet life that I don't possess any sophisticated country clothes. And I haven't had time to go to a hairdresser and my hair is far too long to be fashionable."

"But the result is perfect!" Marie Louise spoke for Glynn. "You really do look amazing, Lindsey."

It was impossible not to feel different, Lindsey thought, as the day wore on. Impossible, here in this bright sunshine amongst such affectionate, complimentary and good friends, not to feel a slow unbending of the tension that had held her prisoner inside herself for so long. Only now, as the years rolled backwards, was she beginning to feel her old self . . . her real self again. How tightly she had enclosed that sensitive, emotional and loving heart beneath a cool, even hard, exterior. That armour had been necessary . . . to keep out any encroachment on her heart which had been so bruised. No man was ever to be allowed to hurt her again. So she had determined . . . and now, in one short afternoon, she was opening like a flower to Glynn's compliments, to his undoubted affection, to his enthusiasm.

By evening, when the children were safely tucked up in bed and she had changed into a fresh off-the-shoulder ballet-length dinner-dress, she felt her heart throbbing with warm excitement. She knew that the palest mauve of the lace frock was becoming to her . . . that her eyes were sparkling and her hair shining. Her cheeks were pink, partly from the sunshine, partly, too, from that heady excitement. She knew that Glynn would contrive a way before the evening was over to be alone with her. His dark eyes had told her so as they talked merrily and inconsequently about trivial things in the presence of Marie-Louise and her husband and the boys. Perhaps this, more than anything else, had brought back the past. How many times had she sat near him, reading those messages while his parents carried on their adult conversations. Yet now, they were the adults, hard to believe though it was. She, herself, was a parent! Yet, since the first hour of their arrival, she had forgotten the fact in this re-birth of her own girlhood. Only the sight of her two small boys, playing for the most part with Michael, to whom they seemed to have taken a great fancy, reminded her from time to time that she was not living in pre-war days; that she was twenty-nine and not seventeen again.

Watching her friend across the dinner-table, Marie-Louise felt a moment's anxiety. There was no doubting the fact that Lindsey looked radiant . . . as radiant as a girl head over heels in love. Could it really be going to work out right at last? Could she be falling in love with Glynn all over again? Yet, at the same time, she felt an inexplicable fear. Had they made it too easy? By meeting again in this same setting, were they in fact putting a false background to whatever might come of it? Glynn and Lindsey were no longer children, and this was 1954. If they fell in love again, it must be because they loved each other as they were at this time, not as they used to be.

Then Marie-Louise shrugged her shoulders and sighed. One

could not, after all, control other people's lives or affections. Her brother was quite old enough to look after himself. He, too, must be aware of the danger of reviving the past. It was up to him now.

Glynn was wasting no chances. He had fallen quite hopelessly under Lindsey's spell. To him, she was his boyhood sweetheart and this new, exciting, maturer Lindsey made into one irresistible woman. He knew without question that he wanted to marry her . . . knew that he would ask her before she went home.

After coffee, which they had in the beautiful drawing-room, Glynn drew Lindsey out on the terrace where the sun still shone although it was now low on the horizon.

"It's a shame to be in on such a lovely evening," he said. "Lindsey, what about a walk? Down to the mill pond? We might even see the kingfisher before he goes to bed."

"Not the same one, surely?" Lindsey asked, laughing.

"For all I know, it is just the same one!" Glynn said, happy that she should have remembered . . . wondering at the same time if she remembered other evenings down by the lake.

"I'll get a coat!" Lindsey said. "I'd love a walk!"

"Good luck to him, I say!" was Michael's comment as he accepted another cup of coffee from his wife with a boyish grin. "I think Lindsey is quite adorable . . . and if it weren't for the fact that I already have a wife, I'd fight Glynn every inch of the way instead of wishing him good fortune!"

"I'm horribly jealous!" Marie-Louise said, but she was not. As Lindsey had once said, she had been lucky to have met and married a man whom she loved and who loved her so truly. She need never be jealous of Mike.

Glynn and Lindsey sat on the wooden steps of the old boathouse and watched the sun set. It was wonderfully peaceful looking out across the quiet water. One or two swallows dipped low across the faint ripples before disappearing into the dusk. Occasionally a fish jumped and the splash broke the silence for a moment or two.

Wordlessly, Glynn took Lindsey's hand. She did not try to draw it away although, curiously enough, she felt a moment of anxiety. It was such a short while since she had sat on her terrace with another man . . . with Paris Rogers, holding his hand. Then she forgot Paris as Glynn said:

"Lindsey, you've no idea how wonderfully happy I am to be here, with you. I'm so glad you came today!"

"Yes, I'm glad, too!" Lindsey said slowly. "It has been such fun, Glynn!"

"We always did have fun, didn't we?" Glynn said reminiscently. "You haven't forgotten, Lindsey?"

"No, I haven't forgotten!" Lindsey said. "But I don't think I ever really believed that it *could* be the same. I think I was afraid to come back here . . . to this house . . . this place . . . in case I should find it changed. Yet nothing has changed . . . nothing."

"I haven't changed, either, Lindsey."

She knew then that he wanted her to say that she had not altered either. But she could not. She was not the same girl who had been here before. Then she had had no fears, no responsibilities, no thought for the future. She had been young and trusting and deliriously in love. And it had been an innocent, young girl's love she had felt for Glynn. There had been passion, too, but not the emotion she had been made to feel when . . . when Paris kissed her.

She shuddered, aware of the cool breeze.

No! She would never allow Paris to kiss her again. It frightened and appalled her. With Glynn, she need not be afraid. Somehow, she knew that. She would be in control . . . not he.

"Lindsey!"

She turned and looked at him and her heart filled suddenly with pure tenderness. He looked so young . . . so much the boy she used to know, sitting there in the half light, looking at her from those dark, ardent eyes.

"Yes, Glynn?"

"I . . . I promised not to mention my feelings for you. I won't break that promise unless you give me leave."

"Don't let's talk about anything like that," Lindsey said gently. "Let's just be happy, Glynn. Let's not think about the future . . . not yet!"

"All right!" the man said. "I won't hurry you, Lindsey. But you have, at least, given me some kind of hope. You aren't sorry you came? You don't hate the sight of me?"

"No, Glynn . . . no to both questions. I thought I hated you once, but I don't now. It's almost as if it never happened . . . our quarrel, I mean."

"It should never have happened!" Glynn cried fiercely. "You belong to me, Lindsey."

"No!" she whispered, fighting against herself as much as him. "I belong to myself, Glynn, and to my two boys. I must always think of them first. I am not the girl you used to know."

"But you are, you are!" Glynn cried passionately, his hand unconsciously tightening his grip on hers. "You have not changed at all, Lindsey."

But even as he drew her into his arms, Lindsey knew that she *had* changed. Time had not stood still for her all these years. She was no longer a young girl in love for the first time.

Then, as Glynn's lips touched hers, she forgot that there had been any time between these kisses and the last time he had held her in his arms. She closed her eyes and let her thoughts disintegrate and become nothing in the growing darkness. Past and present merged and the only focus for her being lay in Glynn.

"I love you, I've always loved you!" Glynn cried hoarsely, breaking his promise as he at last released her and tried to master his emotions. "Lindsey, tell me you love me, too."

But she could not . . . not yet. She was not yet sure if this Glynn were the real man . . . not the boy she once knew. It had happened too quickly . . . this getting to know one another again. He believed she had not changed and she found him with each passing hour more and more the same person. Yet was this truly the man he was now? Was she, really deep within her, the same girl merely grown to woman? Would she want to marry Glynn? To live with him as his wife? Did she want him as father to Simon and Richard? Somehow she could not visualize Glynn as a father!

"Glynn!" she said, drawing away from him, but allowing him to keep her hand imprisoned. "We must above everything be honest with each other. I don't know how I feel about you. I tried to get out of coming here this weekend. I would have done if Marie-Louise hadn't written to say you would be so terribly disappointed. You say you have never stopped loving me. I can't say that. It . . . it nearly broke my heart when I gave you back your ring all those years ago. But I thought I loved Elvin when I married him. Since then . . . well, I haven't loved anybody. I haven't wanted to love anybody. I wasn't prepared to feel like this . . . about you."

"Then you *do* feel something, Lindsey? Even if it is not love?"

"Yes!" Lindsey admitted softly. "But I don't trust myself, Glynn dear!" She remembered again how her senses had betrayed her with Paris Rogers. "I only know that I've been wonderfully happy all day . . . that I wanted you to bring me here, to kiss me. But that's all I'm sure of, Glynn."

He gave a quick delighted laugh.

"That's quite enough for me for the time being, my darling girl. Don't you see that you are fighting against the past because I made you so unhappy before? But I'll teach you to trust me again . . . and then the other will come. I'm sure of it. We belong to each other, Lindsey."

"Do we?" she asked, not unkindly but wistfully. "I wonder what we have in common, Glynn. Are you fond of children?"

"I could be fond of yours . . . because they are part of you!" Glynn said. "Lindsey, surely you have not forgotten what fun we used to have together? We always liked doing the same things!"

"Yes!" Lindsey admitted. "But we couldn't do those things now, Glynn. Climbing out through the attic on to the roof and pelting cherry-stones on to the grown-ups on the terrace. We're the grown-ups, now, Glynn!"

He laughed again infectiously so that she smiled, too.

"Well, there are lots of other things we can do instead!"

She did not ask him what they were. It was true that they had always had a wonderful time together . . . that they had been good companions.

"Tell me about yourself now, Glynn. What do you do when you're not working?"

"Oh, I mess around. I sail whenever I get the chance and I've taken up squash. I go hunting, of course, and I still go to all the local point-to-points and races. Mike and Marie-Louise are keen, you know. I go dancing sometimes."

"Have you many friends?" Lindsey asked, meaning, as Glynn surmised, women friends.

"Yes, but there's safety in numbers . . . no one special!" he told her, grinning. "You're the only girl who ever meant well, wedding bells. I've never wanted to settle down with anyone else."

Silence fell between them and behind the boat-house an owl hooted. Lindsey shivered, and immediately Glynn pulled her back into his arms.

"You're getting cold, darling!" he whispered, but made no move to take her back to the house.

She was not cold . . . only afraid. Somehow she could not see herself and Glynn married . . . not now. Once it had all seemed so right . . . their wedding, their honeymoon, setting up home together . . . such fun! Now she could not imagine what it would be like . . . the picture would not come to her mind. Yet she wanted to be able to think of a future with Glynn . . . to go on being happy for always as she had been all day . . . never to be lonely and alone again.

"Kiss me!" she said, wanting the reassurance of his physical touch . . . wanting to feel herself once again under the magic

71

spell of the day's wonder . . . wanting not to think about the future and only to think of the present . . . the instant which she could grasp and hold and know was hers for as long as it lasted.

Her response was warm and spontaneous and Glynn said at last:

"You do love me a little, Lindsey, I know it."

"Yes!" she whispered back, although there was only the owl to hear them. "Yes, I need you, Glynn. To make me whole . . . to bring me back to life again."

And so saying, she fought her fears and gave him back her trust, and her belief in him.

Seven

B ut it was not to be so easy after all. What had seemed to Lindsey in the starry night so perfect and simple and inevitable, took on a new complexion the following day. That she had fallen in love with Glynn all over again she had no doubt . . . unless it were more true to believe that she had never really stopped loving him! But while Glynn had waved aside her doubts as to the suitability of their marriage, she found that they only increased with each succeeding hour.

Glynn could not seem to realize that she was not the same girl he had known before . . . that she was a woman, above all a mother, and that before anything else she must think of her children.

"Marry me, darling Lindsey . . . now, tomorrow, at once!" he had begged her impetuously before they returned to the house that night by the mill pond. "You say you love me . . . and you know I love you . . . I have always loved you. Don't let's waste any more of our life apart!"

Much as she hated to do so, she had had to remind him that she could not marry for at least another six months . . . that she must from common decency show this outward respect to Elvin's memory.

"Then at least let us be engaged . . . let me give you back your ring!" he cried. "No one need know about it except perhaps Marie-Louise, who will guess anyway, and Mike, whom she is sure to tell! It'll be our secret until you feel enough time has elapsed since your . . . your husband died."

He had not liked to mention Elvin . . . even to think of

him. Lindsey realized and understood that. He did not like to think of those years when they might have been together and she had been married to someone else. But Elvin was dead and she could not mourn him even while she wished to give some respect to his memory. Held against Glynn's fiercely beating heart, she had known his sense of urgency; felt the same wish to belong to him now . . . not to waste any more of their lives apart.

Yet the following day, the doubts crept back and she was afraid . . . afraid of she knew not what. That time might part them again . . . that she would never, in fact, become Glynn's wife if she stopped to consider . . . to wait . . . to think. Yet that, she told herself, was ridiculous. What could happen to prevent her marrying Glynn next year if she wished it? And she did wish it.

But she realized now something could still come between her and Glynn . . . her children. She had had little time to think of them on that Sunday, for Glynn had monopolized her company, and Marie-Louise, let into the secret of their refound love for one another, had kindly and tactfully offered to amuse the boys with Mike's assistance while Glynn and Lindsey spent most of the day alone together.

After lunch, Glynn had had James pack up a picnic-basket for the two of them and driven her up to the top of the downs, where they had lain in the heather, hands entwined, talking, laughing, rediscovering one another. Memories of old adventures they had shared filled their conversation and brought back the past so vividly that Lindsey felt she had lost those years between then and now. She felt light-headed from the sheer happiness and sunshine and knew that only Glynn could have given her this feeling of being seventeen again.

He, himself, was so much the dark, handsome boy she remembered that she could not help calling him Peter Pan.

"You haven't really grown up at all!" she teased him. "The years have left you quite untouched, Glynn."

"They've been such empty years without you!" he said,

half-serious, half-laughing. "Nothing has happened in my life to make its mark upon my boyish countenance!"

Even as she smiled back at him, Lindsey remembered that plenty had happened to her and that she had promised her two young sons that she would be back in time to put them to bed.

She jumped to her feet and tried to hurry Glynn. But he held her prisoner in his arms while the warm breeze stirred their hair and cooled their cheeks, and another five minutes was lost while she returned his kisses.

"Glynn, I must go now . . . I promised!" she said at last breathlessly. "Please, darling!"

But by the time they reached home . . . Glynn's home . . . the boys were already in bed and Marie-Louise was reading to them.

"Darlings, I'm so sorry to be late!" Lindsey said remorsefully as she sat down on the chair between their beds.

Two pairs of eyes regarded her seriously and a little sullenly.

"You promised!" Richard said pointedly.

"I know! I'm very sorry, Poppet!" Lindsey could offer no excuse. It was the first time she had ever broken a promise to them . . . and the last time, she vowed silently.

"What were you *doing* all that time?" Simon asked. "You were gone for ages and ages!"

Marie-Louise, sensing Lindsey's embarrassment and distress, said tactfully:

"You know you must allow Mummy a little time to herself. How long is it since she had a holiday? She's always busy looking after you and your house and giving you a good time. Don't you want her to enjoy herself sometimes, too?"

It was not put as well as she meant, for Simon said astutely:

"Don't you have a nice time with us, Mummy?"

"But of course I do, darling!" Lindsey said.

Marie-Louise left her to it. It was Lindsey's problem, and she could not help. She wondered if either Lindsey or Glynn had stopped to think that the boys might be a problem. They would naturally be jealous of Glynn at first. They had had Lindsey to themselves and they wouldn't want to share her. Nor would Glynn want to share her, Marie-Louise told herself as she went along to her bedroom to change for dinner. Glynn, with his quick, impulsive, emotional temperament, had always been a very possessive child. He wanted things quickly, instantly, passionately, and for a while the object of his desire absorbed him utterly and completely and no one could part him from it. Then, as suddenly, the object was dropped for some other interest. Lindsey was the only person whom Marie-Louise knew to have absorbed him as his childish interests had done, and the only preoccupation that had ever lasted. For it was true that he had always loved her . . . always wanted her. Could it have been because this was one of the few things that had ever been denied him that he had truly desired?

Not that Lindsey had been "denied" him at first. She had been as much in love with him as he was with her, and it had looked so promising for both of them. Then Glynn had had a momentary passion for that silly blonde girl up at Oxford, and in giving way to it, lost Lindsey, the idealist, the romantic. But it was too late to undo the damage, and not long after their broken engagement, Lindsey had married Elvin Carter. Now Glynn was being given another chance and Marie-Louise, loth as she was to interfere, felt she ought to have a sisterly talk with Glynn . . . to try to make him see that he would have to tread carefully if he were not to lose Lindsey a second and last time. She must make him see how important the children were . . . how big a part of Lindsey's life . . . any mother's life. He would have to put himself second . . . certainly until the boys accepted him. At least it was some advantage to Glynn that they had never been very close to their father, even while they had liked and respected him.

Upstairs in her sons' bedroom, Lindsey tried to win back a smile from them. She could not bear that they should be unhappy because of her happiness, and she wished now that she and Glynn had taken the boys on the picnic with them. Yet even as she wished it, she knew that it would not have worked. It was all so new, so sudden . . . this new-found re-birth of their love for each other. They had wanted time to be alone together, to find once more what they had believed lost to them for always. And they had found it . . . the old, laughing companionship, the light-hearted caresses, the youthful, carefree kisses with passion hidden only lightly beneath the surface.

"When are we going home, Mummy?" Richard asked for the second time.

"Tomorrow morning!" Lindsey said. "Do you want to go home, Richie?"

"Yes!"

"But, darlings, you said last night you loved it here."

"Well, I don't like Uncle Glynn!" Richard said.

Lindsey felt the colour leave her cheeks and then slowly return. It was silly to let a child's idle remark upset her seriously. He didn't mean what he said . . . or only momentarily. He was annoyed because Glynn had taken her away from them and blamed him for making her break a promise. He was jealous!

Impulsively, she sat down and drew both the boys on to the bed beside her, hugging them close.

"Sillies!" she said tenderly. "Silly old things, both of you. I love you both better than anything or anyone in the whole world!"

Later, as she sat with Glynn and Marie-Louise and Mike drinking after-dinner coffee, she said ruefully:

"They were jealous . . . at their age! As soon as I told them I loved them best in the world, they were all smiles again."

She missed Glynn's sudden quick look in her direction.

"Children can be very intuitive!" Marie-Louise said thoughtfully. "I don't think you and Glynn will be able to keep anything from them very long. It would probably be easier for you to fool us!"

"But I don't want to 'fool' them," Lindsey said quickly. "I only want to give them time to come to it gradually. That's one of my reasons for not wanting anyone to know . . . for a while, anyway."

"But you said it was because of your husband!" Glynn broke in.

"That is my main reason, Glynn!" Lindsey said quietly. "I've only been a widow four months. I . . . I didn't really think about the children until this evening."

No! thought Marie-Louise. Nor did Glynn. She changed the subject and not long afterwards dragged her husband up to bed.

"But it's only ten!" Mike complained.

"Stupid! I wanted to give them a chance to be alone!" Marie-Louise said, ruffling his hair. "Lindsey goes home tomorrow and I think it's high time they had a serious talk!"

"Well, what have they been doing all this weekend!" Mike replied.

"I doubt they've been doing much talking!" Marie-Louise said, laughing. "Have a heart, Mike. Have you forgotten what we were like at that age?"

"What age?" Mike asked. "We're all the same age more or less!"

A little frown creased Marie-Louise's forehead.

"Well, yes, I know; I meant really the 'falling in love' age, or stage. Somehow I always think of Glynn and Lindsey as they were when they first met."

"Seems a bit odd to me!" Mike said carefully. "I mean, they aren't kids any more, are they? I suppose they really *are* in love?"

"There's no doubt about Glynn!" Marie-Louise said. "As for Lindsey, well, she looks like a woman in love, if anyone ever did. You told me yourself she looked radiant!"

"She did . . . she does! Oh, well, I suppose they know what they are doing. It's all happened so . . . so suddenly and . . . well, too easily, if you know what I mean. You tried to get

Lindsey down here for Glynn, hoping she'd fall for him again, and she has done. It's too pat!"

"But, Mike, I don't think they ever stopped loving each other. Lindsey never loved Elvin. She married him on the rebound, and while I think she did have quite a different kind of affection for him, that all went out of the window when she discovered the truth about Elvin and that woman of his. She ought never to have married him. She should have married Glynn."

"And now she's going to? Somehow, I can't see them married."

"Oh, don't be so gloomy!" Marie-Louise said quickly. "It's not like you to be pessimistic, Mike!"

"Forget it, and come here and kiss me!" her husband said with a twinkle. "Time you and I remembered the falling-in-love stage again, I think!"

Downstairs, Lindsey sat on the floor, her head against Glynn's knees, his hands stroking her hair.

"I wish the boys hadn't been so upset!" she said. "I ought to have been home sooner, Glynn. It was your fault!" She smiled at him tenderly.

"No, yours!" he said. "If you were not so incredibly beautiful and attractive, I shouldn't have wanted to kiss you and if I hadn't wanted to kiss you, we'd have been home earlier. Don't keep worrying about them, Lindsey. They'll get over it."

"Yes, yes, of course!" Lindsey said. "But it was silly to start off on the wrong foot. It's so important that they should like you, darling."

"Don't you think they do?"

"I think they are jealous!" Lindsey prevaricated. "You do like them, Glynn, don't you?"

"But of course I do!" Glynn said. "They both look so like you, how could I help it?"

"But like them for themselves, too!" Lindsey said urgently. "They are individuals, too, Glynn with minds and wills and personalities of their own."

"I'll have to get to know them properly!" Glynn said easily. "Lindsey, don't worry so!" He smoothed the frown that creased her forehead and bent his head to touch her lips with his own. A moment later, she was up beside him in the big chair, his arms round her, hers tightly around him. The future and its worries were forgotten again as the sweet thrill of his embrace held her again in its thrall.

Upstairs, the boys slept soundly, Simon dreaming of guinea pigs and Richard that he and Uncle Paris had caught the biggest fish he'd ever seen.

Eight

J une Helmer recognized herself for a fool! She had known from the very beginning that Paris Rogers was interested in Lindsey. She had suspected, too, that he was a type she herself had never cared for . . . the conceited, self-opinionated man-about-town who looked on women as amusing playthings and used them to take what he wanted and gave nothing in return. She had been able to concede that he had charm . . . a great deal of charm . . . and it went without saying that he was physically as attractive as any man had a right to be. But she did not put herself on guard against him because she had never believed that she needed to do so. Paris Rogers was certainly not wanting anything from her. It was Lindsey, June told herself, who needed to guard against Paris Rogers.

Yet somehow, without cause or reason or desire, he had managed to occupy an ever-increasing amount of June's thoughts. As she worked in the Art department, she found herself giving the hero on her book-jackets an unconscious look of Paris. In one, the man had a lift to an eyebrow which only when she looked at it later did she recognize as being one of Paris' mannerisms; a large firm mouth on another hero with a half-smile at the corner of the lips . . . another of Paris' features. When she recognized it as such, she hastily tore it up and re-drew it. But even then, the eyes of the next hero she painted unconsciously in that startlingly clear blue that was identical to the colour of Paris' eyes.

At first she did not take these indications of her emotions

81

very seriously; putting them down to the fact that it was only natural she should draw inspiration from this new source . . . that Paris made a very good foil for the heroine of the kind of love story she was illustrating.

But he continued to haunt her even in her non-working hours. As she had told Lindsey, she had many friends, men and women, and she was not poring over a book or cooking on a gas-ring in her digs night after night! Nonetheless, she found herself comparing her current escort with a mental image of Paris and not very favourably. Even at the cinema with a girlfriend, she knew that she was identifying herself with the heroine and Paris as the hero!

At first amused, then frightened, then horrified at her own incredible, run-away feelings, June was at last forced to realize that more than anything in the world, she wanted to see Paris again. She would permit herself no further than this wish. Nor did she expect that it would be granted. A little on the plump side, tending to the plain rather than the pretty, she had no illusions as to Paris' interest in her. She was not his type! And now that he had secured his invitation to Lindsey, he would need no further contact with her.

No one was more surprised, therefore, than June when the 'phone went one afternoon at the office and she heard Paris' voice.

"June? I tried to get you this morning, but you were in conference or something! Did you get my message?"

"No, no, I didn't!" June said, glad that her voice gave no indication of the trembling of her hand on the receiver or the odd sensation in her limbs.

"I asked someone to ask you to ring me!" Paris said. "I wondered if by some lucky chance you were free this evening and could dine with me!"

She hesitated. Every sensible part of her sensible brain warned her not to go . . . not to see him again . . . not to play with a fire that could only burn her. Yet she weakened. At her hesitation, his voice took on a new urgency, and he said:

"I know it's very last minute, June, but I really would be very grateful. I . . . I'm rather down in the dumps and I badly need your cheerful face as company."

"Isn't there anyone else you can ask?" June retorted, her voice brittle as she thought of the many women who would probably be far better equipped than she was to cheer Paris up.

"It depends what you mean by that remark. I have other women friends I could ask to dine with me, but . . . well, it's you in particular I wanted to see, June. Do come!"

She had not ever expected him to plead with her and she knew herself lost. She would go . . . just this once, she would go.

"You're looking very attractive!" Paris told her as she joined him in the foyer of the restaurant where they had arranged to meet. "You've no idea how glad I am to see you!"

Impossible not to be pleased by the compliment even while she knew that compliments came easily from men like Paris, and meant nothing . . . nothing personal. They were merely part of his automatic behaviour with any woman . . . to attract by making them feel attractive.

Yet she was looking pretty, definitely pretty, Paris thought as he guided her to the table he had reserved. There was a bright colour in her cheeks and a look about her that . . . well, caused him really to look at her. He liked June. Not the way he "liked" most women, but liked her, as he might have felt for a sister had he had one. And he badly needed to talk to her. Another woman friend, as she had suggested, would not have done. They would not be willing to listen to his outpourings about Lindsey . . . for that, as June soon discovered, was why he wished to see her.

"It's all such a mess!" Paris told her after they had finished eating and ordered coffee. "May I tell you about it, June?"

She didn't want to hear what was coming and yet she was honest enough to know that Lindsey was the only link between herself and this man, and that it could never be anything more. She had never been under any delusion as to this fact and she might as well let Paris talk and get it into her own head that he was in love with Lindsey and she, June, was a fool to do more than wish herself reincarnated in Lindsey's shape!

"Go on and tell me!" she said quietly.

"Well, the last time I saw Lindsey was a month ago! Four whole weeks. I spent Sunday at the cottage . . . the weekend after you and I were down there together. Simon had just got the measles."

"Yes! Lindsey wrote and told me she'd seen you."

"Did she tell you what happened?" Paris asked eagerly.

June shook her head.

"Only that you took Richard fishing and how kind you had been to the boys and how much they both liked you."

Paris bit his lip.

"Yes! But no mention that *she* liked me? Yet I could have sworn she did, June. Of course, I'm hopelessly and quite painfully in love with her. I've never been in love before. I know that now. And I don't like the feeling. I can't think of anyone else and I can't enjoy anything at all. It's hell!"

Despite herself, June could feel sympathy for him. She had already noticed that he looked pale beneath the tan and that the blue eyes looked tired. She felt a sudden ridiculous longing to put her arms round him and say, Don't love her, Paris. You'll only be made unhappy. She's in love with someone else.

For Lindsey had written and told her about Glynn. She had asked her not to tell anyone, and June believed that this was a request not to tell Paris . . . their only mutual acquaintance.

Paris said suddenly and fiercely:

"She wasn't unmoved when I kissed her. There was something between us and she knew it . . . *I know she did*. Yet every time I have rung her up, she has made some excuse not to see me. First it was because Richard had got the measles and was really ill. Then she had friends down for the weekend. The third time she was taking the boys to London for the day shopping. She doesn't want to see me now . . . yet she did!"

She promised me she'd let me take her and the boys to the Zoo. What can I have done to make her dislike me?"

"I don't for a moment suppose she does dislike you!" June said slowly. "But . . . well, I don't know how far things went but perhaps you misinterpreted that last time you were with her. Maybe . . . maybe you just thought she wanted you to kiss her."

Paris drew in his breath and said vehemently:

"No, I didn't imagine what happened. I'll grant that it has little to do with affection . . . *love*. But she wanted me to make love to her just as much as I wanted to. June, I always believed a woman wouldn't let a man kiss her . . . like that . . . unless she at least *liked* him."

"I think that's true," June admitted. "But . . . well, you're very attractive, Paris. Maybe she felt lonely and a bit lost and . . . and you were there."

"There's some other reason, I'm sure of it!" Paris said. "*I think there is someone else*. That's what I wanted to ask you, June. Is there?"

She couldn't lie and yet she did not want to betray Lindsey's confidence. She prevaricated, saying:

"You haven't known Lindsey very long, Paris . . . how many times have you seen her, two, three? Maybe she just does not want the kind of friendship you offer her."

"I'm not offering her friendship . . . I'm offering her my love!" Paris said violently.

"Did you tell her that?"

The blue eyes suddenly smiled.

"Fat lot of chance I have had to tell her. It's quite obvious, anyway, that she doesn't intend to give me the chance. That is what seems so unfair to me, June. I know she was reluctant at first to see me a second time. But after that Sunday, she overcame those feelings . . . I know it for certain. She liked me and she wanted to see me again. Then, suddenly, she refused to do so. As far as I know, there is nothing she can have heard to my discredit. I'll admit my life hasn't been exactly blameless, but it's a fairly open book. In any event, she doesn't know any of my friends, or I hers. So it can't be that. Is there anyone else, June? I can face a rival, but I find it difficult to face failure as an individual!"

She could understand that. There can't have been many women in Paris' life who refused to see him because they didn't like him! Not at the start of an affair, anyway. It was something of a novelty to him to be turned down flat! It would do him good, and yet it seemed unkind to hurt him for no other reason than to make him less conceited. It only then struck June that she had no real cause to think him conceited. It was only in her imagination that she had typecast him. For her part, at least, she had found no unpleasant traits in his character. Maybe the kindest thing to do for him and for Lindsey was to tell him the truth.

Undoubtedly Lindsey would do so if she knew Paris' feelings for her. As it was, it was clear to June that her friend had been trying, unsuccessfully, to avoid seeing Paris because she did not wish him to make his feelings for her obvious.

Suddenly, she made up her mind. As truthfully as she could, she told Paris all she knew about Lindsey's youthful engagement, how it had been broken off and how she had only just met Glynn again after all these years. She told him, too, that Lindsey was going to marry Glynn some time next year. Meanwhile she was waiting for a decent interval since her husband's death and to give the boys a chance to get to know and like Glynn.

"She asked me not to tell anyone," June ended. "But it seemed best all round for you to know."

"And she's really in love with this man?" Paris asked quietly, only his restless hands fiddling with his coffee spoon betraying his anxiety.

"As far as I know!" June said. "She wrote and told me that to be with Glynn was to be a young girl again; that it seemed to both of them that the lost years had never been and that except for the boys, she could believe this was true."

"And you know this man?" Paris asked bluntly.

"I only met him once or twice when he was hardly more than a boy. I thought he seemed very nice in those days . . . if a bit unreliable. But, then, he and Marie-Louise always were a madly impetuous pair. He is . . . was very nice looking."

Paris looked devastated and June felt a sudden rush of compassion for him . . . an almost maternal emotion that longed to comfort and condole.

"I wish I'd known . . . before!" he said at last. "For weeks now I've let myself believe I stood a chance with Lindsey. She's the first woman I've ever really wanted to marry. And I'm sure it would have worked out . . . that I could have made her happy. The children, too . . . I liked them a lot . . . even surprised myself! And they liked me. If it hadn't been for this other fellow . . ."

"I'm afraid he exists nonetheless!" June said gently. "I don't think there's anything you can do."

"I love her!" Paris said, so softly that June barely caught the words. "She belongs to me . . . not to him. I feel it deep down inside me. I'm not going to let anyone else have her. Do you hear me, June? I'm going to fight all the way. If she's so much in love with him, she has nothing to be afraid of from me, has she? I think she has refused to see me because she *is* afraid of me . . . afraid of what she knows in her heart lies between us. Perhaps it isn't a very pretty thing . . . it's too primitive, perhaps, for her to understand. But I *know* we belong . . . and I know that no one else could give her the love I can give her. She needs me, June, *me*."

She might now have thought him conceited and yet, oddly enough, she did not. She saw beneath the rush of words the sincerity of feeling that gave rise to them. He really did believe that some bond existed between himself and Lindsey.

"What can you do?" she asked quietly.

"I don't know. I haven't thought about it. But I'm not going to sit back and watch some silly young fool take her from me."

"Paris, she isn't yours!"

"But she is!" he said, his voice so calm and sure that June was taken aback. She had entirely forgotten her own relationship to this man. She found herself no more than an observer and somehow she had the feeling that here was danger . . . not for her, but for Lindsey.

"You cannot take advantage of what I have told you this evening!" she said a little desperately. "I don't want to lose Lindsey's friendship now that I've found her again."

Paris looked at her directly, seeing her for herself. He put out his hand and covered hers where it lay on the table.

"No, my dear, I won't let you down. You've proved a very good friend to me and I hope we shall always be so. You know, I've never really met any women before that I *liked*. Yet suddenly I've found two. Maybe it is because I haven't taken the trouble to get to know your sex."

"Paris, are you really in love with Lindsey? I know you think you are, but is it really *love*? Are you sure?"

"Yes!" he said without hesitation. "Somehow, deep down inside –" and he placed his hand over his heart "– I am quite, quite sure. It has never happened to me before, but now I know. You have been in love, June? Were you not sure, too?"

It was then that she knew for certain that she was in love with him . . . not the love she had felt for her Australian fiancé in which she had been the stronger and perhaps more dominant partner. But in a different way, she knew herself in love with Paris. She knew it was hopeless, knew it could never come to anything, but that changed nothing of her emotion. Loving meant wanting someone else's happiness before your own and she would gladly give him Lindsey this minute were it in her power to do so.

"You look sad, June. I am sorry to remind you of someone you lost. Yet, for his sake, will you not help me? I know nothing of this man Lindsey says she will marry. He may be very nice, and I am sure he must be for Lindsey to think of marriage to him. But he is not for her. She is not for him.

Don't ask me why because I can only say again that I know she is mine."

"I wish you luck, Paris!" June said truthfully. "I don't know what you will do; what, if anything, I can do. But I will help you if I can."

"There is one thing at least for a beginning," Paris said thoughtfully. "You can find out if she needs money."

"Money?" June asked, surprised.

"Yes! When she approached me as her agent, she told me that she needed to earn money to support herself and the boys. I understand her husband left her nothing but their possessions. I believe these were sold and put in a trust fund to educate the boys, and that she has nothing over. I do not want her to be in need. There at least I can help her. There is always the possibility, you see, that she might be tempted to marry again for security."

"Oh no!" June said quickly. "I don't think she would do that. I don't think many women would do that."

"There are some, though I do not count Lindscy amongst them," Paris replied. "I didn't mean to imply it in any case. I meant merely that lack of money might give her a feeling of insecurity which might lead her subconsciously to a wish to be safe. Even if this is not so, I do not like to think of her in need. As her agent, I can arrange these matters so that she has money when she needs it . . . advances, royalties . . . that kind of thing . . ." he ended vaguely.

"Well, I will try to discover if she's hard up!" June said bluntly. "Does she earn much as a writer?"

"I think sufficient, if she is careful!" Paris lied without difficulty. He would never tell a living soul that he had sent Lindsey a cheque for double the amount French book and serial rights had earned. He knew that Lindsey would find such a gesture unforgivable and he had no intention of letting her discover it. At the same time, he had not hesitated to send her the cheque when he first heard that she needed money. It meant little to him who could well afford it and, in any event, at the time he had done so he had really believed that the day would come when Lindsey married him. Then his money would be hers. Now he could no longer be certain . . . in fact, on the face of it, it looked very improbable that she would see him again, let alone fall in love with and marry him! All the same, he would do it again just as easily and quietly if he learned from June that Lindsey was in need.

It didn't seem to Paris to be in the least strange that he should be doing this. At least, no more strange than the many other emotions he was experiencing which came under the heading of "being in love". He had never done anything like it for any other woman, but then, he had never felt for any other woman what he felt for Lindsey. The only strange part lay in the amazing fact that he was as completely in love as it could be possible for any man to be. He was himself as astounded by the depth of these newly discovered feelings as June would have been astounded to hear that he had sent Lindsey money she had not earned.

"I shall probably be seeing Lindsey next weekend," June was saying. "She has asked me to go down on Saturday. Is there any message I can give her for you?"

Paris considered the question carefully.

"You are not staying over Sunday?"

June gave a sympathetic smile.

"No! I heard Glynn would be spending the day there and decided to be tactful."

"Then I think . . . yes, I am quite sure that I shall decide to be the opposite!" Paris said, suddenly grinning. "I shall interrupt the *tête-à-tête* and find out for myself how things progress."

"Oh, I wouldn't, Paris, really I wouldn't do that!" June cried, but she could see from Paris' expression that her warning meant nothing. Now that he had discovered a plan of action, he was quite his old self, full of self-assurance and with a kind of wicked humour that half aggravated, half amused her. She was beginning to feel sorry now for Lindsey . . . up against such a man as this . . . and sorry for Glynn, too.

"You think I am afraid of this boy . . . this . . . this other man?" Paris asked, his voice and gestures becoming more French as he became excited. "It is he who will be made to look the fool . . . not I."

"I am hoping that it will not be Lindsey!" June said flatly.

"You should really stay and see the fun!" Paris said, laughing delightedly. "I know exactly what I shall do. I shall call to see the children . . . to ask them out to tea on the river. Lindsey will imagine of course that I have come to see her and she will be vexed. But she will be even more vexed when she learns that it is not so. You will see, June!"

"I shall not see!" June said with determination. "I'm taking no part in this, Paris."

He gave another quick smile that was, to June, both innocently mischievous and purely devilish.

"Yet you would be glad if I telephoned you to tell you afterwards what happened?"

June smiled in spite of herself. It did not surprise her that Paris should know so well a woman's curiosity. Nor that he should have devised so clever a plan for arousing Lindsey to some kind of feeling for him. No woman, however much in love she may be with someone else, enjoys a rebuff from the man she believed in love with her. If he really paid her no attention it would be bound to pique her vanity. One simply could not ignore Paris.

"Come, let us go on somewhere where we can dance. I feel very wide awake and happy, June. You are not too tired?"

No, she was not too tired to dance with Paris. Bitter-sweet though it might be to feel his arms around her without any personal meaning for him; yet still she craved these few moments to treasure afterwards. She knew that if she really wished to avoid being hurt, she would stay well away from Paris Rogers. He made no pretence of his feelings for her, and she was not such a fool as to imagine that he might turn to her on the rebound if he should fail with Lindsey. She was far too ordinary, far too plain, too dull, to interest such a man for long. Yet knowing this so certainly made her the more anxious to make the best of this evening. Her life had for so long now been denied excitement or emotion of any sort, that even unrequited love could seem better than nothing.

And Paris was the most perfect companion. He danced beautifully and paid her extravagant compliments which she did not believe, but which she enjoyed hearing nonetheless. She enjoyed, too, the envious looks of other women at nearby tables as they no doubt wondered why a man of Paris' attractions should be out with a plain girl like herself!

Although it was long after midnight when she returned home and she was physically very tired, still she lay awake a further hour, wondering how Lindsey could resist a man like Paris; wondering at the strength of the ties that held her to Glynn, her childhood sweetheart, and how it would all turn out.

Nine

Although it was early September and the summer had been practically cloudless, it rained throughout the Saturday of June's visit to Lindsey. The boys were playing with an electric train set in their bedroom most of the day and she and Lindsey were able to curl up in comparative peace in front of a small fire . . . not really necessary, but to cheer the dull afternoon and dispel the feeling of damp caused by the sound of the heavy rain.

Lindsey had talked of little else but Glynn since the children had left them alone.

"I don't like to say much about him in front of them as they are both a bit jealous!" she admitted frankly. "It's only natural, of course, but it is rather trying, too. You see, they've taken it into their heads they don't like Glynn. It isn't personal . . . I'm sure of that . . . but it might just as well be. They are both 'fed up' because he's coming tomorrow. It'll be an effort for me to keep them polite if this rain continues. If only it is sunny, we can all get out and not be too on top of each other."

June, remembering Paris' promised gate-crashing of the party, hoped for everyone's sake that the sun would shine. She wanted to warn Lindsey, but Paris had made her promise on oath that she would not reveal his plan and she could not let him down. At the same time, she wanted to give Lindsey some idea of what was to come!

"Of course, Glynn is being the soul of patience with the boys!" Lindsey went on. "He pretends not to hear if they are rude and does his best not to be too affectionate when they

93

are around . . . with me, I mean. But the boys sense how he feels about me . . . and how I feel about him. I'm terribly worried, June, in case they keep this up indefinitely. We want so much to be married next spring, but if they still feel this way about him, I suppose we'll have to postpone it."

"Children can be very selfish!" June remarked. "Don't let them spoil your life, Lindsey!"

"I'm not . . . I won't!" Lindsey cried. "But I must consider them too, June. I know Glynn will be a good father to them and that they'll see it when they are a bit older even if they don't now. But from my own point of view, I couldn't marry Glynn and go off on my honeymoon with him if I wasn't sure that the boys were at least happy about it. I just couldn't give Glynn the whole of my thoughts if I were worrying about Simon and Richard."

"It's rather a complication!" June agreed. "What does Marie-Louise say?"

"She thinks if I stop trying to *make* the boys like Glynn, they'll probably do so of their own accord! She's right, too, but somehow the little wretches seem to guess how much I want them to like him . . . to behave well in front of him. I don't say anything to them, but they know it. Last time Glynn was here, Richard did nothing but talk of that fishing expedition he had with Paris!"

"Maybe Glynn should take them out somewhere by himself!" June suggested.

"But they won't go! I suggested it, of course, and Glynn said he'd love to take them both somewhere, but they wouldn't go. It was horribly embarrassing. Glynn was upset, and I suppose I was cross because, apart from anything else, they were very badly mannered in their refusal. Between us, we made matters worse. And, of course, Glynn wanted to know who Paris was and got jealous, although I told him again and again he had no reason to be . . . that I hadn't seen Paris since that Sunday, and wasn't going to see him again ever."

"I don't see how Glynn could be jealous of Paris. After all, you've only met Paris three, four times?"

"I told him that!" Lindsey said, blushing slightly. "But Glynn seems to resent anything in my past . . . anything that happened to me since we used to be engaged. June, I do love him. I couldn't bear anything to come between us again."

"But what could?" June asked quickly. "Surely not Paris? You are not afraid of him?"

"No! Of course not!" Lindsey cried fiercely. "I wish I'd never met him. All I hear all day long from both children is Uncle Paris, Uncle Paris! Last time I saw him, June, he kissed me. I suppose it was wrong of me to let him . . . but, well, it just happened. It was before I met Glynn, of course. Since then he has been ringing me up trying to get me to see him again. I've made one excuse after another, but he doesn't seem to take the hint."

"Perhaps he is in love with you!" June suggested carefully.

"What nonsense! How could he be?" Lindsey said, too quickly, June thought, for it to be a new idea to her friend. "Besides, you said yourself that you thought he was one of those inveterate bachelors . . . out for a good time. Love! Marriage! Those aren't words I'd connect with Paris Rogers!"

"There is a first time for everyone!" June suggested. "Paris could quite easily be in love with you. That was the impression I had."

"Oh no!" Lindsey cried despairingly. "I don't want him to be. I don't want to see him again. I wish he'd leave me alone. I wish he wasn't my agent and that I could just tell him I never want to see or speak to him again."

"What has he done to make you dislike him so much?" June asked. "I . . . I thought he improved on acquaintance!"

Lindsey pushed her hair away from her forehead, the little frown creasing the mark between her brilliant green eyes.

"Oh, I don't know. Nothing, I suppose. But I don't trust him. He . . . he frightens me in some way."

"Why don't you just tell him you are going to marry Glynn and prefer not to see him again? I'm sure he wouldn't try to force himself on you if he really believed you were in love with someone else."

"No, I suppose not! I suppose I could write and tell him Glynn and I are engaged. Perhaps that is what I should do. Yet he hasn't actually ever said anything to provoke that kind of letter, June, if you know what I mean. It might seem strange for him to get such a letter from me. After all, you don't write to casual friends and tell them that you don't wish to see them again because you are engaged to another man. You only do that with rivals! And he has never even suggested himself for that part."

"Then why let him worry you?"

"Because he will ring me up and ask me out!" Lindsey cried. "He accepts the excuse I give him and a day or two later he rings me again. He won't *see* that I really don't *want* to go."

"I should imagine he is being purposely obtuse!" June said, smiling. "Paris Rogers isn't a fool, Lindsey, and I'm sure he can read between the lines if he chooses."

"Then why be so obtuse?" Lindsey asked desperately. "Why not take the hint and leave me in peace?"

"Because he's in love with you, Lindsey."

She watched the colour flood Lindsey's cheeks and then slowly recede.

"I don't want him to be! I can't cope with that, too!" Lindsey whispered at last. "Can't you tell him for me, June . . . to leave me alone?"

"I don't think he'd listen to me. Nor do you believe he would, Lindsey, if you think about it. I mean nothing to him. You'll have to tell him yourself."

"If Glynn and I could only be married *now*!" Lindsey cried. "That would make everything so much simpler. But we can't, not just because of Elvin, but because of the children. Glynn's

96

coming tomorrow and I long desperately to see him, just as I dread to watch how the children will behave. Aren't you glad to be you and not me, June?"

June smiled . . . a smile that hid her true feelings. If she were Lindsey, she would be loved by Paris . . . she could marry him. There just wouldn't be any problem about Glynn. She began to feel the wish that she were, after all, staying until tomorrow to meet the man who could so easily wipe Paris Rogers out of the picture! As she recalled him, he had been attractive in rather the same dark-eyed, Spanish fashion that was Marie-Louise's chief claim to beauty. She remembered a somewhat irresponsible boy who was often laughing. Perhaps that was what attracted Lindsey . . . Glynn's gaiety. Yet Paris could be light-hearted enough, too, as she had discovered for herself!

She sighed, giving up the idea of trying to discover what made people attractive to one another. Lindsey had, so it appeared, no doubt as to her love for Glynn, or of her dislike of Paris. She wondered how Paris was going to face up to the fact that this time he could not have what he wanted! She could even feel sorry for him, for he would not give up easily, and failure would not be easy for such a man.

"Lindsey, what do you know of Paris?" she asked abruptly, her own curiosity getting the better of her.

"Know of him?"

"Yes! He seemed so completely dissociated from everyone else. He must have some connections somewhere."

"I know very little about him!" Lindsey admitted. "I found his name in the list of authors' agents and picked it out from the many others at random when I wrote my book. When he wrote and told me it was accepted, I was naturally delighted. I never thought of him as a person . . . only as an agent, until the day I went up to London to meet him. He asked me out to lunch and I learned a bit about him then. He's half French, which I believe you already know. He was in the Commandos during the war and I discovered recently that Mike has a chap in his office who knew him then; he said Paris had a great reputation for courage and held the *Croix de Guerre* and the G.M., and that he reached the rank of colonel. It's rather odd to find him behind an office desk after that kind of a war career, but of course, his father was in the publishing business, and I suppose it was natural he should take up something in that line. He has some very well-known authors on his lists, and I imagine he's doing very well. I must admit, as far as my work is concerned, I've no quarrel with him."

It was June's opening and she took it.

"How is the writing going, Lindsey? Do you do much?"

"Not a line since the holidays started!" Lindsey admitted ruefully. "I shall have to get down to it very seriously as soon as the boys go back to school. I'm very hard up, June. To tell you the truth, I had no idea it cost so much just to live! I'm not surprised now that Elvin lived up to the hilt. Running that big house with those servants and the horses and our holidays must have taken every penny of his income."

"Yet he never seemed worried about money?"

"That's the funny part . . . he never did!" Lindsey said. "But Elvin was a secretive man in many ways." After all, Lindsey was reminding herself, it had been months before she had discovered about that girl he kept in London! "He paid all the bills except the housekeeping money, and I didn't even handle that as I just turned it over to Cook every week and she made the best of it. I think she did well, now. At the time I was sure she used to pocket half herself! I'd no idea of the cost of living. But I'm finding out."

"Will you manage to keep the boys at school?" June asked tentatively.

"I want to . . . if I possibly can!" Lindsey said. "I think I told you I'd put enough money by for their education when I sold the house and the horses and the big car. If I can keep my head above water until next year, well, I suppose Glynn will be bearing the brunt of our upkeep. You know, I'm very glad I've got that money put away for the boys. It wouldn't be fair to Glynn to ask him to pay for their education. I shall keep on writing to earn what I can to put towards their school clothes and holidays. I don't want Glynn to feel the financial burden too heavily. It wouldn't be fair to him," she repeated.

"Have you talked to him about it?" June asked.

Lindsey shook her head.

"No! I suppose we'll have to one of these days, but . . . well, money isn't a very romantic subject, is it? And I've seen so little of Glynn these last weeks. He knows I've got a fund for the boys, of course. Don't you think it is wonderful that he should be willing to take them on, as well as me? I mean, there are not many men who would marry a widow with two young sons."

"Oh, I don't know, Lindsey!" June replied. "There must be many instances after the last war. I don't see why it should be such a hardship to have two ready-made children . . . not unless you couldn't afford any more. But surely Glynn and Marie-Louise are both very well off. I seem to remember their grandmother leaving them each a small fortune when we were still at school."

"Oh yes! Glynn won't ever have to worry about money," Lindsey said with a sigh. "We shall be able to afford other children of our own . . . if he wants them. But I don't know if he will. I don't know if I want them . . . though I wouldn't deny them to Glynn, naturally, if he does."

"I suppose you would worry about the relationship between half-brothers and sisters!" June said thoughtfully. "You know, Lindsey, you could marry Glynn when the boys go back to school this autumn. Then, when they come back for the Christmas holidays, they'll have known for some time that it will be to a new home, with Glynn there, too, and be adjusted to the idea. Hadn't you thought of that?"

"Glynn suggested it last time we saw each other. But . . . oh, I don't know, June. I suppose the truth is this has all happened so suddenly that I feel I've lost control . . . that I'm being rushed along with the tide. There's no time to sort things out. I *am* sure I love Glynn, but sometimes I have wondered if I ought to marry him."

"But if you love him, why ever not?" June asked.

"Oh, June . . . it's so hard to explain. But Glynn hasn't been married before . . . and he hasn't been a father. He is still so very young . . . inside himself. I don't know if it would be fair of me to saddle him with a family all of a sudden, especially if the boys are going to make trouble."

"You mustn't let them make trouble, either of you!" June said firmly. "It would be criminally stupid to let the whim of two small boys ruin your whole future, Lindsey. They'll grow up and leave you and you'll find you have nothing, if you let them do that. As for being fair to Glynn, well, surely if he loves you, he wants the boys, too? Wouldn't you want them if he were the widower and they his children?"

"I'm a woman!" Lindsey said quietly. "I don't think men feel the same as we do, June."

The arrival of the two children, who had tired of playing trains, put an end to any further confidences. Soon after tea, June left to catch her train back to town. She felt far from elated by her visit to Lindsey. Her friend had not by any means been radiant; Paris would be disappointed by June's confirmation of the fact that Lindsey's thoughts were all of Glynn; and as for herself, she had only a quiet evening in her digs alone, with nothing to look forward to and no safe harbour for her love.

Ten

Lindsey was, for the moment, perfectly and gloriously happy. The day had dawned with that soft dewy brightness that was to precede yet another radiant summer's day. She had promised the children a tub of water in the garden later in the morning when Uncle Glynn arrived, and they were in high spirits, the measles long since over and both boys tanned a healthy golden brown, as, indeed, she was herself.

She dressed with care in a crisp mauve and white check cotton frock with a fresh white muslin collar that enhanced the warm brown of her shoulders and arms and face. She knew that her tan suited her . . . seeming to enlarge the green of her eyes and the reddish tints of her auburn hair. And above all, she wanted to look lovely for Glynn; lovely and young. This, her favourite summer dress, did both for her.

Glynn, to surprise her and to ease his own eager impatience, arrived in time for breakfast! They took out a bright check table-cloth to the garden table and had hot rolls and honey and coffee in continental fashion, and the start of the day augured well for them both. Even the boys managed not to be surly or difficult and greeted Glynn in what was for them a friendly enough manner.

After breakfast, Glynn helped to clear away and wash the dishes and, while Lindsey went upstairs to make the boys' beds, he told himself that soon she would not have to work any more; when they were married, she could have as many servants as she wished.

"I hate to see you doing this kind of work!" he told her, when she came to help him in the kitchen.

Lindsey laughed.

"But why, Glynn? I really quite enjoy it! I'm only just beginning to realize how useless a life I led when . . . when Elvin was alive."

Glynn's face clouded as it always did when she mentioned her husband's name.

"Lindsey, why did you marry him?" he asked, voicing aloud for the first time his curiosity and jealousy at the mere thought of Lindsey married to anyone else.

"I don't really know!" Lindsey said truthfully. "I was lonely . . . and I expect on the rebound from you! And Elvin was much more sophisticated than I. I think I was flattered by his interest in me and . . . well, I thought it would work."

"You belong to me!" Glynn said suddenly and fiercely. "You're mine, Lindsey!" And turning to face her, caught both her hands tightly in his own and stared into the green enigmatic eyes with his own intense, darkened gaze.

"It's true . . . of course it's true!" Lindsey thought as her heart quickened with emotion that was almost fear. Glynn was so demanding, so intense, so possessive. He would be a jealous husband! Yet she need not fear that. When she was married to him, she would prove to him that he need never fear to lose her again. For that, she felt, lay behind his present strange, almost brooding manner with her. Tenderly, she raised her hand and gently touched his cheek and smiled. She was glad to see an answering smile light those dark eyes and the laughter come back to his lips.

"Let's go into the garden!" Lindsey suggested.

"Kiss me first!" Glynn said, his voice teasing now and so much the voice of the boy she had loved long ago . . . the boy she still loved.

She raised her mouth and felt his lips against her own, gently at first but with increasing passion until at last she drew gently away from him, starry-eyed and breathless, saying:

"Darling, please!"

She did not voice her real feeling, which was that they must, at all cost, keep a brake on their emotions for fear the children might find them in a passionate embrace and be horrified. Somehow, she could not doubt that they would be horrified to find Glynn kissing her. She had no doubt that the dislike they imagined they felt for him would turn to hate, and that she could not risk. Before she could ever begin to relax in the happiness of the love she shared with Glynn, she *must* reconcile the boys to the idea that he was to become their stepfather; to overcome the jealousy she supposed was quite natural under the circumstances; never to give them the smallest reason on which to base their antagonism to Glynn.

"Darling," she said suddenly, "will you take out the tin bath and fill it for Simon and Richard? I promised they could have it to splash about in today."

He did not guess at the strategy that lay behind her simple request for aid in carrying the heavy bath. But Lindsey was working on the new idea she had that Glynn should be the one to give the children any pleasant surprise that might be coming to them; that, without knowing it, the boys would begin to associate Glynn with the nice things that happened, and thereby begin to enjoy his company and want him there.

Glancing out of the kitchen window, she watched her two small boys scampering round Glynn as he carried the galvanized bath on to the lawn and heard their shouts and saw their bright faces and felt that she was going to win this little battle. It would be only a question of time and patience and as she had tried so hard to explain to Glynn, they had all the rest of their lives to spend together. A little patience now would make so much difference to the success of their marriage in the future.

Lindsey did not worry when she heard the sound of a car in the drive, believing that it was the milkman, who never came until mid-morning on Sundays. She remained in the kitchen peeling potatoes for lunch, her eyes on Glynn and the children in the sunny garden, oblivious to the fact that Paris Rogers was walking in through the open front door.

Her surprise was so sharp when he spoke to her from the kitchen doorway that she let the small kitchen knife slip, and a second later was clasping a badly cut finger.

Immediately Paris was beside her, apologizing, anxiously mopping at her finger from which the blood was pouring freely with a clean handkerchief.

"I'm so sorry, Lindsey . . . I called out but no one came to the door and I supposed you were all in the garden . . . in fact, I heard the children's voices from the garden. I am so sorry!"

For a moment, Lindsey concentrated on her cut finger, which, while it did not hurt a great deal, was nevertheless managing to bleed profusely. She let Paris reach up to the mantelshelf where she kept her first-aid box, cut a fresh square of lint and bind up the finger with a bandage. As he was doing so, his long fingers surprisingly gentle and efficient for a man, she tried to gather her senses. What was he doing here? What right had he to burst in like this, uninvited, to spoil her day? Surely she had made it clear enough that she didn't want to see him! And any moment Glynn would come back and see him here and she had told him that she intended never to meet Paris again!

"Why did you come here?" she asked, abrupt because she was annoyed and strangely confused by his presence so close to her. How blue his eyes were as they stared into her own . . . a sailor blue! Quickly she looked away, and picking up the first-aid box, covered her confusion in unnecessarily tidying it.

"It was so beautiful a day I thought perhaps you would permit me to take the boys on the river!" Paris said calmly, a half smile on his face as he watched the colour come and go in her cheeks. "I will take the greatest care of them, of course."

"Oh, but I'm afraid . . . it's very kind of you, but . . . well, as a matter of fact, I have a guest."

"How stupid of me not to telephone first!" Paris said in

pretended surprise. "It is most disappointing. I had thought perhaps we could swim and maybe do some more fishing. I realized that the holidays must soon be over, and you had said that I might give them one treat."

"Yes . . . yes, I did, but . . ." Lindsey felt hopelessly unable to deal with the situation. Resolving to be firm at all costs and to put an end to this kind of thing once and for all, she said abruptly: "I ought perhaps to have told you when I last spoke on the telephone, I . . . it is my fiancé who has come down to see me today . . . I'm going to be married . . . I'm sorry . . ." Her voice trailed away.

"But why should you be sorry?" Paris asked smoothly. "On the contrary, Lindsey, my congratulations and very best wishes for your happiness. May I ask who is the fortunate man?"

"He's an old friend . . . his name is Glynn Noble. I believe I hear him coming now with the children!"

"Then I may at least say hullo to the boys and give your fiancé my congratulations before I go?" Paris asked.

Lindsey grabbed at the straw he offered her. After he had seen the boys and Glynn, he would go! Silently, she led him through the kitchen door, on to the terrace where they had sat together in the twilight, and there came face to face with Glynn and the boys.

The moment of meeting between the two men, which might have been awkward, was made easy by her two small sons. They flung themselves with childish abandon into Paris' arms and Lindsey watched, all else forgotten, as they gave him a rapturous welcome. She felt an insane desire to slap them both hard. How could they show such obvious affection for Paris on so short an acquaintance! How dare they make such a difference between their liking for him and Glynn! It hurt and angered her and she dared not look at the expression on Glynn's face.

"Oh, Uncle Paris, what a scrumptious surprise!" Richard was gasping as he clung to one hand, Simon to the other.

"Pop's going to have babies!" Simon clamoured. "He's ever so fat, and I'm sure he's a she!"

"I came to see if your mother would permit me to take you both on the river!" Paris said in his slow calm voice with that trace of accent which made it so unmistakable. "I didn't know, of course, that you had a visitor."

"Oh, but we can go, can't we, Mummy?" Richard left Paris' side to tug at Lindsey's skirt.

Lindsey gave Paris a furious glance which he did not see as he was looking down at Simon with an enigmatic smile. How dare he do this!

"But of course not!" she said sharply. "Uncle Glynn wants to see something of you now he is here!"

"Oh, but, Mummy . . ." Richard began when Lindsey said again sharply:

"Glynn, this is Paris Rogers, my literary agent."

"I believe I am to congratulate you on your forthcoming marriage to Lindsey," Paris said, deliberately setting the cat among the pigeons, for he had learned from June that Lindsey was having trouble reconciling the boys to the idea of Glynn as a stepfather. He did not know that she had not got so far as telling them that she was going to marry Glynn.

The boys were staring at their mother and Glynn alternately, round-eyed and aghast.

"Marriage?" Richard asked, stupefied. "You mean you are going to marry Uncle Glynn, Mummy?"

Lindsey bit her lip and looked at Glynn for help. He said:

"There's no point in letting them think otherwise, Lindsey, is there? They have to know sooner or later. Yes, we are to be married next year!"

"But I am so sorry!" Paris said with surprise that was quite genuine. "I had no idea this was a secret from the children. I . . . I really do apologize."

"But, Mummy . . ." Richard began again when Lindsey silenced him with a fierce glance that he had never seen before on his mother's face and which frightened him as well as stopped him speaking. Simon, who did not fully understand the conversation, and who, in any case, was more single-minded, said:

"But we *can* go fishing with Uncle Paris, Mummy?"

Paris looked at Lindsey questioningly, and a swift refusal sprang to her lips, but before she could voice it, Glynn said:

"Why not, Lindsey, if they want to go?" His glance said unmistakably that he would welcome the chance of a few hours alone with her.

Torn by the conflict of emotions that beset her, Lindsey found nothing to say. The children immediately took her silence for assent and flung themselves on Paris, demanding that they leave now.

"Then it is all right after all?" Paris asked, watching Lindsey's face. "I assure you I shall not let them come to harm, and I will bring them back to you at whatever time you say!"

"I'll get their cardigans!" Lindsey said furiously. "And please don't let them be too late back, Mr Rogers!"

His eyebrows lifted as she spoke this formal method of address and, just for an instant, she felt an hysterical desire to laugh as she saw a glance of pure mischief in those blue eyes. A moment later, she felt an equally hysterical desire to slap his face. She did neither, but walked past him into the house.

In the children's bedroom, she sat down, unable to support herself on legs that trembled. How dare he! How dare he! Agent or not, she would have nothing more to do with him after today. She would tell the children, too, that they were to stop talking about him once and for all as they would not see him any more. He had won this round perhaps . . . but this was the last round there would be. Now he knew she was going to marry Glynn, he must in all decency leave her alone.

Paradoxically, she realized that he had not in fact come to see her today. He had come to see the boys! Could he have intended to take them out and leave her here alone?

For he could not have known that Glynn would be here. Or had he merely hoped that she would agree to go along, too?

Perplexed, angered, disturbed and thoroughly confused by the events of the last half hour, Lindsey made her way downstairs to find Paris and the boys already packed into the car. Glynn was not to be seen.

"Put these on if you get cold!" she told the children, and to Paris she gave their bathing trunks and towels, a feeling of complete unreality assailing her as she added: "Don't let them stay in the water too long!"

"No, Mrs Carter!"

The use of her surname caused her, as he had intended, to look up and meet his eyes, which were smiling again and disconcerting in a way she could not explain.

She turned on her heel and went back into the house, and, a moment later, heard the car roar off down the drive. Everything was suddenly quiet, and with a speed that surprised her, she hurried out into the garden to find Glynn.

He sat in a deck chair, smoking, and as she came up to him, said:

"Have they gone?"

She nodded as she took the chair beside him.

"Not a type I care for!" Glynn said abruptly. "I assume he wasn't expected."

"He certainly was not!" Lindsey said violently.

"Damn nerve!" Glynn said rudely. "Foreigner, isn't he? What did you say, half French?"

Again she nodded. Against her will, she found herself defending Paris.

"I think he is genuinely interested in the boys. He has no family of his own – they were killed in the war – and I suppose he's lonely."

"Doesn't strike me as the 'lonely' type!" Glynn said, his voice irritable. "Hasn't he got any girlfriends?"

"He never mentioned any!" Lindsey said. "But then, we are

not really on those kind of terms, Glynn, as I told you. I know very little about him."

"He doesn't exactly behave like a stranger!" Glynn said jealously.

"Darling, don't let's talk about him!" Lindsey said with a violence of feeling that caused Glynn to glance at her sharply. "I don't like him and if it hadn't been for the boys wanting to go so much, I'd never have let him take them today."

Glynn's expression changed.

"Well, it gives us a break, doesn't it, sweetheart? I suppose they won't be back till after tea. We can count on about seven hours to ourselves!"

She understood his wish to be alone with her, for her own wishes had lately been so similar. Since that first time when she had fallen in love with Glynn again, and they had had all Sunday alone together to rediscover each other, they seemed to have had no more than a snatched moment or two to themselves. They had only met twice in fact since that weekend, both times here in the house with the thought always at the back of Lindsey's mind that the boys were within earshot, and it had been impossible for her to give her whole mind to Glynn or to the magic of his brief stolen kisses. It had been almost as if they were furtive and ashamed of their love, and Glynn had voiced this opinion quite clearly the last time they were together.

"Dash it all, Lindsey, the boys are in bed asleep, and I have to push off in a few moments."

So she had allowed him to kiss her, feeling desperate and anxious and worried and not really giving her whole thought to Glynn as he drew her into his arms.

And when his passionate intensity at last found an answering chord in her, she wished with her whole heart that they were not here in this tiny cottage with the boys so near and this strange feeling of guilt towards them to spoil all their happiness.

Now they had the whole of the rest of the day to themselves and it would be for them both as it had been that Sunday on the hills. She would convince Glynn once and for all that she really loved him . . . that if he would only be patient a little longer, she would soon be his wife.

She said:

"Now that Mr Rogers has told the boys we are to be married it will bring everything to a head, Glynn. I was furiously angry when he did speak but, on reflection, I think maybe it's just as well. They have to know sooner or later and maybe the sooner they do know, the sooner they will accept the idea."

"They seemed to get over the shock pretty quickly!" Glynn commented. "You worry far too much about them, Lindsey. Dash it all, they are only seven and eight!"

"Yet children do feel things very intensely at that age," Lindsey replied thoughtfully. "And the last few months have been full of changes for them, Glynn. Their – their father dying, and moving to this cottage. When there are these kind of changes they need added security. They need to be able to depend on me."

"And why not on me, too?" Glynn said reasonably. "I like them both very much, as you know, darling. If only they'd give me half a chance, I'd make them glad they were having me for a stepfather. But you must admit, they haven't been very forthcoming as yet in spite of my efforts."

"I know, Glynn! They have been awkward. But be patient, dearest, please, for my sake if not for theirs."

But Glynn did not immediately respond to her plea for his understanding. He voiced another grievance.

"They seemed a damned sight more pleased to see Rogers just now . . . greeted him like a long-lost friend."

Lindsey felt the colour race into her cheeks. It had been so patently obvious to them both that the boys had rushed to Paris in a way they had never once gone to Glynn.

"Maybe it is simply that they know instinctively they have no cause to be jealous of him . . . that he doesn't constitute a threat to their possession of me!" she said, more hopefully than truthfully; for until a moment ago the boys had had no cause to distinguish between the two men except as individuals. They had not known she was going to marry Glynn or that she loved him . . . unless, somehow they *had* guessed . . .

Her thoughts reverted suddenly to Paris and the reason for his coming here today. Had he really come just to take the boys out? Had she been wrong in assuming that he was interested in her? That he was really only interested in Simon and Richard, who, no doubt, were a novelty to him?

Then she remembered their strange half hour alone together on the terrace when he had imprisoned her hand and a gentle thoughtful Paris, new to her in this guise, asked for her friendship and told her he believed they could be such good companions. How odd it seemed in retrospect! But then he was an odd man. There appeared no accounting for the unusualness of his behaviour. Maybe the fact that he was half French had something to do with it. Friends! Were men and women ever friends? Surely not men like Paris Rogers! Yet she had to admit that until now he had never offered her anything but friendship.

"I will not think about him!" she told herself for the second time in a half hour. She turned to Glynn and the frown left her forehead and she smiled gently, saying:

"Don't look so cross, darling. Tell me what you'd like to do!"

He turned and looked at her with those dark, burning eyes of his and there was no smile on his face as he said:

"I'd like to put you in my car and drive you miles and miles away, Lindsey! To marry you, this afternoon, and begin our honeymoon tonight. I want to be sure in my heart that now that I have found you again, I shall never lose you."

She bit her lip, quelling the nervousness that threatened her voice, and said lightly:

"But, darling, how could we lose one another now? I love you, Glynn."

He pulled her to her feet and a moment later they were out of the sunlight in the cool shadow of the tiny hall and she was crushed against his heart. Even as she felt herself respond to him with all the awakened ardour of her nature, she thought, We cannot go on like this all day! Neither of us will be strong enough to bear this kind of feeling unrequited for long.

"Glynn, Glynn!" she whispered, desperation in her tone of voice. "Please let me go, darling, please!"

"But why, why?" he asked roughly. "What are you afraid of, Lindsey? There is no one here but ourselves!"

She realized how contradictory she must seem to Glynn if she voiced her reply. At other moments she had left Glynn's arms because the children might find them in a passionate embrace; now that the boys were probably miles away, she found herself afraid to be alone with Glynn. Was she always to be afraid of something? Could she never relax and give herself completely to love . . . to Glynn? Or at least, love him as freely as her standards permitted until they were married.

Tentatively, she tried to tell Glynn that she feared the consequences of too much love-making between them. He did not at first understand her.

"Surely you are not afraid I'll take advantage of you in that way?" he asked, drawing away from her. "You know I wouldn't do anything you didn't want me to do."

"But I might want you to make love to me!" Lindsey cried desperately. "I am afraid of myself!"

And it was terribly true, for she seemed now to be constantly assailed by emotions that were new and frightening to her when, for so many years, she had always had her feelings completely under control; had always known exactly how she would react, how she wished to behave; what she wished to do and say. Yet ever since . . . since she had been jolted out of her rut by Paris, she had lost the precious certainty of herself that made life in the past so easy, so bearable.

"Would it matter so much?" Glynn was asking her. "You are going to be my wife, Lindsey!"

Now it has happened again, she told herself wildly. I don't

want to belong to Glynn in that way until we are married, and I see exactly what he means . . . why should it matter so much since we are to be married in a few months' time anyway? Glynn would not think the less of her although she might think a great deal less of herself for going against a moral principle that was so strong in her. Yet, in the physical sense, she needed Glynn as much as he needed her. She felt that it would bring them to a fuller and more complete understanding and knowledge of each other. In some ways they were still strangers . . . strangers where once they had been such perfect friends. One could not, after all, pick up the threads of that adolescent love where they had been dropped. They had to start again, to build something new together, to learn to know each other again as individuals. They seemed only to be really together in thought and understanding when they were in each other's arms. Then she felt she was where she belonged and she had no doubts as to their future happiness.

Did she ever have doubts? she asked herself, as they went back outside into the garden. She touched Glynn's dark, curly hair with her fingertips, watching him with unseeing eyes as he drew on the cigarette he had lit. Could she make him happy? Did she know how? What did she know of this man who was, after all, different from the boy she had known so well?

"Glynn, tell me more about yourself!" she said as she sat on a cushion, curling her legs beneath her and leaning her head against Glynn's knees. "Tell me what we shall do and say and think when we are married."

His face brightened and became boyish again. The faintly brooding look had gone.

"We're going to have such a wonderful time!" he said eagerly. "I shall buy a house in London, I think, so that we can entertain and go to the best shows and generally be in the swim. Then at the weekends we'll go to Woodley Manor. I've talked to Marie-Louise and she says we can redecorate the top floor and have it all to ourselves as a weekend retreat. In the summer we'll take a cottage in Devon or go abroad for a month and perhaps go ski-ing in the winter. As you know, Dad's business practically runs itself, and as his junior partner I really only have to look in and out occasionally and sit on boards and attend meetings; so life will be pretty easy."

It had never really occurred to Lindsey as important that she was marrying a very wealthy young man. She had known it of course, but not applied it to herself. As Glynn's wife, she could have practically anything she wanted. Yet she did not really want to live in London . . . nor would the boys. She had spent all her own childhood in the country and a love for it was so ingrained in her that she never felt relaxed or well in a big city even while she enjoyed what it offered her intellectually. But home . . . well, home meant a country house and garden.

She thought back again to her childhood. Only child of rather elderly parents, she had always been very much alone. She had been sent to boarding school, to give her companionship, and had made friends – Marie-Louise and June Helmer in particular. She remained independent and was never lonely playing by herself as a child. Her father, a solicitor, was away from home nearly all day and, while fond of him, there had never been any very real or deep understanding between them as there is sometimes between fathers and daughters. But then he was nearing fifty when she was born and the gap in years was too much for them to breach, just as it was with her mother, who was past her fortieth birthday when suddenly Lindsey appeared to end their childless state. First a nurse and then a governess and finally boarding school had served to widen the gap between her and her mother and when, in the second year of her marriage to Elvin, both parents had died within a year of each other, her father from a heart attack and her mother from pneumonia, Lindsey had grieved a little while as she might have done for grandparents, and then readjusted her life without them.

But her childhood, solitary though it had been, had also been a safe, happy one. Her parents had loved her and seen that she was well looked after, and she had had all the beauties of a Sussex country garden in which to grow up and learn and develop her flowering personality. She had realized the benefit of a country life to her and wanted the same for her sons.

But she hesitated to say now to Glynn that it might not be best for the boys to live in town. Instead, she said only that she would prefer not to do so herself.

Glynn seemed surprised.

"But, darling, you don't want to go on living this kind of life, do you? I want to take you away from this . . . to give you light and brightness and gaiety."

"Couldn't we have those things in the country?"

"Well, we could entertain at weekends of course. But most of my friends live in London and they wouldn't come out for an evening during the week. Of course, Marie-Louise and Mike would probably move if I suggested it. Dad really left the house for me while he and Mother are away, but as I had a flat in town and didn't want to be there all week, it seemed the sensible thing to do to let Mike and Marie-Louise have the place and just go down when I wanted. Actually the house is too big for them and Mike is always saying it costs the devil of a lot to keep going."

"But I wouldn't want to turn them out!" Lindsey said quickly.

"And I wouldn't want to share!" Glynn said, smiling at her possessively. "I want you all to myself, darling. Surely the sensible thing to do is to live in town and weekend in the country? Remember what fun we used to have in London in the old days? Dinners in Soho, dancing, theatres, and the ice-hockey matches! We can do all those things again, Lindsey!"

He was so enthusiastic that she did not want to discourage him. She listened silently while he listed the good times they might have together; told her how proud he would be to have her as his hostess at the dinner parties they would give; how they could take the boys to the circus, the pantomime, the museums and ice-shows in the holidays.

His mention of Simon and Richard gave her the opening she sought. She said slowly:

"Could we afford to keep two places going, Glynn? I mean, would it be possible to keep this cottage? You see, Simon's one passion in life is animals and except for the zoo he really isn't very keen on anything else! And Richard wants to ride and fish. They couldn't really do those things in London. I thought maybe we could keep the cottage going just for the holidays?"

If Glynn was reminded sharply that there were two others to be considered now besides himself and Lindsey, he gave no indication of his feelings. He said generously:

"Well, why not? That would solve everything for everyone. We can have the place enlarged, two more bedrooms and another living room. We can get a good reliable nanny or governess or whatever boys of their age have and be free to go up to London if we want. We'll keep the house open for when we need it."

A sharp fear shot through Lindsey's heart, a fear that Glynn would not want to be with the boys during the holidays as much as she would; that he would not be willing for her to devote herself exclusively to them in the few weeks she had them at home! Then she quelled that fear as unreasonable. Glynn wasn't used to being a father and she could hardly expect him at this stage to feel her love and affectionate selflessness for her sons. It was only natural that he, too, should be a little jealous and possessive at first and want her all to himself! During term time she could be all wife to him, and when the holidays came, he would be ready to spare her for a few weeks to her children. Then, of course, they might have children of their own. They could no doubt afford to if Glynn wished it. But she wouldn't talk of that now. It was clear to her that Glynn's mind was taken up completely with her . . . and their future together as man and wife. He had not her experience of married life . . . of family life. His was the

116

romantic outlook of a boy . . . believing that if two people loved each other, everything would be "happy ever after".

And it will! she thought, suddenly as sure of it as she was determined to make it so. When Glynn looked down at her and asked her her thoughts, she smiled up at him reassuringly.

Then she escaped from the imprisonment of his outstretched arms and went into her tiny kitchen to get some lunch.

Eleven

They had fished first, then swam, and now they had eaten an enormous lunch from the hamper Paris had brought with him, and were lying in brief shorts, their bodies soaking up the sun.

Simon was trying to stretch himself so that he could touch Paris' toes, but when triumphantly he claimed, "I am as tall as you, look!" Paris had to point out that he had wormed his head down with his toes and that it was now beside his waist.

"Will I ever be as tall as you?" Simon asked.

"When you're as old as I am!" Paris said, smiling. "But you don't want to be in a hurry to grow up, Simon. It's much more fun being a boy than being a man. When you're a man you have to work all day in a horrible office."

"Yes, I suppose so!" Simon agreed, and then, his freckled face brightening: "But I'm not going to, I'm going to be a vet!"

"Yes, of course!" Paris said seriously. "That reminds me, how is Pop?"

"I'm certain he's going to have babies!" Simon said, propping himself on an elbow to look earnestly into Paris' face. "He's enormously fat!"

"Then he must be a she!" Paris said, trying not to smile. "It could be too much bread and milk though!"

"I know! I thought of that. But I think it is babies. Uncle Paris, could it be?"

"Well, I rather doubt it!" Paris said, concealing the amusement he felt. "Even if Pop were a 'she', there would need to be a father guinea pig if there were to be baby ones."

"We had a father once!" Richard said suddenly, his method of phrasing his remark showing Paris how much longer time's span was for children. After all, Elvin Carter had not been dead a year yet Richard made it sound long ago. "He died, you know."

"Yes, I know!" Paris said, waiting for further confidences which he guessed from Richard's expression would be forthcoming.

"Uncle Paris, if Mummy marries Uncle Glynn, does that make him Simon's and my father?"

"No!" Paris said shortly. "He would be your stepfather. But your Mummy isn't going to marry Uncle Glynn!"

Both boys sat up and looked at him from enormous questioning eyes.

"But he said . . . she said . . ." began Richard.

Paris smiled.

"Grown-ups don't always mean what they say . . . or at least, they mean it when they say it but then they change their minds. If your Mummy marries anyone, she will marry me!"

It was a dangerous prophecy to make, Paris realized, even as he spoke. Not only dangerous in so far as it might not come true, but very unfair to these two children if it did not. How angry Lindsey would be if she knew! Yet he could not unsay the words.

"Oh, Uncle Paris . . . that would be scrumptious! *Super!*" Richard breathed. And Simon, less able to believe without proof, said:

"But how do you *know*?"

"Well, no one can know for absolutely certain about anything!" Paris said slowly. "But I love your Mummy very dearly and I love you two as well, and I think we could all be very happy together. I hope that I can persuade Mummy to feel the same."

"We don't like Uncle Glynn!" Richard said. "We told Mummy and she was cross!"

"Well, naturally she wouldn't be very happy about it!" Paris

119

replied. "After all, he is a very old friend of hers and if she likes him you should try to like him, too. In any case, you haven't any cause to dislike him, have you?"

"He doesn't like us!" Simon said in a rush of words.

"Surely he hasn't said that?"

"No, but we know!" Richard said with conviction. "He wants Mummy all to himself and he won't even share. Uncle Paris, can we tell Mummy you said she would marry you?"

Paris hesitated, but only for a moment. He would not have secrets from Lindsey or ask the boys to conceal anything they might wish to say to her.

"If you really want to!" he said slowly.

Richard pursed his lips.

"Perhaps she'd be cross if she thinks she wants to marry Uncle Glynn. I vote we keep it a secret, Simon."

Simon, who, like all small boys, loved secrets, agreed instantly.

Silence fell for a few moments. Then Richard said:

"When will she change her mind, Uncle Paris?"

"I wish I could be sure of that," Paris said. "It may take a long, long time. I don't know. There may not be a lot of time. Anyway, you can count on me to do everything I can."

The boys were immediately reassured and light-hearted again; they forgot the problems of grown-ups and fell in a heap on top of Paris, cajoling him to a rough and tumble before, hot and sticky with their exercise, they all three plunged back into the river for another swim.

He took them to tea at a riverside café where they ate mountains of ice cream and cakes. Looking across the table at their flushed, contented and absorbed little faces Paris was surprised to discover how contented he was, too! It was true that he had planned today as part of his campaign to bring himself to Lindsey's notice. Yet in the little while he had known the boys he had grown so genuinely fond of them, was so interested in each of them as separate individuals, that the day had passed without any real regrets that Lindsey was not with them. But now, as he instructed the boys to put on their cardigans against the slight chill in the air, he thought of her . . . thought of the cool reception he would get when he took the boys home, and suddenly his heart hurt him. She would be flushed and happy from a day alone with Glynn. She would, no doubt, have his kisses still on her lips, her body still afire from his touch. Furious jealousy smote Paris so unexpectedly that he found he was shivering. He felt a completely uncivilized wish to drive back to Lindsey's house, seek out Glynn and smash in his rival's face with his fists.

Yet even as the thought crossed his mind, he smiled at himself, knowing that this was not the way.

When, soon after six o'clock, he followed the children into their house, the greeting he gave Glynn and Lindsey was cool and smiling.

"We've had a wonderful day!" he said. "Thank you so much for 'lending' me the boys."

"Thank you for taking them!" Lindsey said, an arm round each small shoulder. "They look as if they've thoroughly enjoyed themselves."

Her eyes dropped before Paris' steady gaze and she felt suddenly shy, awkward, confused.

"Glynn, will you give Mr Rogers a drink while I push these two into bed?"

Glynn nodded his head kindly. He had no ill feelings towards Paris now that the day had shown him to his satisfaction that Lindsey was his for the taking. In fact he could feel sorry for the chap who had lost her. He could even feel grateful, too, for the fact that he had taken the kids out of the way. He said as much to Paris when he handed him a whisky and soda.

"I enjoyed it!" Paris said.

"Oh, they're not a bad pair, I suppose!" Glynn said. "But they do rather get in one's way at times!"

"I expect they are jealous!" Paris said smoothly.

"I've no doubt of it!" Glynn agreed. "All the same, they'll have to make the best of it when Lindsey and I are married."

"And when will that be?" Paris questioned.

"Soon . . . at least, I think I've persuaded Lindsey there's nothing much to be gained by waiting. We were discussing it today. My point is that the sooner the boys accept the thing as a fact, the sooner they'll learn to like it."

"I trust you are right!" Paris replied, shrugging his shoulders as if he were not much concerned. "Nevertheless, they could make things awkward . . . for Lindsey, I mean. After all, she loves them, too. It wouldn't be very . . . shall we say, comfortable for her, having to keep the peace between you and them!"

"Oh, it won't come to that!" Glynn said confidently. "I'm prepared to give way a bit myself – I realize they are important to Lindsey – they're her kids after all."

"You must let me know if you want them out of the way on any future occasion!" Paris said, smiling. "I enjoy taking them out and would like to do so again."

"That's very nice of you, old chap!" Glynn said warmly. "I don't altogether understand how you *enjoy* playing nursemaid, but then I'm not all that fond of kids."

"Then please tell Lindsey to let me know if you prefer a day without them!" Paris repeated.

They discussed the latest cricket scores until Lindsey rejoined them and she was a little surprised to find them apparently getting on so well. Paris rose as she came in and said it was time he left.

She made no effort to detain him. His presence was altogether too unsettling for her to wish him to stay. After his departure, she found herself discussing him with Glynn.

"I don't trust him!" she said. "I don't mean with the children . . . but . . . well, you never really know what's behind his actions."

"Oh? I rather liked the fellow!" Glynn said, to Lindsey's surprise. "I admit I was a bit jealous when I first heard you talk about him. But it's clear he isn't interested in you . . . only in the boys. Of course, that's odd . . . but then the fellow's a foreigner, isn't he? That probably explains a lot. All the foreigners I've met dote on kids."

Suddenly Lindsey disliked herself. She had no interest in Paris as a man . . . not now that she was so certainly in love with Glynn, yet she had felt more than a little put out to hear Glynn confirm her own feelings today – that Paris was not the least bit interested in her! What kind of woman was she who wanted admiration from others as well as from the man she loved? How unlikable to be piqued at Paris' indifference! How selfish to prefer him to be a rival to Glynn for her affections.

"I'm surprised to hear you like him," she said to Glynn. "I wouldn't have thought he was your type at all."

"Well, maybe not exactly. But I found him very understanding."

"About what?"

Glynn looked up at Lindsey's tone.

"Well, about us!" he said.

"And what is there to understand about us?"

Glynn looked both hurt and surprised by her angry tone.

"Well, I don't see why you're flying off the handle like this. I merely meant he seemed to . . . to appreciate our difficulties."

"What difficulties?"

"If you're going to be obtuse, Lindsey, we might as well stop the discussion," Glynn said, his irritation getting the better of him.

"I don't exactly enjoy hearing that you've been discussing me with another man . . . a stranger at that!"

"We weren't really discussing *you*," Glynn replied. "As a matter of fact, we talked mostly about the boys."

"So they are the difficulty?"

Glynn stood up and tried to take Lindsey's hand, but she drew away from him sharply. Annoyed by the rebuff, Glynn said:

"Well, we might as well face it, Lindsey. If it weren't for the boys, we could be married next week. You said so yourself this afternoon!"

Conflicting emotions assailed Lindsey, leaving her momentarily speechless. She bitterly resented the boys placed in the light of stumbling-blocks . . . difficulties! Yet she had to admit that Glynn was right.

"We're quarrelling!" she said suddenly. "Glynn!"

He came to her at once, his arms round her and his voice tender.

"I'm sorry, darling, if anything I said upset you."

Yet even as he kissed her, Lindsey felt a stab of unhappiness deep down within . . . a disloyalty to her two little sons for not having defended them. Yet she returned Glynn's kisses with a desperation that he mistook for passion and an hour passed before at last he released her.

"I think I'd better go home now!" he said unevenly. "If I don't, I'll be here all night. Love me, darling?"

"Yes, yes, I do!" Lindsey cried, accepting her need of him and quelling her uneasiness which threatened to spoil even this last moment together.

"And you'll come down to stay with us next weekend after the boys have gone back to school?"

"Yes!"

He managed in time to refrain from saying what was in his mind . . . that it would be a relief not to have to worry about the boys . . . wonderful to have her all to himself.

But after he had gone, Lindsey felt the onrush of loneliness that the boys' imminent departure to boarding school always gave her. She remembered, too, that after the promised weekend at Woodley Manor she must really get down to work. Her finances were on very thin ice and it was time she started on a new novel.

Work reminded her of Paris and she felt herself assailed yet again by indecision. She had said she would get another agent . . . that she would refuse to see Paris again. Yet it would be a poor reward for the pleasure he had given Richard and

Simon today; for the efforts he had made to get her foreign rights sold . . . to speed up her book advance. She could not quarrel with him as an agent. And she could not put her finger on any reason for quarrelling with him as a man. If he had no personal interest in her, no reason existed for making a break with him. Only her instinct demanded that she put him right out of her life . . . prompted her not to trust him or his motives. Even the fact that Glynn liked him unsettled her and puzzled her.

She sighed deeply as she wandered out in the dark garden and past the wooden box beneath the boys' bedroom window where Simon kept Pop. Then she smiled, recalling her small son's pleasure in the little animal and the fact that soon she would have to take care of it for him until next holidays. She wondered idly if she need take it with her next weekend! Then she decided that she could leave sufficient food and water. It would look so absurd for her to arrive complete with guinea pig!

The future, which had seemed so rosy as Glynn talked today here in the sunlit garden, now seemed shrouded in the same half darkness. Alone in the warm, starless night, it was less easy to be sure that everything they planned together would come out right. At least Glynn had agreed that they should keep this cottage for the boys' holidays. Perhaps he believed that once she was taken out of the "rut", as he called it, and into the bright lights and social whirl of London, she would not be so anxious to return. She who loved the country, loved these warm summer nights and days as much as she enjoyed the winter cold and toasted crumpets in front of a huge log fire. In winter, the boys could take their toboggans on the slopes that were covered in snow. They could skate on the pond down by the village. Their holidays went so quickly, even the long summer holidays, and she did so want them to be completely happy and free in a way they could never be in a city.

Of course, Glynn was right when he pointed out that thousands of children did live in towns . . . that they seemed happy enough. Yet in Lindsey's mind, museums and pantomimes and the parks and Kew could not compensate for the adventurous unplanned freedom of a garden in the country. Here a boy could give free rein to his imagination . . . not just accept ready-made entertainments. He could amuse himself and develop as a boy was meant to develop . . . without fear of dirtying his clothes or breaking something or getting run over.

Glynn would appreciate this once he got to know the children better . . . saw them in a different light. Naturally now they appeared to him more as "difficulties" . . . standing in the way of his happiness . . . and hers! He would find out what fun they could be . . . what good company . . . and then everything would be all right.

So comforted, Lindsey went indoors to get ready for bed.

Twelve

L indsey sat in June's tiny bed-sitting-room, drinking tea and smoking . . . too much, June had just told her.

"You've lost pounds in weight since last summer!" she said, casting an anxious glance in Lindsey's direction. "In fact, you look thin and ill, Lindsey!"

Lindsey gave a brittle little laugh.

"Do I? I suppose it's because I'm worried."

The need to confide, which she had until now refrained from doing, became too much for her. She said suddenly:

"It's all so damned difficult, June. Glynn keeps pressing me to give him a date for our wedding, and the more importunate he becomes, the more the children make it clear that they don't like him!"

"Surely that's an exaggeration, Lindsey? He hasn't given them cause to dislike him, has he?"

Lindsey shrugged her shoulders helplessly.

"No! That's what makes it so difficult. Last holidays, just before they went back to school, I was so sure everything would work out right. Instead, everything seems to have gone wrong. I just don't know what to do. Apart from everything else, my writing has suffered . . . I suppose because my mind wasn't really on it . . . and if it hadn't been for the foreign market where, thank heaven, Paris always seems to find a home for my stuff, I'd be forced to take the children away from school . . . or at least, break into the trust fund I put by for their schooling. I haven't sold more than one story on the English market!"

"Does Paris say what is wrong with your work?"

"Only that it isn't cheerful enough! I suppose I have been a bit depressed myself and that it comes out in my writing. Fortunately the French seem to like my gloomy stories and they pay quite well."

"Then why the depression?" June asked.

"The boys . . . and Glynn. He's beginning to doubt my love for him because I won't commit myself to a date for the wedding. But how can I, June, when I know Simon and Richard hate the idea?"

"How can you know? Have they said so?"

"Today was a typical example . . . at least, what led up to today!" Lindsey said. "As you know, they broke up last week. Glynn and Mike and Marie-Louise wanted us to go to them for Christmas. I thought it would be a lovely idea. Quite apart from my wanting to be near Glynn, large parties are fun for the children . . . at least, I thought so. But as soon as they came home and I told them, they argued fiercely against the plan. They wanted Christmas by themselves with me at the cottage! I had just about persuaded them to agree to go . . . reluctantly, I admit, when this invitation comes from Paris to take them both to the pantomime. That did it! They couldn't be in London on Boxing Day for a pantomime and be at Marie-Louise's house over Christmas. They begged and pleaded and badgered me until I had to give in. After all, Christmas is supposed to be for the children's pleasure. So I had to write to Marie-Louise and put off our visit till after Christmas and Glynn was dreadfully upset. I suppose I should have asked him to come to us yesterday, but the boys stressed they wanted to be alone with me! Now I'm afraid I've been wrong to give way to them. If I let them get away with it this time, they'll expect it next time. It isn't fair on Glynn."

"Couldn't *he* have taken them to the pantomime?" June asked thoughtfully.

"Well, yes!" Lindsey said. "As a matter of fact he did offer to take them out but not until after Christmas. We didn't know, of course, that Paris was going to ask them and he sent the invitation direct to Richard. The truth is, June, that the boys much prefer Paris to Glynn and if it came to a choice between who should take them, they wouldn't hesitate. I wish Paris hadn't asked them . . . or at least asked me if it was all right to invite them before posting that letter to Richard. He can't have known how annoying it would be for me . . . I realize that . . . but he always seems to put his foot wrong however inadvertently."

Not so inadvertently! June thought, remembering the evening just before Christmas when she had dined once more with Paris and found him cheerful and hopeful about the future as he outlined it to her. His confidences, and now Lindsey's, put her in an awkward position. She had promised Paris once again not to reveal anything he told her . . . yet Lindsey needed help badly. She really did look ill. How could she help her friend without giving Paris away?

"At one time, I thought Paris was . . . well, a bit interested in me—" Lindsey's voice broke off awkwardly, then resumed: "But I realize I was mistaken. He never tried to communicate with me when the boys had gone back to school . . . except on business. So I can't very well accuse him of deliberately trying to put a spoke in Glynn's wheel, can I? Yet that's the way it always appears! I'm sure if they hadn't met Paris first, the boys would have been all right with Glynn."

"Perhaps!" June said. "I see it makes things very difficult for you, Lindsey. You don't feel like taking a chance and marrying Glynn in the hope that his relationship with the children will improve?"

"I think that's what will happen!" Lindsey said. "Glynn and I have even been reduced to quarrelling . . . and I don't in my heart believe I should let the children come between us. Yet Simon and Richard are my children . . . part of me, June. I can't bring myself to do anything to make them unhappy . . . something that might make them feel I'd failed them as a mother. June, what do other women in my position do? It must have happened before to thousands of war widows. Did they put their children's happiness before that of the man they loved . . . before their own?"

"I can't answer that!" June said sympathetically. "I suppose they each made up their minds to the best of their ability."

"What would *you* do in my shoes?" Lindsey persisted.

"I can't answer that either!" June said sharply. How could she when she was so deeply in love with Paris that, not having had children or known what it was to love them, she would give anything in the whole world to become his wife! How could Lindsey hesitate? Surely her whole problem could be so easily solved . . . except that she loved Glynn.

"You really love Glynn?" she asked.

Lindsey glanced at her surprised.

"But of course. That is about the only thing I am sure of!" she said.

"If you really are sure, I think you should marry him," June said hesitantly. "After all, the boys will grow up and leave home . . . you, and what will be left for you then? Glynn wouldn't wait?"

"I wouldn't ask him to," Lindsey said. "He has waited already for nearly twelve years. I seem to ask very little else of him but to wait, always wait!"

"What a pity you didn't fall in love with Paris!"

"With *Paris*!" Lindsey cried, astounded.

"Yes! I think if you had been free, he might have . . . have asked you to marry him. The boys like him, don't they? It would have been so easy for you then."

"Yes, I suppose it would!" Lindsey said bitterly. "But I don't even like Paris, June, and even if there had been no Glynn, I wouldn't marry Paris if he were the last man on earth. I don't trust him . . . or understand him. Oh, I know the boys like him . . . but then he's made himself a sort of fairy-godfather to them. I wish he hadn't! The kinder he is to them, the more I seem to resent it! When Pop was caught and killed by that cat last term, he went to endless trouble to find

130

another one identical so Simon wouldn't know. It forces me to be grateful to him and somehow I hate being in his debt."

"What has he done to make you dislike him so much?" June asked curiously.

"Oh, I don't know . . . nothing really, if you want it put in words. He just . . . frightens me in some way. I suppose it sounds crazy to you, but I always feel he is threatening me . . . that he threatens my happiness. In an odd way his friendship for the boys has already done that . . . although I know it wasn't intentional. You know, Glynn sent them both a beautiful Hornby electric train for Christmas, yet they were both much more obviously pleased with Paris' presents. And I can't even pick a quarrel about that since Paris' gifts had very little monetary value and the train must have cost Glynn a great deal."

"I suppose children don't judge things by cost!" June said wisely. "Anyway, maybe they are a bit young for trains!"

"But what boy doesn't love a train!" Lindsey said hopelessly. "It isn't that, June . . . it's that they won't allow themselves to like Glynn. They don't say it but it's obvious enough. And you can't even excuse them by saying they want to be alone with *me*. They left me today without a qualm to go off with Paris."

"It looks as if you'll have to be firm about it if you are going to marry Glynn."

"Well, of course I'm going to marry him, sooner or later!" Lindsey said. "And I'm beginning to believe that Glynn is right . . . that it'll be better for us all if it is sooner! I've been a coward about the boys . . . there'll be a scene, I'm sure. But they must face facts in the end."

"I suppose it is easier to do so if there's no alternative!" June said thoughtfully, thinking once more of her own life and how she had been able to accept her love for Paris and his for Lindsey since there had never been any chance for her that things might be otherwise . . . or would be different even when Lindsey was married to Glynn. Paris was not interested in her . . . nor ever would be. She could bear what she had always known to be so, even though at times it was painful for her.

In a half hour Paris would arrive here in her tiny flat with the children . . . and he would not look at her . . . only at Lindsey. She knew how desperately he longed for this brief glimpse of her . . . to hear her voice, perhaps touch her hand. She, herself, longed as ardently to see him, hear him. She could understand. That was why she had so readily placed her flat at their disposal as a meeting place. She wondered if Paris would see how ill and tired Lindsey looked . . . whether he would be tempted to say anything to her.

But when at last they arrived, the children breathless and excited, clinging to Paris' hands, he greeted Lindsey calmly enough, although June, watching him, saw the look of consternation in his eyes.

Lindsey seemed ill at ease with Paris' tall frame crowding the tiny room, and soon stood up to go.

"We ought not to be back too late!" she said vaguely.

Her voice sharpened as she broke in on the boys' clamour to stay just a few minutes longer.

Paris said:

"It's about time we made a move, too, June, if we're to be in time for the show!"

He had given no indication that he wished to take her out this evening, and it was on the tip of June's tongue to refuse from sheer pride. Yet she caught the sharp glance he gave her and realized that he was speaking for Lindsey's benefit. She remained silent.

Paris went in search of a taxi for Lindsey . . . a method of transport she felt she could ill afford but was too proud and tired to make an issue of it. While he was gone, she looked at June curiously.

"Do you often go out with him?" she asked.

"Sometimes!" June said as vaguely as she could.

"Perhaps I shouldn't have said what I did about him!"

132

Lindsey said with an awkward laugh. "I didn't realize you were . . ."

". . . friendly?" June finished for her. "I fill a need of the moment, that's all. Paris is really rather lonely."

"With all his girlfriends?" Lindsey said sharply.

"He doesn't see them now!" June replied, handing Lindsey her coat.

Thinking about this brief conversation as she sat in the train going home, Lindsey found she could draw only one conclusion . . . that Paris was in love with June. For her sake he had given up his many women-friends. Who had told her of their existence in the first place? She could not remember.

Yet, somehow, June did not seem right for Paris' choice . . . not his type! She pulled herself up quickly. How could she judge for Paris who was his type and who was not? She did not really know much about June . . . the adult June. All she did know was pleasant and kindly and good. She was a woman any man might love for herself if not exactly for a quality of glamour she did not possess. Men did not always choose glamorous wives. After all, for she was without conceit herself, Glynn had chosen her, Lindsey thought. Glynn found her attractive because he loved her, and so might Paris see June through eyes of love.

She tried to believe in it yet could not. She remembered suddenly June's curious remark . . . "I think if you'd been free, Lindsey, he might have asked you to marry him!" It was nonsense, of course, yet she herself had, at one time, imagined Paris to be attracted to her. Yes, and she had been afraid of him even then.

Wearily, Lindsey closed her eyes and tried to feel some kind of happy anticipation about the following day. The visit to Marie-Louise had not been cancelled but postponed and the boys were aware that this was so. One of the conditions on which Lindsey had agreed to their going to the pantomime today with Paris had been that they should allow her her "treat" with a good grace afterwards.

"Uncle Paris may be your friend, but Uncle Mike and Aunt Marie-Louise and Uncle Glynn are my friends. You must learn that it is necessary to give happiness to others as well as take it for yourselves," she had said. She doubted if they understood her reasoning but they would have agreed to anything to get their way about Christmas at home and the pantomime with Paris.

Lindsey suddenly became aware how quiet they were. Both were staring out of the windows, but there was nothing to be seen except an occasional light flashing by in the darkness. She felt a strange and unaccustomed estrangement from them. Was she right, after all, to believe so strongly in boarding school? Sending them away from her forcibly for the greater part of the year? They had come home for Christmas almost as strangers to her! Both had grown inches and, of course, Richard was nine now, Simon soon to have his eighth birthday. They were growing up . . . and growing away from her. She could no longer guess their thoughts.

I must not be a possessive mother! she thought, half fearfully. It would be so easy living alone as I do. I must let them free . . . emotionally free.

It occurred to her suddenly that she had taken entirely the wrong attitude to them both over her engagement to Glynn. They had perhaps sensed her hesitation when she spoke to them of marrying Glynn and mistaken what had been her apprehension for their approval or disapproval for a weakness in knowing her own mind. If she had presented them with facts . . . with a calm statement that she and Glynn were to be married in March or April or May . . . they might have accepted it in the same vein. Her worry for their reaction had, in fact, turned upon herself; by communicating it to them she had made them doubt a future in which Glynn played so big a part.

The way seemed suddenly clear to Lindsey. Not tonight, but tomorrow night, after she had spoken to Glynn, she would give the boys a flat statement . . . tell them the wedding date which she would arrange with Glynn and hear no argument about it. Say what they might, she would not let it alter her plans nor deter her, and when they saw she was adamant they would cease to resist.

Her uncertainty gone in the rush of this new idea, worry and tiredness left her. Almost gaily, she asked her two small sons to tell her about the pantomime. Even when they told her more about what their Uncle Paris had said and done than about the story of Robin Hood, she was not angry or perturbed.

Even when Richard said later, as she tucked him in for the night, "Mummy, do we *have* to go tomorrow?" she was not put out as she had been the first time he said it. She said firmly that they did have to go, kissed them good night and went downstairs.

She might have been more perturbed if she could have heard her two small sons discussing her after she had left them.

"It doesn't seem any *better*!" Simon was saying. "It's still Uncle Glynn this, that and the other. I vote we make a stink bomb to drop on him from the bedroom window."

"Better not!" Richard said wisely. "She'll only get cross with us and be all the nicer to him. Uncle Paris said to be patient."

"Well, it's jolly difficult. Suppose he's wrong all the time, Rick, and she really does love Uncle Glynn best?"

"We can run away!" Richard suggested, enjoying the surprise on his brother's face. "That wouldn't half put the wind up her if we did!"

"Gosh!" Simon exclaimed. "You wouldn't really, would you, Rick?"

Pure bravado made Richard reply in the affimative.

"'Seasy!" he said casually. "Just buy a train ticket at the station and disappear."

"But where to?" Simon breathed, thrilled by the prospect of adventure.

"Well, we could go to Uncle Paris, couldn't we? That 'ud show Mum who we want her to marry."

"What a whopping good idea!" Simon said, and yawning promptly fell asleep.

It did not occur to Richard that this "wopping good idea" might so soon be put to the test. Exactly twenty-four hours later he knew he must either run away as he had threatened, or else lose face with his younger brother for ever.

"Uncle Glynn and I are going to be married at the beginning of the summer term!" Lindsey said as she put them to bed in one of the guest rooms at Woodley Manor. "That will be at the beginning of May, I expect. We shall probably go abroad somewhere for . . . for a holiday, and then buy a house in London. In the holidays we'll *all* go back to the cottage." Carefully, she stressed that all of them would go.

She refused to discuss the matter with them, avoiding their direct reproachful eyes and cutting them short by saying:

"We won't talk about it now. I hope you'll both be pleased because it will make me very happy to be Uncle Glynn's wife." She could not bring herself to add that she felt they should be glad to have a stepfather.

"Well," said Simon, as soon as the door closed behind his mother's back, "now what?"

"I never really thought she would!" Richard said, suddenly wretchedly unhappy.

"But you said last night—"

"I know . . . and I meant it. We'll have to run away of course."

"Now?" Simon asked, sitting up in bed.

"No, stupid!" his brother said. "Someone 'ud be sure to ask at the station what we were doing out so late by ourselves. We can go tomorrow."

"How'll we get to the station?" Simon asked breathlessly.

"Walk, of course!" said Richard. "It's only two miles."

"What'll we say if anyone asks us what we're doing?"

Richard thought it out.

"We can say we're going to spend the day with an uncle. It wouldn't be a fib then, would it?"

"What about money for the tickets?" Simon said with a touch of practicality which the more imaginative Richard lacked.

"We've got that five bob each Uncle Paris gave us at the pantomime. That should be enough for ages."

"Do you s'pose we could have lunch on the train?" Simon asked wistfully but without much hope. It was something he'd often longed to do.

"Better not!" Richard discarded the idea regretfully. "We'll need a taxi to get to Uncle Paris' house. I wouldn't know how to get there by bus."

"Where?" asked Simon.

"What do you mean?" Richard questioned. Then he realized Simon's meaning. Where did Uncle Paris live?

"Gosh!" he exclaimed, momentarily deflated. Then his face brightened, and he jumped out of bed and began to search feverishly through the pocket of his grey flannel jacket. He emerged triumphantly with a grubby, crumpled, but apparently legible piece of paper.

"Uncle Paris gave me this . . . he said I might want it some time to let him know if Mummy was ever ill or needing a friend. I think he's jolly decent to worry about her so much when she just worries about Uncle Glynn."

"You're sure he'll want to see us?" Simon asked, still apprehensive.

"Course!" Richard said with conviction. "Him and us is friends for life . . . he said so, didn't he?"

"Maybe he'll take us to another pantomime!" Simon said hopefully, and on this happy thought turned over and promptly fell asleep.

Thirteen

The adventure was pure delight for the two small boys. With commendable intelligence, they made their way unobserved to the station, bought tickets, told a charming old lady in their carriage they were off to visit a favourite uncle, but omitted to give any further information in case she should get suspicious! At Victoria they jumped into a taxi, having waited their turn in the queue, and in a short while were deposited at the door of a block of flats in Knightsbridge where a porter came forward to help them out of the taxi.

When he heard whom they had come to see, he shook his head.

"Mr Rogers'll be at work. Was he expecting you?"

It was against Richard's code to tell a lie, so he said:

"We're probably rather early but we can easily wait."

"What about your lunch? Mr Rogers doesn't come back to lunch."

"Yes . . . well, we can look after ourselves!" Richard said haughtily. "We've been in Uncle Paris' flat before, you know."

The porter shrugged his shoulders. The kids didn't look like hooligans. They were neatly dressed and well-spoken lads and they'd come in a taxi. He supposed their mother had sent them.

"Tell you what!" he said. "I'll take you up to your uncle's flat and let you in and you can phone through to his office and tell him you're there."

"Thank you!" said Richard with dignity.

It was unfortunate that the porter was called urgently to the flat opposite as he was unlocking the door of Paris' flat. He meant to go back but by the time he'd completed the errand demanded of him by No. 43, he forgot about the boys and didn't remember them again till he was going off duty. But as he wasn't really concerned about them, he forgot them again and took himself off home.

Richard had no idea how to telephone Paris' office since he couldn't even recall the name of the firm. He gave up wondering about it and went in search of food with Simon. They found bread and butter and cheese and made themselves large untidy sandwiches and helped themselves to an apple and a banana each from a bowl of fruit on the sideboard.

"Can I have another banana?" Simon asked, his appetite not quite satisfied, but Richard, feeling grown up and responsible, said "No!" Uncle Paris wouldn't expect them to starve but he mightn't like to come home to find everything had been eaten up.

But, by tea-time, his own appetite got the better of him, and he reluctantly agreed that they might have some more sandwiches and another banana.

"Will he be very much longer?" Simon asked wistfully. The lack of action caused by an afternoon cooped up in the flat with nothing to do had somewhat tempered his enjoyment of the adventure. He began to think about his mother and to wonder if Richard really was quite as sure of himself as he pretended.

Richard was not but he knew better than to let his younger brother know. With responsibility weighing heavy on his shoulders, he quelled his qualms and tried to think of an alternative to noughts and crosses.

Once the telephone rang but Richard wouldn't answer it.

"It might," he said thoughtfully, "be Uncle Paris, but it might be the police. People do get the police to look for lost children."

"But we're not lost!" Simon said literally.

"Well, no! But Mummy probably thinks we are . . ." The thought caused him a moment's apprehension but his face cleared as he added: "And Uncle Glynn!"

Having gone straight from the office to a literary cocktail party, it was nearly half past eight by the time Paris reached home. Simon was asleep in the armchair and Richard nodding, fighting against sleep and depression and tiredness. When he heard Paris' key in the lock, he very nearly wept with relief. He threw himself into Paris' arms and gulped noisily.

It was to Paris' credit that the "Good God!" he so nearly said was changed in time to "Great Scott! What in heaven's name are you doing here?"

Calmer, Richard recounted the story from start to finish.

"What else could we do, Uncle Paris?" he ended, near to tears. "You said she wouldn't marry him and now she says she is. We won't go back and share Mummy with Uncle Glynn. He doesn't really like Simon and me at all."

Thoughtfully Paris went to the cupboard and poured himself a stiff whisky. Apart from the shock of finding the boys here, he was deeply shocked at the news Richard had given him. Deep in his heart, he had never believed Lindsey *would* marry Glynn. April or May? Only a few months hence. How could he stop it? Had he any right to try? Had he not already done wrong to let the children believe so implicitly that he knew what he was talking about? He'd forgotten how literal children could be and it was obvious that they had believed him utterly. He had meant it too. Even now he could not fully realize that Lindsey was as good as lost to him.

For a long moment depression held Paris in its grip. What absurd conceit had ever prompted him to think that Lindsey might love him? What evidence had he ever had to even imagine such a thing? One kiss? He must be crazy!

Yet even as he saw the enormity and absurdity of his behaviour, he still could not rid himself of that deep inner belief . . . a kind of instinctive belief, that he and Lindsey belonged together.

He remembered suddenly the small boy sitting beside him . . . realized how desperately worried and anxious Lindsey must be.

"I'll phone your mother and tell her you're here!" he said.

"But you can't do that!" Richard cried. "We've run away!"

"You can't run away from life, old chap!" Paris said gently. "Besides, you must understand how deeply your mother loves you. She'll be desperately anxious about your safety. It is never, never right to cause pain to someone who loves you."

"But she doesn't . . . any more!" Richard said, a break in his voice. "She only loves Uncle Glynn."

"No matter whomsoever your mother might love it will never stop her loving you!" Paris said firmly. "You are her child, Richard, and part of her. No matter what dreadful thing you might do in your life . . . no matter how much you hurt her she will always love you and Simon because you are her sons. Never forget that."

Seeing the boy's white, strained face, and guessing he was not far from tears, he said more gently:

"Look, I'm going to put you and Simon into my bed for the night. We'll sort it all out in the morning. Don't worry about it any more."

In a matter of five minutes he had both boys in bed, Simon never really waking properly at all. Relieved of responsibility, Richard was asleep before Paris' call to Lindsey came through.

"Thank God!" Lindsey cried. "Oh, I've been so worried, Paris. Why in pity's sake didn't you ring me before?"

"Because I have only just got home!" Paris said gently. "They've been here all day waiting!"

"We've scoured the countryside for them!" Lindsey told him. "It wasn't till lunch-time that we realized they were not just off playing somewhere. We all thought they'd been with one or other of us. At tea-time we asked at the station and were told two small boys had bought tickets to Victoria. We rang the police and they said they could probably trace them if they got a taxi. But I wasn't sure if they had any money. I rang your flat just in case they'd gone to you but there was no reply. When I rang the office, you were out somewhere and your secretary said the boys hadn't been there anyway. I'd just about given up hope and was imagining—"

"Don't think about it any more. They're quite safe . . . both fast asleep."

"But why . . . why have they come to you?" Lindsey asked.

"They were looking for a friend . . . and thought of me. I . . . I think I know what's wrong but I can't really talk about it on the phone. Do you think you could come here tomorrow morning? I expect you want to fetch them anyway, and we could talk about it then. It might be best if you come alone."

"I see!" He knew that Lindsey had guessed from his last remark what to expect.

"Why didn't they tell me themselves?" Lindsey said at last bitterly. "We've always been so close . . . they haven't had secrets from me before. To run away—" Her voice broke.

Paris said:

"They're growing up. Perhaps they felt they needed a male confidant."

"Yes . . . I suppose I understand. I . . . well, we can discuss it tomorrow. You're sure they are all right?"

"Quite sure. They haven't starved, either! I find my larder almost bare!"

He was happy to hear her sudden laugh.

"I suppose I shan't be able to be cross with them."

"I'll do that part of it for you!" Paris said. "They won't do it again."

"No, well . . . I'll . . . I'll say good night . . . and thank you for giving me such good news."

He replaced the receiver and poured himself another drink. He knew now that tomorrow would settle many things in his life . . . that his happiness lay on the scales and that this would be his chance. There would be no game to be played tomorrow . . . only the truth to be told. Lindsey should learn how he loved her . . . how he could love her if she would only give him the chance. Would she? Or was she *really* in love with Glynn? The question tormented him and kept him awake long into the night. He could not bear to think that, by tomorrow evening, there might be no hope to cling to. Yet in his heart, this was what he had begun to fear.

A good night's sleep had done wonders for the boys' morale. Even the "jawing" Uncle Paris gave them about hurting their mother could not quell their good spirits or energy, especially when he told them she was coming to talk to him. They had complete faith in his ability to put everything right. As he warned them that this might very definitely not be the case, Paris felt an even greater responsibility and fear add to his emotions. Not only did he stand to lose Lindsey but now also the trust and love of her boys. He realized he loved them too; in their open way they had wound themselves about his heart just as surely as Lindsey had done. He knew he would not see them again if things went wrong for him today.

He packed them both off to the Science Museum for the morning, having given them a beautifully cooked omelette for breakfast. He wished to see Lindsey alone.

As he had anticipated, he did not have to wait long for her arrival. She had caught the first train up and arrived at his flat soon after nine. She wore a soft blue-grey tweed dress and jacket beneath her fur coat, and a tiny fur hat covered only part of the beautiful auburn hair. There were violet shadows beneath the green eyes and he guessed that she, too, had had a sleepless night.

She was ill at ease and shy at the same time, as he took her coat and told her he had sent the boys out. But she did not say he should have kept them in.

"I've made some real French coffee!" he told her as he went

143

out to the kitchen to get the tray he had prepared. "I thought you might have breakfasted very early."

"That was kind!" Lindsey said as he came back into the room. How tired she was! It was true she had scarcely slept all night. It did not take much effort to guess why the boys had "run away". It was their way of showing her that they didn't want her to marry Glynn. After she had heard from Paris that they were safe with him, she had had to go back to Glynn and Marie-Louise and Mike and tell them. It had not been easy, and Glynn had been furious.

"Of all the damned selfish things to have done!" he said violently. "Surely they knew how upset you'd be!"

She knew he was angry for her and tried to explain that small boys of eight and nine didn't make allowances for grown-ups' emotions. They acted on impulse and had done the first thing that had come into their minds.

"Well, why go to Rogers?" Glynn argued.

"Because he has been a good friend to them and I suppose he was the first person they thought of. I don't know. I'm sorry they've messed up this visit for you all."

"It isn't your fault, darling," Marie-Louise said quickly. "I'll come with you, Mike, and make some tea."

Alone with Glynn, Lindsey had felt that she was being torn apart. Try as she might, she could not make him see that the boys had behaved thoughtlessly and not with deliberate unkindness. He could think only of how worried she had been and how their actions might delay their marriage.

"Promise me you won't let this make any difference!" he pleaded with her. "You won't postpone our wedding because they want you to themselves?"

In the end she had promised but she was much more deeply disturbed than she dared let Glynn realize. Her problem was that she could see Glynn's point of view . . . understand how hurt he must be that she considered the "whim" of two small boys before his happiness when at the same time she professed to love him. But then Glynn had no children of his own and could not be expected to understand. Did she herself understand? Was it just a prank to show they were jealous, or were they really antagonistic towards Glynn personally rather than upset by the idea of sharing her?

Lindsey drew her mind back sharply to the present. She knew she had been day-dreaming for quite a few minutes and seeing Paris' eyes she knew he had taken the opportunity to study her unobserved. The colour came to her cheeks and she spoke quickly to cover her confusion:

"You were going to tell me the reason for the boys coming to you yesterday!"

"Yes!" Paris agreed, taking her empty coffee-cup and replacing it on the tray. "But it isn't easy for me to say what I must say to you. You see, it is partly my fault."

Lindsey looked at him curiously, struck by the tone of voice and the expression in his eyes.

"Your fault?"

"Yes! It happened last summer. I had just met you and fallen deeply in love for the first time in my life . . ." He heard Lindsey give a little gasp and looked up suddenly into her eyes. "You must listen to the whole story or you will not understand," he went on quickly. "I knew almost at once that I wanted to marry you and well, I began to hope a little that time you permitted me to kiss you . . . do you remember?"

She did not answer him but he knew by the quick downward sweep of her lashes, hiding her eyes, that she had not forgotten and the knowledge gave him confidence.

"I thought of little else but you, and then I heard about Glynn . . . it was a great shock at first, but I quickly consoled myself with the kind of reasoning *you* may think unreasonable. I told myself that this man was once your fiancé . . . that it is not possible to re-light a love once dead . . . that you were alone and lonely, and that he had come back into your life at the right moment. I felt that in time you would see differently . . . and when I met him I was sure of it. You may have loved each other once, but I was certain that this man was now too immature for you. Please, do not be angry . . . let me tell you the truth. It sounds, no doubt, very presumptuous of me, but I felt from the beginning that you belonged to me . . . that this was our destiny. One afternoon the boys told me they thought you were going to marry Glynn . . . they were very distressed about it, and because I was so certain in my own mind that you would not . . . whatever you might think at the time . . . end up marrying him, I told them I did not believe they would ever have Glynn for a stepfather. I went further and told them that I hoped one day *I* would be their stepfather. I think they both liked me and were glad to think I could be right, and because they wanted it they took my words very literally. I see now how much wrong I may have done to you. Had I not told them this, they might in time have come to accept Glynn. This is the reason they came to me and I expect you are now very very angry with me, no?"

Angry! Lindsey had gone through practically every phase of emotion possible while listening to this fantastic recital. Anger was certainly uppermost, but it was closely accompanied by fear. How dared he do such things? What right had she ever given him to discuss her with her children?

She spoke the last thought aloud.

"Only that I loved you . . . do love you so desperately! And I love your children, too, Lindsey. Forgive me if what I am saying upsets you, but I must say this now, although I had not meant to tell you this way . . . or so soon. You are to be married in May and I cannot bear it. *Don't marry him, Lindsey*. He cannot make you happy. You do not love him in your heart. Perhaps you do not have any love for me but I could make you love me if you would only let me."

"Don't!" Lindsey cried sharply. "Please don't say any more. This whole conversation is ridiculous. Why, it's not yet ten o'clock in the morning!"

Paris laughed, suddenly and spontaneously.

"How English is that remark! Do you think it is not possible to love at ten o'clock in the morning? Perhaps it is not possible for Englishmen, but I would love you every hour of the twenty-four, every day of the week, every week in the year."

"You're mad!" Lindsey cried, conscious that her hands were trembling and that the situation was rapidly getting out of control. "Don't you realize that I am going to be married? I love Glynn . . . I'm going to marry him!"

"Yet you speak defiantly . . . as if you were trying to prove something not to me but to yourself. You are afraid of me?"

"I am not!" Lindsey cried, her own words sounding childish even as she voiced them. She lowered her tone and said again: "I am not afraid of you."

"Then would you kiss me now? Would you dare?"

Lindsey bit her lip.

"It is not a question of would I dare! Have you no sense of honour? I am engaged to someone else. You have no right to even suggest such a thing."

"Is it ever wrong to speak the truth? I believe you will not kiss me because you are afraid you might learn you are not in love with the man you are going to marry. You want to be in love with him and you are afraid to be in love with me. Do not be afraid, Lindsey. Find out the truth for yourself before it is too late."

Lindsey's heart was beating wildly and her thoughts were a medley of confusion. She wanted at once to get up and run from the room and at the same time knew her legs would not support her. She felt that Paris really must be crazy to talk this way and yet there was some truth in his words . . . *she would not dare to kiss him*. She tried desperately to bring Glynn into her mind but she could not even remember the contour of his face . . . the tone of his voice . . .

She started violently as she felt Paris' hand touch hers. Her heart doubled its beat and she knew that she must stop behaving like a gauche schoolgirl and take the situation in hand. She would get up, tell him once and for all that she never wished to see him again and walk out . . . quickly!

"*Linotte* . . . this is what I call you in my dreams. It is the

French word for linnet. You are so like a restless little bird carried this way and that by the strong winds that blow you about. You have no haven where you can be at peace because your heart has no place to rest. So has it been for me until I met you. Then I knew suddenly how beautiful life and love could be. Can you not feel it, too? Can you not feel that you belong here, close against my heart?"

The soft accented voice, his words, seemed for the second time in her life to have some strange hypnotic power. Against her conscious will, she allowed him to pull her gently to her feet and draw her close against him. She could feel the soft silk of his shirt, for he wore no jacket, against her cheek; and hear the fierce unsteady beat of his heart. Or was it her own heartbeat she heard?

"Linotte! Kiss me!"

Her "No!" was crushed back against her lips and was not heard at all except in her mind. Her eyes closed and she felt all the breath she had leave her body in a long sigh. Then, as the tenderness of his touch changed to a fierce demanding pressure, her whole body began to tremble and her arms, which had hung limply by her side, went round his neck. She had one brief flash of coherent thought . . . that she wanted to belong to this strange man with her whole body . . . that whatever her mind might tell her, her senses believed only in this . . . and then she was hopelessly and completely lost.

Her moment of surrender . . . of complete answering desire . . . was Paris' brief moment of content. She loved him . . . of that he now was as sure as of the fact that she and he belonged together. No woman in love with another man could respond as she had done. A woman's emotions were too much involved for her to make love in a purely physical sense as a man might do.

Yet even as this knowledge spread through his whole being, comforting him, reassuring him, thrilling him, he felt her stiffen suddenly in his arms and a moment later she broke away from him, her face white where it had been so delicately pink, her eyes frightened and seeming enormous.

"Please, *please!*" she whispered as she backed away from him. "Let me alone!"

He could have refused her plea. He knew enough of women to understand that her cry was one of weakness, knowing herself too weak for resistance if he should take her in his arms again. Afterwards, he believed he had been wrong to let her escape so easily. Yet he loved her so much now that even this small command was difficult for him to refuse, despite the cry of his own heart.

His hands were unsteady as he reached for a box of cigarettes on the coffee table and handed it to her. Then seeing how those long slender fingers trembled, too, his heart was overcome with tenderness and he said:

"Was it so wrong, Linotte? Where is your need to fear me? I will never hurt you."

"I . . . am . . . not afraid . . . of you!" Lindsey said desperately. "I believe that you . . . you think you are in love with me. But this must never happen again. I . . . it was very wrong. I'm going to marry Glynn. I love Glynn."

Paris drew hard on his cigarette, his eyes never leaving her face.

"You cannot . . . now! You cannot!"

"Yes, yes I can. This is madness . . . a madness of the senses. It has nothing to do with love. It was wrong of me to permit you to kiss me . . . I don't love you . . . you mustn't think I do."

"But I do not believe what you say!" Paris said quietly. "I do not believe that your kisses lie . . . only that your lips lie when you deny what is in your heart!"

Lindsey twisted her hands together in her lap.

"Can you not understand that I love someone else?"

"And you feel in his arms as you feel in mine?"

The question unnerved her. It was true that she had never in her whole life, even in the early days of her engagement to Glynn, felt this devastating electric current rack her body and

149

leave her senses reeling. But that meant nothing more than a biological attraction she had so often read about in books and never fully understood. It was a primitive emotion . . . strong and . . . and frightening and even wonderful . . . but it had nothing to do with love. Love came from the mind . . . and what did she know of this man's mind? Nothing . . . nor did she wish to know . . . she loved Glynn, even if she did not feel the same fantastic reeling of her senses when he held her in his arms.

"There are other things . . ." she said slowly.

"So you will marry him . . . and forget the magic that could be ours?"

She stood up, suddenly resolute.

"Of course I will forget, *must* forget, that it ever happened. I should never have allowed it. You must never talk of love to me again."

He stood up, too, his face drawn yet still handsome.

"I shall not forget, Linotte! Nor will you. Every time you lie in *his* arms, you will remember mine. Since you wish it, I will not speak of love to you again. But you must not forget that I do love you . . . that I believe in my heart you love me. There are still four months before you are to be married . . . four months left before I must give up hope. But I shall never do that. Even when you are married I shall not cease to believe that one day you will be mine. It was meant that way."

"You are mad and none of what you say is true! I'm sorry to hurt you but I must say it. Try to understand that I am not in love with you . . . that I *will* be married in May. In the meantime, I think it's obvious that we should not meet any more. It is not that I am afraid, but there is no point in it and for the boys' sake I think it would be best."

"So you will not allow that I should see Simon and Richard any more?"

"I know that you are fond of them . . . that they are very fond of you. But it simply is not fair to Glynn. Perhaps, after the wedding, when they have accepted Glynn as their stepfather . . . you might see them then . . . if you still wish."

"I would wish it very much."

"Then, in return, would you do something for me? I don't want to seem cruel . . . to the boys. I think it would be best if you could make it seem that you are unable to see them rather than that I forbid them to see you."

"Very well!"

"Thank you!" Lindsey caught her lip. "I . . . I'd better go now. I'll take a taxi to the Museum and no doubt I'll find the boys there. Thank you for caring for them last night!"

"So you will walk out of my life now? Just like that?"

She turned to him, her eyes pleading.

"Can't you understand that I have never been part of your life? You must not think you love me . . . please!"

"I do not think it . . . I know it, here!"

He placed his hand across his heart. Even now he could not believe he had really lost her.

"I shall say '*au revoir*'," he said, watching her face. "I cannot accept this as good-bye. You are still afraid of me . . . of love. You are running away."

I shall feel sane again once I am back . . . once I am back with Glynn . . . Lindsey told herself. Everything will be normal, and I shall cease to feel as if I am acting a part in a dream.

"I am not running away . . . I am going away!" she said with a calmness she was far from feeling. "Can't you let me go in peace?"

"You will only have peace of mind if you marry the man you love," he said cruelly, because he was so desperately hurt by her denial of him.

"I love Glynn!" Lindsey said, and because his words to her had been cruel, she added: "You cannot believe I don't care for you only because you have always had your way with women. Well, I'm not like the others . . . I am not in the least in love with you. I'll admit that you kiss very well . . . I expect most

151

Frenchmen know how to make a woman feel . . . feel the way they want. But passion is not love and you are mistaken if you think so."

Her hand was on the door, her back turned towards him as she moved away, but the last word was, after all, to be Paris'. He caught her arms and twisted her round so that she cried out. Then his lips came down on her mouth ignoring her struggles to free herself, and this time there was no tenderness in him. Weakly Lindsey struggled, hating him passionately and yet, because he seemed to be able to evoke this weakness of her body, wanting him, needing him, too.

Again and again he kissed her while her hands beat helplessly at his shoulders. She felt his strength, his firmness and knew that she had no chance against him. A tiny spark of fear caught hold of her when she realized that she was quite alone here in his flat with him and that even if she cried out, no one would hear. When his hands touched her body, she struck furiously downwards with her arm and knew that she had hurt him, but he made no move to release her. Slowly, languor stole through her limbs and only her mind fought him, yet hating him, hating his power over her. She was not even aware that her lips were voicing her thoughts over and over as she cried out against his mouth:

"I hate you, hate you!"

"*Et je t'aime, je t'aime!*" he answered back in French.

She had never hated him so wildly or intensely as, when the last of her resistance left her, and she would have let him have his way with her, he pushed her suddenly and roughly away from him, his eyes smouldering, his breath coming in deep rough gasps that were in time with her own.

"Go then and forget me!" he all but shouted at her. "Forget that I love you . . . forget that you are mine!"

With a little cry she stumbled through the door he had thrown open for her, and with her hand against her bruised mouth she ran towards the stairs.

Fourteen

S uch was Lindsey's panic as she rushed headlong down the stairs and out through the entrance to the block of flats, that she paid little heed to the traffic. As the day porter stood watching her, his curiosity turned to anxiety and then to horror as a motorist, travelling over-fast on the busy road, shot past a stationary taxi and with a screech of brakes pulled up too late to avoid Lindsey. She was knocked to the ground and lay motionless, a tiny pool of blood spreading out across the tarmac as the crowds began to gather.

It was one of the daily miracles of London life that within seconds of the accident a policeman was in charge of the situation. The porter was already in the roadside explaining how Lindsey had run across the road behind the taxi. He was sent back to the flats to phone for an ambulance. Meanwhile, the police constable had blown his whistle and two of his ilk were keeping back the crowds.

The motorist, white-faced, was giving an incoherent account of what had happened. Within five minutes the ambulance was there, and it was as they were lifting Lindsey on to a stretcher that Paris came out into the street and saw her.

"*Nom de Dieu!*" he cried in French, his face chalk white. "What has happened?"

"The lady ran out into the road and the car couldn't stop in time . . . going too fast, I say!" the porter informed him, quite enjoying his part in the melodrama. He was pulled up short, however, when Paris caught his arm in a grip that was bruising in its severity.

"She's not . . . not dead?"

Without waiting for a reply, Paris ran forward and clutched the policeman who was talking to the ambulance driver.

"Where are they taking her? I'm a friend . . . I know this lady. What hospital?"

"St George's casualty department!" the policeman told him. "If you know the lady, sir, would you kindly give me her name and address and her next-of-kin if you happen to know it?"

Again Paris cried out in his fear.

"She's not . . . not dead?"

"No! Concussed, I think. They won't know the extent of the injuries till they have examined the lady. Now, sir, would you give some information?"

The quiet, measured tones of the constable calmed Paris' momentary shock and horror. He waited while the ambulance drove away and the crowds were dispersed, and then taking the police constable into the flat entrance, announced himself ready to answer questions.

"Mrs. Lindsey Carter, widow . . . aged about twenty-nine . . ." He spoke automatically until the police constable asked him for her next-of-kin. Of Lindsey's relatives he knew only of an aunt who lived in South Africa. He found himself reluctantly telling the constable that Lindsey was engaged to a Mr Glynn Noble.

Writing in his notebook, the constable forbore to look at the tall, good-looking, distraught man as he asked:

"And could you tell me, sir, what she was doing here at the time of the accident?"

Paris bit his lip.

"Mrs Carter was . . . visiting me. She had come to collect her two little boys. In fact, they are at the Science Museum . . . they had spent the night with me . . . and she was hurrying off to collect them. I believe she is staying with her fiancé in the country at the moment and was taking the boys back there."

"I see, sir. You're not a relation?"

"No! I'm Mrs Carter's literary agent. Look, someone will

154

have to look after the boys. I'll be responsible for them. I'll phone Mr Noble's sister and suggest she comes to fetch them. She is a close friend of Mrs Carter and the boys will be all right with her."

"Very good, sir. And in the event of it being necessary for you to give us further information, I can find you here?"

Paris gave his flat number and office address and soon afterwards the police constable departed.

Paris went back to his flat and put a phone call through to Marie-Louise.

"But how ghastly!" Marie-Louise cried as Paris repeated to her the story he had given the police. He had no intention of revealing to anyone that Lindsey had left his flat in terrible fear of him. That was something he must have on his conscience all his life. He knew that he and he alone was responsible for the accident and his heart was unbearably heavy with the knowledge. He loved her . . . had wanted nothing more than to love and cherish her all her life . . . to protect her . . . above everything to protect her from a second unhappy marriage. He had staked everything in one wild confession of his feelings for her and then, losing his head, he had tried to prove to her something he had only sensed but could not know . . . that she cared for him, too. Panic-stricken she had run away from him . . . run into a passing car and was perhaps even now . . . dying . . .

"Of course I'll come . . . at once!" Marie-Louise was saying. "Glynn will drive me up immediately . . . we should be there in an hour."

"Thank you! I'm going to the hospital now and then I shall go to the Museum to collect the boys and bring them back here. It will be their lunch-time and you could all have a meal in the restaurant downstairs."

A moment later Paris was racing downstairs, not waiting for the lift, to call a taxi to take him to the hospital.

As the taxi drove round Hyde Park Corner, Paris noted the time on the clock outside St George's . . . eleven fifteen. This morning seemed to have lasted an eternity and his nerves were like tense violin strings. He paid off the taxi and ran up the steps and into the hospital.

At the enquiry desk he could hardly bring himself to voice his quest for news of Lindsey, so afraid was he that she might be dead. It seemed hours before the man told him that Mrs Carter had only come in a quarter of an hour previously and was in the operating theatre at the moment.

"If you care to wait, sir, I can perhaps give you some more news in a half hour when she'll be back in the ward."

"I would like her to have a private room!" Paris said quickly. "Can that be arranged, please?"

His words were spontaneous and he gave no thought to whether or not Lindsey might wish him to concern himself as to her comfort, far less be the one to pay the expenses of a private room in the hospital. Just as spontaneous was his action in going out to buy enough flowers to fill a whole ward. At least it gave him something to do while he waited that endlessly long half hour.

When he called at the desk the third time, he was at last given news . . . news that caused him to sit down weakly with relief. She was all right . . . concussed and suffering from shock. But her heart was sound and there were no internal head injuries, only a superficial wound at the back of her head which had had eight stitches. If he cared to phone in the morning, they would advise him if she could be visited. It would depend of course on whether she came out of the state of concussion.

It was only as he walked out of the hospital into the bitter east wind that he realized Lindsey would not want to see him, tomorrow or any day. He had no right here . . . not even the right of a friend. He had forfeited his part in her life by his own reckless, crazy behaviour.

He felt desperately lonely and depressed and the need to share his emotions with someone . . . anyone . . . took him to a phone box, where he dialled June's office number. As briefly as he could he told her the story . . . not the version he had given Marie-Louise but the truth. June listened in silence, guessing from the tone of his voice just how low he was.

"Poor Paris!" she said simply. "Try not to worry about your part in it too much."

"But it was my fault . . . my fault!" Paris cried. "She was running away from me . . ."

"Perhaps that fact alone justifies what you did!" June said enigmatically. "Why else should she run from you but because she was afraid? Not of *you*, Paris, but of herself. She cannot have feared you would do her physical harm. To put it bluntly, you were not exactly trying to rape her, were you! If she objected so violently to your making love to her, she could have been quietly angry, disgusted, annoyed, but not afraid. The door was open and she had only to go through it to escape you. I think she ran because she knew she could not trust herself. At least, that is my woman's point of view!"

"You are kind . . . and a great comfort to me!" Paris said. "But you do not convince me, June. Thank you all the same. I suppose . . . you could not join us for lunch? I find it difficult to face Lindsey's . . . fiancé . . . with equanimity. If you were there, too, it might help."

"What's the time?" June asked. "Twelve thirty. I can get off now, Paris. Suppose I take a taxi to the Museum and we find the boys together?"

June had felt that the boys might take the news of their mother's accident badly. But she had forgotten how simple a young child could be. When the boys were reassured that their mother was all right . . . that she was being well looked after and would be back with them in a short while, they took the fact calmly enough, with childish self-concern.

Simon clung to Paris' arm and said:

"Does that mean we can stay with you, Uncle Paris?"

And Richard said darkly:

"If she's ill for a long time, she won't be able to marry Uncle Glynn after all, will she?"

Meeting June's eyes across the children's untidy heads, Paris gave a rueful smile. Lindsey might not care a row of pins for him but at least her children did!

"Selfish little beasts!" he said, but they paid no attention since the tone of his voice was so warm. "Firstly you cannot stay with me . . . your Aunt Marie-Louise will be at the flat waiting to take you back to her house till your mother is better. Secondly, I've had a long talk with your mother and she has every intention of marrying Uncle Glynn. It's no good making a fuss about it . . . you must just get used to the idea the way I have to."

If he had overestimated their concern for their mother's accident, he underestimated the feeling his last words were to evoke. Richard went white and clenched his teeth and said:

"I won't get used to it. I don't want Uncle Glynn for a father. I don't like him. I want Mummy to marry you!"

Simon's face was scarlet and he looked not far from tears.

Quickly, June said:

"Let's buy an ice-cream before we go back to lunch. There's a man selling them just outside the door!"

But she had only temporarily avoided a scene which had to be faced sooner or later. Back in Paris' flat, Marie-Louise and Glynn were waiting. Richard refused to shake hands with Glynn, although he managed a surly nod to Marie-Louise. Simon burst into tears which the visitors misconstrued quite naturally to be shock. June, with her usual tact, took both the boys to Paris' bedroom for a "tidy-up" before lunch and left Paris to explain.

"I expect you want to know about Mrs Carter first," he said as he busied himself handing round drinks.

"As a matter of fact, we made use of your phone," Glynn said. "Hope you don't object but we were naturally worried, especially when we arrived to find you still out. The porter let us in with his key. They told us at the hospital that Lindsey was in the private room you ordered for her. I presume you did that on my behalf?"

Paris bit his lip. "Yes, I arranged it," he admitted. Perhaps

158

after all it was better to let it come from Glynn. He, himself, had no right to give Lindsey anything. But at least the flowers should come from him . . . that he could do.

"There's no further news?" he asked, trying to hide his own deep concern.

"They think the concussion is wearing off . . . that by this afternoon she may be conscious," Marie-Louise told him, studying him curiously. This was the man the boys had run away to! Well, she could understand how they might hero-worship such a person. He was attractive enough in his way. Quite different from Glynn, of course, but nevertheless extremely good-looking. No woman could ignore that fact. Yet Lindsey seemed to dislike him! It was odd.

"It's all been very unfortunate!" she said with a sigh. "I'm afraid the boys are desperately jealous of their mother. I suppose it's only to be expected but they resent the fact that she intends to marry my brother."

"It's time they learned a little unselfishness!" Glynn said roughly. "It's really their fault that this accident has happened."

"But we must not let them think we blame them for it," Paris said quickly. "Really, I am most to blame. You see, I have perhaps spoilt them a little and they have grown fond of me. Boys of that age . . . I do not know much about children . . . but I suppose they need a man sometimes . . . a mother is not enough. In their minds, I am identified as . . . as their friend. If . . . if I had not encouraged their affection for me, they might well have given it to . . . to your brother."

Glynn raised his eyebrows.

"I see. You're really saying that they would willingly have accepted you as a stepfather where they won't have me!"

"I did not say that!" Paris replied, handing Marie-Louise a cigarette and lighting it for her.

"He means that they *think* they wouldn't object to him as a stepfather because there is no fear of it happening!" Marie-Louise said mistakenly. "They are willing to give him affection because it holds no danger for them. You're the enemy, Glynn, because you're going to take their mother from them."

"This psychology is beyond me!" Glynn said, shrugging his shoulders. "I've always done everything I could to get on well with them. I'm not trying to take their mother from them . . . that's ridiculous. Rather the boot is on the other foot . . . they've done everything in their power to take Lindsey away from me!"

"We've been over this so often!" Marie-Louise said, worried by Glynn's darkened expression. She knew how hurt and anxious he was and tried to conceal her own feelings. "Personally, I'm sure it will all be all right once you *are* married. You seem to know the boys pretty well, Mr Rogers. Don't you agree?"

"I really can't advise you," Paris said, his outward calm still apparent but a sudden inner emotion taking possession of him. "You see, I am not exactly an impartial observer. I'm in love with Lindsey myself."

He turned away to pour himself another drink and to avoid the incredulous expression on their faces. But he was halfway prepared for Glynn's reaction. The younger man stood up and said furiously:

"So that's it! You've been trying to influence those damn kids against me . . . so Lindsey wouldn't marry me and you'd stand a chance. That's a filthy dirty trick to play!"

Paris swung round, no longer in control of his words.

"If she loves you so much, what have you to fear from me? Are you afraid she loves her children more?"

"Damn you!" Glynn said violently. "I might have guessed something like this was afoot—" He broke off as Marie-Louise stood up, laying a restraining hand on his arm.

"Please, Glynn . . . the boys are next door . . . they might hear you!"

"Hell to that!" Glynn cried, breathing deeply. "Let our fine-feathered friend here deny he's been trying to put a spoke in my wheel . . . pretending to be interested in the boys when all he really wanted was to get Lindsey for himself!"

Glynn's loss of control steadied Paris and even while anger and frustration whitened his face his words were slow and measured.

"I have never pretended an interest in the boys. I love them for themselves as much as for the fact that they are Lindsey's children. When I first made friends with them, I had no idea she was going to marry you. I had already told Richard and Simon I hoped one day to marry their mother. In that perhaps I was wrong. But I have never run you down to them . . . how could I when I knew nothing about you except what little Lindsey herself told me of you? I admit I still hoped until this morning that Lindsey might find herself mistaken in thinking she loves you. I was wrong . . . as I learned for myself."

"So she put you in your place!" Glynn said with a triumphant little laugh.

"She told me she intended to marry you, but I am still of the belief that she doesn't really love you!" Paris said with a conviction he was far from feeling. Only June's words gave him the courage to say . . . to hope so much. "I believe she will marry you and there is nothing in the world I can do about it!"

"Except trick those boys of hers into making life damned difficult for her!" Glynn said furiously.

"I have given her my word not to see the boys any more . . . or at least until some time after her marriage," Paris said. "I am not in the habit of breaking my word."

"Then the sooner we get out of this place the better!" Glynn said.

"While I appreciate your sentiments and approve them, the boys need a meal. I think you will find it a somewhat awkward task getting them away. If I may suggest it, you will put your own feelings aside as I have to do and consider them first. They want, in fact, to remain here with me."

"I think Mr Rogers is right!" Marie-Louise said quickly, before Glynn could say anything more. "I'm sure he will try to make this easy for us all if he has said he will do so. Lindsey wouldn't thank you, Glynn, if she heard you'd dragged the boys screaming out of the block."

"Very well! What do you suggest?"

Paris said:

"That we try to appear on good terms during lunch. I will make it clear to the boys that I cannot possibly have them here. It is also obvious that they cannot go home alone. Miss Helmer will help in any way she can. We will all point out that this is what their mother wants them to do. I think if Mr Noble says very little, it might be for the best. You will, after all, have the rest of your life to win them round, Mr Noble."

The boys were brought back into the sitting-room, both looking cleaner and tidier and considerably subdued.

"We're going downstairs to have lunch," Paris told them, his tone carefully casual, although he put an arm around each young shoulder in an easily affectionate manner. "After lunch I'll have to go back to the office and so will Aunty June. We're both working people, you know. Your Aunt is going to drive you back to her house, where I hope you will both behave yourselves very well. We are all sufficiently worried about your mother without wanting to be bothered with runaway kids."

"Mummy *is* going to be all right?" Richard asked.

"Yes! But she'll get better much more quickly if she knows you are both doing as she would wish. I promised her this morning I would do my best to extract a promise from you both not to repeat yesterday's performance. Now she is ill I am sure neither of you will want to add to her troubles. Will you both give me your word of honour to behave as she wants you to do?"

"But . . ." Simon's sentence was not completed, for Richard, with a strangely adult resignation, interrupted him saying:

"It's just no *use*, Simon. All right, Uncle Paris, we promise!"

162

"There's a good chap. Now, what about some lunch? I expect you are all starving!"

When, in little over an hour, the boys were driven away, Paris and June were left alone in the flat.

"I really must go back to the office," June said with a sigh. She felt exhausted, emotionally and physically. It is always tiring to be in the middle of an emotional cyclone, even when you are only remotely involved, she thought.

Paris looked tired, too, and more depressed than she had ever seen him.

"It's strange, but I hated letting the boys go!" he said. "I suppose they are my last link with Lindsey. It's all over now. For a few days . . . a week or two . . . I can ring up the hospital for news of her. Then she'll get better and go away and marry that . . . that—"

June smiled.

"He's really very nice, Paris, although I don't expect you to see it!"

"He's immature!" Paris said violently. "He knows nothing at all about women."

"I believe he's had a number of girlfriends in his lifetime!" June said with another smile. "Probably just as many as you've had, Paris."

"I didn't mean that! And you know it. Noble is the kind of fellow who never outgrows the undergraduate stage. He doesn't and won't ever understand a woman's mind . . . won't want to. Lindsey isn't his type. Oh, I'll grant he finds her attractive . . . what man wouldn't? But he won't be able to make her happy. He isn't sufficiently . . . how can I put it . . . of the mind? He will imagine that, if he possesses her physically, he will possess also her soul. He wants her because she has always been so elusive, so unforgettable. Even now he is not sure of her. Let him once tie her to him with a marriage bond and he will see things very differently."

"In what way?"

"For one thing, he will consider as the main object in life

that they have 'fun'. This is all very well but it is not enough. Lindsey is domesticated, too. She will want a home and a husband and a father for the boys. He is taking on the boys because he has to, but he resents them bitterly. As to being a husband, he will want her to lead his kind of life his way. And she will do so because she will never admit that she made a mistake . . . never let him know it."

June gave a little shrug of her shoulders.

"You are a strange man, Paris. How is it you know so much of what goes on inside people? You haven't been married and yet you talk as if you know women and what they need from life. How can you know?"

Paris gave an enigmatic little smile.

"Love is the answer to that question, June. When you love someone as I love Lindsey, it gives you a special kind of power over them . . . an insight into their characters. I can feel inside my heart what it is that *she* needs from life. If I really believed Noble could make her happy I would let her go to him with a quiet mind, even while I love her and want her for myself. I want her happiness before my own. Noble is only concerned with himself."

"I hope you aren't right!" June said after a moment of silence. "Because I think Lindsey will certainly marry him."

"So do I!" Paris said with a wry smile. "That is why I am so unbearably depressed. I feel in my heart that she is lost to me. My thoughts are nothing but pain to me. Will you come round tonight, June, and cheer me up?"

"All right!"

Paris suddenly reached out for and took her hand, giving it a friendly squeeze.

"You know, you are a good friend to me, June. I never thought to have such a good friend in any woman."

June gently withdrew her hand, firmly squashing the fierce beat of her heart or any hopes that came with it that Paris might turn to her on the rebound. Friends they might be . . . might remain if she could control her own feelings, but nothing else. Paris' need of her could only be temporary. She could never make him happy . . . never be the kind of wife he needed. She could understand now what he had meant when he said to love someone gave you an insight into their needs; that to love them truly was also to mean unselfishly. Even if Paris were to ask her to marry him, she would refuse him for his sake, knowing that it would never be within her power to make him happy.

"I really must go!" she said again with a smile that concealed her reluctance to leave him. "I'll come straight here from the office when I knock off tonight . . . about sixish!"

But when she returned, Paris was not in the flat and she had a long wait for him. The porter, who admitted her to No. 47, told her that Mr Rogers had phoned during the afternoon to say that he had been called to the hospital and might be detained. Would she be so good as to wait?

It was nearly four o'clock when Paris' secretary told him he was wanted by the hospital on the telephone. She watched curiously as his face turned grey and jumped when he barked at her to put the call through instantly and see he was not interrupted.

As he lifted the receiver, Paris felt as if his own life lay in the balance. It was possible . . . all too possible that they were ringing him to tell him that Lindsey had had a relapse . . . even that she had died. There could be no other reason for wanting to get in touch with *him*. It was hardly likely that she had asked to see him.

These thoughts flashed through his mind in the brief second before he said:

"Rogers here!"

It was the ward sister who introduced herself.

"I'm so glad we have at last got in touch with you. You left only your home telephone number and when we had no reply, we presumed you would be at work. Fortunately the police constable who witnessed the accident was in the building and told us your firm's name and address. Mrs Carter has been asking to see you for the last two hours, Mr Rogers. Would it be possible for you to come immediately?"

"Asking . . . to see . . . *me*?" Paris asked incredulously.

"Yes, Mr Rogers. She is still suffering very severely from shock and the concussion has not entirely worn off. Doctor does not wish her to be worried by anything and it seems she has something very much on her mind she wishes to tell you."

"She is not worried about her two sons? They are quite safe."

"No! She seems to understand that."

"Of course, I'll come immediately!" Paris said, suddenly spurred to life. "I'll be there in about ten minutes."

Wild hopes chased themselves round his brain as the taxi sped him to the hospital. Could Lindsey at last have seen reason? Could she have discovered now, at the last minute, that she loved him?

But his hopes were considerably sobered when the Sister met him with the quiet caution:

"You must not expect Mrs Carter to be herself. She is partially drugged, Mr Rogers. I do not know what it is she wishes to tell you, but if it is within your power to put her mind at peace, we should be extremely grateful. I do not think she will remember when she is fully recovered anything she might say to you now . . . or you to her. It will seem more like a dream to her. So that any promise you might make her need not be binding. Do you understand me? It is simply that it is important for her recovery that she is not worried."

"I understand!" Paris said. "May I see her now?"

With her knowledge of human nature, it had not taken Sister Ann long to surmise that Paris was in love with Lindsey. It showed in every expression on the mobile, sensitive face. Yet she knew that the pretty young woman upstairs was engaged to be married to someone else. Her woman's emotions were intrigued by this tangled romance, even while she spoke without emotion as her training demanded. She knew she

166

could safely leave Mrs Carter alone with Mr Rogers . . . that he had only her good at heart. Had she doubted it, she would have left a nurse in the room with them to watch that Mrs Carter did not get over-excited or overwrought. As it was, she told Paris at the door of Lindsey's room:

"See that she keeps as quiet as possible, and ring the bell if you are in the least worried at any change in her condition."

Then she opened the door and Paris went in.

Lindsey lay on the high hospital bed, her face nearly as white as the spotless sheet and counterpane that were drawn up to her neck. Covering the beautiful auburn hair was a circle of white bandages. Her eyes were closed and only the delicate colours of the masses of roses he had sent to her softened the harshness of so much white.

With a quiet movement that seemed unnatural in so large a man, Paris went across to the bed and sat down beside it. His heart felt near to breaking with tenderness as he took the lifeless hand that lay palm upwards in silent appeal.

"Lindsey, Linotte, *chérie!*" he murmured.

At the sound of his voice, her head moved on the pillows and, slowly, the long lashes lifted from her cheeks and he saw the soft hazel green of her eyes.

"Linotte, it is I, Paris, here beside you!"

The head turned and the eyes searched and focused on his face.

"Paris!" Her voice was scarcely more than a breath.

He wanted more than anything in the world to sweep her into his arms and cover that beloved face with kisses – kisses that must bring the colour back into her cheeks, the life to her eyes. But he knew he must not do so. Only his voice betrayed the intensity of his feelings as he said:

"I love you so much, Linotte. I have always loved you since the moment I first saw you."

The calm contented expression on her face changed suddenly and became strained and anxious.

"Why can't I love you, Paris? Why is it wrong?"

He realized then with a sickening jerk of his heart that Lindsey wasn't really in her right mind. Sister had warned him that she was drugged, yet her quiet acceptance of him had momentarily tricked him into thinking that she was herself.

Her hand moved restlessly in his and her face turned from side to side on the pillow.

"Why not? Tell me why not?"

He bit his lip. This was so much more difficult than he could have imagined possible.

"There is no reason why not, *chérie*!" he said at last. "I love you, with all my heart. If you love me too, there is nothing to stand between us."

"There is, there is!" There were tears in her voice and on her cheeks. "I want to love you but I must not. I must not! You must never believe that I love you . . . no matter what I do. There is a barrier between us for always."

Disjointed though her sentences might be, her words were coherent and sensible, and he found it more and more difficult to remember that she could not really know what she was saying. Nor could he understand her meaning. What barrier could she be referring to? Her engagement to Glynn?

"Is there someone else?" he asked softly. "Someone you love more than me?"

Her hand twisted from his grasp and caught a fold in the sheet.

"There was someone . . . once . . . long ago. So long ago. I was so hurt. No one shall hurt me again. You want to hurt me, too."

"No!" The words were wrung from him. He thought she was referring to the terrible scene in his flat . . . could it be only this morning? It seemed already an eternity ago. "No, I want only to love you, to care for you always."

For a brief moment calmness stole across her face and her eyes smiled at him with an innocent sweetness. Then her brow furrowed and the expression of her eyes changed again and she said in a voice full of bitterness:

168

"You want only my body . . . you have had so many women in your life . . . but I will not be one of them. I will never marry you . . . no matter how much I love you. I wanted to tell you that for a long time . . . I wanted to tell you that when you kissed me—"

Now . . . now at last he had the truth. Now he could begin to understand what Lindsey meant when she spoke of barriers between them. Glynn had no part in this. It was something that lay between the two of them. And it explained so much. Almost triumphantly he understood what had been an enigma to him. He had felt so surely and so deeply that she, too, had felt that curious thing called "love" for him. He had seen it in her eyes, felt it in her touch, known it in his mind and body. Yet her every word and action had denied it . . . only her kisses could not. Now he knew why she had fought against him so desperately this morning . . . *She had been afraid* . . . afraid to give him her love.

Paris tried to control the fierce beat of his heart. So much was explained . . . even her engagement to Glynn. He, at least, since she did not love him, could not hurt her again. Deep down inside herself, she had closed her heart to love because long ago she had been wounded by it. So she had run away from him, Paris, afraid not of him but of her own emotions for him, and sought safety in her engagement to Glynn.

Suddenly, her words became clear to him as he repeated them in his mind . . . *so many women in your life . . . I will not be one of them!*

Well, if it were true in the first part, it was never true in the second. How could he make her understand that? He had had many girlfriends . . . the war itself had put such a strange construction on his way of life just as it had on other men's . . . on other women's lives, too. No one had been sure if they would survive . . . least of all those like himself who courted death daily. Was it so unnatural that he should seek solace and relief in light, feminine company? He was, after all, a man, and women found him attractive. But love . . . it had never come into his life until the day he met her. From that moment no woman had so much as entered his thoughts, except to break the few threads that still held him to various friends . . . girls he took to parties or the theatre or dancing when the mood necessitated company.

In his own way, Paris had had a strict code of behaviour by which he lived. He never showed the slightest interest in another man's wife; and he never played games with a woman's emotions. The moment he suspected that her interest in him had become more than his own mild interest in her, he ceased to see her. On the other hand, there had always been a certain set of women who lived much as a man might live, taking pleasure where they found it, lightly and casually as a man might do. Paris had enjoyed their society in his light-hearted, irresponsible and emotionally aloof way.

But meeting Lindsey . . . falling in love . . . had changed all that. He wanted no other woman in his life, and he knew beyond all doubt that had he met her years ago, there would never have been another woman in his life. She suspected that he was a philanderer, a flirt, out for what he could get from a woman. It was bitterly untrue. Yet he could not deny that he had taken what was offered him.

With a cry that was torn from his aching heart, he said:

"You are the only one . . . the *only* one I have ever loved!"

He saw her head turn back towards him and her eyes stared into his, slowly becoming soft and lucid.

"Oh, Paris!" she whispered. "Don't you know that I belong to you? When I am ill, I want you with me. When you are away, I am only half myself. I am in love with you and I love you and that is not the same thing at all yet both are true."

"Lindsey!"

Her eyes smiled with the deepest tenderness into his radiant face. Then they closed and she said:

"I am so tired, so tired . . . my head hurts . . ." Her voice

170

trailed away to a whisper and Paris, suddenly frantic with apprehension, rang the bell violently for the nurse. Within a moment the door opened and a young nurse came in and went quickly to Lindsey's bedside. Her capable hands were on Lindsey's wrist, feeling her pulse, then she smiled and turned to Paris.

"Mrs Carter is asleep, sir. It is what we hoped for. She seemed so restless in her mind, as if she could not let herself relax."

"Can I stay with her, Nurse?" Paris asked.

The girl looked doubtful.

"Perhaps you would like to have a word with her doctor, sir? He could give you permission to stay."

Paris stood up and glanced down at the sleeping woman, his face giving no disguise to his feelings. Watching him, the young nurse thought unprofessionally, I wish some man loved me like that!

Then she led him out of the room and along the spotless corridors. Paris saw nothing of the people they passed, nurses hurrying on their duties, two porters pushing a trolley on which lay a silent patient, a ward maid carrying a tray of empty dishes. His whole being was wrapped in a glorious golden cloud that the knowledge of Lindsey's love had woven for him . . . *when I am ill, I want you with me. When you are away, I am only half myself. I am in love with you and I love you, and that is not the same thing at all yet both are true . . .*

He could still hear the soft beloved voice speaking those words which meant life itself to him. He had forgotten that he had been warned Lindsey was in a state of semi-delirium; that she might not remember afterwards anything she said to him in this condition; that she was drugged and concussed and could not be held to her words.

It was only when he was talking to her doctor that he was brought back to this cold, bitter fact.

"I don't think it is possible for you to remain with Mrs

Carter, although I naturally appreciate your wish to do so. You're her fiancé, aren't you?"

Paris gave the doctor a quick uneasy stare, liked the honest face of the man opposite him, and decided to tell him the truth. He did so as briefly as he could.

"Thanks for being so frank with me!" the doctor said as he finished. "It makes it easier for us to care for Mrs Carter properly now we know the state of her mind. I'm afraid I have to tell you that you may be in for a shock. When Mrs Carter wakes, she will probably have no recollection of this last half hour you were with her. If she remembers at all, it will be most probably as a dream which she will try quickly to forget."

"But everything she said . . . I know she was speaking from her heart!" Paris argued wretchedly. "She couldn't have pretended."

"No! But you have summed up the situation fairly well for yourself. You told me you thought she was afraid to let herself love you. Such a thought lies in her subconscious and influences her conscious thought and action. There is nothing at all you can do about it, except hope that she will call off her present plan and get married of her own accord . . . her own free will."

"But there must be something I can do!" Paris cried.

"You tried . . . and failed!" the doctor pointed out as kindly as he could. "You can't very well abduct her!" Even Paris managed a brief smile. "If she refuses to see you, which is quite likely, we can't insist that she does and it is naturally our duty to see that she is left as undisturbed as possible. You, yourself, would not wish to jeopardize her chances of recovery?"

"Of course not!" Paris agreed wearily. "But there is so little time left . . . she arranged to be married in May. Must I stand by and watch her ruin her life? I *know* it is me she loves. I could make her happy and she will not be happy with the man she is going to marry."

172

The doctor looked at him with a good deal of sympathy showing in his expression.

"Perhaps I shouldn't say this, but my advice to you is to try to find some way to get the wedding postponed. It may not be possible, of course, but if you can, there might come a chance for you to convince her you're right! She may find it out for herself."

Paris stood up and held out his hand.

"You've been very kind!" he said. "I know you will see personally that . . . that the hospital gets in touch with me again if Mrs Carter asks for me. I'll try not to expect to hear from her."

"Sorry, old man!" the doctor said, shaking his hand. "Women are strange creatures . . . perhaps that's why we love them. It's sometimes easier to love them than to understand them."

"If only it were as easy to fall out of love!" Paris said. "Thanks again!"

He remembered the doctor's words as he walked back to his flat. How could he possibly get the marriage postponed? There was no way. Marie-Louise was obviously on her brother's side. He had himself given Lindsey a promise that he would not see the boys any more or try to influence them. There was nothing . . . no one who could help him . . . except . . .

"June!" he thought, and suddenly remembered that she was waiting for him in his flat and his slow pace gave way to a mad rush home.

Fifteen

"There is only one way I can think of," June said when she heard his story. "It may well succeed in postponing the wedding but on the other hand it is practically certain to make Lindsey your enemy for life!"

Paris looked at the girl with desperation.

"I would risk that. If she broke her engagement, I would at least have time to make her see the truth . . . even if it took years."

"You really are in love with her, aren't you!" June commented. "All the same, Paris, it is a risk . . . my way."

"What is your way?"

"To let Glynn know you've been giving Lindsey money!"

Paris drew in his breath sharply.

"But he'll be sure to question Lindsey—" He broke off as he suddenly realized that this was what June had meant when she warned him he might risk losing Lindsey for always.

"Well, I can't think of any other way!" June said helplessly. "And it's not such a good idea anyway. Lindsey can quite truthfully deny any knowledge of it and Glynn can hardly blame her. They might both lay the blame at your door where it belongs and be thrown even more precipitately into a hurried wedding!"

"I dare not do it!" Paris cried, and in the same breath, added: "Yet it is a chance. He might turn against her—"

"Don't forget that he's in love with her, too. Put yourself in his shoes, Paris. What would you do if you learned that same thing about him, and Lindsey was engaged to you?"

Paris paced the floor in an agony of indecision.

"I should probably want to kill him!" he said dramatically, and then laughed at himself in a quicksilver change of mood. "But that is ridiculous! I should write him a cheque for the amount and see Lindsey had another agent in future!"

"Glynn can do just that!"

"Yet it is not quite the same . . . he is jealous of her . . . of me. *He is not sure of Lindsey's love for him.* He might doubt her . . . question her . . . and she would not like that."

"No! And she would like you even less than she liked him, Paris. She will feel humiliated and betrayed, and if Glynn and she quarrel she will lay the blame at your door for the rest of her life."

"I would prefer even that than that she should make a second unhappy marriage."

"Then if you can really be certain in your mind that she will be unhappy married to Glynn . . . and if you are prepared to risk her hating you . . . I suppose the chance is worth taking. But you must love her a great deal, Paris, to choose such a near-certain way of losing her."

Unexpectedly, Paris smiled, his face transformed and radiant with an inner happiness.

"You were not there in the hospital with me an hour ago, June. Lindsey loves me. The doctor himself explained that it was probably her subconscious mind directing her to say the things she did. But that means only that she was speaking from her innermost heart. One day . . . some day, she will allow her heart to speak again . . . and I will be waiting."

Impulsively, he turned and went quickly towards his desk, sat down and drawing a piece of notepaper towards him, began slowly and carefully to write.

As she listened to the scratching of his pen on the paper, June studied the back of his head, the curve of his broad shoulders, the long straight back. Her artist's eye imprinted the unconscious pose on her mind and she knew that one day she would draw him like this – his face hidden from her, his back towards her, symbolic, perhaps of his relationship to her in life.

Strangely enough, she felt no ache in her heart. He was not lost to her since she had never allowed herself to believe in a future that joined his life to hers. One cannot lose what one has never possessed. Yet at the same time, she did possess something of him . . . his friendship. And she knew quite certainly that she would never lose that. In a way, this relationship was enough for her. It was to her he came when he was in difficulty, just as a boy might go to his mother, or a brother to a well-loved sister whom he trusted.

"Listen!" he said, interrupting her thoughts. "Tell me what you think of this." He read what he had penned:

> *"My dear Noble,*
>
> *There is no time today to discuss anything privately with you so I am writing to advise you of certain facts which will concern you when you and Mrs Carter are married.*
>
> *As you are now aware, I had hoped at one time that Lindsey would one day marry me. At the time, she was in some financial difficulty and as her agent, I advanced her a certain sum of money against sales of work. Unfortunately I was not able to sell more than a very small percentage of her work and being aware that she would be unable to return the sum I had advanced her without breaking into capital she had put aside for the boys, I decided not to ask for a return of the money. It did not seem to me to be of any importance since I hoped to take over Lindsey's financial commitments in any case when we were married. However, this does not now seem likely and I believe that Lindsey will probably wish to acquire another agent when she is out of hospital.*
>
> *You will no doubt wish to spare her any undue anxiety while she is convalescing so I am advising you of the position so that you may use your influence to*

dissuade her from changing her agent at least for the time being.

Yours truly,

Paris Rogers

P.S. My partner is unaware of these transactions as I made up the differences from my personal account."

"Well?" he asked, as June made no comment.

"I don't know. I'm a bit frightened of it now, Paris. You may be laying yourself open to some kind of criminal proceedings! Falsifying accounts, or something!"

"I've robbed no one but myself!" Paris said simply.

"All the same it was a mad thing to do. I can't think how Lindsey will feel when she hears about it. She will hate you, Paris."

"She thinks she hates me already!" Paris said with a wry grin. "At least she will not be indifferent to me. And is there not an English saying that love and hate are akin?"

"You know, I'm sorry for Glynn. You are a very deadly enemy, Paris."

"You encourage me, June. You speak as if he is going to lose her!"

June smiled despite her anxiety.

"One cannot help being influenced by you . . . you seem to convince yourself."

"I am convinced only of my own sentiments . . . and that Lindsey loves me. Once I doubted that but now I don't. And if it is me she loves, she cannot be happy married to anyone else."

"People do have happy marriages without love!" June said thoughtfully. "Perhaps sometimes they are happier marriages than the ones where two people are in love."

"You are cynical, June. You mean that love does not always last but that habit does. In France we have many marriages without love but while they might appear happy on the surface, they are not really marriages at all . . .

177

not as marriage could mean . . . a unity of heart, mind, body, soul."

"Surely it is not possible for any two human beings to be so perfectly united?" June argued. "Certainly not people of strong character and personality. I agree it can happen where one partner is of a weaker character and merges herself into the other person's being, thinking his thoughts, doing his will, becoming a kind of shadow for the stronger one."

"But that is not as I wish it!" Paris said. "I do not want a shadow of myself. One would be inexpressibly bored with such a partner. There must of course be two separate individuals with separate characters and personalities and differences of opinion. But that need not jeopardize the inward knowledge of belonging, of unity, of being only half a person without the other. It is possible to be separated by many hundreds of miles and yet be near to someone. I discovered this in the war . . . with a compatriot who was eventually killed. I never thought at the time that I would have this same feeling with a woman, yet I see now that this is the perfect expression of love . . . to have a physical as well as mental unity."

"Tell me about your friend who was killed," June asked.

"He was a Frenchman, a Commando. We had not met till the night we found ourselves in the same aeroplane waiting to be dropped into occupied France. Things went wrong and we were in hiding in very dangerous circumstances for three weeks. In that time, we got to know one another and to appreciate one another so well that we knew even what the other was thinking. It stood us in good stead later on when we were caught by the Gestapo. We were questioned separately and yet we both told practically identically the same story. We had, of course, prepared a story but it so happened that in the circumstances in which we were caught, it was not possible to use that version. We were released and got away. Two months later he was again landed in France, and this time he was caught and shot. I was in England at the time, and I knew the night he was killed although I was not told of the fact till a year later."

"I'm sorry!" June said.

"After the war, I went back to France and killed the man who betrayed him. I think he must have known I would seek revenge, although it was not easy to trace the man so long afterwards."

"You knew his name?"

"No, I did not know it. But I knew I would be able to find out. As soon as I came face to face with him, I knew him for the right man. He knew it, too. He saw me staring at him across the table in the *Bistro* and he stood up, a glass of red wine in his hand, and he said: 'You can't prove it . . . there is no proof!'"

"Yet you killed him?" June asked.

"Yes! I did not need proof. I killed him. Before he died, he said: 'I'm glad now. He said you'd come back to kill me . . . I've waited so long in fear.' He died at peace."

It was a new insight into Paris that June had not known before. His civilian occupation hardly seemed in keeping with the courage and endurance of his part in the war.

"And you have never wanted to live in France again?" she asked curiously.

"Not then. I had lost too many friends and relatives. I had to make a fresh start. Everyone did. I love England and I had never contemplated going back to live in France . . . but now . . . well, if I should lose Lindsey for always, then I doubt if I could bear to stay in this country."

June gave him a doubtful smile.

"Where is your confidence of a moment ago? You were so certain then that you would end up with what you wanted!"

Paris gave a deep sigh.

"Perhaps I merely talk with confidence to bolster up my own flagging spirits . . . I don't know. One moment I feel certain that I am right . . . that she loves me as I love her. Then I begin to wonder how much I am making myself believe this because I want it so desperately. June, do you think she loves me?"

"She is crazy if she does not!" June said unguardedly, then

179

quickly covered herself by saying: "Any woman would be mad to throw away so much devotion laid at her feet!"

"And this fiancé of hers . . . you do not think he loves her as I do?" Paris asked abruptly.

June shrugged.

"I can't tell you that, Paris . . . I don't know him well enough. You must not ask me for advice. I think I have already advised you wrongly. You will end up hating me because I shall ultimately be responsible for you losing your Lindsey."

"How could I blame you?" Paris said reasonably.

June frowned.

"Because you will be so unhappy, Paris. It is easier to blame someone else. Please, tear up that letter to Glynn . . . don't send it. I am sure that Lindsey will never forgive you when she discovers the truth. It was a crazy idea."

Paris was silent for a moment, thoughtful and preoccupied. Then he said slowly:

"Yes, perhaps it is a little mad. Yet surely this is the time for just such madness. I have tried in every reasonable way I know to make Lindsey see the truth. Still she remains blind to her own feelings and deaf to mine."

"Paris, at least wait till you see whether Lindsey wishes to see you again . . . when she is recovered, I mean. The doctor could have been wrong . . . she could have known exactly what she was saying to you in the hospital. She may say it all again tomorrow. Then you would wish with all your heart that that letter had not been posted."

"True!" Paris admitted. "All right. I will wait . . . always wait. I thought I had learnt patience in the war but it is foreign to my nature. It is action I crave. And now, my poor little friend, you must be starving. I am the worst host possible . . . and the most ungrateful friend. Yet that is not really true. I shall never forget how kind and understanding you have been to me."

He took one of June's hands and pulled her gently to her feet, his eyes smiling.

"Don't look so serious!" he admonished her, misunderstanding her expression. "Surely you do not doubt how much your friendship means to me?"

"No!" June agreed, her heart sore and yet strangely comforted. "I don't doubt the quality of your friendship, Paris, and I value it enormously. Now, let's eat as you suggest."

There was no word from the hospital when they returned to the flat later that evening, and at Paris' request, June telephoned for information. She was told that Mrs Carter was still sleeping and that there was no further news available as to her condition.

With a promise to Paris to telephone again in the morning, June went home to a sleepless night. Try as she might, she could not put the problem of Paris and Lindsey out of her mind. She knew that worrying about it would solve nothing, and yet here, away from Paris, she felt his case to be far more hopeless than she did when with him. He was so certain, that to hear him speak made one certain, too. Yet now she began to doubt the happy outcome for him. He had forgotten how much Lindsey had once loved Glynn . . . ignored the fact that had it not been for her two boys, she would have been married to him by now without a doubt. It was easily enough explained if one took the view that it was Glynn she loved and Paris she really did fear because he held some compelling physical attraction for her. Contrary to the somewhat Victorian belief still in existence, June considered that it was possible to love one man and at the same time be attracted to another.

She twisted and turned and tried to find sleep but it eluded her until the early hours when she nearly overslept and had to hurry with breakfast and run for a bus to work. She found a moment during the morning to phone the hospital but was told nothing beyond the fact that Mrs Carter was fully conscious and very much better.

"Would you ask her to have someone let me know if she would like to see me?" June asked, giving her name and office telephone number.

181

She relayed this information to Paris, who, unable to bear the suspense any longer, himself put a call through to the hospital and asked to speak to Lindsey's doctor.

"I'm sorry, Mr Rogers. She has not mentioned your name."

"I see!" Paris said wearily. "Then am I to understand that you were right? She doesn't remember me coming yesterday?"

"I'm afraid not! Or if she does, she is not willing to speak of it. She has asked to see Mr Noble. I believe he is coming up by train this morning and will be here this afternoon."

"Thanks for telling me." Paris' voice did not disguise from the doctor his acute disappointment. "I suppose it is out of the question that I should call to see Mrs Carter anyway?"

"As her doctor, I cannot advise that. She must not be worried or distressed in any way. I will, however, tell her you phoned. If she would like to see you, I will ring you immediately."

I'll give it till tonight! Paris thought. Then I'll post that letter. It's my last chance.

Lindsey lay propped against the pillows, her eyes closed, her body completely relaxed and at peace. She knew she had had an accident and had been concussed for twenty-four hours. She knew, also, that she had nothing to worry about. The boys were safe at home with Marie-Louise, and this afternoon Glynn would be here to tell her about them.

She knew, too, that she had been running away from Paris when the car hit her. Her mind was quite clear up to that moment of impact when it became a blank until she had woken up this morning. Everyone had been so kind . . . the young nurse, Sister, the doctor. It was wonderful to lie quietly like this and relax, knowing that there was nothing she could do . . . nothing she should be doing except to lie here, at peace.

Somewhere at the back of her mind there was a problem she had to solve. She knew it had to do with Richard and Simon and the fact that they had run away because they did not want her to marry Glynn. It had hurt her desperately to realize this and yet now it did not hurt. It was just a fact she accepted the way she accepted that she was here in this warm pleasant room with the beautiful flowers someone had sent her. She had meant to ask the nurse but she had forgotten. She would ask in a little while.

I suppose I am drugged! Lindsey thought. That is why my thoughts are floating in this strange way. They don't seem to be connected with me.

Her eyes closed and for a moment she nearly slept again. Then her face tensed suddenly at the thought of sleep. She had had such strange dreams. Paris had come to her and held her hand and in her dream she had loved him.

Dreams always go by opposites! she thought drowsily. Yet it had been a strangely comforting dream. She had been so alone . . . and frightened, and when Paris took her hand everything had become right as if by a miracle. It was a mad thought because really it was Paris who had made her life so difficult. If it had not been for him, the boys would have accepted Glynn as their stepfather and it could all have been so easy and happy for her. Paris had played on the boys' emotions behind her back and she knew she should hate him for this, yet in her curious half-drugged state the knowledge was there but in a passive form. The hate did not need to be expressed.

Of course, he used as an excuse that he loved her. June had warned her that he did but it had come as a shock to hear him say so. Not that he knew the meaning of the word. For a man like Paris, it meant merely that he was attracted to her. He knew nothing of the finer depths of the most powerful emotion in the world.

She thought suddenly of a poem Glynn had sent her when they were first in love. She had treasured it long after she had burned his letters when, at the time, she had believed him to have fallen short of the standards the poem quoted. Hesitantly, she said it to herself now:

"Give all to love;
Obey thy heart;
Friends, kindred, days,
Estate, good fame,
Plans, credit, and the Muse—
Nothing refuse.

'Tis a brave master;
Let it have scope:
Follow it utterly,
Hope beyond hope;
High and more high
It dives into noon,
With wing unspent,
Untold intent;
But it is a god,
Knows its own path,
And the outlets of the sky.

It was never for the mean;
It requireth courage stout,
Souls above doubt,
Valour unbending;
Such 'twill reward;—
They shall return
More than they were,
And ever ascending."

Strange how appropriate this poem was to her and to Glynn. In the first instance, it said that love required souls above doubt. She had doubted Glynn when they were young and because of it she had made such a hopeless mess of her life. Not that she would undo her marriage to Elvin now, for Richard and Simon were children of that marriage and dearer to her than anyone in the world. Yet at the same time, the poem said that love required courage. She had been weak . . . weak in her resolve to marry Glynn. It was strange to her now, seeing her own weakness, that he had not lost patience with her long ago. Well, it would be different from now on. She would see Glynn this afternoon and tell him that they would be married as soon as she left hospital if he wished it. Simon and Richard could have nothing against Glynn personally and she no longer worried about them. Without Paris to influence them, they would soon become adjusted.

She would never see Paris again. He must know that as surely as she did after that dreadful scene in his flat. If she were to continue with her writing, she would find another agent and then Paris could disappear from her life just as suddenly as he had entered it. He would get over his kind of loving easily enough . . . there would be some other woman soon to console him.

Lindsey sighed. It was silly and yet she could not quite rid herself of that feeling of peace her dream of Paris had given her. It was so illogical to dream that he could give her peace when he was in life the one to disturb that peace. All the same, she could remember, almost as if it had been real, the touch of his hand, the look in his eyes, her own glorious surrender of herself to his keeping.

Surrender! The word itself brought back truer memories of Paris . . . memories that were facts, not dreams . . . the way she had really felt when he had kissed her so passionately. No! That was danger and unhappiness . . . never peace, never love. Only with Glynn was there safety.

When, at this moment, the doctor came into her room and told her that Paris had phoned, for the first time since she had woken this morning, her calm left her.

"No, please, Doctor!" she cried. "I don't want to see him . . . I won't see him—"

"Of course not, if you don't wish it!" the doctor said quickly, soothingly. "There was also a call, I believe, from a Miss June Helmer. She wished you to know that she was free to come to see you if you wished to see her."

Lindsey hesitated. She would have liked to see June and yet, curiously, June was associated in her mind too closely with Paris. She quickly shook her head.

"The quieter you keep the better!" the doctor said again. "You have eight stitches in the back of your head and you had a very nasty knock as well."

"How long . . . shall I be here?" Lindsey asked.

"A week . . . ten days . . . if you keep quiet!" the doctor said. "Then I advise a holiday if you can manage it . . . by the sea, perhaps. You're very underweight, Mrs Carter."

"I . . . I was thinking of getting married soon," Lindsey said. "Perhaps I could combine a holiday with a honeymoon."

The young doctor could not help but feel sorry for Paris, yet, at the same time, his advice was purely professional when he said:

"So long as you have a complete rest, Mrs Carter. Do you think you might get abroad somewhere . . . where there's some sun?"

"My fiancé is . . . very well off," Lindsey said. "I am sure he would take me abroad if I asked him to."

"That would be the best thing for you. Now, let's have a look at that dressing . . ."

Sixteen

Glynn was shocked by Lindsey's appearance. Somehow, he had not expected her to look so ill. He sat by the bed, holding her hand, feeling uncertain and unhappy. His expression must have shown on his face, for Lindsey said:

"There's no need to worry about me, Glynn. The doctor says I'll be out in a week or so."

Glynn nodded.

"Yes, he told me outside. But you look rotten, darling."

"I don't feel so bad," Lindsey said to reassure him. "It's rather nice . . . having a rest, I mean. I'd no idea I was so tired."

"The doctor said you needed a holiday when you come out," Glynn said. "He said you'd spoken to him about it and had something to say to me. Lindsey, are you going away?"

It had not occurred to her that Glynn could have reached the stage where he could imagine she might have decided to leave him . . . for that, surely, was what he meant.

"Did you think I might?" she parried.

Glynn scowled, looking so much like Richard in the same mood that she nearly smiled. Yet it was no smiling matter.

"I suppose I did. After all, things haven't been going too well . . . between us, I mean, have they? And yesterday . . . well, I gather that Rogers fellow is in love with you—"

"That's rubbish!" Lindsey interrupted angrily. "He may think he is, but anyway, why should that concern you . . . or me? Glynn . . . you didn't think . . . you don't think that . . . that I . . . that—"

187

"Well, is it so unreasonable?" Glynn broke in, his voice still surly, his eyes avoiding her direct gaze. "It's perfectly obvious whom Richard and Simon prefer . . . and you think so much of the boys' opinion, I thought maybe—"

"Oh, Glynn!" Lindsey could almost smile at such childishness and yet, at the same time, it worried her. Glynn was older than her by five years and yet at times she felt so much more mature . . . so much older, in wisdom. He had not really changed since the days when they first met.

He looked up, suddenly hopeful.

"You mean, you aren't going to break our engagement?" he asked.

"Of *course* not!" Lindsey said, shocked that he could have put it into words . . . made it sound so possible. "Glynn, how could you have thought so? Why, I promised I'd marry you next May."

"Well, yes, but then the boys ran off like that and then . . . well, I don't know . . . but last night I thought it all out and when you asked to see me today, I believed that was what you wanted to tell me."

"I see!" Lindsey said, suddenly quiet. "And if it were true, Glynn, what would you do?"

"Do?" Glynn questioned. "What could I do?"

"You could refuse to take no for an answer!"

"Well, I could make a fuss, I suppose, but I'd rather not marry than be married to someone who loves someone else!"

"Glynn!" Her voice was now sharp. "I don't love Paris Rogers . . . I hate him, hate him . . . do you hear me, I—"

"Steady on, old thing!" Glynn said quickly. "The doc said you were to keep quiet. I only thought maybe—"

"Well, you're crazy!" Lindsey said, her voice quieter but her face now flushed and her eyes bright as her temperature rose. "I never want to see him again. And if you really want to know why I wanted to see you, it was because I wanted to say that I hoped we could be married now . . . as soon as I'm out of hospital."

For a moment the enthusiasm flooded back into his face and he gave her hand a quick squeeze. Then his expression changed and he said:

"Marie-Louise said last night I had no right to rush you . . . not unless you were absolutely sure."

"But I am sure . . . I am!" Lindsey cried desperately. "Why should you all think I've changed? I've always loved you, Glynn. You know that."

"Well, yes, but there's been this problem about the boys. Still, if you are sure, Lindsey, then you know there's nothing in the world would make me happier."

"I am sure!" Lindsey said violently. "I can't help the boys being upset. They'll get over it. It was all Paris' fault, anyway. He told me yesterday what had happened. Months ago, last year, he told them *he* was going to marry me. They believed him and naturally it was a shock for them when they found it wasn't true after all."

"Of all the dirty tricks . . ." Glynn said, his temper flaring as she had so often seen it when he was really upset. "I'll—"

"No, Glynn! There's nothing more to be done. He's given me his word he won't see the children again. Let's leave it now. I want to forget all about him, and the sooner the boys do so, the better."

"I'd break his neck if I could!" Glynn said. "What right had he to say anything of the sort? Lindsey, you never . . . never let him think that—"

"No, I did not!" Lindsey broke in. "It was something he thought up for himself. "I've told you before that I had only just met him . . . on a business basis, really, when you . . . when I met you again. I hardly knew him. Oh, please, Glynn, let's forget about him."

For Lindsey's sake . . . she really did look feverish . . . Glynn dropped the subject. But later, as he went home in the train, he remembered it and felt a nagging unease. It was all very well for Lindsey to go on like that about "hating" but how could a fellow tell her two kids he was going to marry their mother if he hadn't *something* to go on? And the way he used to come and take them out last summer . . . that had seemed odd at the time, too, even while he had been glad enough to have Lindsey to himself. Just what had been going on behind his back that he had been too blind to see? Lindsey swore that the only position Rogers held in her life was that of her literary agent. But he certainly hadn't behaved like one.

Did he doubt Lindsey? He tried not to. She had promised him over and over again this afternoon that she would marry him as soon as she came out of hospital. They had made plans for a quiet register-office wedding and then a month in the south of France, leaving the boys with Marie-Louise until they went back to school. She had seemed as anxious as he was to be married. Surely it was stupid of him to worry about anything now he was at last getting his own way? Once Lindsey was his wife, he'd make sure that fellow never came near her again . . .

Glynn tried to throw off his depression. It had all seemed so wonderful at first . . . finding Lindsey again, falling in love with her all over again. It had been so perfect, what had gone wrong? First, of course, the children. He had known all along that if he married Lindsey, he must naturally accept the boys. And he would have done so quite happily if they'd shown a little more affection for him. He'd made allowances for their being jealous . . . in a way, he was just as jealous of them, if they but knew it! More, in fact, since Lindsey had postponed their wedding because of their feelings. Now, at last, she had made up her mind to marry him despite the boys. He should be triumphant and yet he was only depressed. He could not understand why. He loved Lindsey more than ever. Yet she frightened him in some strange way. She used to be so bright and full of life. Now there was a seriousness . . . a tension about her that he could not understand.

Maybe it will disappear when we're married, he thought as the train drew into the station. I'll be able to bring back the colour to her cheeks. We'll have a whole month without the boys to worry or depress her. That should be long enough to make her see how silly it is to worry about two kids.

His face cleared and when finally he arrived home and opened the front door and called to his sister, his voice was full of renewed confidence. He lifted Marie-Louise off her feet and swung her round twice.

"Everything's all right!" he told her, grinning. "We're going to be married as soon as she's out of hospital. The doctor says she needs a holiday in the sun so we're going to honeymoon in the south of France—"

He broke off suddenly as he looked over Marie-Louise's shoulder and saw two grubby scowling faces glaring at him with resentment and dislike from the foot of the stairs.

Due chiefly to June's repeated requests Paris did not send the letter he had written to Glynn after all. He was influenced in spite of himself by her continual reiteration:

"Paris, surely you must see how she will hate you if she finds out. She will be so humiliated. If anything will fling her into Glynn's arms, it will be the knowledge that you were giving her money."

"What does it matter if she hates me?" Paris argued. "She has not asked to see me . . . and from her letter to you, she will be married by the beginning of next month. What have I to lose?"

"There's always a chance something may go wrong before then," June pleaded with him. "And it isn't worthy of you, Paris . . . to do such a thing. You'll only make her unhappy, and Glynn stupidly jealous to no purpose. Don't do it. I ask it as a personal favour."

So the letter remained on his desk and Paris worked wearily through the following days, living only for the brief hours in the evening when he would meet June and could feel some nearness to Lindsey in talking of her. He had no knowledge of June's feelings for him, yet he nevertheless appreciated the friendship she offered, just as much as he valued the amount of her time she gave to him.

It was from June he learned that Lindsey was to come out of hospital the next day, and, since it was a weekend, had asked June if she would meet her and take her back to her own cottage.

She wrote:

> ... *I need some clothes and to tie up various loose ends there. It is a month now since I left and I'm not even sure if I emptied the fridge. On Monday I shall go over to Mike and Marie-Louise and I plan to be married quietly to Glynn the weekend after. I was hoping you would be able to come to the wedding ... the only guest we are inviting as we want it to be very quiet. But you can tell me if you will come on Friday, that is if you are free this weekend. A p.c. to the hospital will reach me in time ...*

"Frankly, I'm surprised. Lindsey has refused to see me during this time she has been in hospital. Now she wants me to go down to the cottage for the weekend, and be the only wedding guest. I don't understand."

"I understand only that in ten days from now she will be married!" Paris said bitterly. "June, is there nothing . . . nothing at all I can do?"

"A pity *you* aren't taking her to the country tomorrow!" June said with an attempt at humour which fell flat, for Paris was looking at her with an "alertness" she had not seen in him for days.

"That's it!" he cried. "Don't you see? This is my chance. This is Fate."

"What is?" June asked quietly.

"That you should know she is going to be there . . . alone!"

June looked at Paris in dismay. Surely his mind could not be running to anything so crazy as . . . as . . .

"Paris, please explain!" she said quickly.

For Always

"It is simple!" Paris said. "Tomorrow you take Lindsey back
to the cottage. On Saturday, you receive a phone call from . . .
from a sick relative . . . me! Lindsey is left alone. I shall go
down on Saturday afternoon—"

"But to do what?" June cried. "She won't see you. You can't
force your way into her house, Paris. This is England, 1955."

"Will you deny me this last chance?" Paris asked. "I do not
intend to abduct Lindsey, if that is what you are thinking . . ."
he gave her a wry smile, "but maybe she will listen to me.
Believe me, I shall not try to touch her."

"But, Paris, you . . . you had your chance . . . you said
so yourself, the morning of the accident. Why should she
have changed her mind since then? I don't want to seem too
depressing, but I cannot understand what you are hoping for,
unless it is a miracle."

"Miracles can happen, although I do not expect one in this
case. But I can see that I took the wrong line with Lindsey . . .
I frightened her . . . let her think I was trying to prove my
physical power over her. That is why she ran away from me.
This time I shall make my appeal to her mind."

"Oh, Paris, I hate to say this but I can't believe there is any
use in all this. If ever a girl said 'no' to a man, Lindsey has
said that to you."

Paris seemed unmoved by her calm statement of the truth.

"There are times when a woman's 'no' can mean 'yes'."

"Yet she has made arrangements to marry Glynn ten days
from now. I can't find it in my heart to believe there is any
hope for you, Paris."

"We shall see!" Paris said. "That is, if you will allow me
to see Lindsey on Saturday. I realize this means you may
ultimately lose Lindsey's friendship. I know that she will
see through your excuse when I appear on the scene, and
that if I fail, she will blame you. That is why I need your
permission."

June drew a deep sigh. Of course he did not know, but he
could ask anything in the world of her, and she would give it.

193

Yet now she wondered if it might not be better for him, for Lindsey, for all of them, if she denied him what he called his "last chance". It could only bring him further disappointment and unhappiness. To Lindsey it could bring only distress of mind. And Glynn . . .

June tried to think of Glynn with at least some pity. No doubt his love for Lindsey was as sincere as Paris', and he had not had an easy path to tread. Yet if she were some kind of fairy godmother who could wave her wand at this moment, she would grant to Paris Lindsey's hand without hesitation. Poor Glynn . . . yet it was really Lucky Glynn, wasn't it?

"And the letter?" she asked Paris abruptly. "You won't send it after all?"

"Yes, I shall send it!" Paris said firmly. "You see, June, this will put a lot of things to the test. Glynn won't like it one bit. I would like Lindsey to see how he reacts when he is thwarted."

"You're mad, Paris. You'll lose Lindsey if you do. You're letting go your last chance."

"No! I am staking everything on a last throw!" Paris argued.

June could see that his mind was made up. For one moment she toyed with the idea of asking Paris to give her the letter to post and then withholding it unknown to him. But it seemed suddenly useless to try to take a hand in the affair. Paris would go his own way, and if it seemed to her to be ruthless, she could also admire his tenacity. There were not many men who would fight so long and through such difficulties for the woman they loved.

The following morning Glynn received the letter at the breakfast table and his face went white as he read it. In silence he handed it across the table to his sister.

"But, Glynn, that can't be true. I don't believe it for a moment!" Marie-Louise said quickly.

"You think any man would dare to put such facts on paper if they were untrue?"

194

Marie-Louise looked serious and unhappy. If it were true that Lindsey had accepted money from Paris Rogers, it explained so many things which had puzzled her. Lindsey's hesitation in agreeing to marry Glynn in a hurry . . . no doubt she wanted time to pay back the money first. Then there was Paris' part in the affair . . . he had all along acted as if he had more of a personal right in Lindsey's life than that of a mere business friend. But how could Lindsey have accepted a loan from a man who was a stranger to her? Had she in fact encouraged him, accepting the money on the understanding that she was going to become his wife eventually and then changed her mind when she met Glynn again? Yet that did not seem in the least like Lindsey, who was always so straightforward and honest.

As if following her thoughts, Glynn said:

"I don't know what to believe. Lindsey assured me he meant nothing to her, yet how can she have taken money from him if he did not?"

"Perhaps she did not know!" Marie-Louise said, suddenly brightening.

"That almost makes it worse!" Glynn argued. "For if she was unaware of it, then *he* must have been pretty certain in his own mind that she intended to marry him, and if he was so sure, she must have encouraged him."

"We must not judge Lindsey in her absence!" Marie-Louise said unhappily. "She has a right to see this letter, Glynn."

"I suppose so! I hope she can explain it away. I hope it is a lie and I can sue that . . . that damned Frenchman for slander or libel or whatever it is!"

"You couldn't do that in any case!" Mike said quietly. "It would put a wretched publicity on the whole thing that you couldn't possibly want for Lindsey, even if . . . if you don't marry her."

Glynn and Marie-Louise were both shocked into silence. It had not yet occurred to either of them that this might alter Glynn's plan to marry Lindsey. Yet they could both see now that Lindsey would need to prove herself ignorant of what had happened. It was impossible that she should have accepted money from one man while being engaged to another, no matter how hard up she might have been.

"Damn it, surely she knew I would have helped her financially if she needed it!" Glynn said wretchedly. "She knows I've plenty of money. Why go to him?"

"He's her agent. She is quite entitled to accept an advance from him," Mike said thoughtfully. "You must not confuse in your mind the man and the businessman."

"I'm beginning to wonder if I really know Lindsey at all!" Glynn said. "She's always worried and preoccupied and personally I'm beginning to wonder if she's been in love with Rogers all along."

"Glynn, how silly!" Marie-Louise said sharply. "She has agreed to marry you nine days from now. As to her being worried, she has had every cause with those boys, as you well know. Moreover, she has obviously had financial worries, too. You mustn't fail her now, Glynn."

"Fail her!" Glynn cried furiously. "It's Lindsey who has failed me!"

"That may not be true!" Mike put in gently. "I trust Lindsey, and I think you at least could do as much, Glynn. Show her the letter and let her tell you what happened."

"When?" Glynn said, more quietly. "She's leaving hospital this afternoon and going down to her cottage for the weekend. I shan't see her till Monday."

"Couldn't it wait till then?" Marie-Louise asked, yet she knew herself that she would not want this hanging fire for three days. "Why don't you go up to town this morning? You could see Lindsey before she goes to the country."

Glynn stood up, the letter clenched in his hands, his face white and determined.

"Very well! I'll go. And heaven help that fellow if he's lying."

Lindsey had had a short rest after lunch and now she sat in the armchair by the window, staring out at the rain, waiting for the hours to pass until five-thirty when June was calling to collect her. She wondered now if she had been silly to arrange this weekend at the cottage. It would be late when they arrived and the beds would have to be aired, a meal cooked, fires lit. Nothing would be prepared or waiting for them. It had seemed such a good idea at first and now, suddenly, she was depressed.

"Maybe I'm just tired!" she told herself. The doctor had warned her that she would tire very easily for a few weeks yet, until she regained her full health and strength and put on a little weight. She must have lost a stone since she came here! She had lain in bed half the morning, returned to bed after lunch for a rest and yet already she was tired again! How silly to have decided to go home when she could have allowed Glynn to call for her in the car and take her back to his house where she would be spoiled and nursed by everyone. She would have seen Simon and Richard, too. It was nearly three weeks since she had seen them and they were due back at school next week. What could have happened to her that she was willing to forgo a precious three days of their remaining holiday?

Suddenly honest, Lindsey knew that one of her reasons for going back to the cottage was because she wanted to avoid her two children. The thought frightened her and she tried to disbelieve it. Yet it was true. Her mind, even more than her body, had become exhausted. She had lived through so much emotionally these last months that her conscious mind was directing her actions to avoid any more emotion. And she knew that if the boys once began to beg and plead with her not to marry Glynn, she would break down completely. And she could not do that to Glynn. No one should come between them and their wedding next week. She had made up her mind and given her faithful promise to Glynn. She would not let him down. Yet she dared not trust herself to face her children.

I suppose I'm a coward! Lindsey told herself ruefully. At least there was no going back now. June had agreed to come at short notice and had arranged a taxi to take them to Victoria and another to take them from the station to the cottage. . . .

The thought of her little home gave Lindsey a sudden pang. It was not entirely one of pain nor yet of pleasure. She had not really lived there very long and yet her whole life seemed to be tied up in the place. It was almost as if her life had begun there . . . and now it was to end there, too, for she would never go to it again except as Glynn's wife.

She felt a quick, urgent desire to see Glynn . . . to hear his cheerful boyish voice, see his smile; be reassured by his love and need for her. With Glynn she would be safe. He would take care of her . . . protect her . . . from what? What did she fear? Why was she afraid? Was this feeling of apprehension, even of danger, merely a symptom of her illness, or was this depression?

The rain beat more heavily against the glass window panes and involuntarily Lindsey shivered. She wished the doctor, or one of the nurses, even the rather starchy matron, would come in, if only to relieve her of her loneliness.

As if in answer to her silent prayer, the door opened and one of the orderlies came in.

"Mr Noble is downstairs and would like to see you. Shall I show him up?"

Lindsey's face was suddenly radiant. How wonderful of Glynn to come just when she most needed him! She had told him not to come today and now she was never more glad to see anyone.

"Glynn!" she said, holding out her hands as he came through the door. "How lovely!"

There was no answering smile from him and her hands fell to her sides, unclasped by his. Her heart gave a sickening jolt.

"Glynn, what's wrong. The boys . . . ?"

"Damn the boys!" Glynn said furiously. He was the more angry because the sight of Lindsey's thin, pointed little face moved him to a sudden pity. She looked ill . . . and those green eyes of hers seemed enormous. He knew that he ought to be gentle with her, yet his sense of betrayal by her made him the more rough.

"Glynn, what is it?" Lindsey asked, her face as bewildered as her thoughts.

"This!" Glynn said, holding out the letter.

He saw her colour change as she read, misjudged the swift rush of pink to her cheeks for guilt, and his heart hardened.

"Well?" he asked.

"You think . . . *that I knew*?" Lindsey did not know how she managed to bring out the words coherently. Her heart was hammering inside her throat and she wanted desperately to be alone . . . to think . . . to hide her humiliation. It was not just the thought of what Paris had done . . . but that Glynn should believe she had known about it; that was worst of all.

"I'm asking you to explain!" Glynn said, taking the letter from her and banging it with the back of his hand. "You don't deny that it is true?"

"I suppose it must be. Paris couldn't lie about . . . about a thing like that!" Her voice was so full of pain that even Glynn, in his anger, heard it and was momentarily touched again to something like pity.

"Look here, Lindsey, there must be some explanation!" he said more gently. "You couldn't just take money from him."

"I didn't know about it," Lindsey said quietly, her face turned once more to the rain on the windows that seemed symbolic now of the tears in her heart. "I didn't know, Glynn."

"Then he tricked you? He's been trying to use this as a kind of blackmail . . . to make you marry him?"

Lindsey shook her head.

"No, he didn't tell me. I knew nothing about it. He sent me cheques from time to time for stories he said he had sold abroad for me. I . . . I wondered sometimes why he was never able to sell anything in England. It's true I needed the money. I suppose he knew it . . . I must have told him."

"But you can't just do those kind of things!" Glynn argued. "I mean, not without reason."

"I . . . suppose . . . he thought he had a reason!" Lindsey said quietly, helplessly. "People like Paris . . . don't conform to . . . to ordinary standards."

"You mean because he loved you he thought it gave him the right?" Glynn asked uneasily.

"I . . . I never really believed he loved me!" Lindsey said, again in that quiet voice, devoid of emotion. "He told me so . . . before my accident . . . and that he'd really believed I would one day marry him. I suppose if he really thought that, to advance me money I hadn't earned was . . . well, at least a safe bet!"

"But he couldn't have thought you'd marry him unless you'd given him some encouragement!" Glynn said accusingly.

"I suppose it is difficult for you to believe me when I say that nevertheless he did!" Lindsey said, an appeal in her voice now. "One can't very well prove a thing like that, Glynn."

He walked round the room, his face unhappy, his whole body showing his uneasiness.

"Naturally, I don't doubt your word, Lindsey, but . . ."

"But you find it hard to believe?" Lindsey finished for him. "Yet I do swear to you now, Glynn, that there was nothing between us . . . except . . . once he kissed me good night. It was before I'd met you again. There was no talk of love . . . or marriage . . . just a good-night kiss."

"You never told me about it before!" Glynn said accusingly.

"I suppose I didn't think it was important!" Lindsey said wearily. More than anything in the world, she wanted to throw herself into his arms, to plead with him for understanding, trust, belief in her. Yet pride forbade it. Glynn must make his own decisions and if he could not trust her now, then it was better that they should learn it before their wedding.

"It was obviously important to him!" Glynn said. "Dash it all, Lindsey, none of this makes sense. Are you quite sure you really do want to marry me?"

"Nothing has happened to make me change my mind," Lindsey said after a moment's silence. "That is, not unless you feel differently . . . about me, I mean. There is a poem I know . . . one you sent to me, Glynn, years ago. I expect you have forgotten it, but I was thinking of it the other day. It says that love *'was never for the mean; it requireth courage stout, souls above doubt . . .'* Do you doubt me, Glynn? Do you doubt yourself?"

"Hell, I don't know any more what I feel!" Glynn said. "It's all been so hopeless all along . . . it seems to me, Lindsey, as if you're the one to ask yourself that question. Even now I'm not sure that it is *me* you love. You've always found some obstacle to put in the way of our marriage and now . . . now there's this."

"I am not making this an obstacle!" Lindsey said simply. "It is you who are doing that, Glynn."

"Can't you see how difficult it is for me? If I was quite sure in my own mind that you loved me, I suppose I wouldn't be here wondering if . . . well, wondering if perhaps you've really been in love with someone else all along."

"I think if I were to see Paris Rogers again I should kill him!" Lindsey said violently. "I hate him in a way I never thought it possible to hate anyone."

He ought to have been convinced, yet with a perception that was foreign to his nature, he said:

"Are you sure, Lindsey? People often make that trite remark that love and hate are akin."

She turned on him then, her face ravaged and her eyes brilliant.

"If that is what you believe, then you'd better go, Glynn. It will be no marriage if we are to live with Paris Rogers' ghost between us."

"Look here, Lindsey, I didn't mean . . ." he began, but he broke off, seeing the tears gathering in her eyes and the desperate unhappy twist to her mouth. He remembered suddenly that she was still not fully recovered from the accident and that he ought not to have come here and made a scene to upset her. Of course, it was ridiculous to suppose that *he* wanted to break the engagement. He loved Lindsey as much as ever and when she was feeling a bit better he'd tell her so.

"Won't you please go!" Lindsey cried. "Can't you see I want to be by myself!"

"Well, all right. But at least promise me you'll forget all about this . . . this row we've had," Glynn said awkwardly. "I'm sorry to have upset you, and you're not to worry. I'll see you on Monday, shall I?"

But she gave him no answer and at last, unhappy and ill at ease, he turned and left the room, closing the door behind him. He'd send her some flowers by way of reconciliation, he consoled himself. Yet he could not do that since she was leaving hospital this evening. Well, he would ring her at the cottage tonight when she'd no doubt be in a better mood.

For a moment he toyed with the idea of walking into Paris Rogers' office and giving him a piece of his mind, but the impulse left him. The sooner they all forgot him the better. He was pretty sure now that Lindsey didn't care for the fellow and once he'd cleared the debt they need never mention his name again.

Alone in the hospital room, Lindsey cried silently, the hot tears scalding her cheeks. There was no anger in her now . . . not even bitterness. She had learned at last that Glynn was only a boy . . . the same boy she had loved when she was young, *but wasn't in love with any more*. She had thought to find safety and security with him, not physical safety or financial security, but of her mind and heart. How blind she had been not to see how ill-equipped he was by virtue of his very immaturity to give her these things she had needed so much. Yet she had loved him . . . or was it only the memory of him she had fallen in love with? Had she really only been trying to recapture the wonder of first love? What *had* brought her so near to marrying the man who had just left her? His persuasive, ardent wooing? Or her own need of someone in her life at that psychological moment?

She could still marry Glynn . . . she knew that . . . if she wanted to. He would forget about Paris' letter and his suspicions of her duplicity if she chose to make the effort to convince him of her innocence. But she would not do that. Pride forbade it . . . and a strange suddenly recognized honesty. She was not innocent. She had tried to fight against the knowledge of Paris' attraction, yet even in her unconscious dreaming she had wanted to be in his arms.

The thought terrified her. For her hate for Paris was the uppermost emotion in her mind. Never, never could she bear to be in the same room with him again. He had humiliated her unforgivably, and she could see now to what lengths he had gone to try to force her to love him. Undoubtedly he was mad. Looking back over the various facets of his behaviour she could see that he was utterly ruthless in his efforts to obtain what he wanted. He might give it the name of love, but she would never believe that . . . never. If he really loved her he could not have set out so clearly to have brought her life to this present state of utter misery. Had it not been for him, she might by now have married Glynn. . . .

Lindsey paused in her thoughts. Perhaps, after all, he had inadvertently saved her from a second mistaken marriage. She could see all too clearly now that Glynn was weak, prey to quick, easy emotional sway. Had he really loved her, he could have refused to accept those constant postponements she had made for their wedding. Yet was that fair? Had he not agreed to wait for her sake . . . because of the boys? Was he not justified in everything he had done since her own indecision had been so obvious?

"I have only myself to blame!" Lindsey thought wearily. "It was not Glynn's fault. Had I been sure of my love for him, I would not have let the boys hold me back!"

She remembered suddenly something Paris had said to her in the flat that morning of her accident . . . *you are afraid to kiss me because you are afraid to find out that you do not love the man you are going to marry . . .*

Perhaps, after all, he had been right. Love, as she had always believed, excluded all other emotions. If she had belonged heart and soul to Glynn, could she not have scorned Paris' kisses instead of fearing them? He had seen her weakness and played on it, just as he had made use of her ignorance of business to put her into his debt. That much at least she could undo. She would write from the cottage tonight to her solicitor, asking him to draw money from her capital trust fund for the boys and pay back every penny she owed him.

Her cheeks burned at the thought. Anger mounted in her again, superseding her unhappiness, her loneliness, her despair. How dare he have done such a thing!

Anger gave her the strength of action. When she left the hospital with June later, she walked with a buoyant step that misled the doctor into thinking that she had made a better recovery than he had till now believed.

But by the time the two women were sitting in front of a roaring fire, the beds in the boys' bedroom made up and airing with hot-water bottles, supper over, Lindsey's face was white with exhaustion and June looked at her anxiously.

"I think you should go straight to bed," she suggested. "You really do look ghastly!"

"It's only nine o'clock. I couldn't sleep yet," Lindsey said desperately. "I'm resting here, June."

Until now, they had talked lightly and impersonally . . . about life in the hospital, the boys, June's work. By unspoken understanding they had not mentioned either Glynn or Paris. But now Lindsey said suddenly:

"I'm not marrying Glynn, June. I . . . I think he may ring up this evening. If he does, will you tell him I'm in bed asleep? I can't talk to him tonight!"

June felt her heart thumping. She nodded her head, waiting for Lindsey to say more.

"You don't look very surprised!" Lindsey said after a moment of silence.

June looked uneasily at Lindsey. She felt a sudden sharp need for honesty. Lindsey had asked her down here as a friend . . . perhaps one of the few friends she had. She ought at least to know that her friendship was not unqualified.

"Perhaps I ought to tell you something before you say any more," June said quietly, staring into the fire. "You see, you may not want to trust me with your confidences when you know."

"What is it, June?" Lindsey asked. "Surely you know I trust you completely?"

"Then you should not!" June cried. "Can't you see . . . haven't you guessed . . . I love Paris!"

Lindsey stared at her from those enormous green eyes, her face so shocked that June's seriousness left her momentarily and she laughed.

"Darling, don't look so horrified! *He* doesn't know."

"June, you can't love a man like that . . . you can't!" Lindsey cried. "Don't you see how . . . how *evil* he is?" She proceeded to tell June what she already knew . . . that he had sent her money she had never earned. So Paris had sent that letter after all!

When Lindsey finished, June said quietly:

"I can see that if you don't love him, you might very well hate him for what he has done. But you must not doubt the reason, Lindsey. He loves you the way . . . the way I'd give my eyes to be loved by him. You are his . . . his obsession, Lindsey. For months and months I have heard nothing but your name on his lips. I think he might even commit murder for you!"

Lindsey gave a nervous little laugh.

"But that's all nonsense, June. If . . . if he talks about me . . . that way, it's just because I'm the one girl he's wanted and couldn't have!"

"That may be true. But you are also the first woman in his

life he has wanted to marry . . . the only one he has ever loved. I know those two things to be true, Lindsey."

Lindsey choked back a feeling of hysteria mounting in her.

"Why do we have to talk about him!" she cried. "He won't leave me alone. Why must he come into my life the way he did and ruin everything for me? I might have been happy with Glynn . . . the boys might have been different . . . I could have been at peace."

June said quietly:

"Is Paris the reason you are not going to marry Glynn?"

"No, no, *no*!" Lindsey said. "I just don't want to marry Glynn any more. I . . . I thought I loved him . . . and in a way, I still do. But . . . I can see our marriage wouldn't be . . . well, what I had imagined. Glynn has never really grown up. He hasn't changed since I first knew him . . . and I . . . I have changed. Glynn wants a carefree companion to laugh and dance with him through life. I'm not like that. I want someone to . . . to lean on, to trust, to look after me."

"But, Lindsey, surely marriage could mean both? I grant that Glynn is not perhaps the person to have responsibilities . . . that he is . . . well, Peter Pannish. But surely marriage can offer lightness and gaiety and fun and at the same time give you security and protection?"

"Yes, I suppose so!" Lindsey said, her voice infinitely weary. "That would be the ideal. But I can see now that it is not for me. I shall never marry again, June. I've made a hopeless mess of my life and marrying Glynn now won't get me out of it. I suppose I thought it would. But I don't love him and it wouldn't be fair to him to marry him knowing that."

"You could marry Paris. He would look after you . . . and the boys . . ."

A sudden tightening of Lindsey's face gave June an unexpected moment of fear. Had this all been too much for her on top of her accident? She looked almost . . . out of her mind. The laugh that came from her lips was without humour.

"How pleased the boys would be!" she said in a hard, unnatural little voice. "How satisfied Paris would be to think that his letter had got him what he wanted. I'm almost tempted to marry him, you know, just to spoil his life the way he has spoiled mine."

"That's childish!" June said calmly. "Paris has never harmed you intentionally."

"Hasn't he? I think he has. It would be a fine reward for him, wouldn't it, if I married him . . . let him believe I loved him until after the ceremony and then left him, flat."

"Let's stop this discussion!" June said quickly. "I think you are overwrought, Lindsey. I'm going to make you a hot drink and then you're to go straight to bed!"

Lindsey laughed.

"Oh, I know you will take his side, June. I was forgetting for a moment that you love him. I should be doing you a good turn if I put him out of circulation. I pity the woman who becomes his wife. You're far too good and sweet to be married to a man like that."

"I'm not going to be married to him," June said, striving to keep calm as she recognized the hysteria in Lindsey's voice. "For one thing, he hasn't suggested it. For another, he doesn't know I love him and he never will. So you will be harming no one but yourself, Lindsey, and him, if you persist in this silly notion. But then, you are not serious and I refuse to take you seriously."

She stood up and left the room with dignity.

But when she came back with two cups of hot cocoa, Lindsey was still staring into the fire, her face flushed and her eyes brilliant.

"You are in love with Paris, so you are blind to the kind of person he really is," she told June. "I can see him clearly. He has always got what he wanted from life and there has never been anyone to teach him a lesson."

"You are the one who is blind!" June said simply. "You think he has walked through life treading on people's feelings. It isn't so. You condemn him because he is handsome and attractive to women, but he has never made use of those assets to hurt anyone. He is a loyal, good friend, and capable of great love. And he loves you, Lindsey, with all his heart."

"He has twisted you round his little finger!" Lindsey said bitterly. "You believe only what he wants you to believe of him. You'll do anything he asks you because he has hypnotized you."

June was momentarily silent, remembering how she had agreed to go away tomorrow and leave Paris free to see Lindsey alone. It was true that she had complied. Now she wondered if she should go . . . or at least if she should warn Lindsey first. Clearly, Lindsey was ill . . . ill in her mind as well as her body. Paris, too, should be warned.

"Lindsey," she said, "it is true that I will do anything I can to help Paris. I agreed to . . . to go away tomorrow because he wanted to come down and see you alone. I am telling you this because I shan't go now . . . I don't think you ought to be left by yourself."

Lindsey looked at June as she might have regarded a dangerous snake.

"You mean you . . . you and Paris . . . planned this . . . ?" June nodded.

"It isn't so terrible a thing to do. Paris means to be very gentle with you. He wouldn't have touched you. He only wanted a chance to explain to you that—"

Lindsey broke in with a wild laugh.

"Don't go on . . . you think I'm crazy the way I have behaved, but you are the crazy one, June. He's using you . . . the way . . . the way a murderer plans to kill his victim with an accomplice. Well, you can go if you want. Let him come . . . let him be gentle and sweet and charming. Let him propose to me and he will see what happens to him."

"I refuse to continue this ridiculous conversation!" June said with an effort. "We are both being dramatic and . . . and . . .

silly. I shall not go away tomorrow and I shall warn Paris that you are not well enough to see him."

"You will not!" Lindsey cried. "This is my house and I shall see whom I please in it. Stay if you wish. I don't mind whether you do or not. It's time someone showed both you and Paris that you cannot plan other people's lives for them."

"Good night, Lindsey. Try to get some sleep!" June said, hoping to calm the fevered girl. But Lindsey only laughed and called back to her:

"Pleasant dreams, June. You'll thank me one day for what I'm going to do!"

After June had left her alone, Lindsey leant back in the chair, her eyes closed, her head throbbing violently. She felt very ill and yet at the same time she felt elated. It was almost as if she were two people . . . one who was desperately tired and wanted only to sleep and sleep and be at peace; the other who wanted to hurt the way she had been hurt. The two people warred in her overwrought mind. Could she really go through with that crazy, spur-of-the-moment plan to marry Paris and then walk out on him? What good could it do to anyone? None to herself . . . perhaps even harm to the boys, and certainly harm to Paris. She thought of his feelings on their wedding night . . . triumphant that he had at last made her love him; then discovering that she hated him, hated him . . .

Then the pain in her head became unbearable and she rose swiftly and went to the bathroom to find some codeine tablets she remembered keeping there. She took three and went to her bed and was almost instantly asleep.

At nine o'clock the next morning, when June awoke after a restless night, Lindsey was still dead to the world. Hurriedly, June dressed and went downstairs to the telephone. As she put out her hand to pick up the receiver, the bell rang and she grabbed it off its rest. But it was not Paris . . . it was Glynn.

"I don't like to wake Lindsey," June said truthfully. "She was really not at all well last night and she needs sleep. I'm going to get the local GP in this morning to check up on her."

Glynn wanted to phone again, but June asked him to wait till Lindsey rang him. He reluctantly agreed.

As soon as she could get rid of him she did. She waited for the dialling tone to come through and then quickly put a call in to Paris' flat. But there was no reply.

"There must be!" she cried desperately. "It's only nine fifteen. I'm sure there's someone there!"

"I'll ring them again!" said the operator.

But there was still no reply and June put back the telephone helplessly. She must somehow warn Paris not to come. She had no doubt this morning that Lindsey was ill. Even if she had not meant what she threatened last night, it was clear how she felt about Paris and it could serve no purpose him coming. It would upset Lindsey still more, and Paris would be made utterly wretched to see how intensely she hated him. Yet how could she warn him now? Lindsey might wake at any moment . . . and clearly Paris was on his way.

She stood undecided by the telephone. Then shrugged her shoulders. There was nothing she could do . . . except hope that when Lindsey awoke she would be in a more normal frame of mind. She would try to persuade her to stay in bed and if necessary enlist the help of the local doctor. Then, when Paris arrived, she would explain to him and send him away again.

She decided suddenly that she was being silly to take last night's conversation in the least seriously. Lindsey could not possibly have meant what she said. People did not use marriage as a way of getting their revenge on someone they imagined had hurt them. It wasn't logical or civilized.

Lindsey was still asleep when half an hour later Paris drove up. He looked at June anxiously.

"I'd hoped you'd be out of the way by now!" he said with a half smile. "I suppose I am early, but I couldn't wait any longer."

June took him into the sitting-room where a warm log fire blazed, and in a lowered voice told him what had happened last night. Far from the expected concern on Paris' face, she saw only a quiet triumph.

"I knew she loved me!" he said when she stopped talking.

June looked at him dismayed.

"Don't you understand, Paris? She's threatening to do this to hurt you! I don't think for a moment she'll go through with it, but at least you can judge from it how she really feels about you. She said she would pretend affection for you until your wedding night . . . then she would reveal to you just how much she hated you."

Paris put a hand on June's arm.

"Don't get so ruffled, my dear!" he said. "It is unlike you to lose your calm. Can't you see that everything is going just as I hoped? First, she breaks her engagement to Glynn, or if she hasn't done so, it is as good as accomplished. She knows now that she does not love him. She blames me . . . and she is right. It is because of her feeling for me that she can't just sit back and relax, saying: 'I'm free now!'"

"You mean, you would marry her, knowing she hates you, despises you?" June asked.

"She only thinks those things . . . it is not what she really feels!" Paris said calmly. "Can you imagine marrying a man you really hated, really despised, just to spite him? No! You cannot . . . and nor would Lindsey or any woman. It is just that she is not ready to admit she cares. Oh, I am so happy I could sing!"

"I think you are both crazy . . . quite mad!" June said desperately. "And I think you are playing a very dangerous game, Paris. Lindsey is ill . . . I'm sure of it. I will not be party to any of it."

"You have done more than enough for me!" Paris said, his voice now serious and sincere. "Trust me a little further, June. I know what I am doing. You speak of danger, but there is none. If Lindsey is ill, it is because she is fighting all the time against herself. She will be well again when she discovers how to be her real self again. I learned this in the war. It gave freedom of action to many people for whom it might otherwise have been impossible. They had made themselves conform to standards of behaviour that were against their innermost convictions. Men for instance who had spent all their adult lives working in a certain job believing that this is what they must do for the rest of their lives, convincing themselves they enjoyed it or wanted it that way. Then they were forcibly removed from that work and they knew then how terribly it had gone against the grain. They never went back to those jobs. After the war they became something else . . . the person they were meant to be."

"You think that applies also to . . . to marriages?" June asked, impressed by Paris' reasoning.

"Yes, I do. I believe many women marry men they only believed they loved. They lead the lives such marriages demand of them, making themselves the partner their husband wishes them to be, convincing even themselves that they are happy . . . that this is what they want. Yet deep inside is the knowledge of a life wasted . . . or feelings that have to be trodden on because they can never be given expression for fear of where they might lead. It is always fear. It takes courage to learn to be yourself . . . utterly yourself."

"I suppose that is true!" June agreed. "Yet is it not possible to be yourself without being very selfish?"

"The truth often hurts!" Paris agreed. "But are we not less hurt in the end by recognizing the truth? You are essentially a very honest person, June. Would you not rather face the truth than spend your life convincing yourself it was otherwise?"

June was silent. Above all, this was true of her. She had admitted so long ago that there was no hope of Paris' loving her . . . faced it and even found happiness of a kind in merely being Paris' friend. Suppose she had talked herself into believing he might one day love her . . . how bitterly disappointed and disillusioned she would be by now.

"You so often surprise me, Paris!" she said. "To meet you at first, one would not believe that such profound thoughts went on behind that handsome forehead of yours!"

"That is one of the silly notions of our modern world," said Paris, laughing. "That beautiful women and handsome men are necessarily empty-headed."

He broke off suddenly as Lindsey came into the room. She was dressed in a warm fisherman's knit jersey over a pair of tartan slacks. Her face looked dead white above the bright scarlet of the scarf tied at her throat, but she seemed perfectly self-possessed and calm.

"You should not have let me over-sleep, June," she said, and then holding out her hand to Paris:

"I won't pretend this is a surprise. June told me you were coming."

"I hope you are pleased to see me?" Paris asked, standing up and holding her hand until she withdrew it with a sudden rush of colour to her cheeks.

"Delighted!" she said, but she moved away from him to the window and said, a hint of nervousness in her voice: "I see it is still raining. Doesn't the sun ever shine?"

"In the south of France, the sun will be shining," Paris said, smiling.

"I'll get some coffee," June said abruptly, and went quickly out of the room. Let Paris manage this as he might . . . she wanted no part in it.

"How tactful!" Lindsey murmured. "Did June tell you that I'm . . . that I . . . I'm not going to marry Glynn now?"

She trembled with anger at herself for hesitating over her carefully prepared speech.

"Yes!" Paris said. "I expect you realize what the news means to me? You know I'm in love with you, Lindsey . . . that I've wanted for a long time to ask you to marry me. Now you are free I can do so."

Lindsey bit her lip and said quickly:

"You . . . you don't ask me if I'm in love with you?"

"No!" Paris answered. "I am only asking that you should marry me. Not tomorrow or the next day or next year but now . . . today."

As he had expected, he had ruffled her composure. She turned from the window to face him, her expression tense, her eyes frightened.

"But that's ridiculous. It's impossible!"

"Nothing is impossible if you wish it enough!" Paris said simply. "I can take you in the car now . . . to the village church, and kneel down before God and say: 'I take thee Lindsey, to be my lawful wedded wife . . . with all my worldly goods I thee endow.' And you can make the same promise to me."

"But that's . . . that's crazy," Lindsey said. "That is no wedding . . . no marriage . . ."

"It could suffice until I can obtain a special licence. Then we can be married in the eyes of the law as well as in the eyes of God."

When she made no reply, he said gently:

"Are you afraid, Linotte?"

Her eyes narrowed suddenly at the name. He had seldom called her this before and yet she recognized it . . . ". . . I love you so much, Linotte. I have always loved you . . ." She remembered now where she had heard him call her Linotte before . . . in her dream . . .

"Afraid?" she repeated desperately, her mind now in hopeless confusion. Was she afraid? What was happening to her mind? Which was true . . . her dreams or this terrible reality?

Slowly, Paris walked towards her, and just as if it were a dream, she could not back away from him. His fingers touched her hand . . . the barest contact, and yet it brought the colour flaring to her cheeks and set her heart beating wildly.

"I am afraid . . . I am afraid!" she cried desperately.

"Of yourself, not of me!" Paris said steadily. "You know that I love you . . . *in your heart you know it is true.* You are afraid to love me, because for you to love is to give, and if you give yourself into my keeping you give me also the power to hurt you. Isn't that true?"

She stared at him, breathing deeply.

"You have hurt me . . . you have come between me and the man I was going to marry . . ." she cried desperately.

"I have come between you and the man you did not love!" Paris corrected her. "You didn't love him, Linotte. Be honest with yourself at last. You wanted to love him, but that was all. But love does not always come where it is wanted. Now, for us, this miracle has happened. It has come to both of us when we are free to let it be so. It might have been otherwise. There is nothing between us but your fear of me . . . of loving me. See, my darling, there is nothing to fear . . ."

His arms were round her and with the deepest tenderness he drew her close against his heart.

She leaned against him, her eyes closed against the infinite surprise and wonder that was flooding through her. She had believed herself full of hate . . . full of a desire to hurt and take revenge. Now it was as if a dark cloak had fallen away from her leaving only this unbelievable feeling of peace. She lifted her face so that she would see into his eyes and read in them only the depth of his love. There was, after all, nothing to fear, nothing to fight against. Here, in his arms, was perfect safety.

"Paris, I . . . I don't understand!" she whispered.

"Love is not easy to understand!" he replied. "But let us not question it, Linotte. Let us take it by the hand and treasure and guard it for always, for surely it is the greatest gift that can be given to us in our lives."

"Shall we be happy . . . always?" Lindsey questioned, like a small child placing her trust in his keeping.

He smiled down at her.

"Always!" he said. "I am not a very rich man, Linotte, but there are some things I can always give you . . . love, laughter, and care. I offer them now to you . . . and to Richard and Simon, whom I love also. Will it be enough, *chérie*?"

She smiled through her tears.

"I do love you, Paris!" she whispered, and it was as if the rain had suddenly stopped and the sunshine had flooded warm and full of promise into her heart.

THE SEARCH FOR LOVE

One

1955

Beverly replaced the tin of talcum powder on the bathroom shelf and had already half turned on her heel to hurry downstairs when she caught sight of her reflection in the mirror above the basin. She frowned and suddenly looked at herself with more than the usual glance. What she saw shocked her and added quickly to the day's growing depression.

I look a sight! she thought, touching the tip of her shiny *retroussé* nose, then trying ineffectually to tidy the mop of dark hair that seemed to be straggling rather than curling over her forehead. Her mouth gave her no encouragement either. Over large, it looked its best brightly outlined with lipstick and with her lips smiling and upturned at the corners. But now it grimaced at her from the looking-glass and her eyes lifted swiftly away from this feature to stare directly into themselves. Green eyes, beautiful eyes, Jonnie called them, fringed with dark curling lashes, but now red-rimmed from a bad night's sleep and ringed with violet shadows and tiny lines of fatigue.

Her expression became defiant.

"It's not my fault! When have I time to get my hair done? See to my make-up? My clothes?"

She looked away from the mirror and down at her none-too-clean tweed slacks and slightly too tight twin-set. The slacks needed pressing and she needed a new jersey – three new jerseys, come to that. But there wasn't time or money to cope with these things.

It's not my fault! she repeated silently, but it was to her mother she was really speaking in her mind. Only last weekend Mummy had torn strips off her for going around looking the way she did.

1

"It's so *unlike* you, Beverly! You were always the fastidious one, the most fussy, most clothes-conscious, of my two daughters. And look at yourself! I can't think how you can bear to have Jonnie see you this way!"

"Oh, he doesn't notice," Beverly had replied vaguely. "And, anyway, I haven't time nowadays. Nor would you if you had five young children to care for and no money!"

Of course, that had been Mrs Bampton's cue to restart the old argument about Beverly and Jonnie taking a small allowance from her. She could well afford it, as they both knew. But Jonnie was proud. He hadn't forgotten that Beverly's mother had tried to prevent their marrying. "Far too young," she had said, "and Jonnie hasn't sufficient money to support you the way you've been used to, Beverly."

"Seventeen isn't young these days, Mummy. And, besides, Jonnie's boss has promised him a rise next year. You just haven't any faith in Jonnie or in me. Because you've always given me everything, you think I can't do without it. Well, I'd rather have Jonnie and do without the so-called luxuries."

In the end Beverly and Jonnie had won over Mrs Bampton, and, although she still maintained they were too young, once she had given in she had been very nice about everything, giving them the house as a wedding present and Beverly a magnificent and sensible trousseau. Really, Beverly hadn't had any new clothes since then, and it had turned out to be just as well she'd had such a large trousseau, for they couldn't afford luxuries like new clothes on their budget. With the ever-rising cost of living, even Jonnie's payrise hadn't helped, except to keep them out of debt. And Jonnie wouldn't accept a shilling-piece from his mother-in-law. Deep inside her, Beverly agreed. It was a question of pride, hers as well as Jonnie's. They'd said they would manage and they would! All the same, it was a terrible struggle and seeing herself now in the glass Beverly realized for the first time just how badly that struggle was showing.

It wasn't just herself – it was all over the house. They couldn't afford to have the sitting-room carpet cleaned this year and it looked spotty and shabby. They hadn't been able to buy new bathroom curtains; the children's clothes were patched and darned and nothing matched. It was the same with the china . . . all odds and ends because they no longer had a full set of anything.

They might have managed pretty well if it hadn't been for the children. Beverly could admit this to herself, though not to anyone else – least of all to her mother.

Nicky had been the first; they hadn't planned to have Nicky but he'd come along all the same exactly nine months after their honeymoon. She'd just had her eighteenth birthday when the baby was born. Although they had meant to wait a few years before they took on the responsibility of a family, they'd none the less been thrilled and happy about Nicky and with the very young's adaptability had reversed all their original ideas and decided to have the family first and a good time afterwards.

Jonnie had agreed whole-heartedly after the first surprise and delight in finding himself a father. Nicky had been such a good baby and they'd hardly noticed the extra expense at first. One of Beverly's aunts had given them a pram, her elder sister, Pam, a cot and baby bath and most of the larger items like a playpen which her own two children had outgrown.

"Let's have another, soon!" Jonnie had said. "It's nice to have two boys growing up near to each other in age."

So eighteen months later Philip had been born – the brother they had wanted for Nick.

The second baby had somehow seemed to affect their finances more than the first. Maybe because they'd worked out on paper that he wouldn't cost anything. In theory he should not have done. He had all Nick's things to grow into. Yet in practice they began to find themselves really hard up.

"I hope that's an end to it!" Mrs Bampton had said firmly.

Beverly eyed her mother stubbornly. Privately, she thought they wouldn't have any more children – not yet awhile anyway. But Mrs Bampton's remark somehow seemed like a challenge, a doubting of hers and Jonnie's capabilities.

"Why not, Mummy? Jonnie and I would both like a daughter."

Her mother's shocked reply strengthened Beverly's belief that a daughter was now the most desirable thing in the world to have.

"Besides," she argued, "it wouldn't be fair to have one child all by itself, say, in five years' time. It would be almost as bad for it as being an only child."

Twelve months after Philip, Julia completed the family. This time, Mrs Bampton knew better than to discuss any possibility of adding to the numbers. She didn't need to. Beverly had her hands full with three children under four and even an outsider could see how precarious were the young couple's finances.

Mrs Bampton was a widow, still young and extremely smart in her appearance. She needed to be for she was quite a personality in the fashion world where she had gone into business on the death of her husband ten years previously. Mr Bampton had left her very well provided for, but with her two daughters away at boarding school, she felt the need for some occupation and with her good dress sense, her social contacts and natural head for business matters, she had quickly risen to a position of authority in the fashion house who had given her a job.

Now she was by way of being very well off. Both her daughters were married and she had only her smart little London flat to keep up. There was more than sufficient money for her to have given Jonnie and Beverly a helping hand in the way of a regular allowance. But they wouldn't take it. Secretly, she admired them both for their spirit of independence, but she could not see that it *could* continue. Granted Beverly was nearly twenty-one and would come into an income from her father's legacy of a hundred and fifty pounds a year. Jonnie had eight hundred a year which was pretty good for a boy of twenty-three. All the same, they were five in the family now and neither Jonnie nor Beverly were really *trained* to manage economically. Jonnie had never considered giving up his Aston Martin sports car, nor his membership at the golf club – not that the latter cost him so much, but naturally he had to spend a bit of money at the club, rounds of drinks in return to those who treated him. And they liked to entertain, to offer their friends gin, whisky, sherry. It was important, too, for Jonnie to look smart at his work, and he had a new suit every year, tailored for him. No wonder they were poor! And Beverly might blame her appearance on her lack of time to see to herself, but the fact remained that more money could have bought Beverly a little domestic help and more time; not to mention clothes.

Then it had happened! Not intentionally – even Mrs Bampton had no doubt that they'd meant to confine their family to three children. But all the same, Beverly had found she was going to have another baby, and even her bravado had been finally shaken when later on an X-ray confirmed that "it" would be "they" – she was to have twins!

It was plain bad luck, Mrs Bampton said, but Beverly, after the first shock, had refused ever to allow her mother to call her two new babies "bad luck". She loved them, even while she resented deep down inside her the hopeless mess they were slowly but surely making of her life. She loved all five of her children when she had time and wasn't too worn out with the domestic chores to even think of them as individuals.

I look worn out! she told herself now, turning away from the glass with tears of self-pity filling her eyes and spilling down her cheeks. And no wonder! Just look what my days are like!

She was up at six every morning, feeding the twins, then getting the other three children dressed and breakfasted with Jonnie so that he could be away by eight. By the time he'd left the house, she felt she'd done a day's work already! But the day had only started. There was the twins' mid-morning bath and feed to interrupt the mountain of washing and the housework. There was lunch to get, to be washed up, the twins to be fed again at two while the other children rested. Then ironing, or mending, tea, and the bedtime rush and scramble with the twins' evening feed and then Jonnie's supper. Granted, Jonnie helped all he could; he did shopping in his lunch hour, and as soon as he was home he took over the washing-up, the fires, the wood cutting, the coke and coal hauling. He even gave the twins their late-night feed.

But he wasn't home all the time. He had the supreme advantage of being able to get away from it five days a week for eight hours a day, and he had his golf every Sunday morning.

How she resented that golf.

"But, darling, I must have a few hours off in a week," he had answered her request to him to give it up.

5

"And when do I get any rest?"

"Well, you can put your feet up every Sunday afternoon," he'd suggested. "I'll mind the kids."

But of course it didn't work. How could she go to her bed and lie down and enjoy an hour or two with a book, knowing how hard she would have to work to make up for all the jobs not done while she had her rest? After the first try she'd given it up.

The continual round, day in, day out, had begun to tell on her nerves. Jonnie had suffered, for her temper became short and irritable. After their first, blazing quarrel, she had lain in their big double bed, sobbing in his arms.

"Look, darling, the trouble obviously is that you don't have enough fun. Neither do I, come to that. Do you realize we haven't been out dancing for a whole year? From now on we're going to go out once a week, without fail. We'll shut the door behind us and go out and enjoy ourselves."

"But we can't afford it!" Beverly wailed.

"Yes we can. We must! We won't go anywhere expensive. Leave it to me."

The first time had been wonderful. Until six o'clock next morning when Beverly realized that a late night, several drinks when you're not used to them, and four hours' dancing are not a good prelude to a heavy day's work beginning at six in the morning.

The night out had become fortnightly, then monthly, and finally ceased altogether. Slowly but surely, the days, weeks, months went by, and now, suddenly, Beverly realized that she looked more like a woman of forty than of twenty-five. She was shocked, depressed, and suddenly wildly angry with Jonnie . . . with life. Between them they had cheated her out of all the fun a young girl should have had. It wasn't even as if she and Jonnie were madly in love any more.

This, really, was the key to her discontent. Whilst they loved one another, all the hard work, the economizing, the doing-without, had been worth while. Now, quite suddenly, overnight, it wasn't worth while any more.

But I do still love Jonnie, I *do*! Beverly argued with herself. But in her heart, she was forced to admit that love seemed to have flown out of the window. Granted, she and Jonnie still shared the big double bed, but they no longer slept in each other's arms. Only occasionally did Jonnie's arms reach out for her, and recently she had steeled herself against her natural inclination to be loved by him. Resentment stopped her. Jonnie couldn't expect to have it all ways. If he couldn't be bothered any more to kiss her when he came home at night or when he went off in the morning; if he never had time to pay her a compliment or bring her some little surprise, then he had no right to claim her body just because he suddenly felt in the mood. Gradually, even that had stopped and they lived like strangers who happened to share the same bed, the same house, the same children and nothing else.

Downstairs, Beverly could hear one of the children crying. It sounded like Philip. He cried easily and noisily but it was never for long. Julia, once she started, could go on for hours, but at least she sobbed quietly, to herself.

Let him yell! Beverly thought rebelliously. It's just what I feel like doing.

As she went into the kitchen to put the kettle on for one of her never-ending pots of tea, she knew that at long last she was beginning to weaken. Hitherto, she had been heart and soul with Jonnie about accepting financial help from her mother. But the moment came, she told herself, when the camel's back was broken, and that was how she felt this morning. A pound or two a week would give Beverly some domestic help, and her mother had said a thousand times that *she* wouldn't miss it. After all, why should she go on wearing herself literally to the point of a breakdown just to bolster Jonnie's pride? He should see for himself that his wife had far, far too much to do. Every one of their friends seemed staggered to find she *could* cope, even though Nicky had started school. A daily help two or three hours a day. What an incredible difference it could make to her life! Jonnie ought to see that it wasn't fair to put his pride before her health. Tonight she would tell him so outright, to his face.

A little strengthened by the cup of tea and by her own new-found determination to remake her life, Beverly turned to the pile of washing. As she worked, her mind ran on, planning swiftly and with some of her old quick enthusiasm. With a daily help, she could get out to the hairdresser occasionally and have her hair done . . . it needed it so badly. She might even save up for a new dress. There would be time at last to sort out her things and give herself a few beauty treatments. Soon Jonnie would begin to notice the difference and he would fall in love with her all over again. It was his indifference that hurt so much.

Of course I do still love him, Beverly told herself by lunchtime. I'll always love Jonnie, all my life. It's just that we've grown apart . . . we are not the same two people who fell in love with each other. Jonnie's never fun the way he used to be. But we'll be able to get back to being ourselves.

By the time Jonnie came home, Beverly looked a very different girl from the wife who usually greeted him. She had found a moment to brush out her thick dark hair . . . to powder her nose and put on some fresh lipstick. She had even changed out of her slacks into a dress. Because her thoughts had carried her so far ahead of Jonnie in her planning of the future, she was totally unprepared for the fact that it was the same Jonnie who had left the house eight hours earlier. He glanced at her briefly and said:

"Oh lord, Beverly, we haven't got people coming in, have we? I wanted to go through my accounts tonight."

Hurt by his tone as much as by his failure to kiss her, Beverly turned away from him and said coldly:

"No, no one is coming. Tonight is just the same as any other night."

"Then why all the dressing-up?" Jonnie said, but without waiting for her answer: "Supper ready? I'm hungry."

Beverly controlled herself with an effort. Jonnie was always hungry and until he had eaten, it was best to let all she had to say to him wait. Silently, she dished up the supper and silently they sat opposite one another eating. Dutifully, Jonnie helped her with the dishes and then left her to make coffee. When she took the tray into the drawing-room, he was already buried in a mound of papers.

"Jonnie, I want to talk to you," she began as she handed him his coffee. He didn't look up, but said:

"Not now, Bev. I'm busy."

"Yes, now," Beverly said, her voice suddenly sharp and angry. "And you know I hate you calling me Bev. It sounds like that bottled coffee or whatever it is."

Jonnie made no reply, and Beverly felt anger rising in her. How unfair Jonnie was – how rude to her these days. All he could think of was his work. A year or two ago he had come in about six and given her a hand with the children before supper. Now he was never in before seven and sometimes it was eight or nine. At least when he did get back he could pay her a little attention.

"Jonnie!" He looked up, his broad forehead creased in a frown of irritation. Beneath the forehead, the bright blue of his eyes stared at her with no love in them. There were lines beneath them that Beverly hadn't really noticed before – lines of worry and fatigue that maybe shouldn't be on the face of a man still in his twenties. Beverly's anger drained away as suddenly as it had come. Impulsively, she knelt down on the floor and leant her head on his knees.

"Darling, please listen," she said, her voice now soft and appealing. "It's something to do with us – with our life . . ."

"With us?" Jonnie's voice was sharp, questioning. She had his attention now   all of it.

"Yes! Jonnie, I've been thinking all day about – well – about the life I lead . . . you lead – both of us, and how everything seems to be a bit on top of us. It's true, and you can't deny it," she added as she heard him draw in his breath sharply as if he might have been going to contradict her. "Jonnie, I want you to let me accept Mother's offer to help out a bit. I know how much you feel we *should* manage without, but it wouldn't be because of any failure on your side – it's me. I just can't cope. I get tired and irritable with the children, and I look a sight. Just a couple of pounds a week would make all the difference to all of us. You do see that, don't you?"

Jonnie let his breath out slowly. "I suppose you really mean you want me to give up the club?"

Beverly turned her head so that she could look at him fully, but his eyes dropped and he did not hold her glance.

"No, Jonnie. I don't think that. I think you should have at least one pleasure outside your home. It isn't any reflection on you. It's just that it would make life easier and happier for me if you'll let me take something from Mother."

Surprisingly, staggeringly, Jonnie said briefly: "OK! If that's what you want. I don't mind."

Beverly was too astonished to reply – even to thank him.

"Then . . . then you really don't mind?" she repeated.

"Not if it will make you happier."

Beverly reached out her arms to fling them round her husband, but his lap was covered by files and letters and somehow he did not seem to notice the gesture. Slowly, her arms fell to her sides and Beverly felt a little of her triumph subside. She had been all prepared to talk Jonnie round and there wasn't any need. Maybe that was why she felt this anti-climax.

"Are you going to have to work long?" she asked.

"At least a couple of hours," he replied briefly, already back in his books again.

"Then I'll do some ironing," Beverly said, sensibly but without enthusiasm. "Try and hurry up, darling. We might have half an hour's talk before bed."

But he wasn't listening; she knew his attention had gone before she reached the door. Tiredness hit her with a sudden sharp ache in her back. It had been a long day and a wearisome one. Maybe after all she'd have a bath and go to bed early. It would do her good, and an early night might get rid of some of the shadows beneath her own eyes. Jonnie wasn't the only one to look worn out.

Uncertainly, Beverly walked slowly up the stairs and began to run her bath.

Two

"It's no good, I can't, Elinor. You just don't understand."

"But, Jonnie, darling, aren't we ever going to have more than a few kisses? Maybe it's enough for you, but I love you. I want more than a flirtation."

Jonnie looked at the slim but voluptuous woman he held in his arms and abruptly moved away from her. The devil of it was, he too wanted more than a few kisses. Elinor attracted him in a way Beverly had never done. She was made for love and, Jonnie had no doubt, was thoroughly used to being loved. During these two months since he had met her he had known he could sleep with her just whenever he wished. Oh, he wanted to all right, but he hadn't. Loyalty to his wife prevented him.

I ought to stop seeing her, Jonnie thought for the thousandth time. It isn't fair to any of us, and least of all to poor Beverly.

But he couldn't make the break. Once or twice when he had tried, Elinor had quickly reopened the affair, ringing him up at the office, or managing to be at the club when she knew she would be bound to run into him on a Sunday after golf. It wasn't easy saying 'no' to a woman like Elinor. She took it for granted a man wanted her, and she was right to do so. Most of the chaps at the club – the unmarried ones – were after her. And why not? She was a young, rich and very, very attractive American widow. She knew her way around, especially with men. She was lonely and she wanted Jonnie. It was as simple as that.

"Elinor, it's just no good our letting this flirtation develop. It can only end by hurting everyone . . . you, me and most of all Beverly. You must see that. I can't ever divorce Beverly."

But she did not seem to understand even then.

11

"Why not? You say you aren't in love with her any more."

"But I still love her in a way. I couldn't hurt her," Jonnie said. "Besides, even if there weren't Beverly, there are the children. I have five kids, Elinor . . . *five*. And I haven't a penny-piece to my name. I couldn't leave them and I couldn't afford a divorce."

"OK, so you have five kids. What of it? That's no bar to divorce. We'd be in the dog-house, of course, but we could take that, and as to the money, well, I've got close on half a million dollars, my sweet."

Jonnie had flinched. Of course, he didn't blame Elinor for feeling the way she did – it was flattering. But he couldn't see it that way. They'd just been brought up differently, that was all. Besides, he wasn't sure he wanted to leave Beverly anyway. Elinor seemed to take it for granted that because he had confessed to being in love with her, he must necessarily have stopped loving Beverly and the children.

"Honey, you can have your cake and eat it!" Elinor's voice broke in on his thoughts. Her arms were round his neck and he could smell her perfume, an exciting, provocative perfume that exactly suited her.

"Nobody can," Jonnie said gloomily.

"Sure they can! You don't have to divorce your wife if you're so set against it. I'm not the one who suggested it – you brought it up. Why can't we just have fun together, you and I? You've every right to slip away for the odd weekend occasionally; your wife can't expect you to stay put all the time. What are you afraid of, Jonnie? It's so easy!"

"Is it?" Jonnie tried to steel himself against his mounting desire to stop fighting against her and comply with her demands. She might want him but he wanted her just as much. His desire for her was beginning to war with his own innate belief in what was right and wrong. "Suppose Beverly finds out?"

"Why should she? It's easy enough to find an alibi – golf with a friend, or something. I'll rent a little house at the seaside somewhere and you can run down whenever you can get away. It'ud be such fun, honey . . . just you and me."

They were in his car, parked in a side lane on the far side of the golf course. Jonnie was ostensibly working late, his unoriginal excuse to Beverly whenever he was stealing an hour or two after office hours with Elinor. Elinor had a small but very luxurious cottage a mile or two away and she wanted him to go back there with her, but he'd always refused. It was too dangerous. Beverly might get to hear of it, and how could he explain what he was doing in Elinor's house when he should have been at the office? Meeting Elinor anywhere was appallingly risky, but she just didn't seem to care. She cared about nothing except him. That was why it was so exciting to be with her. Once he'd meant everything to Beverly, but then the kids had come along and she had always been far too busy for his wants or his needs.

Come to think of it, Jonnie told himself morosely, he'd never really had much fun, getting married so young and with so many responsibilities always. It was enough to make any fellow feel a hundred years old. But with Elinor he felt like a new man. She was so tremendously exhilarating. She had enormous vitality and "go", a zip which carried him along even when he, too, was tired.

Of course, when their relationship had first begun a few months ago, he'd never meant it to develop into anything serious. She'd caught his eye over a drink at the golf club bar and he'd smiled and she'd called "Hi!" and suddenly they were talking to each other and finding they had lots of things in common. He'd kept an eye open for her next time he was in the club and, sure enough, she was watching out for him, too, and because his car had a flat tyre, she offered to run him home.

He'd never guessed she meant to stop on the way. In fact, he'd even been a little shocked when she switched off the engine and turned to him, saying:

"Well, aren't you going to kiss me, Jonnie?"

It would have seemed boorish to refuse. Afterwards, he'd let her go reluctantly and somewhat shamefacedly confessed he was married. Again, Elinor surprised him.

"So what? We haven't committed any crime!"

It was Elinor's utter lack of guilt about their association that made it so difficult for him to sort himself out. One half wanted to stay completely faithful to Beverly, to his own beliefs in what

13

marriage should mean. The other half saw himself through Elinor's eyes and he could see that to her he seemed bourgeois, narrow-minded, far too straight-laced for a man of his years.

Gradually, her influence became stronger as his own desire for her increased. He knew she wanted him to go back to her house and let their love-making go a step further, but somehow he still hadn't been able to do so. There was always Beverly and the children, and he almost hated them for their innocent hold on him. It just wasn't fair. There were plenty of men who had the odd affair on the quiet. Why shouldn't he? Beverly need never know. As Elinor said, there were ways of arranging these things . . . and it could be such fun!

They were back at the point of Elinor's last remark. It would be such fun. It never occurred to Jonnie that this was all Elinor wanted – the excitement of an illicit affair.

Elinor Wilmot was in her early thirties and smart and well groomed. She was essentially feminine and yet there was a hard core in her that paid little regard to the true attributes of femininity; gentleness, tenderness, unselfish love – these were totally absent from her make-up. Love to her meant sex, and sex was as necessary to her as food and drink. There had been plenty of young men before she married and she had not even been faithful to her husband. After he died she decided to make her home in Europe and although Jonnie did not know it, it was an affair with an older man which had first brought her down to this remote part of the country. When she tired of the man, she made up her mind to sell the lease of her cottage and get back to London, but just before she accepted a fairly reasonable offer for the place, she ran into Jonnie.

It hadn't meant much at first; she was attracted to him and she wanted him. But when weeks went by and she still had not been able to get him to do more than kiss her, her casual interest in him was fired into something more – a strong determination to make him put her before anything else. She told the estate agent she had decided not to move anyway until the autumn, and settled down to firing all her guns in Jonnie's direction.

It wasn't difficult for Elinor, who had met Beverly once, to find little ways of running her down.

"She should take a little more trouble with her appearance, my sweet, if she wants to keep an attractive man like you. After all, there's no need to look forty when you're not yet thirty."

"It isn't really her fault, she's too busy with the house and the children," Jonnie had tried to defend his young wife. But when he thought about it later, he found himself agreeing with Elinor's point. A woman should always find time to look attractive if she wanted her husband to stay interested in her. Sometimes when he got home Beverly hadn't even bothered to put on any make-up at all. Not that she wasn't pretty in a way without it; she had beautiful eyes and naturally wavy hair. But somehow she wasn't as pretty as she had been when they were first married. He supposed it was make-up that made the all-important difference. He couldn't see that the loveliest eyes, red-rimmed and shadowed with tiredness, would not show their best; nor did wavy hair curl becomingly if it was limp and lifeless from lack of attention.

What has happened to Bev and me? Jonnie thought for the hundredth time. We used to be so crazy about each other. Beverly had been such a darling, so sweet and gentle and loving. Had she really changed so much? Ought he not to try to put their marriage right somehow and not accept Elinor's view that once the gilt had worn off the gingerbread, it couldn't be put back? Once or twice he'd tried to get close to Bev again, tried to make love to her. His pride smarted still under her refusal.

It's her own fault! Jonnie thought bitterly. I wouldn't look twice at Elinor if Beverly really wanted me!

"Say, Jonnie, you haven't said a word in ten minutes. We're wasting all our precious time together, honey."

Roughly, Jonnie leant across and pulled her back into his arms. He looked into the dark eyes and saw only desire in them . . . desire for him.

His hold on her tightened and his mouth came down on hers, bruising her.

"All right!" he said at last as he pulled away from her embrace. "All right, but not now, Elinor; not here in a car. I want it to be quite perfect for both of us. We'll fix up something somehow, soon."

"Soon!" Elinor echoed triumphantly, content to relinquish her immediate need in favour of certainty. To over-persuade Jonnie now might mean to lose him altogether. Tomorrow, she'd try to find a cottage away from this village. It was too near Jonnie's wife for his peace of mind. Once away from Beverly he'd be all hers and that was all she wanted.

Three

"Well, of course you shall have an allowance, darling. I'm only too glad you've finally come to your senses. We'll see about finding you a good daily help right away."

Beverly looked at her mother gratefully.

"I did think I might get a foreign girl to live in," Beverly said hesitantly. She wasn't used to confiding in her mother and now that she wanted to, it didn't come easily.

When Beverly had married Jonnie, she had broken away completely and although Mrs Bampton visited them fairly frequently because she loved her five grandchildren dearly, Beverly had never imagined it was because of *her* her mother came.

She was, in fact, wrong. Mrs Bampton was primarily interested in her daughter's happiness. She did, of course, adore each of her five grandchildren, but it was Beverly she worried about. The eight years of her marriage had wrought a great change in her youngest daughter. She'd lost a stone in weight, had added years to her looks, and the sweet, sunny, gentle disposition was now slightly bitter, irritable, quick-tempered. The once pretty mouth was turned down at the corners and she was far too severe with the children, not to speak of "short" with Jonnie.

Yet Mrs Bampton could understand why. Beverly had far, far too much to do. Her nerves were in shreds and small wonder. Secretly, Mrs Bampton admired Beverly's courage in having stood out so long against accepting help . . . help that had to come in the end. Maybe if the twins hadn't arrived, she might have managed. But come they had, and only Beverly's stubbornness and pride had prevented her from accepting an allowance before now.

"That's a splendid idea, darling. I know a woman in town with

17

two children. She has a French girl. I think she only has to pay her thirty shillings a week. Her keep shouldn't come to very much since you have seven to feed already."

Beverly leaned back in the arm-chair and just for a moment closed her eyes. She and her mother had just packed the last of the children into bed and now they were waiting for Jonnie to come home so they could have supper. How she hated cooking! Not that she had always disliked it. Once it had been fun, she and Jonnie doing it together. But since those days there seemed to have been a hundred years of meals to shop for, cook, dish up, eat and clear away. One interminable meal after another, in fact! But soon she would have someone at hand to do the vegetables, wash the dishes. What heaven it would be.

"I'm terribly grateful, Mum!" she said, opening her eyes and smiling at her mother with genuine gratitude. "I can't think why Jonnie and I didn't agree to it before."

"Well, dear, it's always nice to be independent if you can, and I admire you both very much for the way you have managed – you especially, Beverly. I never in my wildest dreams imagined you could cope with one child, let alone five, the way you have. But I'm glad you're going to get a girl at last, you look so dreadfully worn out, darling!"

The unexpected and unaccustomed sympathy touched deep down inside some inner core of weakness. Unaccountably, Beverly found herself in tears. A moment later, she was sobbing uncontrollably in her mother's arms. For a few moments Mrs Bampton did not speak, but sensing that Beverly's crying was bordering on hysteria, she became brusque all at once and said:

"Pull yourself together, my poppet. Jonnie will be home soon, won't he, and you don't want him to see you like this!"

Beverly sniffed and then blew hard into the handkerchief her mother pressed into her hand.

"Perhaps it would do him good. I don't think he begins to understand how worn out I am. Oh, I know he works hard – too hard. It's been nothing but one late night at the office after another. All the same, he never thinks of me . . . never even looks at me now. Oh, Mummy, something's gone all wrong between us, and I don't know what it is!"

She hadn't meant to say it . . . to confess to her mother of all people, that she wasn't one hundred per cent happy with her lot. Yet she had to tell someone, and somehow in beginning a simple complaint about her own utter weariness, it had turned into a complaint against her marriage, too – against Jonnie.

Mrs Bampton appeared outwardly calm. Inwardly, she was appalled by what she was hearing. Beverly had always been so insistent about her happiness. Only last week she had waved her goodbye after just such an evening as this, saying brightly:

"I am lucky, aren't I, Mum, to have Jonnie and the kids!"

Personally, she thought Beverly's life was more an ordeal to be endured than to be enjoyed. But then she appreciated that two young people as much in love as Beverly and Jonnie could find happiness even under such circumstances. What had gone wrong, other than the first sweet flush of marriage wearing off? Or was that it?

"Eight years is quite a long while, darling. You can't expect Jonnie to behave the same way now as he did when you were first married. It just doesn't happen that way – with men, anyway. I'm sure Jonnie does understand how tired you are. Why, if he didn't, surely he would not have agreed to your letting me help you a little?"

Beverly sighed. Maybe her mother was right. She had been terribly surprised when Jonnie had said "yes" to her request, and without even an argument. Perhaps he had noticed her after all. Poor Jonnie; he looked tired, too, and worried. Yet he'd sworn to her all was going well with his work. There was even chance of further promotion next year, and if he made the grade it would be a really good rise in pay.

"Of course, I've got to work for it," he'd said vaguely. "I–I might possibly be kept late fairly often at the office. I may not always be able to let you know about supper, I mean, or which train I'm on. Just shove mine in the oven if I'm not home by the usual train and go ahead and eat yours."

He'd looked almost guilty as he said it, as if he expected her to jump down his throat. Well, maybe she deserved it. She very often did jump at him for nothing at all and he'd probably thought she wouldn't like him being home too late to help her at the children's bedtime. It was true she missed his help. By the end of the day they were all tired and the children could be difficult. Somehow with Jonnie, it was all laughter and fun; he made a game of it and they responded and were quite different with him. The more *she* tried to hurry them, the more maddeningly slow they were. All the same, it was worth it if Jonnie really did get a partnership. The extra two hundred a year would be a godsend.

"Maybe Jonnie and I need a holiday alone together," Beverly said thoughtfully, remembering a magazine story which had sounded very much like her own life with Jonnie. In the end the couple had left their children with their grandmother and gone on a second honeymoon and fallen in love all over again. "You know, Mummy, except for that one week at Selsey two years ago, we've never had a holiday since our honeymoon."

"Well, dear, once you get your help settled in and are quite sure you can trust her, why don't you and Jonnie go off together for a few days? I think it's a splendid idea. In fact, I'd been wondering what to give you for your birthday next month. Suppose I give you a cheque instead of a present. It would help towards your expenses, wouldn't it?"

Beverly smiled. "It's very generous of you, Mummy. And this time, I'm not going to refuse. I think Jonnie and I both need to get away. Of course, he won't like the thought that you're paying for it."

"My dear, don't be so silly as to say where the money is coming from. There are some things best kept from one's husband, you know, and I think this is one little secret you and I could keep to ourselves."

"But he knows I haven't any money of my own."

"Well, say you have saved a little each week from your house-keeping – he won't question it; or that you've sold some of the children's old clothes."

Beverly looked at her mother in astonishment. "Mummy, *you* telling *me* to tell lies? I can't believe it!"

Mrs Bampton smiled. "Not real lies, dear, just fibs. They're permissible to save Jonnie's face, for I know he is fearfully proud about taking help from me. I'm afraid that is my fault, too, for the way I once talked to him. Perhaps this way I can make amends. You see, if I hadn't been quite so scathing about the possibility of his supporting you when he asked my permission for you to be married, maybe you wouldn't have had to go so long without help, and then maybe you and Jonnie wouldn't have – well, grown a little apart. You know, dear, it stands to reason that love and poverty just don't go together; they never will. I'm not saying you have to be rich to be happy, far from it. But you must have enough to enable you to have a little time free for being together, for keeping your love fresh."

"I think you're right," Beverly said. "All the same, I don't like the idea of leaving the children with a young girl. I'd never trust her, however, capable she was."

"But you'd trust me, and I'd come down and stay here the week you were away. I'd enjoy it. I haven't been able to suggest it before because I don't pretend I could do all you do and last even a day. But with the girl here to do the fetching and carrying, I'd manage the children quite well."

"Mummy, you're an angel!" Beverly cried, flinging herself upon her mother and hugging her in a way she had not done since she was a young child. "Oh, I do wish Jonnie would hurry up and come home so I can tell him!"

But although they waited another half-hour, Jonnie still had not arrived, so they had their own meal and put the casserole back in the oven.

Four

S pring had come, and with it Beverly had felt an increasing restlessness. She found she could no longer concentrate on the day-to-day routine and that her mind wandered away thinking and planning her week's holiday. Of course, she had a little more time for day-dreaming since Annette had arrived. Annette was nineteen, French, and very pretty. Beverly had liked her enormously from the first moment they had met three months ago. Since then the young girl, inexperienced though she was, had become Beverly's right hand. She no longer knew how she had ever managed without her. Not the least of Annette's assets was her wonderful way with the children. They all adored her, and they all behaved far better with her than with their own mother.

If Beverly had been a little more self-opinionated, she might even have felt jealous of Annette's endless qualities! No matter what she was asked to do, the young French girl did it, efficiently, coolly, calmly and with a smile.

"I don't know how you stay so calm!" Beverly had once said to her. Annette smiled, and in her very halting English, replied that this was her nature.

Questioned as to his feelings about their young "help", Jonnie had been satisfactorily indifferent. "She seems a nice kid," he'd said briefly.

"Don't you think she's pretty, Jonnie?" It had been pure feminine jealousy that had prompted this question and Beverly waited a little anxiously for Jonnie's reply.

"Pretty? I suppose she is. I never really noticed. Not my type, though – too insipid!"

It was true, in a way, Beverly had to admit. There was nothing glowing or vital or exciting about Annette. She was pale-complex-ioned, fair-haired, her eyes a light misty blue. But perhaps this very "paleness" detracted from her sex-appeal, at least, in Jonnie's eyes. None the less, Beverly thought her both pretty and sweet, and was doubly grateful for the fact that she wasn't Jonnie's type.

"Not that I'm the jealous kind, Mummy," Beverly had related this episode to her mother. "At least, I don't think so. But I did wonder rather if I'd been a bit silly having so pretty a girl living in the house right under Jonnie's nose."

Mrs Bampton had smiled. "Of course, you're jealous, darling. Anyone with any real depth of feeling is jealous. That doesn't mean they don't control their feelings. If you weren't jealous of Jonnie, I would really be worried about you both. Anyway, you needn't worry about Annette. I'm so pleased she is such a success. What about that holiday you and Jonnie are going to have?"

"I think I'll plan it all and then just tell him about it when it's all fixed," Beverly said, musing.

"But suppose he can't get off work at the last moment?"

"I know he can get off in May," Beverly replied triumphantly. "He was taking about it the other night. He said he had a week's leave due and that he wished he could get off somewhere for a bit of golf. I thought I'd try to find some little hotel on the south coast near a golf course. I might even take my clubs and play, too. That's been the whole trouble with us, Mummy. We just haven't been able to do things together."

Now it was all arranged, and Beverly was excited and happy anticipating the week away with Jonnie. She meant to tell him tonight . . . put the letter from the hotel finalizing their bookings in front of him and say:

"It's all arranged, darling. The first week in May."

He'd have a whole month in which to fix his leave to coincide with her arrangements. Her mother had long since promised to be away from her work that week and Annette was more than capable of managing the children with her mother's assistance. Nothing could go wrong, unless Jonnie couldn't get away.

Staring out over the heads of the yellow daffodils bordering the lawn, Beverly suddenly shivered. Maybe she'd been wrong to spring this as a surprise. Suppose Jonnie had something special coming up at the office which would prevent him getting away?

Then she saw Annette come towards the house pushing the twins' pram, Julia running behind her, her rosy face alight with laughter. She was calling something to Annette but Beverly couldn't catch the words – only the happiness on this glorious April day. Her own spirits soared upwards again.

It was going to be all right. She and Jonnie would have their second honeymoon, just as she had dreamed and schemed and planned.

How like Jonnie Julia was growing. The same springy corn-coloured hair, the same eager eyes and firm set of the jaw. She could be very stubborn, but mostly she was an easy-going placid little girl with a great deal of charm; a child everyone loved. Philip was thinner, wirier, not unlike herself at the same age. Or so her mother kept saying. He was always right up or right down; he felt things keenly and his childish disappointments were tragedies just as his happiness at other times was pure golden joy. Yet he seemed popular enough with the other children at his nursery school. He was like her, in temperament, anyway. It seemed she was herself right up or right down and the pendulum could swing one way or the other in no more than a minute.

Well, at the moment, it was right up. She was happy . . . happy . . . happy! Glad to be alive on this lovely day, glad to be the mother of five such perfect children – all the more perfect now that she knew she could get away from them for a little while. And most of all, glad that she had married Jonnie. She felt suddenly terribly sad for Annette, who was nineteen and who, by her own admission, had never yet fallen in love. Why, at nineteen she had been married and twice a mother! Poor Annette, to be growing old without life's most wonderful experience.

Beverly laughed and ran downstairs to begin the lunch. The day passed in its usual routine manner but without its usual minor upsets. Nicky came home from school with two red stars for good behaviour. None of the children quarrelled during playtime after tea. The sponge cake Annette had made – her first under Beverly's instructions – turned out perfect.

Jonnie was home early for once, as if he, too, were trying to do his best to make this one of those days where everything sought to make her happy. Dinner was over, washed up, and Annette had gone upstairs to wash her hair.

Beverly handed Jonnie his coffee and sat down beside him on the worn sofa. Her hand trembled a little as she handed him the envelope containing the hotel's bookings. It was crumpled from the heat of her body for she had carried it around all day in her apron pocket.

"Jonnie, will you look at this?"

She watched his face as he took the letter from her and read it slowly. She watched the colour drain from his cheeks and something in his expression froze the smile on her lips.

"Darling, what's wrong? You *are* going to be able to get away, aren't you?"

He avoided her direct glance, looking down again at the letter in his hands.

"I . . . I'm not sure . . . I . . . I don't think so!"

"But, Jonnie, it's a whole month from now. Surely you can arrange it? You said you were due for some leave. You *must*; it's all arranged – just the two of us. Jonnie, you can't say no."

He couldn't – he hadn't the heart or the stomach for wiping that look from her face. He hadn't been too blind to notice the change in her this evening. Not just her looks, but her whole person had radiated happiness and excitement. This explained it. How *could* he dash her hopes to the ground?

"Jonnie, you're not worrying about money? It's all fixed. You won't have to pay for anything but the petrol to get there."

But he wasn't thinking of money. He was thinking of Elinor. He'd promised he'd wangle at least a long weekend in May so that they could go away together. Elinor was counting on it. Why, why had Beverly to spring this on him now? What had put such an idea into her head? Now of all times!

"What . . . what made you think this up?" he asked hesitantly.

Beverly looked at him in hurt surprise. "You mean, you don't *want* to go? You don't think it's a good plan? I just don't understand, Jonnie. We haven't had a holiday alone together since Selsey.

I've thought of little else for months. With Annette here and Mother to give her a hand, it means we can go at last, and now you ask me *why*."

He heard the hurt and bewilderment in her tone and bit his lip in sudden remorse. How could he explain? How could he say, "I do want a holiday, but I want it with Elinor – not with you."

"Jonnie, you said you were due some leave, that's why I went ahead without asking you first. Is that what's worrying you? Because I didn't ask you first?"

Weakly, he nodded his head. Better let her believe this than the truth. Yet he hated lying to her. Dishonesty was foreign to his nature and he longed suddenly and quite desperately to say: "I'm crazy about someone else; I can't get her out of my mind; the thought of her is tormenting me. She wants me and I want her, and I *have to* have her." How many thousands of times had he gone over just such a longing to confess? How many times had he quelled that longing, believing that it was better to deceive her than to ease his own conscience at the cost of her happiness. What good could it do either of them? Beverly was hardly the kind of wife who'd say, "All right, go ahead and have your fun, I'll turn a blind eye. I don't care." She would care, he'd be forced to a decision he never wanted to make: to give Elinor up or to leave Beverly and his children. There would be rows, scenes, tears, recriminations, and for what? He didn't want a divorce, and to go on living with Beverly once she knew how he felt about Elinor would be to ruin all hope of happiness for either of them.

"I . . . I expect I can fix it," he said helplessly. Beverly flung her arms round him and kissed him swiftly on the mouth. Some automatic instinct prompted him to return that kiss, but even as he did so, his mind swung back to Elinor. What would she say? Would she walk out on him when she knew he was throwing away their long weekend together? Would it mean he'd have to stop seeing her . . . knowing her, before their love affair had really started? Or was there still some way out? Perhaps at the last minute pressure of work might stop him going. But he couldn't do that. Beverly was flooding him with a hundred plans and hopes for their holiday and heaven alone knew, she deserved one.

He felt ashamed, and at the same time, angry with his wife who made him feel so. It was all so terribly unfair. And, anyway, how could such a holiday be a success when his own thoughts were concentrated on Elinor? Beverly was speaking now of "a second honeymoon". Well, he couldn't. It was Elinor he wanted now; Elinor with her exciting perfume, her violence, her experience. Instinct told him that it would be different with such a woman. She would lead and he would follow. With Beverly, he had been the master, he had done the teaching – and he had not wanted it any other way. But he hadn't known women like Elinor existed then.

"Jonnie, I don't believe you are listening to a word I'm saying. What *is* wrong? You are pleased, aren't you? Don't you see how important this is to us? For years now we've just taken each other and our love for granted. It . . . it's been bogged down amongst the daily routine. We'll have a chance to find each other again."

He looked at her blankly, not because he didn't understand but because he understood too well. Beverly, too, had begun to find their marriage dull and lacking in its essential needs. Well, that made two of them. But she wanted to try to fan the old embers into a new flame, whereas he was already afire with a longing for someone else.

Something of his inner bewilderment must have shown itself to her for she said softly:

"I didn't mean to hurt you by those last remarks, darling, but I think it's time we were honest with each other. Jonnie, don't turn your face away like that. How can we hope to know what we feel or want from each other when you try to hide yourself away from me? I know I'm not easy to live with; I know I've probably been perfectly beastly to you, but it's just because I was tired and nervy. I'm sorry, darling, and I want a chance to prove I still love you as much as when we were married. Say you understand."

Guilt swept over him again, souring, hateful. To be honest with each other – how could he? You don't say to someone who has just told you they love you that you love someone else.

"It . . . it hasn't been your fault, Beverly; it's mine. I'm the one who should say I'm sorry and apologize."

Beverly laid her cheek against his hand and said softly: "It doesn't

27

matter, Jonnie, just so long as we do find each other again. I don't ever want to lose you. It's so lonely living by yourself."

He reached out his other hand and gently stroked her hair. No one could be more generous than Beverly. One had only to offer her half an inch and she gave a yard in return. How could any man help but love her? That was one of the puzzling things about his feelings for Elinor. He was violently and quite madly *in love* with her so that he thought of little else, yet he would always love Beverly. His feelings for her were almost those of an elder brother – protective. They'd more or less grown up together. Maybe that was the root of the trouble, marrying too young. They'd neither of them really known what life was all about, and they'd just fumbled along its roads side by side, hoping for the best. Only it hadn't turned out for the best. If only he'd never met Elinor, never let her get under his skin. Beverly didn't want an elder brother, she wanted a husband, a lover. Yet he couldn't belong to two women.

"Oh, Beverly," he whispered in an unconscious appeal for the understanding she could give him.

"Yes, darling? What is it?"

"Nothing, nothing. Just life, I suppose. It seems so strange, the way things work out."

"We've been lucky, haven't we," Beverly said, her voice rich with content. "Do you realize, Jonnie, that there are probably thousands of men and women, sitting together like we are, but wishing desperately they could be together always and knowing they can't? Yet here we are, with our own home where we can shut ourselves away from the world and just be together, like this, whenever we want. And we have the children, too. Think of all the couples who *can't* have children – and we've got five lovely healthy kids. I'm so happy, Jonnie; so very glad I'm married to you."

It should have ended differently. It was the first time in months that Beverly had spoken so openly and intimately about their relationship and their marriage. Had it not been for Elinor, maybe he could have shown her the response she must be hoping for; told her how glad he was to be a married man with five children. But he couldn't – not with every nerve longing for freedom and release from the very responsibilities he had taken on.

He tried to smile but felt that the result must be more a grimace. He felt beastly and treacherous, and hated himself. If only he could hate Beverly, too, instead of feeling this overwhelming pity for her. She was so innocent, so good, so sweet! How could he feel anything but love for her when she was like this? Yet he didn't want to feel tender towards her. It made everything he was thinking and feeling about Elinor so tawdry, so mean and deceitful.

"I . . . I think I'll go out for a walk!" he said, suddenly and abruptly. "It's a lovely evening and I could do with some fresh air."

Beverly jumped to her feet. This was like the old Jonnie, impulsive and unpredictable.

"What a good idea. I'll come with you. It's so nice to be able to say just that . . . I'll come with you. I just can't get used to the wonder of having Annette here. I'll go and get a coat."

Jonnie slumped back in his chair, his face pale and taut. He'd wanted to be alone, to escape from Beverly. He couldn't trust himself any longer – not under such circumstances. If Beverly went on being so enthusiastic and happy about their life, sooner or later he would blurt out the truth: that for him, their marriage had become a disaster . . . a failure. Yet that wasn't true. Nothing had failed – yet. If he could only keep some control of the situation, nothing need go wrong. But how could he keep control when the reins were out of his hands? On one side Beverly, planning to have a "second honeymoon", and on the other, Elinor, planning a weekend on the quiet.

Blast Elinor! Jonnie thought, trying to hate the woman who had completely uprooted all that was sensible and secure and dependable in his life, and made him see the fun and excitement he was missing. Did every man reach this same feeling about his marriage? Or was Elinor right when she had said:

"Ours won't be just an *ordinary* affair . . . we love each other. It's something we can't control – too strong for us. If it were just a casual interest, I don't believe you would have thought of being unfaithful, darling, you aren't the type. But this . . . well, you feel the same way, don't you, Jonnie? We're made for each other and we have to belong."

Once he had been so sure that he and Beverly had been "made for each other". They'd been so terribly in love, but as Elinor had argued, he'd been only a boy then. What a boy demanded from life could be quite different from what a *man* needed from the woman at his side. Beverly hadn't "grown up" the way he had. Elinor was right about that, too. She still looked like a rather untidy schoolgirl in spite of bearing five children. The children; there lay one of the most disturbing elements of this whole wretched affair. It was possible that Beverly might have found someone else. She was still young and pretty in an unsophisticated way. But there were the children – his children. He loved them all deeply; Nicky most of all perhaps. Now he was seven years old, he was becoming a real companion to Jonnie. He was getting on fine at school and in another year he'd be off to Jonnie's own prep school – as a day boy, of course. They couldn't afford boarding school fees, and in any case, Jonnie wanted him where he could keep in touch. He and Nicky had a lot of fun together, when there was time. Just lately there hadn't been so much time. Weekends that he and the boy had spent mostly entirely in each other's company, Jonnie had lately spent more often in or around the golf club with Elinor. Nicky had been a bit hurt.

Of course, the boy couldn't understand *why* his father had suddenly decided he wasn't suitable to "caddy" his clubs. Jonnie's excuse that he'd be better employed playing about the garden had sounded pretty feeble to both of them. After all, it had been Nicky's job for the last year now, to push the trolley round the course every Sunday morning.

Fortunately, Nick had suddenly become great friends with a lad who lived at the other end of the village. Jonnie didn't know much about him except that he was a year or two older than Nick, but they were now pretty continuously in each other's company and Nick no longer pestered Jonnie to give him some time.

Much better for the boy to have someone his own age to play around with, Jonnie told himself uneasily. But he wasn't quite happy about it. Nick seemed to have managed to get along without him so easily, it wasn't exactly flattering. He'd believed he was his son's idol.

"Darling, you aren't ready? Aren't you coming out after all?"

Jonnie jumped to his feet.

"Yes . . . yes, of course. I was just thinking about Nick. Beverly, what is that boy's name, the one Nick's always playing with nowadays?"

"You mean Paul Marshel?"

"Yes, that's the one. What do his people do?"

"I'm not quite sure," Beverly said, as they closed the front door behind them. "I think his father is a lorry driver. I've never met him but the mother is very nice. She "does" for Sue Bates. I think she goes a couple of hours every day as they aren't very well off. Paul goes to the same school. He's a bit slow but that's probably why the boys get on so well. Nick's bright and that levels out the difference in their ages. Paul's ten, you see."

"Slow?"

"I think he's just behind with lessons not in other ways. At least, I've always found him quite intelligent. He's always very polite when he calls for Nick. But shy. He never quite looks you straight in the eye."

"Do you think it's all right Nick spending so much time with him?"

Beverly glanced up at Jonnie surprised. "Why yes! Mrs Marshel is as nice as could be and Sue says as honest as the day is long. So I don't see why you are worrying about Paul."

"No . . . but, well Nick seems to be changing a bit lately. Perhaps he's just growing up."

It was on the tip of Beverly's tongue to tell Jonnie that he'd been neglecting Nick the last few months but she bit back the remark. With this new-found happiness, she did not want to take any chances. It wasn't as if Jonnie meant to be selfish about his "spare time". He had a right to spend part of the weekends the way he wanted. Men needed physical exercise and golf was Jonnie's only sport now.

Just because he had to work late so many evenings in the week and *she* saw so much less of him, there was no valid reason to suggest he give up his one hobby. Maybe the answer was for her to take up golf again. She had played before they were married, in fact she'd been learning when she first met Jonnie. If it hadn't been for golf, they might never have met at all. It certainly wouldn't be reasonable to expect a young man with Jonnie's temperament to be tied to a household of young children all day long. But at one stage he had been so eager for Nick's company; unable to wait for him to grow up so that he could take his son out alone and teach him things – golf especially. Nick adored his father and had been his shadow. But when Jonnie rejected his company to be his caddy Nick had suddenly turned against his father and transferred his hero-worship to young Paul Marshel. Beverly had been pleased that Paul had turned up at the psychological moment, as for a week or two Nick had mooched around the house like a bear with a sore head. Paul had been the very companion Nick needed and now the two boys were always off on some jaunt together.

Once or twice, Beverly had been a bit anxious about them. Nick, was on the young side to go roaming about the countryside. But he was a sensible little boy, and he was always home at the time Beverly stated; muddy, dishevelled, but content with some wild game they had been playing; and he glowed with health. Beverly had stopped worrying and given the two boys her blessing. If Nick had become a little less well-mannered, she did not really blame the new friendship for it. Nick was bound to go through a stage of "showing off" and wanting to appear "tough". The use of an occasional "blast" or "damn" was what she would have expected of him. She thought that it was a thoroughly good thing that Nick should learn to mix at an early age.

"No, Nick's all right," she said again. "It's Philip I'm worried about. He's so dependent on Julia. We always meant him to be a companion to Nick, didn't we, but it just hasn't worked out that way. Nick and Phil are so different it doesn't seem as if they'll ever be really close companions. Phil is nervous and sensitive and thoughtful. I think that's why he attaches himself to Julia – she's never unexpected. But it can't be right for a boy of six to be so reliant on a girl only just five, yet Julia organizes him and bosses him as if he were a younger brother."

Jonnie frowned. He'd never been able to make much headway with his second son. Phil seemed neither like him nor Beverly. He didn't understand the boy the way Beverly seemed to, even though he wasn't like her either. He cried easily and Jonnie felt he was a bit of a sissy. Yet in some ways, Phil was sharper than Nick. When it came to games that demanded thought and observation, Phil soared on top despite the year's difference between his age and Nick's. He was doing well at school, too. Probably the child would turn out a brilliant scholar. Nick's brilliance was nearly all sporting.

To Jonnie's relief, discussion of their children occupied the remainder of their walk and continued even when they had gone to bed. Not only did it keep Beverly from becoming too personal, but it kept his own mind off Elinor. Nevertheless, once the light was out and he lay awake in the darkness, listening to Beverly's soft, regular breathing, his mind turned again to the fresh problem this evening had evinced. What would he say to Elinor? How could he tell her the weekend was off? How would she take it?

It was a long while before Jonnie fell asleep.

Five

J onnie followed Elinor into the drawing-room of her cottage and
looked around him with a mixture of curiosity and interest.
He'd known Elinor nearly six months now and yet this was the first
time he'd been to her home. Of course, it wasn't really hers, as she
was pointing out to him now – only a rented cottage. But it had
acquired her personality and her perfume. It unsettled him, reminding him why he was here.

He watched her go to a corner cupboard and find some bottles
and two glasses. He did not take in what she was saying. He could
think only of the line of her body as she lifted her arm to reach for
a glass and stood for a moment, poised, slim, mysterious yet
familiar.

He began to tremble and clenched his hands. He knew that it was
only a matter of moments before he would have to take her in his
arms. He wanted that moment to come, and yet he dreaded it. Until
now, he had never made love to her fully and completely. Until
today, he'd withstood the temptation to come back with her to the
privacy of her house.

He'd argued against it nearly all afternoon as they had walked
round the course together, not thinking about the game, but only
about each other. He'd told her the week they'd planned together
was off. He had expected a scene, or at least, for Elinor to argue
violently against it. But she hadn't. Surprisingly she had not said a
thing.

"Elinor, I'm terribly sorry. It—"

"You don't have to make excuses, Jonnie. No woman likes to be
given reasons why the man she loves doesn't want her."

"Elinor, that isn't true; you know it isn't. Want you! Good

34

heavens above, I can't sleep, eat, think for wanting you. You *know* that."

"If you loved me, Jonnie, you'd have found a way to be with me. It's nothing but a thousand and one excuses from you – it always has been. Don't let's talk about it any more."

"But we have to talk about it, darling. You've got to understand why—"

"I'm just not willing to discuss this here and now, Jonnie. If you like to come back to tea at my house, I'll listen to anything you have to say. But this is too big a thing to thrash out on a golf course. If I'm getting the brush-off, I'd rather have it in private."

After that he hadn't had the face to make further excuses not to go to her cottage. As if reading his thoughts, she had said:

"And if you're afraid to come back to the cottage, I suggest you get over that one by being perfectly open about it. Come back and have tea – just that. Then you can tell anyone who might drop in, or your wife when you get home, that that is how you spent the hour between four and five. Having tea with me."

So he had come, openly and without deceit. As Elinor pointed out, there was no law against him going back to tea with her. They'd played a round of golf together and it was quite natural she should ask him back. If it had been anyone else but Elinor, he would have gone without a second thought about the propriety of such an action.

Now he was here, really alone with her, and "tea" was going to be champagne, it seemed.

"Cheer up, honey! We might as well drink to the end of a glorious friendship in style. Why so gloomy?"

But he couldn't laugh. Her own light-hearted tone of voice, slightly bantering, goaded him almost beyond bearing.

"How can you talk like that, Elinor? Doesn't it mean anything to you after all?"

"Doesn't what mean what and why? Drink up, my sweet."

She clinked her glass against his own and drank, her eyes never leaving his.

"You know, you're even more attractive when you're scowling. You look like a cross old bear."

"Elinor!"

She was in his arms now, her half-empty glass dropping unheeded to the floor, the contents spilling over the carpet making a stain neither of them saw.

He kissed her wildly and desperately, believing that this might indeed be the last time he held her in his arms. Her mouth was open and responsive, and then suddenly she broke away from him.

"No, Jonnie! It's silly to go on behaving like two school kids. Frankly, I've had enough of it."

Jonnie leant back against the wall, his breath coming in deep uneven gasps. How Elinor remained so cool and calm was beyond his understanding. She always seemed to be the complete master of her emotions. Yet she did not lack passion. Every line of her face and body breathed fire that he knew to be within her.

"You . . . you want this to be goodbye?" he asked, his voice hoarse and barely audible.

Elinor stooped and picked up her glass and went slowly across the room to refill it. She took a deep sip before she replied.

"It's *you* who want to end it all, Jonnie. *I* never said it's what *I* wanted."

Jonnie looked at her in bewilderment.

"But—"

"There are no 'buts', Jonnie," she broke in, coming over to where he stood and leaning against him provocatively. "It's quite simple to understand. I'm not mad at you because you can't make that weekend we were planning. I'm sure you've got a good reason for calling off. It's just that I can't go on any longer not being sure of the way you feel about me."

"Not sure!" Jonnie echoed stupidly. His arms went round her and he tried to bring his lips to her mouth, but she half turned her head and said:

"No, I'm not sure, Jonnie. If you loved me, you'd have proved it to me by now. Even now you're hesitating. You don't need me the way I need you."

White-faced, Jonnie caught her chin in his hand and forced her head round so he could look deep into her eyes. He knew now what she meant – that he had always avoided the actual act of unfaithfulness to Beverly. So long as he did not give way completely to his desires, he could still go on at home more or less as if nothing had happened. But now it couldn't go on like that any longer. No man ever needed anyone more than he needed Elinor. He had to have her. Beverly; the future; nothing mattered any more beside the terrible alternative of losing her completely.

"Jonnie, honey, I'm so crazy about you. I'm not ashamed of the way I feel. I'm a woman – all woman, and I want you just the way you want me. You do want me, don't you? It could be all that was ever meant to be, between us, Jonnie!"

Her soft voice was drumming in his ears and he knew he had reached the end of control. For too long he had tortured himself and her with kisses, embraces, words which were all just symbols of what they really wanted of each other. And Elinor was making it all seem so easy, so natural. It wasn't as if she expected him to break up his home, mess up his life, to do anything more than he wanted himself.

For nights upon nights he had lain awake, imagining this moment when he would make her his own. Now there could be no turning back. Already she had slipped off the thin cashmere cardigan she had worn for golf and the blouse beneath, of some transparent nylon, clearly revealed the creamy rounded shoulders, the long bare column of her neck, the tiny pointed breasts.

"Elinor!" he murmured before she turned, and smiling at him with a strange, savage triumph, wound her arms around his neck.

An hour later, he drove himself slowly towards his home. The mad, incredible emotions of the past hour seemed already like a strange unearthly dream. He wanted to forget, to put Elinor out of his mind; but tired and depressed though he was and apprehensive about his coming meeting with Beverly, he kept remembering snatches of time spent with Elinor as if he were seeing flashes of film. He'd never known a woman could be like Elinor. It was as if he had held a wild warm panther in his arms. She made no attempt to control the swift tide of passion that engulfed her and himself, too. The very force of her feelings was sufficient to arouse in him every nerve, every sense, but of the body rather than the mind. It was a mating of the senses rather than the spirit; swift, cruel, but intensely satisfying. The primitiveness of their behaviour only now in retrospect had the power to shock him a little. Was this how man and woman were meant to love? Had he and Beverly only touched on the delicate fringes of real emotion? Or was this thing that existed between himself and Elinor born of something greater that made them behave not as gentle, loving people, but as hungry insatiable creatures.

Love! Where had there been time or place for love in that mad hour? There had been only desire and now, the after-effects of guilt and shame. No shame for the way they had behaved for it seemed as if with Elinor there could be no other way, but shame for what Beverly would think if she knew.

Thank God she would never know. It was something he could never ever explain to her; something she could never hope to understand. For Beverly, the act of love had been an act of giving, and Jonnie had taken and given in return. But Elinor had not stopped to give – only to take and take and take again, and in her wild, uncontrolled need she had given herself with an abandon which Beverly would never understand.

Jonnie stopped the car, and was suddenly physically sick into the ditch by the roadside. The nervous and mental strain was beginning to take its toll of him.

When at last he reached home, Beverly took one look at him and said: "Jonnie, what is the matter? You look ghastly. Are you ill?"

He could thank God now for the lack of need to lie. "Must be something I ate or drank," he said weakly. "Just been terribly sick."

"You go straight to bed," Beverly ordered. "I'll call Dr Massie."

"No. No, don't, Beverly, please. I'm all right now. I'll go upstairs and lie down, but don't call the doctor. It's all over, anyway. If I ate anything to upset me, it's not inside me now."

"Then I'll bring you up a hot-water bottle," Beverly said anxiously. She was well aware how Jonnie hated being ill and to have the doctor was something he would always avoid until he was so ill he had to give way. There was a little more colour in his face now, but he'd looked really terrible as he came into the house, grey, tired, almost shocked.

A few minutes later, she went up to their room with two hot-water bottles. Jonnie had undressed and was lying between the sheets, his eyes closed. She slipped the bottles beneath the bedclothes and whispered:

"Sure you're all right, darling?"

He opened his eyes and looked at her, fully in the face, as if, Beverly thought afterwards, he were uncertain who she was. Then he said slowly:

"Yes, thanks . . . and . . . I'm sorry, Beverly."

"Poor darling," Beverly told Annette downstairs. "He was half asleep but he still managed to apologize for being ill. As if it mattered. I suppose he was thinking of the supper being spoilt. Well, we'd better have ours and then I'll go up again and see how he is. If he isn't better in the morning, I'm going to call the doctor, whatever Jonnie says."

Suddenly the phone rang. Beverly went to answer it, expecting her mother. Instead it was Elinor.

"Is that Mrs Colt? This is Elinor Wilmot speaking. I wonder could I speak with your husband a moment?"

"I'm afraid my husband isn't very well. He's gone to bed." Beverly said, puzzled, "Could I take a message for you?"

There was a brief pause, then Elinor said: "I guess it isn't important. Your husband was kind enough to run me home after golf this afternoon and he left his cigarette-case in my house. I thought he might be worried, which is why I called. He can stop by and pick it up any time. Say, I hope he's not real sick?"

"Well, I don't think so. We think it's probably something he had to eat."

"Say, we had a drink at my house but I guess it wasn't the champagne. I had the same myself and I'm OK. Well, I won't keep you talking. Please tell Jonnie 'hullo' from me and say I hope he'll be OK tomorrow."

39

"Thank you. It was good of you to call."

"That's OK, Mrs Colt. You must come to tea one day so we can have a chance to get better acquainted."

Beverly was pleased. "I'd like that very much. I don't get out much. Do you and Jonnie often play golf together?"

"Oh, we make up a four when an odd man or girl's needed," Elinor said casually. "Your husband's got a better handicap than I have, but he gives me an occasional lesson when there's time. You don't play, Mrs Colt?"

"Well, I used to, but I'm just a beginner, and I've no time now," Beverly said, laughing. "Look, won't you come and have tea with me, Mrs Wilmot? Why not tomorrow?"

"Say, that's too sweet of you to ask me, but I can't tomorrow. I'll call you again and we'll arrange something soon."

"She sounds fun!" Beverly thought as she went back to the kitchen to rejoin Annette for their evening meal. "I must ask Jonnie about her. Funny he hasn't mentioned her before. She seems to know him quite well."

A sudden swift pang of jealousy struck her. Suppose Jonnie and this woman . . . but how silly! Jonnie wasn't like that. Besides, in a village like Buckley, what possible hope was there of any man taking any girl anywhere without it being all over the place five minutes later. If Jonnie had been out with Mrs Wilmot, she would have been told about it long before now.

Yet although she dropped the idea almost as soon as it had come to her mind, somehow she could not quite forget the American voice on the telephone. She had hoped Jonnie might wake during the evening, but he slept on, as if exhausted, and did not even stir when she went to bed herself.

Unable to find sleep, Beverly let her mind wander. Would it matter so terribly if Jonnie were unfaithful to her? Would she divorce him if she found out or would she forgive him? Her vivid imagination invented a dramatic scene with a mythical American woman as her rival. For ten minutes, she faced Jonnie, white-faced, trembling, telling him that he must give up this woman or else.

Beverly relaxed and turned over on her other side, one arm resting

40

on Jonnie's warm familiar body. How silly to think of such things. Better to lie and imagine happy thoughts such as their holiday together.

Smiling, warm and content, Beverly slowly drifted into sleep.

Six

"Beverly, I can't make the holiday after all. I . . . I'm terribly sorry!"

Beverly looked up from her sewing, her face white with shock. "*Not go*? But, Jonnie, you said—"

"I know!" he interrupted swiftly, getting up and walking across to the window with his back towards her, so that she could not see his face while he destroyed the joy in hers with a lie. "I thought I could, but now, well, a works study has come up during that week and I just have to be there."

Beverly relaxed and drew a deep breath. "Oh, darling, if that's all, you can come, you silly! Then the day you're needed you can catch a train to town. It wouldn't take more than an hour. For one awful moment I thought the whole week was off!"

Jonnie sighed.

"I don't see how I *can* get away. I know this will be rather a disappointment, but I can't help it. There'll be work to do before and after the day I'm needed in town. Couldn't we postpone the week and take it later on in the year?"

Beverly put down her sewing and swung round so that she could look at him. But he still stood with his back towards her. Her heart was beating double time, but she managed to keep her voice level and quiet as she said:

"What's the matter? Don't you want to come?"

"Don't be so childish, Beverly!" The words were out before he could stop them. He knew in his heart that his only method of defence against her shot in the dark was to attack. But was it just a shot in the dark? Had Elinor said something during that phone call?

She couldn't have been so silly. Besides, Bev had shown no more than an idle curiosity about her.

"Childish!" Beverly's voice was higher pitched now and taut with the disappointment that welled up in her. "Jonnie, don't you know what this week means to me? I've been looking forward to it for weeks on end . . . counting the days. Mother had planned to take time off especially from her work and it's all arranged. You *can't* back out now!"

"You can't blame me. I have my work to do and it must come first or I'll lose my job, you know that. I'm sorry about the holiday, but *you* can still go."

Jonnie's voice was stiff and cold. It seemed as if one lie must inevitably lead to another and he hated himself at this moment more than he had ever done in his life before. Yet he couldn't go on this holiday; *he just could not go.* It would be a far worse tragedy to give in and then disappoint her when they were away together; because disappointment was certain. Beverly had not tried to hide her dreams from him. She meant them to become lovers again and he knew he could not pretend. It would be impossible to hold Beverly in his arms now, if ever again, since Elinor . . .

"I see! It doesn't seem to have struck you, Jonnie, that it wasn't because I wanted a holiday that I planned all this. It happens that I wanted to go away with *you* be alone with you. Perhaps that is just what you are trying to avoid?"

Another shot in the dark but how near the truth. Involuntarily, Jonnie shivered. One read in so many books about a woman's intuition. Did it really exist, this kind of sixth sense? Or was it he himself who was giving the show away by his behaviour?

"If you want a quarrel, Beverly, then I suggest you find someone else to quarrel with. I've told you the reason I can't go; now let's leave it at that."

Beverly stared at her husband in silence. Her feelings were so strong that for a moment she was left speechless, unable to express the appalling disappointment, the fear, the anger, the surprise, all of which shook her in turn. It couldn't be Jonnie saying this! It was a bad dream and she would wake up. But she knew it *was* true. He did not intend coming with her. It was on the tip of her tongue to say to him bitterly, "You know I wouldn't go without you," but she bit back the words, pride suddenly surging uppermost in her emotions. She wouldn't let him see how desperately she had wanted this week with him. If he could say quite casually that it was all off, she could be equally casual. At least, he should not have the pleasure of knowing how much he had hurt her.

"All right. I'll go alone. I'm not going to have Mother's plans upset for nothing."

She turned and walked out of the room, her head held high, the tears that threatened carefully held in check until she reached the privacy of their bedroom. Then she flung herself on the bed and burst into tears . . . tears of frustration and disappointment.

But she did not cry for long. Soon Jonnie would be coming up to bed and she didn't want him to see her with her defences down. On a sudden impulse, she picked up her pillow and night-clothes and marched through to the tiny spare room where the bed lay made up for her mother's visit next week. She would sleep in here tonight. That would show Jonnie just how deeply she felt about all this.

Silently, unhappily, she undressed and climbed in between the cold sheets. She longed for a hot-water bottle, but it would mean going downstairs and she did not wish to speak to Jonnie again that night. After what seemed hours, she heard Jonnie come upstairs and go to their room. A moment later he called her name. She did not answer.

"Beverly?"

This time his voice was louder and she was afraid he might wake Annette or the children. She got out of bed and crossed the room.

"I'm sleeping in the spare room," she said coldly, through the locked door. "Good night, Jonnie."

He had heard her for he stood for a moment on the other side of the door.

"Let him want to come in . . . let him try the door!" Beverly prayed silently. "Don't let him leave me here alone!"

But he neither called her again nor tried the door handle.

A moment later she heard his footsteps return to their bedroom and the door close behind him.

Beverly climbed back into bed shivering uncontrollably. What had she done? This was the first time in all the years of their marriage that they had slept apart. Far from making things better, her action had only made things worse. How could Jonnie leave her like this? Didn't he care any more? What had happened to their marriage?

Frightened, cold and utterly miserable, Beverly lay dry-eyed and tense. Not more than two hours ago, she had been perfectly happy, perfectly secure, certain of Jonnie's love and the difference that their holiday would make to them both. Now the ground had been swept from under her feet and she was no longer sure of anything. Had Jonnie ceased loving her? Months had passed since he had last made love to her, but then that may well have been her own fault, for before that she had rejected his attempts and in doing so might well have hurt his pride. Somewhere along the road their love had dwindled from a glowing, living flame, to a tiny spark. It was this spark she had counted on to build a fire once more . . . and Jonnie had simply and quietly put it out.

Tears came now, hot and salt, rolling down her cheeks and wetting the pillow. She felt bruised and hurt deep down inside herself. No matter whether Jonnie really had work to do to prevent him coming away, he still need not have shown how little he cared by leaving her alone like this! Any man who really loved his wife would have tried to break down the door, force his way in and take her in his arms and tell her not to be so silly!

Beverly choked on a sob and sat up straight in bed. She was shocked by her own train of thought. Where had it led her? To the conviction that Jonnie no longer loved her. It hadn't really anything to do with their holiday; that had just been the last straw. For months and months now Jonnie had had no time for her. He even tried to avoid her company, or so it seemed in retrospect. She hadn't worried because she was so certain in her own mind that this second honeymoon would put everything right. Now there wouldn't be this chance and what would happen to their marriage?

"I can't live with a man who doesn't love me," Beverly whispered into the darkness. "I'll go away and leave him." Yet she knew it wasn't possible. She had five children, and she didn't *want* to go. She still loved Jonnie – if not in the same way she had once loved him, then in a different older way. But was it so different? Remembering their early days together when she had still been uncertain whether Jonnie was going to propose or not, she could find a similarity to her present predicament. She'd taken Jonnie and his love for granted, and now suddenly she was without confidence.

"Perhaps I'm being silly," Beverly reflected, trying to find hope. "Just because Jonnie has called off this holiday is no reason to believe he has stopped loving me. If he really has work to do, he can't help not being able to go." As to his calm acceptance of her removal to the spare room, it could be that he, too, had his pride and wasn't going to force himself on her when she'd shown so clearly she wanted to be alone.

For a moment Beverly toyed with the idea of complete capitulation. She would unlock her door and go along to their room and tell Jonnie she was sorry. He would put his arms round her and tell her to stop crying and not to be such an imaginative little goose. But the moment did not last. *Why should she?* It was not for her to make the first move, it was for Jonnie. He had been responsible for the rift. He must have known how much his cancellation of their holiday would mean to her.

"I hope he's as miserable as I am," Beverly thought wretchedly, lying back on her pillow.

Jonnie was indeed as wretched if not more so. His relief at finding Beverly had moved into the spare room had been mixed with consternation. Could she have guessed at the real reason for his backing out of the holiday plan? If not, why should she take the symbolic action of leaving their shared bed? Never, even after the most serious of their arguments in the past, had they slept apart. Beverly must be feeling this very deeply to have made this gesture. Of course, he knew she was terribly upset that their joint holiday was off. But this departure to the spare room signified more than disappointment. It meant she had finally rejected the significance of their marriage.

He was torn by uncertainty. Privacy was what he had longed for, yet without Beverly's accustomed presence beside him he could not settle to sleep. Her absence was more effective than her presence could have been. If she had been here to argue or storm at him, he might have stayed on the crest of the wave of his irritation with her. Now he felt confused and deeply guilty. He had refused the holiday and now there might be repercussions that would permanently affect their marriage. Was this what he wanted? Did he want his marriage to alter in its meaning, if not to break up? Was this behind his reluctance to force his way into the spare room and make her come back? How was it possible that one hour alone with Elinor in his arms could make so much difference? She had sworn nothing need touch his marriage, that he could keep his liaison with her quite apart from his life with Beverly. Well, Elinor was wrong; he could not. He couldn't make love to Elinor one day of the week and to Beverly the next. The idea revolted him and he felt that Beverly, if she were to know the truth, would never have let him come near her.

He turned restlessly in bed. If he could only hate Elinor, he could put an end to an affair which was against his every principle. But he could not find anything but intense excitement in the thought of her ivory body twisting itself around and against his own. Her face, her eyes, her expression were but a dim haze; he could not even bring her features to mind . . . only the tempting, glowing, passionate body needing him as much as he needed it.

Jonnie bit his lip. Renewed desire for Elinor could only complicate matters further, and he did not want to think of her now. He wanted to think of Beverly, poor little kid. She didn't deserve this; yet in a way it had all begun because she had not wanted him the way he wanted her. It wasn't her fault. Maybe she was just less passionate by nature than Elinor.

He forgot that Beverly had once been wholly and completely everything he desired in a woman; forgot that for years they had been contented and happy lovers. He forgot that Beverly had borne him five children within almost as many years and that she must have been tired, physically very tired, and not always able to respond when *he* was in the mood. He remembered only her rejection of him and his own unsatisfied need . . . a need that had persisted until Elinor had come into his life. Their love-making had been catastrophic and overwhelming and completely and perfectly satisfying, even if he had been a little frightened, too. It was almost as if he had been placed under some primitive spell; as if

Elinor possessed some black magic which gripped him even while his innermost beliefs still warred against her. He hadn't wanted it to happen, yet it had happened, and now there was no turning back. All week he had thought of her. He could not break it off now. He must see her again . . . *he must*, no matter what it cost. And he could not go back to living with Beverly as if nothing had changed. Everything had changed. He was somehow a different person and beyond Beverly's reach. To go away with his wife for a week now would be to court disaster, for he knew he could not be a real husband to her any longer.

Jonnie's mind closed sharply at the thought "and never again". Such thoughts were too dangerous. It was easier to think of Elinor. He heard her voice saying:

"This is only the beginning, honey. Next time will be even better, you'll see. I'll love you the way you've never been loved before, Jonnie . . . Jonnie . . ."

"Damn, damn, damn!" Jonnie swore aloud, his fingers tearing at the bedclothes as he tried to still that voice, to stop his thoughts. Somewhere in the next room, one of the children cried out. He held his breath listening, and then relaxed as the house went quiet. How he hated himself! How could he look young Nick, for instance, in the face? Only yesterday he'd caught him out in a fib and given him a good ticking off, telling him that there was nothing so nasty as a lie. Yet here he was living a lie and without the slightest intention of trying to break away. His hatred for himself once again had its physical effect on him, and he had to get up hurriedly and go to the bathroom where he was very sick.

On the way back, he heard the spare room door open and saw Beverly's shadowed figure standing there, white-faced, looking at him.

"Was that you, Jonnie? Are you all right?"

For one desperate moment, he wanted to go to her, to feel her arms round him warm and comforting, to be able to tell her how very wrong life had become – and why! Beverly was so gentle and sweet and full of tenderness whenever he or the children were ill or distressed. She was really a born mother, and it was as a mother he needed her now. He wanted her to comfort him, to put things right.

The relief of confession would be so enormous, yet he could not do it. He swallowed and stepped away from her.

"Quite all right, thank you," he said coldly, and without looking back at her, returned quickly to their room.

Beverly nearly followed. She had been wide awake when Jonnie went to the bathroom and she had heard him – known he was being sick again. Twice in a week; he couldn't be well. No wonder Jonnie kept away from her. If she went to him now, she could tell him how sorry she was, make him admit he wasn't well; that he was overtired, overworked. He needed a holiday . . . the thought pulled her up sharply. Of course he needed a holiday, and this was the one thing he wouldn't take. So what use in going to him now? He would only believe she was trying to nag at him. If he got really ill, the doctor would tell him he had to go away.

Slowly, Beverly went back to the spare room. Now she was kept awake by a fresh wave of uncertainty. Should she go without him? If she called it off for the time being, maybe Jonnie would get away later on – would have to get away for his health's sake. He looked ill and was pale and tired and lined around the eyes. And he had no appetite. Maybe she would cancel all the arrangements and let Jonnie make the next move. Sooner or later he was going to crack up physically. No man could take his hours of work with no rest and not crack up. She could have a chat with Dr Massie and get him on her side.

Comforted at last, Beverly fell asleep, little knowing that Jonnie's health, happiness and well-being no longer lay in her hands.

The morning brought a fresh crop of worries. It was Saturday, and soon after breakfast Nick appeared in the kitchen in jeans and a yellow polo-necked jersey, waiting for Paul Marshel. He seemed preoccupied and continually asked her the time as if he were incapable of seeing the clock for himself.

"What is the matter, Nick?" Beverly asked at last. "Is Paul late or something? Where are you going, anyway?"

"None of your business," was Nick's staggering reply.

White-faced, Beverly faced her small son. He'd never been so rude to her in his life before and this morning she was in no mood for making allowances. No matter what was bothering Nick, he had to learn he couldn't talk to her like that.

"Go up to your room, Nick. When Paul comes, I shall tell him you won't be going with him."

Nick took a step forward and looked up at her aghast. "But I am going . . . I promised!"

"Don't argue or I'll send you to bed as a further punishment. Now, upstairs, quick!"

For a full minute, the boy remained in front of her, looking straight at her defiantly. But slowly, his eyes fell and he half turned towards the door. "If I say I'm sorry I was rude, can I go with Paul when he comes?"

"No, you can't!" Beverly said. "You can spend the morning tidying your desk and drawers. I'll think about letting you go out this afternoon."

Nick made no further effort to apologize but ran out of the room and upstairs, banging the bedroom door hard behind him.

Beverly sighed. This was a fine start to a new day! If Jonnie hadn't gone out to golf immediately after breakfast, *he* could have dealt with Nick. Maybe the boy wanted some heavy masculine discipline; he was getting a bit too much for her. Well, Jonnie could speak to him at lunchtime.

The morning wore on with its usual round of domestic activities. Annette took the four younger children for a walk, the twins in the pram, Philip and Julia walking beside her. They were going to pick wild flowers and they at least were happy.

At eleven o'clock, Beverly made herself a cup of tea and took a cup of cocoa up to Nick's room. But when she tried to open the door, she found it locked.

"Nick, open this door. You know I don't allow you to lock it."

There was no reply. Angry, but not yet frightened, Beverly called again. "If you don't unlock this door by the time I count three, you'll spend all day in bed and without a book!" she called.

Still no reply, and suddenly anxious, Beverly put down the cocoa and leant her ear against the keyhole. There was no sound at all. Nor could she see anything for the key on Nick's side of the door was in the lock.

Panicky, Beverly ran downstairs and picked up the wood chopper from the coke-hole floor. She ran back upstairs and tried to wedge

50

open the door, using the chopper blade as a lever. After five minutes, the lock gave and the door swung inwards, Beverly fell in on her hands and knees, grazing her cheek against the chopper, which she still clenched in her hand.

The room was quite empty. The window was wide open, the curtains blowing gently in the breeze. Seeing them, Beverly rushed over and only then saw the old rope ladder Jonnie had used when he was making a tree-house with Nick last summer. Nick had attached it to the metal window frame and it dangled down almost to the ground outside. Nick had made his escape!

Relief that he had come to no harm flooded over Beverly, making her want to laugh and cry at the same time. All anger had gone and, deep inside her, she felt quite pleased with her young son at such daring. It was a good fifteen feet down to the garden below, but clearly he hadn't hesitated. He must have known he'd pay for it eventually, but whatever he and Paul Marshel were going to do today obviously was worth a punishment.

"Jonnie will have to give him a good talking to," Beverly thought as she went downstairs again. "He can do it when they both come in to lunch."

But although lunch was late, neither Jonnie nor Nick appeared. Giving the other children their meal, Beverly glanced up at the clock every few minutes. She felt the first feeling of fear gnawing again at her heart. Where was Nick? Had he got up to some mischief? Perhaps Jonnie had been called somewhere to see to him? Perhaps he had had an accident and Jonnie had gone to the hospital? Yet how would anyone have known where to find Jonnie? The police would have come home first to find out where Jonnie was.

"Not to worry, Madame. Mr Colt he probably lunch at the club, no?" Annette suggested, seeing Beverly's anxiety.

"But he always rings, Annette! And where's Nick?"

"Perhaps Madame could telephone the club-house to find if Mr Colt stay there for his dinner?"

"Yes!" Beverly agreed, relieved. "Then I can tell him Nick isn't back."

But her fears only increased when the club secretary informed her that Jonnie had been on the course that morning but had left about midday in his car.

"It's one-thirty now and Jonnie knows we never lunch later than one. Where *can* he be?"

"Maybe that the car break down?" Annette suggested.

"Well then, where's Nick?"

Beverly sat down and tried to eat her own lunch. But nervous anxiety made it all but impossible. She pushed her plate away at last and told Annette to put the children down for their rest and wash up. Then she went to the telephone.

Sue Adams answered almost immediately but she could not help. Mrs Marshel had left at midday and wasn't on the phone. So Beverly could not find out if Paul had returned for his lunch. She was sure the boys were out together.

"If you're really worried, can't you run down in the car to the estate? It wouldn't take you five minutes, Beverly."

"I haven't got the car," Beverly said. "Jonnie went out to golf this morning and *he* isn't back either."

"Then he must be lunching at the club," Sue said in an attempt to soothe her.

"He isn't. He left at twelve or thereabouts. It's so unlike Jonnie; he always telephones if he's going to be late or miss a meal. Oh, Sue, I really am worried."

"Look, I'll get Pete to run you down in our car to Mrs Marshel's if it will help, Beverly. I can't go myself because I'm feeding Jane in two minutes. You know how she gets if she's late for her bottle. But Pete won't mind going."

"I can walk, Sue. Thanks all the same," Beverly said.

"Nonsense – it'll take you twenty minutes, and I know how long that can be when you're on tenterhooks. Pete's here beside me now. He says he'll be along in five minutes."

Beverly thanked her lucky stars for these two good friends. Sue Adams was a little younger than herself and Jane was her first baby. They hadn't been in the village long but the two girls liked each other from the start and were rapidly becoming close to each other. Beverly saw more of Sue than of anyone else. Pete was nice, too. He was a year or two older than Jonnie and they sometimes played golf together.

When Pete arrived, Beverly climbed into the old Austin beside him and said, "I suppose I'm making a lot of fuss about nothing, but I can't help feeling worried." She told him how Nick had had to be sent to his room and how he climbed out of the window.

Pete laughed reassuringly. "I expect he thinks he might as well be hung for a sheep as a lamb. He'll be back by bedtime, if not before. Boys will be boys, you know."

Beverly smiled. "I suppose so. I wish Jonnie was home to deal with him. You didn't play golf this morning, Pete?"

"Why, yes, and I saw Jonnie. He was playing with Mr and Mrs Ward and that American woman . . . can't remember her name now. They were on the eighth tee just as we finished the seventh, and we had to wait for them to get ahead of us."

"You mean Elinor Wilmot," Beverly said slowly. "Pete, what is she like? Do you know her?"

"Only vaguely," Pete replied as he turned down into the council house estate. "Rather a striking woman. Bags of sex appeal, of course; very American. Not my type though. Too sophisticated. But she plays a good round of golf."

Beverly felt suddenly and unreasonably jealous. Was it Elinor Wilmot's golf that attracted Jonnie – or something else?

But she forgot Jonnie as Pete stopped the car outside the Marshels' house. Mrs Marshel answered the door, asking Beverly to step into the spotless little hall of her home.

"I just came to ask if Paul was home," Beverly said. "I think he and my Nicholas were playing together this morning."

"No, he's not home," said Mrs Marshel, pushing the greying hair back from her forehead. "Isn't your boy back neither?"

"No, he's not, Mrs Marshel, and I'm very worried. Nick's never missed a meal before . . . he knows he has to be home for meals. Did Paul say if he was coming to fetch Nick?"

"I left home 'afore John this morning," Mrs Marshel replied. "You see, I leave for Mrs Adams' house at eight-thirty and John hadn't got up, not by then, he hadn't. I know he's most often up at your place. It's very good of you to have him around so much."

"Well, I don't see a great deal of him; the boys are usually off somewhere in the woods or fields. Does he often stay out all day?"

"He's got used to fending for himself, and I don't worry none about him, not Paul. He can take care of hisself. You see, I'm often as not not here myself. I do for another lady as well as Mrs Adams, and we don't bother much with lunch. We have our main meal come teatime."

"I see!" Beverly said. "Well, I'm sorry to have bothered you. At least it looks as if the boys are out together, so I'm not quite so worried. Paul would have told someone if anything had happened to Nick, I'm sure."

"That he would. Paul's no fool. For all he can't do his school work, he's brighter than most boys of his age in other ways. Don't you worry about your boy, Mrs Colt. If my Paul comes home and he hasn't been with Nick and seen him home first, I'll send him along right away to tell you."

"That's very good of you, Mrs Marshel. Thanks," Beverly said.

Pete treated the matter much in the same way as Mrs Marshel. "He's just showing you how independent he's become," he said as he drove Beverly home. "I know you will worry, but I'm sure there's no need, really. Would you like to come back for a bit and chew it over with Sue?"

Beverly shook her head. "No, I'd rather be home. Maybe Jonnie is back by now and he can take the responsibility. It's just that if he, Nick, I mean, hasn't turned up by dark, I really shall be frightened. But Jonnie will know what to do. He may go out in the car and have a look around for him. I expect you and Mrs Marshel are right and he's out with Paul somewhere."

But there was no sign of their own car in the garage as Pete dropped her back at home, and by three o'clock Jonnie was still not back. Nor was Nick.

Beverly was by now nearly frantic, alone with an imperturbable Annette, who seemed not to be able to understand any of Beverly's fears for Nick's safety. Her very placidity only increased Beverly's powers of imagination. Suppose Nick had been run over . . . kidnapped . . . had fallen off a tree and broken a leg and was even now lying alone calling for help in some wood.

At last, unable to bear the waiting any longer, Beverly telephoned the golf club again. Jonnie had not reappeared.

"Annette, I'm going out to try to find Nick. If he comes home while I'm gone, or if Mr Colt comes, please tell them both not to go out again in any circumstances. Do you understand?"

Beverly hurried out of the house and along the lane that led to the woods. It was a lovely spring day, mild, sunny, agreeably drowsy except for the busy chatter of the birds in the hedgerows. Everywhere was green and fresh and full of growth. Great clumps of primroses clustered in the banks and occasionally she saw patches of mauve and white where the wild violets were growing beneath some tree.

Where *was* Nick? She'd be so relieved to see him it was doubtful if she'd even be cross if she caught sight of him now. Perhaps she was silly to fuss. Jonnie would probably have told her not to be so silly. Where was Jonnie, come to that?

"I beg your pardon!"

She had collided unseeingly with a tall rather large man who had been walking towards her. A moment later she recognized him; it was Mr Forbes, Nicky's schoolmaster.

"It's Mrs Colt, isn't it? I am so sorry."

Beverly smiled. "I am looking for Nicholas. I suppose you didn't happen to have seen him on your walk, Mr Forbes?"

"Nicholas? No, I can't remember meeting anybody. Is Nicholas lost?"

"I don't know," Beverly said truthfully.

Suddenly, her companion laughed. Beverly looked at him in surprise. Allan Forbes had the reputation of being a very quiet, shy man, difficult to converse with. She had only met him once or twice at school gatherings and had not really paid much attention to him as an individual; merely interested in the man who was Nick's teacher, and in what he had had to say about the boy's progress at school.

But Nick seemed to like him, though he, too, said he was "different" and that "he never laughs, you know. He just sort of smiles."

Well, he was laughing now, not stiltedly or nervously, but with a deep-throated kind laughter that seemed to make the nightmarish quality of the day no longer real.

"I suppose that did sound rather silly!" Beverly said, smiling. "But I've been so worried I hardly know what I'm saying."

"Then suppose you sit down here on this log, have a cigarette, and tell me all about it?"

Beverly looked at the man beside her, really seeing him now for the first time. He was older than Jonnie; nearing forty perhaps, with dark hair greying very slightly at the temples. He had a nice face with hazel-coloured eyes set wide apart, a long straight nose and a gentle, sensitive mouth still curved a little in laughter. Beneath, his jaw was square and firm.

"He's really very good-looking," Beverly thought, as she accepted the cigarette and sat down obediently beside him. "I never noticed it before."

Allan Forbes was in turn studying the girl beside him. Perhaps he should have thought of her as a woman, but she looked so incredibly young with her dark hair curling carelessly over her head, her coat hanging loosely from her shoulders as if she'd flung it on in a hurry, her nose shining and, not least, a large dark smudge across one cheek. He wondered if she knew it was there and decided not.

"What are you staring at?" Beverly asked, seeing his glance and the amusement in his eyes.

"Well, it's rude to make personal remarks, but I think you probably ran out of the house in a great hurry, having just made up the boiler, brushed your hair back from your cheek and left a black streak on it in doing so."

Beverly grinned, wrinkling up her nose in an unconscious gesture of self-disapproval. "Oh lord . . . and I haven't got a hanky!"

"Then borrow mine."

He offered her a clean white handkerchief, but when she scrubbed the wrong cheek, he took it gently from her and lightly rubbed away the mark.

"There; now you're perfect," he said – and meant it. This was the way a woman should look – without artificial make-up, the colour in her cheeks and lips natural, and the light in her eyes as she began to laugh again, making them sparkle and shine. He liked the untidiness of her hair, too. The curls were just as the wind might have blown them. She looked like a wood nymph.

Beverly heard the compliment with some surprise. The words had been spoken so easily, so naturally, that it was somehow quite wrong to question them, yet they were curious words to come from a complete stranger. This whole crazy day had a strange and quite unnatural and unending quality that did not add up. To be sitting here on a log with Allan Forbes listening while he told her she was "perfect" when she had set off from home in a panic to look for Nick.

"I have lost him," she said suddenly and inconsequently. "Nick, I mean. I shut him in his room after breakfast for being rude to me and he got out of the window by climbing down a rope ladder and he hasn't come back to lunch."

The man beside her nodded his head as if she were recounting a perfectly normal episode in Nick's life.

"Of course I'm worried. I must find him!" she added less forcefully.

"I wouldn't try to find him. I'm sure it's just what he hoped you'd do when he set off. He was trying to scare you. If you go after him, you'll have done just what he wanted."

"But suppose something has happened to him?" Beverly said anxiously. "Suppose he and Paul went tree climbing and they fell off or something."

"Paul?"

"Paul Marshel. Of course, he's older and I suppose he would come home and tell me or his mother if Nick had had an accident. But Nick's never missed a meal before . . ."

"It's my bet he won't have missed a meal today. Paul probably had some food with him and shared it with Nick. I don't suppose he even thought about lunch till he got hungry, and by that time he'd no doubt forgotten why he dashed off the way he did. He wouldn't want Paul to know and he wouldn't want to have to explain his reluctance to go home for lunch. I expect they just said, 'Let's have lunch here', and had it."

Beverly looked up at the calm face beside her and said: "You don't seem to think I ought to be worried. But it's very naughty of Nick. I shall get Jonnie to give him a thoroughly good dressing down when he gets back."

"Good! Now you're at least certain he'll be back. A moment ago you had the young rascal dead in a ditch. I expect Paul has put him up to this. He's not exactly a good influence, you know."

"Paul Marshel? But his mother is such a nice woman."

"Yes, I know," the man said. "I like her, too, but the father's a thoroughly bad lot. Drinks too much and is pretty unsavoury one way and another. Paul's a strange lad. It's my belief he could do a lot better at school if he wanted, but he doesn't want to, and he distracts your Nicholas. His marks are right down this term. As a matter of fact, I was coming along to have a talk with you about him sometime, but, well, I just haven't had time."

"Oh dear!" Beverly said miserably. "I wish I knew what to do. Nick and Paul are such good friends, and I've encouraged them to be. You see, my husband is away from home a lot and Nick needs someone . . . a companion. I thought Paul seemed a nice enough boy."

"I'm not saying he's a *bad* child," Allan Forbes said thoughtfully. "All the same, I don't think he's the best companion for a boy like Nick. Nick's at an impressionable age, and liable to set far too much store by an older boy's example. He's quite all right in class until Paul starts a shindy, and then he follows suit and ends up the worst of the lot. I don't think he'd behave like that if it weren't for Paul."

"Then you think I should try to break up their friendship?"

The man looked directly at her as he spoke. "I don't like interfering with children's friendships," he said carefully. "It makes for complications if you do. But in this case, I think if Nick were my child, I would. He's a particularly nice little boy. I like him. I wouldn't want him growing up into a bully."

"Nick – a bully! But he's always so gentle with the younger children."

"At home, maybe, but not at school."

"But why didn't you tell me before?" Beverly asked. "I had no idea Nick wasn't behaving the way he should."

The man beside her laid a restraining hand on her arm as if sensing her anxiety. "Because so far nothing very serious has happened. It seemed to me to be just a phase he was going through, and in fact I'm sure that is all it is. He's a very nice boy at heart. He's intelligent, too. I knew he was copying Paul and guessed he'd been a little too much impressed by an older boy's ideas of what was right and what was wrong. I did not know he was seeing a great deal of Paul out of school. I had hoped he might be an influence for the good on Paul."

"Does Mrs Marshel know what you feel about her boy?" Beverly asked abruptly.

"Well, I have spoken to her once or twice, but, you know, it isn't always easy for a master to criticize a child to its parents. Parents have a way of being quite certain it isn't their child at fault."

Beverly's face relaxed into a smile. "Well, you can't accuse me of that. You are the one who has been trying to exonerate Nick. Goodness only knows what he's up to this minute, but I know Jonnie will give him a good telling off and a severe punishment to go with it when he gets back."

"Not too tough," Allan Forbes said quietly. "After all, he's only a little boy yet. Besides, it's so easy to give vent to one's own feelings in that way and it doesn't always meet the bill . . . a thrashing, I mean."

"Then you are against corporal punishment?" Beverly asked curiously.

"No, not really. But it should be applied in moderation, I think. Did you ever read that poem by Coventry Patmore called 'The Toys'?"

"I don't think so," Beverly admitted. "Say it to me. I love poetry."

Quietly, the man beside her began to speak. Beverly watched his face, seeing in the steady profile a sudden inexplicable sadness, hearing it in his voice, too. Then her mind became fixed on the words he was quoting.

"My little Son, who look'd from thoughtful eyes
And moved and spoke in quiet grown-up wise,
Having my law the seventh time disobey'd,
I struck him, and dismiss'd
With hard word and unkiss'd,
His Mother, who was patient, being dead.

Then, fearing lest his grief should hinder sleep,
I visited his bed,
But found him slumbering deep,
With darken'd eyelids, and their lashes yet
From his late sobbing wet.
And I, with moan,
Kissing away his tears, left others of my own;
For, on a table drawn beside his head,
He had put, within his reach,
A box of counters and a red-veined stone,
A piece of glass abraded by the beach,
And six or seven shells.
A bottle with bluebells,
And two French copper coins, ranged there with careful art,
To comfort his sad heart.
So when that night I pray'd
To God, I wept, and said:
Ah, when at last we lie with tranced breath,
Not vexing Thee in death,
And Thou rememberest of what toys
We made our joys,
How weakly understood
The great commanded good,
Then, fatherly not less
Than I whom Thou has moulded from the clay,
Thou'lt leave Thy wrath, and say,
'I will be sorry for their childishness.' ''

Both were silent for a moment or two when his voice stopped at the poem's finish. Beverly was moved and extremely curious about the man beside her. What a strange person he was – not a bit as she had imagined him to be; not a bit like the usual school-master in a village school. He was obviously very well educated, a man of sensitivity and perception.

"You're not married?" she asked suddenly.

"No. I was, once. But my wife and our small son were killed the last year of the war."

So that was why that face was so full of sadness just now. He must have been thinking of the terrible tragedy of his own life.

"It seems so inadequate to say one is sorry . . ."

He turned and looked at her and smiled, a quiet, gentle smile, as if he were comforting her. "You mustn't be upset on my account. It happened eleven years ago and I've learned to accept it in that time. I don't very often talk about them, but there's something about you which reminds me a little of Louise. She must have been about your age when . . . when she died."

"Do you live alone now?" Beverly asked curiously.

"I have a cottage just this side of Bartel village. It's tucked away under a hill, so I don't suppose you've ever noticed it. Sometime you might care to walk over with Nick and have tea with me."

"Oh, I'd like to very much. I love walking; though I don't often have a lot of time nowadays. There's four more at home, you know, besides Nick."

"Four? I knew there is Philip in the kindergarten class and a sister coming next September – I didn't know there were five."

Beverly laughed.

"I'm afraid so; the twins are just toddlers. But I've more time now we have a French girl staying with us. If you really mean that invitation to tea, we'd love to come. How long would it take us?"

"From here? About half an hour if you go by the lanes. How about Wednesday week? It's half term so Nick and I will both be off from school. If you like, I'll walk over and meet you both here."

Beverly nodded. Then suddenly remembered that she was supposed to be going on holiday. But she knew now that she wouldn't go alone. She'd wait till Jonnie could get away, too. Besides, from all accounts it sounded as if Nick was going to need some extra care and attention. It wasn't fair to leave her mother in charge if Nick was going to be troublesome.

The thought of her small son brought her to her feet.

"I really ought to find Nick," she said. "I wish I knew where to look though."

Allan Forbes stood up and laughed. Beverly noticed inconsequently how much younger he looked when he smiled. He was attractive in a rugged, masculine way.

"If I were you, I'd go home and wait there for the young scamp. I'm sure you've no real cause to worry."

"Well, if you really think that, perhaps I will go home. Look, if you're not doing anything, why not come home with me and let me give you some tea. Jonnie – my husband – may be home by now and I'd like you to meet him and the other children, too."

"I'm sure you've enough to do without me there," the man said hesitantly.

"But I'd like you to come," Beverly insisted. "That is, if you wouldn't be bored. Maybe you have enough of kids at school."

Again he laughed. "Well, fortunately I love them all, or I wouldn't have picked on being a school-teacher. If you really mean it, I'd like to come."

They began walking back along the lane towards Beverly's home, talking lightly and easily as if they were old friends. Beverly felt happier than she had done for days. She did not analyse her feelings, but the sudden lifting of her spirits was there, none the less, and she smiled often and her steps were light.

Mostly they talked of Nick and school. By the time they reached the house, the last of her fears for Nick's safety had vanished; what a reassuring man Allan Forbes was!

The children rushed to her as they heard her voice at the front door.

"Is Nick back?" Philip asked eagerly. "Annette said he'd escaped. Has he run away? Will he get a bad punishment?"

"*I* think he's silly!" Julia remarked placidly. "There's crumpets for tea and if he isn't back soon, we'll eat them all." She turned her rosy-cheeked, chubby little face to the stranger. "Who are you? Phil and I thought you might be Daddy, but I suppose he's still playing golf. Are you staying for tea? We're having crumpets."

Beverly allowed them to lead Allan into the sitting-room and was glad of the chance to stop a moment and think. Jonnie wasn't back. Where had he got to? Should she ring the club again? Surely he couldn't stay out all day? Or was he trying to punish her in some way because of the way she'd behaved last night?

Her chin rose stubbornly.

If that was the way he wanted it to be, he could have it. The last thing she wanted was to let him think she cared whether he ever came home. At least, when he came back, he'd find her enjoying herself for a change. It might do him a power of good to see Allan Forbes entertaining his wife and children.

"I'll go and see if Annette has started tea," she told Allan. "Now, Julia, don't climb all over him."

When she came back into the room Julia was curled up in Allan's lap, her head against his shoulder, Philip leaning against his knee, both silent and absorbed in the story he was telling them. Julia put a hand to her lips to show Beverly she must not interrupt.

". . . and so Thumbelina found her Prince, married him and lived happily ever after."

"Tell it again!" Julia said promptly. "Please!"

Allan laughed and lifted her off his knee, dumping her fat little body down beside her brother's.

"Another time," he said. Smiling at Beverly, he added, "Can I do anything?"

"No, thank you. Tea is ready. We're having nursery tea, if you don't mind; the twins are far too young to eat in the drawing-room and, anyway, Julia and Philip are better behaved if they're sitting at table."

He followed her into the dining-room where the twins, already in their high chairs, were stuffing small squares of bread and honey into their open mouths. Annette joined them and they sat down to a noisy meal, Julia and Philip talking incessantly to their visitor who seemed to know just the right way to converse with them.

Beverly looked at them happily. This was the way family meals should be; and how nice Nick's school-teacher had turned out to be. What a pity they hadn't met him long before this. He must be lonely living by himself; maybe this kind of home life was just what he needed. And she so badly needed a friend, especially now.

It was six o'clock and Allan Forbes was just about to depart when Nick, filthy from head to toe, burst in through the kitchen door. He made no attempt to conceal himself but went straight to Beverly, his face rosy and his eyes bright.

"Gosh, Mum, I've had a super day!" he said. "Paul and me walked all the way to Bartel Wood and we nearly caught a squirrel, and, Mum, we pinched some potatoes from a farm and made a camp-fire and baked them, and they were super. For lunch, I mean. But I haven't had any tea yet—"

He broke off as he suddenly caught sight of his school-teacher. His young face suddenly stiffened as he remembered that this was no ordinary day. He was in dire disgrace and he was supposed to have spent the morning in his room. It had seemed such an enormous long time ago that he'd rushed into the house forgetting all about it. Mr Forbes and his mother, standing together, suddenly reminded him.

"Gosh!" he said flatly. "Gosh!"

"You seem to have forgotten you weren't supposed to have gone out," Beverly said. "And I don't suppose you've stopped to think once how worried I've been."

"Gosh!" was all Nick could find to say.

"Suppose I have a chat with Nick?" Allan said with a glance at Beverly's face. "Alone!"

Beverly returned the glance with gratitude.

"Would you? Thanks. Nick, go into the dining-room, please. And take off those filthy boots first."

"Seems to have had a good day," Allan said with a grin which Beverly could not but imitate. "Still, he's got to learn he can't do this kind of thing. Don't you worry. I'll deal with it."

"But you won't—"

"Strike him and dismiss him with harsh words . . .?" the man quoted simply. "No, I don't think it's necessary. See you in a minute."

In the dining-room Nick stood with his back to the window facing his teacher with wariness. He had a very healthy respect for Mr Forbes, and he was impressed that his mother had thought fit to call him in to deal with this crime. He must have done something pretty serious for her to do that.

"Well, Nicholas, I hate to spoil what has obviously been a thoroughly happy day, but, all the same, I think it's time you accepted a few responsibilities. You're quite old enough to know what you're doing. Your mother has been in a terrible state of fright about you. Is that what you wanted? Did you want to hurt her because she had had to punish you for being rude?"

Nick shifted on to another patch of carpet. "No, I didn't want to hurt her. I just wanted to go out. It's silly to stay indoors on a super day like this morning. I don't see why I shouldn't go. She said yesterday I could. Besides, Paul was waiting for me. He'd have thought I was a sissy to stick in my room just because my mum said so."

"What Paul might have thought isn't in the least important, Nick, not when you weigh it up against your mother's feelings. Paul is just a rather silly boy. Oh, I know you think he's clever and that he's a friend of yours, but he's not a bit clever really. If he were, he wouldn't be in a class for seven-year-olds when he's past ten."

"Well, he's clever at other things!" Nick defended his friend loyally. "Things like tying knots and carving your name on a tree and tracking squirrels and things. And he's jolly good at pinching potatoes. He had to go right into the yard and he crept in so quietly nobody saw."

"I see! So you think it's clever to steal?"

Nick flushed. "It wasn't stealing. We were just pinching a few for our lunch."

"Pinching is stealing, Nicholas. The potatoes weren't yours and you weren't paying for them, so you stole them. I would have thought *you'd* know better. Escaping from your bedroom down a rope ladder was naughty but not bad. Stealing *is* bad, and I'm sure you do know that. Just the same as hurting someone who loves you is bad. If you had stopped once today to think about your mother, you must have known she would worry. Mothers always do, unless they know you are safe somewhere and what time you'll be home. Then they don't fuss."

Nick grinned. "Gosh, that's right! Mum doesn't really fuss much. Did she think I'd run away or something?"

"She didn't know what to think. Don't do it again, Nick; not if you love her, which I'm sure you do. And don't ever steal again either. You do know that was wrong, don't you?"

"Y-yes! I s'pose so. But it was jolly good fun!"

"There are plenty of ways of having fun without resorting to theft!" Allan said quietly. "And you know, Nick, Paul is by no means the only person who can tie knots or track squirrels or bake

65

potatoes. Why, although you're only seven, I could teach you all those tricks in one afternoon, and I dare say a good many more difficult knots than Paul can tie, too."

"Gosh, would you?" Nick asked eagerly. "Paul says he's got to be the leader because he can do things better'n me. But I could be leader if I knew more'n him, couldn't I?"

"Yes, you could. What's more, I think you *should* be leader if Paul's idea of leading means leading into mischief. But you'll need to pull up your socks, Nick, before you're captain of anyone else. Captains have to think before they act. What you did to your mother today you did without thinking first."

"Well, I can think all right when I have to," Nick said with conviction. "I had to think about tying that rope ladder to my window to get out. I say, sir, do you think a granny knot would hold with my weight on the end? I'm sure it wasn't a proper reef knot I tied. It's right over left and then left over right, isn't it? Will you show me?"

"Not now, Nick. I want you to go and find your mother and tell her how sorry you are. You are sorry, aren't you? Deep down inside, I mean?"

"Gosh, yes!" Nick said. "Mum's jolly nice really, and – well, I s'pose I was rude. I like her much better'n Daddy."

Allan Forbes was shocked, not just by the child's words but by the casual tone in which they were delivered. Why didn't Nick care for his father? What kind of man was he? Surely a decent enough fellow if a woman like Beverly Colt loved him. And he must be fond of kids or he would never have had five!

"I expect you just said that because it's usually your father who administers a little discipline," he said lightly.

"You mean Daddy does the punishing? Not much," Nick said scornfully. "He's never here. He's always working."

"I see. But at the weekends when he's home . . ."

"Oh, he's always playing golf. Silly game, golf! I'm not going to play golf when I grow up. I'm going to be a footballer like Stanley Matthews."

"Yes, well, run along now and find your mother," the man said quickly. The puzzle was beginning to fall into place. The boy's tone of voice when he spoke of his father was a pretty clear indication of how he felt about him – jealous and resentful. It was usually something of the sort that started a thoroughly decent kid like young Nicholas off on the wrong road. But how could he suggest to Beverly that her son needed a little more of his father's time and attention?

As if he were the devil whose name had just been spoken, a man's voice could be heard in the hall. Then Beverly's:

"But, Jonnie, where were you all afternoon? I was worried to death because Nick had disappeared and you chose the same time to do a disappearing act."

"I was at the club, of course."

"But, Jonnie, you weren't. I rang at lunchtime and they said you'd left."

"All the same, I was there. Whoever spoke to you couldn't have looked very far for me."

"Time I went," Allan Forbes thought, suddenly tired and dispirited. A domestic quarrel was obviously about to ensue and he knew that he would not be able to feel impartial. He'd already taken a strong liking to Beverly Colt, and from what young Nick had just said, an equal dislike to his father.

He went out to the hall and held out his hand to Beverly.

"Thanks very much for giving me tea. I enjoyed my afternoon, and I don't think Nick will do anything like it again," he said.

"Oh, Mr Forbes, this is my husband," Beverly said quickly, nervously. "Jonnie, this is Nick's teacher. I don't think you've met before. We met when I was out looking for Nick and he very kindly came back with me."

"I've just given your young son a good 'talking to'," Allan said, and could not refrain from adding, "since you weren't here, and Mrs Colt felt a little masculine influence would be a good thing."

Jonnie flushed. "I see! What did the boy do?"

"Not a great deal, but enough!" Allan said. "He climbed out of his bedroom window and took a day off with Paul Marshel. I gather they stole some potatoes from a farmer and baked them over a camp-fire. I should say the biggest crime was worrying his mother, though I don't honestly think that occurred to him till I pointed it out. He's a good kid, Mr Colt, but I don't think Paul Marshel is any too good a companion for him."

"Oh! Well, thanks for dealing with it. Won't you stay and have a drink?"

"No, I must get home," Allan said quickly. He turned back to Beverly and noticed how pale and tired she looked. "Don't worry!" he said. "Nick's all right. I've told him if he likes to come over sometime to my place I'll teach him a few things he wants to learn. Thanks again for asking me here."

Beverly stood watching him as he walked away down the garden path. She felt as if some strong support were being dragged away from beneath her. Now she had to face Jonnie and find out where he'd been all day.

Jonnie was in the sitting-room pouring himself a drink when she rejoined him. He avoided her eyes, and it was quite plain to Beverly that he was nervous.

"Where were you, Jonnie?"

"I told you . . . at the club. For goodness' sake don't start nagging, Beverly. I wasn't to know Nick had done a bunk, or even that you'd had to punish him this morning."

"You weren't very likely to know since you weren't here," Beverly said, coldly, her hands clenched at her sides. "It seems as if you prefer to be out of your own home than in it these days. The children and I rarely see you now except at the weekends, and if you're going to start spending Saturday as well as Sunday playing golf, you might as well stop away altogether."

"I don't see what you've got to complain about. You said if you had Annette to help in the house, you'd be more than satisfied."

Beverly flushed. "I didn't engage Annette as a replacement for my husband's company, Jonnie, and I do expect a bit of help from you with your children. If you'd been here today none of this would have happened with Nick."

"Just because the boy had the guts to climb out of his window and stay out the whole day—"

"Don't defend him, Jonnie. He was extremely rude to me after breakfast and he had to be punished. I wouldn't have kept him in his room all day. If you'd been here you could have dealt with him and then he wouldn't have had to be punished further."

"So it's all my fault!" Jonnie said truculently.

"Yes, I think it is! And I think it's time we had a good long talk about our marriage, Jonnie. It's not just today, or Nick or the golf. It's . . . it's everything!"

Nerves, tiredness, tension, all combined to bring Beverly to the point where she could no longer restrain the threatening tears. She sat down in the nearest arm-chair and for a moment or two sobbed uncontrollably.

Jonnie looked down at her, appalled. He'd never seen Beverly cry like this . . . not in all their years of married life. Was this what he had done to her?

"Bev, don't!" he said wretchedly. He took a step towards her, his hand held out to touch her bent head, but slowly he withdrew it. He was afraid to touch her, afraid of what might be said; afraid to face up to the mess he'd made of their life together.

He'd been with Elinor all afternoon. He'd gone back to lunch with her in a mood of defiance. Elinor, probing his mood while they played a round of golf during the morning, had lost no time in taking full advantage of the situation.

"If she moved out of your bed, honey, she must have stopped caring altogether. I don't know why you worry the way you do. Chances are she couldn't care less about us if she did know."

"But you don't understand her, Elinor. She was dreadfully disappointed because I'd backed out of the holiday. I think she acted on impulse. It was her way of showing me how upset she was. She'd have come back if I'd asked her."

"You mean she expected *you* to be the one to eat humble pie!" Gradually, Jonnie's feeling of guilt about last night had vanished and it had seemed as if it had all been Beverly's doing.

But now here alone with Beverly, he felt mean and deceitful and he hated himself. There was no excuse, and deep down inside he knew it and fought against it hard. Beverly had every right to complain and to demand an explanation, but there wasn't any explanation he could give her. He couldn't say: "I spent the afternoon with Elinor Wilmot. I was making love to her. I was being unfaithful and because I'm so weak, I'll probably be unfaithful again. Elinor fascinates me. I can't leave her alone. When I'm with her, she bewitches me. It all seems so completely right. Now it seems wrong, but I can't give her up. I can't."

"Beverly, please stop. There's nothing to cry about. Nick's safe home, and that chap Forbes seems to have dealt with him quite satisfactorily. I'm home and I'm not going out all tomorrow. Suppose we take the kids on a picnic if this nice weather holds?"

She looked up then, her face wet with tears. "Jonnie, you mean that? It would be wonderful!"

"'Course I mean it," Jonnie said, feeling better now that he was offering something by way of compensation. "Now, what about some supper?"

Beverly blew her nose and tried to straighten her hair. "All right," she said shakily. "But before I go, will you tell me what you *were* doing this afternoon? I–I suppose it's silly of me, but I keep thinking . . . well, Jonnie, were you with Elinor Wilmot?"

Jonnie's whole body tautened at the name coming so unexpectedly, and without warning, from his wife's lips. A quick denial rose in his mind but he hesitated a moment, and in that moment, gave himself away.

Beverly's face was white as she said: "So you *were* with her? Jonnie, why? What does she mean to you? Are you attracted to her?"

"I like her company," Jonnie said stiffly. "She's good company and amusing, and . . . well, fun to be with," he finished lamely.

"And I suppose I haven't been amusing and fun to be with! All right, I'll accept that, though it isn't easy to be fun and amusing when you have five children to care for and a house to run and very little time alone with your husband. That's why I was counting on this holiday, Jonnie. Don't you see? It's because I've known in my heart that we were beginning to lose each other and perhaps a little of our love, that I knew we had to have time by ourselves to be the people we really are. Jonnie, you're not in love with her, are you?"

"Don't be so damn silly!" The words came out roughly and his tone frightened Beverly.

"Well, it may have seemed a silly question to you, but not to me.

She must mean something to you for you to prefer her company to mine."

"She's just a friend," Jonnie lied quickly.

"Then you believe men and women can have platonic friendships?" Beverly asked pointedly.

"Why not? I suppose you and this Forbes fellow are friends? Just because you asked him back to tea, I don't imagine you've been falling into bed with him."

"Jonnie!" Beverly's voice was shocked. "That really is silly. I only met him this afternoon. As if I'd even consider Allan Forbes in that way."

"Then why attribute ulterior motives to my friendship with Elinor Wilmot?"

"I suppose because I'm just jealous," Beverly said miserably. "But if your friendship with her is so innocent, why did you lie to me about being at the club?"

"Because I knew you'd make a scene if I told you I'd been with her," Jonnie said. "Now let's put an end to this, Beverly. I've told you I'll take you out tomorrow. Isn't that enough?"

"I don't know!" Beverly's voice was almost a whisper. "I think I'd rather you said 'I love *you* . . . that's why she doesn't mean anything to me.' Oh, Jonnie, don't turn away like that. I don't mean to nag about this, but nothing will ever be right again between us until I'm sure. Are you going to see her again?"

"Are you going to see Allan Forbes again?"

"Yes, but I wouldn't if you asked me not to; if I thought you were really jealous."

"Then I think you should grant me the same freedom. I may very well see Elinor again or I may not. But you've nothing to be afraid of. I've no intention of walking out on you and the children."

This last remark, more than anything else Jonnie had said so far, shocked Beverly. For him to have said such a thing was in itself an indication of how far in his own mind he had been thinking about Elinor Wilmot. He had *felt it necessary to reassure his wife that he wasn't going to leave her* . . . as if it had ever entered her mind.

She was silenced at last. Slowly, thoughtfully, she got up from her chair and, without looking at Jonnie, went up to their room to tidy herself and try to remove the traces of tears. Annette was putting the children to bed and they called out to her, but for the moment she could not face them. Without any real consciousness of her actions, she once again took her pillow and night-things from the bed where she had replaced them that morning, and went with them into the spare room. She couldn't bear the thought of lying beside Jonnie while her mind was in this turmoil. She wanted to be alone to sort things out. Or at least, sort out the facts she knew. And even then, Beverly asked herself bitterly, did she know half the truth? Elinor Wilmot! Elinor Wilmot! The very name rang like a warning bell in her ears.

Seven

"Elinor, I can't see you again. It's got to end now before something awful happens!"

Jonnie walked away from her where he could no longer feel the touch of her hands on his arm, nor look at that provocative mouth so close to his own.

"Something awful? What are you trying to say, honey?"

Even across the width of the room, he could still smell that heady perfume of hers. He felt desperate and utterly miserable. The day had been a terrible strain both on him and, as he rightly guessed, on Beverly. He had kept his promise to take them on a picnic, and the children had been wildly excited. Fortunately, their eager chatter had made it unnecessary for him and Beverly to talk to each other. Beverly was very quiet. There were great dark rings of violet beneath her eyes and he guessed that she, too, had had another sleepless night. If it hadn't been for the tension between them, the day would have been so perfect. The weather was warm, sunny and soft. The kids had been allowed to discard cardigans and run about with their faces upturned to the sunshine or bent studiously over hot handfuls of wild flowers they had gathered. It could all have been so perfect if only he had not had Elinor crowding every thought; making him feel guilty and a cheat. How he hated himself! How right Beverly was to hate him!

When at last the day was over and they were home and the children tucked up in bed, Jonnie had known he could not go on like this any longer. He had to put an end to his association with Elinor, or else see his marriage break up. He couldn't go on deceiving Beverly, seeing her pale and miserable and suspicious, knowing something was horribly wrong. Sooner or later she would find out what it was, and then he knew he would have to face up to a decision; unless Beverly made it for him and asked for a divorce.

But he didn't want a divorce; he never had. He only wanted Elinor – sometimes. She'd never suggested marriage to him and he'd never contemplated it.

"Beverly knows I was with you yesterday. It can't go on, Elinor. I'm no good at this hole-in-the-corner kind of affair."

Elinor looked at him sharply. She knew that she would have to play her cards carefully if she were not to lose him. And she had no intention of losing him yet awhile, anyway. Their affair had barely begun.

"That's only because it's the first time you've been unfaithful," she said calmly, matter-of-factly. "It comes easier after you get used to the idea. Still, if you want it to be goodbye, I'm not going to try to prevent you. You're a man, not a boy, and you know what's best."

Jonnie swung round, his face twisted. "That's just it, Elinor. I don't know any more what is best. I know we are absolutely right for each other; that we must have been made for each other. You said so yesterday, remember. It's as perfect for you as for me, isn't it?"

Elinor smiled at him. "Why, you don't have to ask me, honey. No man has ever made me as happy as you do. I guess there never will be anyone else quite the same."

"No, but there probably will be someone else. That's the trouble, Elinor; you don't feel the same way about all this as I do. You aren't in love with me. You just want me."

"Sure I want you. Is there anything wrong in that? Love – well, I thought you wouldn't want my love, Jonnie . . . that's why I never told you I loved you. I didn't want to make things more difficult for you. After all, you've been very fair with me. I've known all along you were married and that you didn't intend to leave your wife for me. It hardly seemed my place to ask you for love."

Jonnie felt even more of a heel. He wasn't sure he had wanted love from Elinor, but pride demanded that he meant more to her than just a casual lover.

"Then you do care?" he persisted, taking her in his arms and looking deep into her strange, inscrutable eyes.

The Search for Love

"Shall I show you how I care?"

"No, no!" Jonnie said quickly, drawing away again. "You mustn't tempt me, Elinor. You've got to help me to be strong about this. I just can't go on being unfaithful to Beverly. Don't you think . . . Elinor, can't we just be friends?"

For a moment she began to laugh, but seeing the expression in his eyes, she quelled the laughter quickly and said:

"I guess not, Jonnie; not if we're going to be honest about all this. I think the link between us is too strong. But I'll try, darling. I'll try real hard rather than lose you altogether."

Jonnie felt like a man reprieved from the gallows. He need not lose her completely, and at the same time he could still play fair with Beverly. If he were not actually unfaithful to his wife, he need have no conscience about her or the children.

"I don't know why you bother with me," he said meekly. "It can't be much fun for you, darling."

"I'd go through a great deal just for an hour or two alone with you, Jonnie. That's how much you mean to me."

"Oh, Elinor, darling!"

She was back in his arms now and he was kissing her mouth, trying to keep a brake on his emotions and on hers. He could quite understand that it would be more difficult for her. She had no reason to hold back, no one to whom she would be unfaithful when she gave herself to him. But he had to be strong for both of them, for Beverly's sake; or if not for her directly, for his marriage.

"Elinor, I'd better go home. We'll both be weak if I stay here now. Let me go, darling!"

She gave in easily, too clever to reproach him or to try to take a further trick. It sufficed for the time being that she had prevented him breaking with her completely. Jonnie was weak . . . he'd give way again soon enough. Meantime, his uncertainty gave an added piquancy to their relationship, at least as far as she was concerned. She was bored with the man who too easily and too readily became her slave. It was really the "hunt" she enjoyed, and then the fruits of victory were all the sweeter for being delayed. She never gave Beverly a thought. If a woman couldn't keep her husband's affections, that was her folly, her misfortune. It had nothing to do with Elinor. If

75

Beverly wanted to keep Jonnie, let her fight for him. But somehow Elinor didn't think she need worry much about her opponent.

Jonnie returned home feeling virtuous and for once able to look Beverly squarely in the eyes. But Beverly had gone to bed in the spare room, and he had no opportunity to talk to her. It was frustrating to say the least. Moodily, he went along to their bedroom and alone to bed.

By the Wednesday of half term, no further word had been spoken about the holiday except for Beverly's brief comment that she had decided against going alone. Jonnie announced that he might be late home from the office that night.

"I may be late home myself, anyway," Beverly replied coolly. "Allan Forbes rang up on Monday afternoon and he has asked Nick and me to tea."

Jonnie felt a pang of annoyance. It was a bit much to swallow that Beverly should be able to go off and have tea-parties until all hours while he slaved away at his desk. And he really was working late on that Wednesday. He decided he did not like Allan Forbes. Nick had developed an annoying habit of mentioning him on every possible occasion, and he was sick of the man's name.

"Personally, I think Forbes had better pull up his socks a bit; you can tell him I said so," he told Beverly at Wednesday morning breakfast. "Nick's manners are getting worse and worse. He only just stops short of being rude to me every time I speak to him."

Beverly raised her eyebrows. "I don't see what that has to do with Allan Forbes. He's supposed to teach Nick lessons, not manners. That's our job, Jonnie."

Jonnie flushed and his lips tightened. "Well, a little more discipline at school wouldn't be a bad thing," he said, and left the room. Beverly had a way of turning a phrase so that it always seemed as if *he* were in the wrong. It was her job more than his to see to Nick's manners. He was not home enough to be able to control the boy properly. If Beverly didn't take care, he'd begin to think he was being a fool to deny himself the full pleasure of Elinor's company for her sake. If Beverly wanted him around more, then it was time she tried to make things a little more pleasant for him.

Beverly was preoccupied with similar thoughts as she and Nick walked across the fields in the direction of Allan's cottage. She hadn't seen him again since the Saturday, yet somehow she felt as if she were going to tea with an old friend. Maybe it was because Nick talked about him so much. It seemed that Nick must always have someone to fill his universe. Once it had been Jonnie with "Daddy says . . . Daddy does . . ." until she nearly went crazy. Then it had been Paul Marshel until Allan deflated that bubble by showing Nick the older boy really wasn't so clever after all. Now it was Allan himself. "Mr Forbes said I could read the best in the class . . . Mr Forbes said I might go up to Form II next term if I keep on working so hard. Mr Forbes said he'd show me a Bowline knot and a Surgeon's knot when we go to tea on Wednesday . . . Mr Forbes has got an aviary full of budgerigars and he's got a pet one that talks . . ."

She'd learned a lot about Allan Forbes since their last meeting.

He came to meet them, walking across the fields towards them with long, easy strides. Beverly watched him approach with a sudden unaccountable shyness. Maybe it was because Jonnie had flung it in her face that this man was a possible "boy-friend" – a hateful thing to have said.

"Hullo, Mrs Colt. Hullo, Nick!" He seemed quite at ease and he chatted quietly, as if aware of Beverly's shyness, and wanted to put her at ease as well.

"It's another beautiful day," he commented as Nick swooped ahead of them to chase a large Brimstone butterfly. "Nick seems to be full of his usual good spirits."

"He's been so looking forward to today," Beverly said. "He has talked of little else. Moreover, he's been as good as gold since you spoke to him that afternoon. What did you say to bring about such a transformation?"

Allan smiled. "I just told him mothers were there to be loved and taken care of. I don't think it ever occurs to young children that their parents need looking after, unless it is pointed out to them, either by word or example."

Beverly understood what he meant. A boy copied his father in such matters and Jonnie's abrupt, uncaring attitude to her had been

Nick's yardstick for the last six months. She was not sure whether she resented Allan Forbes' implied criticism of her husband. It was too near the truth and he had no right to say it!

As if guessing her thoughts, Allan said quietly: "I hope you don't think I'm criticizing Nick's home in any way, Mrs Colt. He's one of the lucky ones. So many of the lads I deal with come from broken homes, or their fathers drink, or the mothers just don't care. You'd be horrified if you knew how many such homes there are. I suppose it is the inevitable aftermath of war, but it seems as if people can't be satisfied any more with the simple things of life . . . the beautiful things. All they want are bigger cars, television sets, money to spend on this or that. Of course, there are many very good homes – far more than bad ones. But it always upsets me when I learn of another broken home. It so often means a broken child, too."

"You are an idealist, Mr Forbes. I suppose I am, too. But life isn't kind to idealists. I think one needs to be a realist these days, and, you know, it isn't as easy as you suppose to be happy on twopence. I used to think my mother was being old-fashioned and narrow-minded when she warned me that love flies out when poverty flies in, but now I'm not so sure."

"Of course, money makes things easier," the man agreed. "But it can't make two people happier if they can't get along with each other."

Beverly felt her heart beating with a strange rapidity. This man was so wise, so sympathetic. Why not confide in him her fears for her own marriage? But Jonnie would hate to think she had discussed their marriage with an outsider. And he would feel Allan was an outsider. Strangely, she did not.

"You don't agree with me?" Allan prompted, watching the changing expressions on her mobile face.

"Yes, I think I do! But you can't always see all the facts from the outside. You condemn those parents who break up their homes – but do you really know what caused the break-up?"

"Whatever little thing caused the final break, it can only really be because two adults are unable to reach a compromise; that they have failed in their efforts to live together. Surely if they have children, they should realize that their own desires must come second to their children's need."

They had reached Allan's cottage now and Nick had seen the aviary. He was staring into the wire cage, entranced.

"You can go inside if you want, Nick!" Allan said. "Some of the birds are quite tame and if you keep very still, they'll come and perch on your arm or shoulder. Then you can look round the garden and see if you can find some groundsel for them."

Nick nodded in delight and Allan indicated to Beverly the two deck-chairs placed on the flagstone terrace.

"I'll show you the cottage in a moment," he said. "Let's enjoy the sunshine here for a few moments. Tell me, Beverly, what is it that is troubling you? Perhaps I can help?"

His use of her Christian name seemed as natural as his incredible sensitivity to her thoughts and moods. She noticed both but neither seemed strange.

"I . . . I want to talk about myself, but somehow it seems disloyal, in a way. Allan . . ." She turned to him and looked directly into his eyes, her own bewildered and unhappy. "Allan, although in one way it seems as if you and I have been friends for a lifetime, yet I know we are comparative strangers. Would it be right for me to discuss my marriage with you?"

Allan Forbes looked away. He had invited her confidence, had encouraged her to say what was on her mind. Yet could it be right for her to discuss her husband with him? He wanted so much to help her and to see her radiant and happy. How could he achieve this without knowing what was wrong? He'd thought so much about her since that first meeting.

I'm falling in love with her! he thought. She doesn't know it, but she senses it. I love her because she is like Louise. I feel the same desire to protect her, care for her, worship her. But such a love can only hurt her. She belongs to another man.

He stared down at his hands, clasped together loosely between his knees. Fulfilment obviously was not meant for him in this lifetime. The thought saddened him but could not make him bitter. This girl with her beauty and her sadness, her smile and her spirit was like a ghost from the past, evoking memories and stirring desires. As long as he remembered that his love was gone for ever, he could not harm her by giving her his devotion, his sympathy, his understanding.

"Whatever it is that is causing you so much worry will not go on, Beverly," he said slowly. "Nothing in life stands still, even when we would have it so. It will get better or worse."

"But it's the not knowing!" Beverly cried out. "I cannot live with this uncertainty. Allan, I think my husband is falling in love with someone else. I think he is finding me, the children, and his home, a burden and not a pleasure. I'm afraid. I feel I must have failed him in some way and that it's my fault."

It was said. If disloyalty it was, it was too late now to withdraw the words. She wasn't even sorry. Allan would never betray her confidence. She knew that without any assurance from him.

"It won't help to apportion blame, Beverly," he said gently. "What matters is the future. You love him very much?"

Beverly drew in her breath sharply. "I don't even know that any more. I loved him more than anyone in the world when I married him. I didn't believe it was possible for two people to be so happy. But now I feel as if he is a stranger. I don't understand him any more. He isn't the same person, Allan. He lied to me – once that I know of, but how many times I don't know about? How can you love someone who lies to you?"

"You would go on loving Nick how ever many lies he told."

"Nick? Yes, but he's just a child, Allan."

"And Jonnie? Perhaps he, too, is a child. Most men are, you know. He may only have lied to spare you hurt. I can't believe he means to leave you and the children."

"Maybe not that. But he must have been thinking about it. What ought I to do, Allan? Try to go away for a while? Try to get him to go, too? Pretend I don't know what's going on? Or fight for what is mine?"

"Do you know 'what is going on'?"

Beverly grimaced. "Well, no. But I'm pretty sure. What I'm not sure of is what I should do. Shall I force the issue? Yet in a way, I feel it is my fault. I desperately wanted Jonnie to marry me when he did. We were both terribly young. There'd never been anyone else in either of our lives. Maybe I should have waited, let Jonnie sow a few wild oats before he settled down."

"I can't sit in judgment on him, Beverly. You wouldn't want me to, and, anyway, I don't know your husband. I'm not sure what advice I should give you, if any. But I don't think it would be right for you to do anything at all until you are sure this is more than a passing attraction. It is surprising how attractive the unobtainable can be – to a man, anyway."

"The forbidden fruit?" Beverly's voice was half serious, half amused.

"Yes. Especially to the young. Your husband is young, Beverly. I suspect that marriage has matured you but not yet done the same for him. Give him a little time. He must be a fine character for you to love him, and sooner or later he will find out for himself the unhappiness he is causing you."

"I think he knows already. I'm not very good at hiding my feelings. Nor is he. Allan, do you believe a man can be unfaithful to his wife and still go on loving her?"

"Depends on the man. Personally, I could not. Love and sex go together. But I know that isn't so of all others. If you want your marriage to work out, you must have it in your heart to forgive. Forgiveness and love go together."

Beverly made no reply. Would she be able to forgive Jonnie if she knew for a fact that he'd been unfaithful? Was she capable of the high-mindedness, the depth of love of which Allan spoke? She knew what he said was right; true love can forgive and go on forgiving. Did she really love Jonnie? Had she ever really loved him with her whole being? Somehow, she could not truthfully find it in her heart to tell herself their love was of this enduring quality. They had both been too young to know or to understand.

"I was so sure!" she said, more to herself than to the man beside her. "So sure!"

"It is only as we grow up that we become 'unsure'," Allan replied. "The more we learn of life, the less well based do our early convictions seem. Now, if you were to ask Nick what he would most like to have if he could choose the one thing to make him completely happy, he would probably name some object – a football or a model yacht. Ask him again in twenty years' time and he would say, 'Love'. Life would have taught him a set of values, just as it teaches all of us."

"Then you don't think the young can ever judge what is best for them?"

"Not really. Only by instinct."

"Then when do you think we can know? How old must we be?"

"I doubt if we ever know completely. How could we? I think we must simply trust in God."

"Then you believe in God? Really believe, I mean?"

"Yes. There has to be Someone or some Reason. Nothing in life makes sense if there is no God and no life hereafter. When Louise died, I knew that she couldn't just have gone for ever."

"Tell me about her," Beverly said gently.

"I'm not sure if I can. To me she was all I wanted in a woman. To look at – well, you are very like her. Perhaps that is why I wish so much to be able to help you."

"You have helped me with Nick already. He admires you tremendously. I don't think he could have been more fortunate in his school-teacher!"

"Thank you!" Allan said, smiling. "But it isn't entirely motiveless, you know. A happy child is a good worker."

Beverly smiled back. "Even if he were not in your class at school, I believe you would do as much for him."

"But that, if it is true, might also have another motive. I might be anxious to please you so that you can recommend me at a later date for a headmastership. Now, let me show you the cottage. It's simple, but I think has a lot of charm."

Bored now with the aviary, Nick came running up to them. Allan suggested a brief tour of the cottage and Beverly was enchanted with it. His innate good taste had chosen the right colours, materials, rugs. There were flowers arranged in a vase on the polished circular oak table. It was clear that here was a man who loved beautiful things and most of all the beauties of nature.

"You must be very happy living here," she said as they went once more into the sunlit garden, each carrying a tray of tea things.

Allan did not reply. It was true he had found happiness here, of a kind. But it was of a lonely kind.

The same thought had struck Beverly and she wished her remark unsaid. Somehow she must contrive to see he was less lonely.

The rest of the afternoon gave no further opportunity for such talk, as Nick was with them, demanding his share of attention. Beverly sat quietly, listening to her small son and his companion who were obviously already such very good friends.

She had no wish to do so, but against her will she found herself comparing Allan again with Jonnie, and the comparison was always in Allan Forbes' favour. She liked his quiet, slow voice; the things he said; the sensitive hands as his fingers manipulated the intricate knots Nick wished to tie; the unconscious good manners towards both of his visitors; the gentle smile that occasionally flooded across his face. Everything about him was gentle, kind, and above all, peaceful. With this man she could relax completely and feel as if the outside world with its haste, its bustle, its worries and perplexities no longer mattered.

"You'll come again, won't you?" Allan asked her as he walked part of the way home with them. "I have enjoyed our afternoon."

"And so have I," Beverly said truthfully. "It has been a kind of escape from reality. I love your cottage."

"It's there, whenever you feel the need to escape again," Allan said with his friendly smile. But she knew that he did not mean the cottage only – he meant his friendship was waiting, too.

She felt a sudden premonition of danger.

"It's not always easy for me to find the time to get away from home," she said in a sudden flurry of nervousness. "But I will try."

He did not press the invitation and they parted quietly, leaving Nick to do the talking as usual.

"I wish . . ." said Nick as they rounded a bend in the lane so losing sight of Allan's tall figure. "I don't half wish *he* was my father. Don't you, Mum?"

Beverly looked at her small son in quick horror. How could he be so disloyal, so unkind to Jonnie. Sensing her disapproval, Nick said sullenly:

"Well, it's true. And, anyway, he's much nicer than Dad."

"Nick!" Beverly pulled him up before he could say more. But even as she did so, she felt her heart hesitate. Wasn't Nick right after all? Allan was "nicer" than Jonnie to Nick. And perhaps, given different circumstances, he would have been far "nicer" to her, too.

Hurriedly, she took her small son home.

Eight

As they entered the house, Beverly felt strangely guilty. Jonnie had come home from the office early after all. She could hear him playing with the younger children in the sitting-room. The noise was uproarious and she knew, with the familiar sinking of her heart, that the children would be difficult to calm down and get to bed. All the same, she had been silently criticizing Jonnie in her mind for neglecting the children and here he was, home early, presumably in order to play with them.

The noise stopped abruptly as she opened the door. Jonnie looked up from the floor where he was lying and the smile died on his face.

"So you're back," he said shortly, removing the twins' hands from his jacket and climbing to his feet. "Do you realize it's after six?"

"Is it? I'd no idea it was so late," Beverly said truthfully. "I'm sorry, Jonnie. Have you been home long? Did Annette give you some tea?"

"Annette had quite enough to do giving the kids their tea!" Jonnie retorted, his face sullen and angry. He had known she and Nick would be out to tea with Forbes, but he'd forgotten it when he had decided on the spur of the moment to give the office a break for once and go home early. When he reached home he was furious with himself for forgetting and with Beverly for going.

Beverly felt resentment rising in her at his tone of voice.

"I suppose if you feel it is too much for Annette to give four children their tea, it wouldn't also occur to you that it might be too much for your wife to give five children breakfast, lunch and tea on Annette's day off? If so, I'm surprised it hasn't also occurred to you

85

to stay home and help rather than play golf all afternoon with your American girl-friend!"

Jonnie's face flushed. "If you're going to start that—"

Aware of the children's curious glances, Beverly broke in quickly, "Let's finish this conversation after I've got the children to bed!"

"No, we'll finish it now," Jonnie said, knowing Beverly was right not wishing to argue in front of the children, yet unable to curb his temper.

"I said later," Beverly replied quietly, and, taking Philip's and Julia's hands, she led them quickly out of the room.

Her self-control fired Jonnie still further. For a moment, he considered going after her, having it out there and then. But on reflection, he decided not to. There was a better way to deal with Beverly; he'd not be here when she felt ready to talk.

He went to the bottom of the stairs and called up in a loud voice: "I'm going out. I won't be back to supper."

There was no reply, but Jonnie felt sure she must have heard. He waited a moment for her to call him back, but no sound came from the landing, and furiously he flung on his jacket and went out banging the front door behind him.

As he drove automatically towards the club-house, he fanned his irritation into a real grievance. It wasn't that Beverly had been out to tea. No, it was her attitude to him that made their life together impossible nowadays. She was always critical, coolly and maddeningly critical. It undermined a fellow's belief in himself to have a wife who continually criticized him. Nothing he did was right any more. And it was all the more unfair since he'd decided of his own free will to give up Elinor, or at least, give up any idea of taking what he wanted from her. Beverly's attitude was hardly helping the situation. She should have been grateful, understanding, admiring. Instead of which, she taunted him with Elinor's name!

Well, she could take the consequences. Other fellows had a bit of fun outside their homes and now he was beginning to understand why. They probably had wives who went for them the way Beverly was always going for him. It was enough to push a chap into another woman's arms, especially if the other woman was like Elinor, sweet and thoughtful and knowing how to treat a man.

It was one thing to want to stay faithful to a wife you knew loved you. But it was becoming increasingly obvious that Beverly wasn't in love with him any more. It had begun the night she'd moved into the spare room and locked the door against him; that showed the way her mind was working.

Jonnie conveniently forgot the reason Beverly had moved into the spare room – a reason well founded, although she wasn't to know it. The why was not important. That she had done so was, for it helped him convince himself she didn't care. He didn't want her to care. Her love for him had kept him from having what he wanted.

If she goes on much longer, I shall tell Elinor I've changed my mind, Jonnie told himself as he drove into the car park.

He really meant to stay there an hour or two, have a couple of drinks with someone at the bar, have a meal and go home. That Elinor should be in the bar, alone, was an unlucky if not unlikely coincidence since she spent so much of her time at the club-house. He wasn't to know it had been deliberately planned by her. She'd rung his office, hoping to persuade him to drop in for a drink on the way home. When Jonnie's typist had told her he'd already left, Elinor jumped to the conclusion he might be coming to see her. She'd waited at home for an hour, and then hopefully gone along to the club-house. She hadn't been there ten minutes when Jonnie arrived.

"Surprise – nice one!" she said as he seated himself on the bar stool beside her. "I'll even buy you a drink, honey!"

"I could use one," Jonnie said, warmed by her obvious pleasure in seeing him.

Elinor's thin-painted eyebrows were raised questioningly. His tone of voice indicated his frame of mind. Her eyes narrowed. "Sound as if you'd had a bad day. Here, drink this!" She pushed a cocktail glass into his hand. "It's one of Mike's special cocktails . . . my recipe," she said, smiling as she watched him drink it and quickly ordering two more from the barman.

Within half an hour, Jonnie was feeling a little more than light-headed. He knew he shouldn't have drunk so many cocktails on an empty stomach, but in the mood he'd been in, he just hadn't cared. Now he wasn't in a mood any longer. He felt light-hearted as well as light-headed and everything Elinor was saying to him was making him laugh. He felt nothing but goodwill towards the world now, and towards Elinor in particular. Trust her to know when a fellow needed a drink. She understood men all right.

"You unner-sshand me," he told her, leaning his head close against hers. "Beverly doesn't . . . always cross. T'shn't fair!"

"You've had enough, Jonnie," Elinor said, her voice suddenly sharpening. She didn't want him too drunk.

"S'right! Had enough – enough of being boshed about. Do what I want now . . . I'll show her . . . I show you all!"

He swept out an arm and knocked over a glass and grinned sheepishly at Elinor.

"Come on, honey. We'll go home and have some coffee . . . and something to eat. You must be hungry!"

Jonnie acquiesced without argument. He didn't want the coffee but he could do with a meal.

Half an hour later, he began to sober up. A plate of cold chicken and two large cups of black coffee had done the trick. His head began to clear and he looked up from the deep sofa in which he was lying and caught sight of the clock on Elinor's mantelpiece. It was eight o'clock.

"Gosh, I'd better be off!" he said. But Elinor's arms were round his neck and he was suddenly aware of her soft slim body lying against his own.

"Not yet, Jonnie . . . not yet!" she whispered, her voice husky in his ear. "There's no hurry! Your wife won't care if you're late. After all, she was late home from her assignation."

Jonnie had been talking as well as drinking. He began to re-member what had brought him here, back with Elinor again. She was right, of course. Why should he hurry? Beverly had stayed as long as she wanted with Forbes! But it wasn't true she wouldn't care if he stayed on here with Elinor. He knew it, even if Elinor didn't. Beverly would be jealous all right. Would she be hurt? Could you be hurt if you weren't in love?

"Jonnie darling, you need me. I only want to make you happy. It can't hurt anyone – you know that. Kiss me . . . please, Jonnie."

One kiss, Jonnie thought, then I will go, before it's too late. But

Elinor wasn't content with one kiss, nor with several. Her body was alight and his caught fire from hers. He knew it was wrong; knew it was weakness, madness, but he couldn't stop himself. Her perfume was all about him, weakening his senses as the drink had done earlier, and there was no cooling the ardour that was in this vital woman who lay in his arms.

"Jonnie, I want you. Take me, darling!"

"I love you!" he cried, as he crushed her closer and closer against him. He didn't stop to wonder if it were true. Beverly didn't care – it didn't matter. Nothing mattered any more but the complete surrender to their desire.

It was nearly midnight when Jonnie drove himself slowly home. He was sober enough now. Although he felt physically completely inert, his mind seemed charged with electricity as one thought after another chased round his head.

It was wrong. He'd known all along it was madness to give way to Elinor and to his own desires. It wasn't all Elinor's fault. He'd wanted her as much as she had wanted him; and in a strange way, their union had been perfect. No – not perfect, there was a savagery in Elinor's caresses that were frightening even while they stimulated him. He'd felt almost as he might have felt in the presence of black magic. There was a primitiveness in Elinor that spoke of the jungle, of times before man and woman became civilized. Was sex meant to be like this? Exciting, yes! But lacking in gentleness, in tenderness, in love?

Did Beverly still love him? The thought of her made him despise himself for what had just happened. She must never know. She couldn't possibly understand. She was so different from Elinor. He disliked himself for making comparisons and yet he could not stop his thoughts. Beverly was nicer than Elinor. Deep down he did not really *like* the American and yet she had this strange hold on him. He knew he'd want her again, yet it couldn't go on, how could it? Beverly would be sure to find out and then – well, did he want to be divorced? Did he want to lose his home, his wife, his children? Did he really want to spend his life with Elinor?

He knew he did not. This was playing with fire and he had to put a stop to it.

Uncontrollably, his thoughts went back to the woman he had just left. He saw her naked, milk-white body stretched out among the cushions on that large sofa, saw the soft arms held out to him and the wild, strange expression of her eyes. What a woman! And it seemed she found him as satisfying as he had found her. She made him feel special, important, all man. Beverly lately made him feel like a silly schoolboy. Well, it was a pity she couldn't learn a few lessons from Elinor. Then he might not have been unfaithful to her.

Blaming Beverly helped him to stifle his conscience – but not for long. When he reached home, he found himself tiptoeing up the stairs, his heart in his mouth as if he were an escaped criminal. He felt unclean and it was not until he had locked himself into the privacy of the room he had once shared with Beverly that he felt he could breathe normally again. But he could not sleep. Dawn came before he dozed off and then the twins woke and he heard Beverly go along the passage to their room and try to quieten them before they woke the entire household. For a moment, he felt a desperate urge to get up and go to her; to tell her what had happened and beg her to forgive him, to give him a chance to start again. But even as the feeling swept over him, it passed away. He couldn't tell her . . . couldn't face up to the look in her eyes. And what good could it do? It wouldn't make her more loving – he could hardly expect that. It couldn't stop him wanting Elinor, damn her!

Jonnie buried his face in his pillow and fell into a deep sleep.

By the time he had washed and shaved next day, Jonnie had thought out his explanation of his late arrival home. When Beverly looked over the coffee-pot at breakfast and asked him coolly:

"What time did you come home? I didn't hear you!" he had his answer ready.

"I was pretty late. I had a few too many drinks at the club and slept it off in the car before driving home."

His voice, despite his efforts, sounded sheepish and he was unable to meet her direct gaze. She knew he was lying and he guessed she knew. But she didn't question him. She said:

"You'd better hurry or you'll miss your train!"

After he had left the house, Beverly went up to her room – the spare room – and sat down on her bed. She knew that last night had brought things to a head. Something would have to happen now. They couldn't go on like this, living as two strangers.

She was quite sure Jonnie had not been telling the truth, and she knew she could find out. She had only to phone the club and find out when he had left. If, as he said, he'd got slightly drunk and had decided to sleep it off in the car before driving home, his car would have remained in the car park and someone must have seen him. The club-house was shut up at 11 p.m. and the steward would have gone through the car park on his way home. He would certainly have noticed Jonnie asleep in his car!

But did she want to know? If he hadn't been there, it meant he had been somewhere else and somewhere he should not have been since he felt it worth lying. Elinor! Suppose he had been at Elinor's cottage. What had he been doing till midnight? Talking? Or making love?

Beverly felt sick with her own thoughts. Jonnie, her husband, and another woman. If it were true, she didn't want to know. She couldn't bear to live with it! Yet how could she go on with these horrible suspicions unanswered and poisoning her whole life with Jonnie?

I wish Mother was here! she thought. Yet she knew even if Mrs Bampton were in the room now, she couldn't bring herself to admit she thought her husband was being unfaithful. It was too humiliating. This was something she must fight alone.

"But I can't! I don't know what to do!" Beverly whispered aloud. This was something that happened in books, not to her and Jonnie.

What would she do if it were true? Divorce him? Did she want to spend the rest of her life alone with five children? Did she really want Jonnie out of her life?

Beverly stood up suddenly, her face white and determined. It was far worse to imagine these things than to know. She would telephone the club.

Before she could change her mind, she went quickly into Jonnie's and her bedroom where there was a telephone extension. Trying not to see the large double bed where she had spent so many nights in Jonnie's arms, she put a call through to the club-house.

"This is Mrs Colt," she said when the steward answered. "My husband thinks he might have left his clubs in the bar last night and asked me to ring you and see if you have found them."

"His clubs, Madam? I don't think he had them with him when he came in. Let me see . . . no I remember now, he came straight to the bar when he came in and – yes, that's right – he joined Mrs Wilmot. I was serving them one of Madam's special cocktails. I'm sure he hadn't his clubs with him."

"He might have put them on the floor!" Beverly said, her voice carefully controlled and casual. "Did you notice when he left?"

"I'm afraid I didn't actually see him go. I was cutting sandwiches for a foursome who couldn't wait for dinner to be served. When I came back to the bar, Mr Colt and Mrs Wilmot had both gone."

"That's right; they came back here to a dinner. Well, if you find them, perhaps you would give my husband a ring!"

Beverly put down the phone and sat down on the bed. It was easy, so easy to find out the truth. Surely Jonnie must have known she would find out. Perhaps he didn't care. Perhaps he wanted her to know. Perhaps he wanted a divorce, so he could marry Elinor.

"I hate her . . . I hate her!" Beverly thought, tears trembling on her cheeks. "She can have him. I never want to see him again!"

There was a knock on the door and Annette came in. She looked at Beverly curiously.

"The children are gone away to school, Madame, and I have washed the breakfast things. What should I do now?"

Beverly tried to give her mind to the domestic routine. That had to go on even if her whole life was being broken into little pieces. There was still the washing, the cooking, the ironing, the shopping.

"The shopping, I think, Annette!" she said as calmly as she could. "Take the twins in the pram with you. I'll get on with the washing while you are out. You'll find the list on the kitchen table, and some money."

With Annette out of the way, she could at least have time to think.

As the morning wore on, Beverly tried to make herself believe that she was jumping to the wrong conclusions. Just because Jonnie had spent an hour or two with Elinor there was no reason to condemn him completely. He'd been annoyed and he might just have wanted to teach her a lesson and make her jealous! Jonnie wouldn't be unfaithful to her. He couldn't want to break up their home and leave her and the children.

"I don't care for myself!" she told herself. "It's the children I mind about. Why should they have their home broken! I won't let Jonnie do it for any American female."

It was all Elinor's fault. Ever since Jonnie had met her, their life had begun to go wrong. They'd been quite happy until then.

Impulsively, Beverly flung down the bundle of washing she had been about to put into the machine, and went to the hall telephone. She was annoyed to find her hands trembling violently as she leafed through the pages of the local directory for Elinor's number. But eventually she found it and dialled it.

"20315, Mrs Elinor Wilmot speaking."

"This is Beverly Colt. If it's convenient, I'd like to come round and see you!" Beverly was proud of her cool tone. Her heart might be thumping nervously but at least her voice did not betray her.

There was a moment's pause, and then Elinor's light nasal laugh. "Sure, honey. Come right over! I'm not up yet but I'll pull myself out of bed and make some coffee."

"Don't trouble, please!" Beverly said with icy politeness. "It dooon't matter to me what you look like and I don't want coffee, thank you!" Not quite so polite but Elinor might as well know this was not a social call.

"I'll be seeing you!" was the amused rejoinder and the line went dead.

It took Beverly ten minutes to walk to the station and pick up the car Jonnie left in the yard. Twenty minutes later, she pulled up outside Elinor's cottage and by now was regretting the impulse that had brought her here. Suppose she was wrong? Suppose Elinor wasn't interested in Jonnie! How gauche and stupid she would think her coming here like this! But better Elinor's poor opinion than to go on in uncertainty.

In the half hour since Beverly had phoned, Elinor must have bathed and dressed. She was carefully and skilfully made up. The face she presented to the younger woman was sophisticated and had the same amused look that must have been there when Beverly phoned.

"Come right in and make yourself at home! I've made coffee good and strong and black . . . I need it. Sure you wouldn't like some."

"*I* haven't a hangover!" Beverly said childishly and sat down awkwardly in the arm-chair, putting herself at a physical disadvantage for Elinor now stood poised gracefully by the table, looking down at her.

"Well, what did you want to talk to me about, Mrs Colt?"

"About my husband!" Beverly said on an indrawn breath.

"Does Jonnie know you're here?"

Beverly shook her head.

"Of course not, Mrs Wilmot." She stopped short to look up at Elinor's face, her own suddenly appealing as she met those cool grey eyes. "Mrs Wilmot, was Jonnie here with you last night?"

"Not if Jonnie says he wasn't!"

"Then you mean he was?" As Elinor did not reply, Beverly went on haltingly: "You see, I have to know the truth. If you are having an affair with Jonnie, I'd rather know!"

"And if I'm prepared to say we are, what then?"

Elinor lit a cigarette which she put in a long amber holder and studied Beverly's white face through the smoke. She felt no pity for the girl – only a mild contempt. She must know this wasn't the way to get Jonnie back. He'd be furious when he knew his wife had been prying into his private affairs. If the girl didn't want to lose him altogether, she'd better change her tactics. It didn't occur to Elinor, who was always working out some preconceived plan, that Beverly was acting on impulse, from the heart and without reason.

"I . . . I don't know!"

"You want a divorce?"

Beverly was stung into feeling. How dare this woman question her about a divorce!

"Perhaps you aren't aware of the fact that Jonnie and I have five children!" she flung at her companion.

"Poor Jonnie! No wonder he feels the need for a change."

Beverly flushed. "I'm not going to stay here to be insulted by you," she said violently. "I just wanted to know—"

"If Jonnie and I had been having an affair. Well, I'll tell you, just to satisfy your wifely curiosity. We've started an affair and if I have my way, it will continue. Now you know."

Beverly was once more shocked into anger. "Don't you care about anything but your own horrible feelings?" she cried. "Doesn't it matter at all that you are breaking up my home and my marriage?"

"Care? Why should I care? You don't mean a thing to me. It's up to Jonnie, honey! If he wants me, I'm here. You can tell him I said so. It isn't my fault if he's bored with you!"

Beverly stood up and with a last horrified look at the woman Jonnie presumably loved, she turned and ran out of the room. Behind her, she heard Elinor laugh and one half of her mind was capable of sheer amazement at this woman's callousness. It didn't seem possible that any real person *could* speak as Elinor had done. She hadn't an atom of shame, embarrassment, feeling for anyone – unless it were herself and Jonnie.

Jonnie! Beverly felt sick with shame and humiliation. How could he? How could any man enjoy this woman's company?

Again, one half of her mind remained aloof from her heart, coolly accepting that Elinor was attractive, that there was something feline and powerful about her that made her a dangerous rival; she was ruthless, too. She would break up a home and a marriage as easily as she would crush a fly if it suited her.

She shan't have him! Beverly thought furiously. Not if I can stop it! He can't marry her unless I divorce him and I won't, I won't! Why should I make it easy for them? I won't ever divorce him.

She had a sudden appalling vision of her future, married for the rest of her life to a man who loved someone else. She felt cheapened, revolted and desperately afraid. It was too late now to wish she'd never come, never found out the truth. At least while she was ignorant, she had some hope her suspicions were unfounded. Now there was none. Tonight, Jonnie would come home and they'd have to have it out. Elinor would surely tell him of her visit even if she did not do so herself. What would they say to each other? What was there to say? Jonnie would ask for his freedom and she would refuse him. Or maybe he would be penitent, sorry, ask for her forgiveness.

As if she ever could forgive him or ever be a real wife to him again after this!

The day wore on interminably, Beverly alternately longing for the sound of Jonnie's return and then dreading it. Nick and Philip returned from school and momentarily at least she was too occupied with them to think of much else. But even as she played with them, her mind kept thinking, weighing up, trying to consider what she should do with her life and say to her husband. Perhaps he wouldn't come back! Perhaps he'd go straight to that horrible woman and only come back in the early hours of the morning.

If he does, he won't find me here! Beverly thought violently. Yet immediately followed the question, where could she go? How could she walk out and leave Annette with the responsibility of the five children. What would they think? It wasn't so easy to end a marriage. A mother couldn't just walk out.

I can lock the door against him so he can't come back! Beverly thought. He's forfeited any right to his home and his children.

Yet she had only Elinor's word for it. It wasn't inconceivable that Elinor had lied about last night. She couldn't be sure until Jonnie admitted it.

Shall I tell her? Jonnie was thinking as his train neared home. Wouldn't it be better to tell her? Then I can't be tempted to see Elinor again. Once Beverly knows, she'll make it a condition I never see Elinor again. I'd have to give my word, and then it would all be over.

But did he want it to be over? Wasn't it better to leave things as they were until he was sure what he wanted? He could go and see Elinor and talk it over with her. But that was just an excuse. He knew what would happen when he got inside her house. They couldn't be alone together without passion flaring up between them.

In a few minutes, he'd have to face Beverly. What could he talk about? What lies would he be forced to tell if she questioned him again about last night? He felt mean and utterly miserable. It would have to end. He couldn't go on like this. It had been a rotten day at the office. Everything had gone wrong and he knew he hadn't been concentrating and that most of the mistakes had been of his own making. He was tired and ashamed and appalled by the burning need to see Elinor again soon. At least he might have hoped for some respite after last night.

Jonnie was first surprised and then furious when he found the car had gone from the station. It meant he'd have to walk home. Twice before it had happened when Beverly had needed the car urgently and it was understood between them that she would only take the car without telling him when something unexpected cropped up. What could have happened today?

Jonnie stood stock-still in the station yard as a sudden thought struck him. Had Beverly found out the truth and left him? Had she wanted the car to take herself and the children away to her mother's perhaps?

He was frightened and because he was frightened, he was angry when he reached home and saw the car in the garage. He flung open the front door and shouted for Beverly.

"Why wasn't the car at the station?"

Beverly came to the kitchen door and surveyed Jonnie's flushed face with a curious calm. His anger steadied her.

"Because I needed it!" she said coolly.

"So I have to walk home!" Jonnie said furiously. "If this is your way of teaching me a lesson, I can tell you I shan't put up with it."

"Won't you, Jonnie? Maybe you won't have to much longer!"

"And what's that supposed to mean?" Jonnie asked, following his wife's retreating figure into the kitchen.

"Simply what it suggests; that you may not have to put up with me any longer."

"And why, if I may ask, this hysterical outburst?"

Beverly hesitated. It had come, the moment when she must tell him and he must answer. Perhaps he'd try to lie. But she'd know.

"Jonnie, I took the car today to go and see Elinor Wilmot. She admitted you were having an affair with her. She took care to point out that it had only just begun. Well, I think you should know without me telling you that I'm not going to be the kind of wife who sits quietly in the background and turns a blind eye. Those are the women who want to keep their husbands at any price. I don't want you at any price, Jonnie. That's what I'm telling you."

Jonnie was astounded. He'd never once thought Beverly might go to Elinor. And how could Elinor have been so crazy as to admit the truth?

"Don't try to think up a lie, Jonnie. It's a waste of time. I know what time you went to her house last night and I know what time you left. I'm not so naive I think you sat and played rummy all that time!"

She held her breath, waiting for Jonnie's indignant denial, but it didn't come. Her heart sank. She could not meet his eyes.

"I'm sorry, Beverly. I never meant it to happen. I got a bit tight and—"

"Oh, shut up!" Beverly cried, her nerves at breaking point. "I don't want to hear your apologies or your excuses. I think you're disgusting and contemptible. I hate you! Hate you!"

She pushed past him, and ran out of the room.

"Hell!" Jonnie walked over to the window and stood looking out unseeingly at the garden.

He felt ashamed and unnerved. He knew Beverly would be on her bed crying; he knew that he really ought to pull himself together and try to patch things up. Yet he dreaded the thought of her accusing eyes, her justifiable complaints. He hadn't been such a bad husband, except for this one lapse. Beverly could at least show a little tolerance and understanding. If she tried to help him now, maybe he could get over Elinor! If she'd flung her arms round him, begged him not to do it again, told him she loved him, he would have *wanted* to please her.

What did she mean to do now? Would she ask for a divorce? He was suddenly afraid again. Better go up and see what she intended to do.

He knocked on her door twice before she answered in a muffled voice, "What do you want?"

"Let me in, Beverly. I can't talk out here on the landing."

Beverly unlocked the door and Jonnie went in. They faced one another in an embarrassed silence.

"What do you want?" Beverly said again. Her face was streaked with tears and she knew she looked far from attractive. But she didn't care . . . she wasn't going to care.

"That's what I was going to ask you. What you want to do, Beverly. Do you want a divorce?"

"Do you?"

"No! Apart from us there are the children. I've said I'm sorry, Beverly."

"Go on, say it won't ever happen again. I wouldn't believe you. I'll never believe anything you say again, Jonnie. I just don't understand you any more. *How could you*? Are you in love with her? Do you want to marry her?"

"Good God, no!" That at least he was sure of. "It's so difficult to explain, Beverly. I don't expect you to understand. It's just that there's something between Elinor and me that we can't deny. We've fought against it and I swear that's true. I never meant it to happen."

"But you wanted it to happen!" Beverly said. "Deep inside you wanted her, Jonnie, the way you once wanted me."

"No, it wasn't the same!" Jonnie said with conviction. "There is no love, Beverly. Try to understand."

Beverly drew in her breath sharply. "I don't think I want to understand. I find it all quite revolting. I suppose it's all sex if it isn't love. That makes it more disgusting in a way. You've betrayed me and the children for something completely worthless."

"I . . . I suppose you're right. It won't happen again."

"Won't it? How do I know? How do *you* know, Jonnie? You said you fought against it. Yet you weakened in the end. It could happen again, and again, and again. I'm not sharing you, Jonnie, understand that. You've got to choose between your American mistress and your wife. She might be willing to share, but I'm not. Either we move house or she does. If the attraction between you two is so devastating, then the greater the distance between you the better."

Jonnie shrugged his shoulders. "I don't see how it can be done. We can't afford to move house and Elinor certainly won't go just because you or I ask her to. You'll just have to trust me, Beverly."

"Trust you?" Beverly cried. "How can I? You've lied and cheated, Jonnie. It'll be a long time before I trust you again."

"I see! It's pretty obvious the pleasant choice I'm faced with; to continue this wretched kind of existence with a wife who's always suspicious of every moment I'm not with her, who admits she no longer cares about me; or to lose my home and children if I want to be with the woman who does love and appreciate me."

"Appreciate you? In bed, I suppose you mean. I agree you make a very good lover, Jonnie, and no doubt you excel yourself with your precious Elinor. But love? I doubt if you or she know the meaning of the word. I don't see how you can expect me to love you again. Not a very happy prospect for me, either. But it's a decision of your own making. I hope you're very very happy about it."

Jonnie hesitated. In a way it was such a tremendous relief not having to lie any more, that he couldn't feel as appalled as he knew he should have done. Now at least he could look his wife in the face.

"Look, Beverly, I *know* I've behaved rottenly. I know how terrible it must seem to you. I understand how you must hate me. Try to believe me when I tell you that I hate myself probably much more than you do. I've betrayed everything we both valued and I know it. But can't you *try* to understand? I don't love her; I don't want to break up our home and leave you and the kids. It's just that . . . well, I couldn't promise never to see her again. I don't know if I could keep that promise. I've been trying for weeks to fight against this need for her. Give me a little time; let me fight it my way."

Beverly clenched her hands against her sides, her mind in a turmoil of doubt and indecision. The more mature side of her nature spoke a warning: You don't want to lose him. Do as he asks and don't force the issue. He says he doesn't really want her," but the passionate, impulsive, loving side cried out in bitterness. Why should he get away with this? What right had he to hurt her, humiliate her? What kind of a woman could this be to try to take a man deliberately from his wife, his children; smash up a home as if it meant no more than a pack of cards? And for this female, Jonnie was asking her to sit back and take second place.

"There isn't going to be a fight, Jonnie. I'm not going to wrangle with any woman for my husband. It's really quite simple. Give her up and we'll try to make a new life out of the ruins. Go on seeing her, making love to her, and I'll divorce you. I won't *share* you, Jonnie."

Her voice was vibrant with feeling, her cheeks flushed a bright red, her eyes flashing with the outraged feeling that hurt pride had brought to the fore. Inopportunely, Jonnie thought suddenly: How pretty she is! Then the meaning of her words sank into his consciousness and he knew that she was giving him an ultimatum.

"But I don't like ultimatums!" He spoke his thoughts aloud, his voice strangely quiet, cool.

"Oh, no!" Beverly cried scathingly. "You want your cake and you want to eat it as well!" Jonnie remembered Elinor's use of the same quotation. "Well, you're my husband, Jonnie, and if you want another woman in your life, then you can pay the price. I'll divorce you all right. And I'll get the children. You aren't fit to be their father. No wonder Nick's growing up the way he is. A fine example you turned out to be . . ." Suddenly her voice broke and, without warning, the tears coursed down her cheeks. Angrily, she brushed them away, and, pushing past Jonnie, she left the room.

"Hell!" Jonnie said aloud to the empty room. "Damn, blast and *hell*!" and hurried downstairs to the dining-room.

He walked across to the sideboard and poured himself a stiff drink. It steadied him and stilled the desire to run after Beverly. Let her go! Let her think for a moment what divorce would mean. Once she realized its implications, she wouldn't think it such a fine thing. Where would his income go with two homes to run? It was all very well for Elinor to say *she* had money. As if Beverly would ever touch a penny of her money. Or would she? Maybe she would get every penny she could from Elinor. Enticement, wasn't it? But he'd hate to think of Elinor's money helping to raise his children.

The kids . . . always the kids. Divorce might be easy enough when there were no children. But they had *five* and he loved them. Whatever Beverly said about him being a bad father, he'd always loved them.

White-faced, Jonnie paced the room. His anger turned against Elinor. This was all her fault. Until she'd put in an appearance, his life had been pretty trouble free. Oh, it had been difficult at times and dull, maybe, and devoid of that heady excitement. But at least it had been a calm, ordered life without these ghastly rows and scenes.

They couldn't go on. In a way Beverly was right. There wasn't a compromise. Either he must give up Elinor or give up his home.

"I'll give her up!" Jonnie thought, suddenly calm. "I'll go now and tell her it's all over. *She* won't make a scene. I'll do it now, this minute, before I grow weak again."

He went to the kitchen door and as calmly as he could, told Annette he was going out for an hour.

He drove to Elinor's cottage in five minutes flat. This time he felt no anxiety as to whether the car would be seen, recognized. He slammed the car door and without knocking or ringing, strode into the living-room.

Elinor was stretched out on the hearthrug like a large Persian cat. Her hair, which she was drying before an electric fire, was spread all around her bare shoulders. A loose towelling bath-robe had slipped down so that it only half covered her beautiful up-turned breasts. She didn't move her body, only turning her head to smile at him lazily and say in that deep-throated voice of hers:

"Jonnie, *darling*! What a lovely surprise."

"God, you're beautiful!" he said, standing there, staring at her, knowing that he must never hold that body in his arms again, never possess her again, never be possessed. The mere thought only increased her desirability. Had she been forewarned of Jonnie's arrival, she could not have put herself in a more favourable light. The glow of the electric fire flickered on her shoulders, was softening to the lines about her mouth and eyes. The gentle flow of hair was somehow young, innocent looking. Never had she looked less evil.

And I had been telling myself she was bad, bad! Jonnie thought.

"Well, come and sit down, my sweet!" Elinor said, holding out her arms invitingly. "Why, Jonnie, what's the matter? Aren't you well?"

"It's Beverly!" Jonnie said flatly, dramatically. "She knows everything, Elinor. I've come to say goodbye!"

Elinor picked up her hairbrush and slowly began to brush her hair in steady, smooth strokes. Her face was turned away from him now, in profile. He believed she was suffering from shock and trying to control her unhappiness. In actual fact, her mind was teeming with conflicting thoughts.

What a bore this is! Why can't he forget about that stupid girl he married? He's so young – so immature! But that's what I like about him too. He doesn't know all the answers; he's gentle and kind and romantic. It's such a lovely change after . . . But this is too tiresome, this hopping about between us. Is he worth fighting for any more? We have fun . . . there's no one else and he's young and sweet.

"Elinor, for pity's sake say something. Say you understand."

He wanted her to reject him and to make going easier for him. She knew it but her ears were deliberately deaf to the appeal in his voice. She said softly:

"You've always been straight with me, Jonnie. You never pretended you loved me. I can't blame you. I don't want to. I just want to go on loving you, Jonnie. Oh, life is so unfair!"

He saw her suddenly quite differently. This was no longer the sophisticated, self-assured young widow. This was a lonely, unwanted woman rich in everything but love. He knew he was hurting her, and hated himself for it just as he had hated himself for hurting Beverly. What a mess he'd made of it all!

"Elinor, you've got to understand. Beverly's given me an ultimatum. If I go on seeing you, she'll divorce me. I'll lose my children."

He went across the room and, kneeling beside her, took her two hands in his own. Her hair was falling across her face and he could not see if she was crying though he felt her body shaking.

"Elinor, you'll find someone else, you're so lovely. If you knew how lovely, how utterly desirable you are . . ."

She lifted her face then, and a moment later she was lying against him, her arms holding him tightly, her body pressed against his own.

"I don't expect your love, Jonnie. I've always known I had no right to that. I don't ask you to divorce her. I only want to be able to see you sometimes, be with you, be close to you. Surely she can't deny me this small part of you? She can't be so selfish that she wants to deny you everything. She doesn't need you the way I do."

Jonnie struggled against his own desperate weakness.

"Don't you see, it isn't like that, Elinor? She has been brought up differently. She could never accept the kind of terms you are willing to accept. She's my wife and she has a right to expect me to – to be faithful."

103

"Has she, Jonnie? Does a piece of paper and a ring give her the right to own you, body and soul? Isn't it really only love that gives a person that right over another human being? Does she love you? Can she love you the way I do?"

"No, no, it's not your way." The words broke from him. "It's different, Elinor, but it means as much to her."

"I wonder if it does," Elinor said softly. "Real love means giving, doesn't it, Jonnie? If she really loved you the way you seem to think she does, she'd want you to be happy. Even if it meant she had to give up one of her ideals. I'd give you up, Jonnie. I won't try to keep you, not if that's the way I *know* you want it. You've got to convince me that you don't want me or need me any more. Don't you, Jonnie? Look at me, darling. Say you don't care."

"I can't, I can't!" The man all but groaned the words. "When I'm with you, only this seems right. Everything else pales into insignificance beside my need for you. I don't know if it's love – I don't know what love is any more. But when we're not together I know this is wrong."

"How can it be wrong?" Elinor said softly, one hand gently stroking his hair from his forehead, the other warm and soft against the back of his neck. "We're meant for each other, we were made for each other. You know that and I know it. We can't be apart, Jonnie."

Suddenly, abruptly, he stood up, pulling her hands roughly away from him. His face was chalk-white; his whole body trembled as he said: "I've got to try to live without you. I've got to. Maybe I won't succeed. Maybe I'll be back, if you still want me. But I must try . . . I must."

He'd given her the one loop-hole she needed, the one card left to play.

Slowly, gracefully, like a cat, she rose to her feet. Gently, she bent forward and kissed him, the mere touch of a kiss against his lips. "All right," she whispered. "I know in my heart you'll come back, and I'll be waiting, Jonnie. I'll be waiting all the time."

With one last tortured look at her, Jonnie fled from the room.

Smiling, Elinor heard the door bang, then the car door, and finally the sound of the car engine disappearing into the distance.

All men were weak, Jonnie more than most. "Maybe I'll be back
. . ." he had said, even at the moment of going. Yes, he'd be back,
and next time he returned, it would be for keeps.

She curled herself once more in front of the fire and slowly began
again to brush her hair.

Beverly heard the front door close behind Jonnie and a sudden icy
chill settled over her heart. What had she done? What had she done?
He'd asked for her help, her understanding, and she'd given him
neither. Now he'd gone. Perhaps for always. Perhaps this was the
end – the end of love, of marriage.

"Did . . . did Mr Colt say where he was going?" she asked the
startled Annette.

"He just said that he was going out for one hour," Annette said in
her halting English. "At least, I think he said for one hour. Is
something wrong, Madame?"

Beverly did not answer. What could she answer? Jonnie had gone.
He could only have gone to Elinor. She had sent him there. She had
no one but herself to blame.

What can I do, what can I *do*? she thought frantically. To whom
to turn for help, for advice? Her very nature demanded action – any
action. It would be a physical impossibility to sit here in this house,
waiting to see if Jonnie was coming back.

She could phone her mother. But she knew what her mother
would say. She'd say that Beverly must wait, and when Jonnie came
in, behave as if nothing had happened; wait for him to show his
hand. He'd said he didn't want a divorce. He couldn't get free unless
she chose to divorce him and she wouldn't – not ever. Elinor should
never have him.

But it wasn't true that he couldn't go. He'd gone. Maybe he didn't
care about a divorce. Maybe Elinor didn't even want to marry him.
She had cast some spell over him so that he'd lost all decency, all
knowledge of what was right and wrong. He might be with her now,
holding her in his arms . . .

"Annette, I have to go out for a little while. There is nothing to
worry about. It's . . . it's Mrs Adams," she lied swiftly, easily. "She
isn't very well and we are all rather concerned."

105

"But of course I manage," Annette said imperturbably. "Please not to worry, Madame. All will come well to the end."

Slipping a coat over her shoulders, Beverly ran out of the house. In the cool darkness, she paused, uncertainly. She'd meant to go to Sue, but now that her first steps were turned towards Sue's house, she knew she couldn't go. Pride forbade it. Sue would feel so sorry for her and she couldn't bear anyone's pity.

Then where else? She had so few really close friends. Allan? Allan Forbes? He would understand, guard her secret. He would tell her what to do.

She began to run, increasing her pace as a kind of hysterical panic took control of her. Now the night had suddenly become an enemy. The half-light seemed full of shadows, the branches of the trees long, ghostly arms that were reaching for her, to clutch at her and prevent her escape.

Blindly, she ran on until the narrowness of the lane that led to Allan's cottage forced her to slow her pace. Her heart still raced and her thoughts were still incoherent but somehow she managed to stumble forward, tearing her stockings on hedgerow brambles, uncaring, unseeing.

When at last she saw the orange square of light shining from the window of Allan's cottage, she gave a gasp of relief. He was there; it was all that mattered. Allan was there and soon she would be safe.

When he opened the front door to her feverish knocking, the man stared aghast at the dishevelled figure who fell forward into his arms.

"Beverly!" he said in a shocked voice. "My dear, whatever has happened?"

He drew her quickly inside the room and closed the door against the darkness. Then he led her towards his own easy-chair and gently pushed her into it, smoothing the tangle of her hair back from her forehead and then turning away from her to switch on the electric fire.

Beverly watched him with a rapt concentration, unaware of the tears running down her cheeks. She knew she was shivering and she was so glad of the fire. It was all she could think about, she felt so cold.

"I'm going to make a cup of tea and lace it with brandy," Allan said with a calmness he was far from feeling. "I won't be long. Wait here."

"No, no, don't go, don't leave me alone!"

Her voice arrested him half-way to the door. More quietly, she added:

"I don't want anything, really, Allan. I'm so sorry. I shouldn't have come . . ."

Despite her protest, he went to the corner cupboard and poured her a glass of brandy. Then he stood by her until she had had at least three mouthfuls. Slowly, the colour began to return to her cheeks, burning more brightly until they were a feverish red. His anxiety for her mounted. What could have happened?

"Feeling any better?" he asked, his voice so full of his concern for her that suddenly Beverly felt she could not bear it. Kindness now was too much. This time she cried openly, noisily, like a child.

His face twisting with the sudden rush of emotions that had overcome him, Allan leant forward and took her in his arms.

"Don't, don't!" he whispered. "I can't bear to see you like this. Beverly, *darling*. Don't cry. Whatever it is will be all right, I promise it will. I'll make it all right."

In the midst of her own hysteria, she heard his voice, his words, and knew suddenly that this man loved her. It surprised yet somehow did not shock her. Deep inside, she felt she must always have known how he felt.

That's why I came to him, she thought, her mind suddenly cool and clear. I knew deep down inside that I could trust him, that he'd help me.

"Oh, Allan!" she whispered. "I know I shouldn't have come. I'm so sorry, but I . . . I needed you so."

"I'm glad you came." She heard his voice, filled with tenderness, against her hair.

Gently, he released her and, walking away from her, sat down on the other side of the fireplace, looking down at his hands for a moment. Then, with studied calm, he began to fill his pipe. By the time he had it lit, both were once more in control of themselves.

"Want to talk about it?" he asked as casually as he could. "Maybe I can help?"

Beverly pushed the hair away from her eyes and drew a deep, trembling breath.

"I do want . . . I came . . . it's . . ." She saw his eyes crinkle at the corners in that sudden sweet smile, and then she too was smiling. "I'll try again. Allan, I came because I couldn't think who else to turn to. I just rushed out of the house in a kind of blind, crazy panic. I didn't know what to do, you see, and I could only think of you. You've been so kind . . ."

Her voice trailed away uncertainly.

"Beverly, I'm *glad* you came. Let us be completely honest with each other and trust one another. I think you came because you knew how I felt about you. I've tried not to admit it even to myself, but when I saw you in the doorway just now, I couldn't deny the truth. I love you. I think I loved you the very first time I saw you. I know you don't feel this way about me and that's a good thing, for we have no right to love one another. You're someone else's wife and I've never forgotten that. I want only that you should know of my feelings so that you will understand that you can ask me anything, tell me anything, trust me. There isn't anything in the world I wouldn't do for you."

"Oh, Allan," Beverly whispered. "I know I ought not to be glad, but I am, I am. I can't be a very nice person, can I? To be pleased about something like this? I suppose it's vanity. But if you knew what had just happened to me, maybe you'd understand."

Allan drew deeply on his pipe and looked across at her.

"Then tell me. Clearly you'd had a shock, a bad one. You are not the kind of woman to rush out of your house at this time of night without cause. Beverly, your husband hasn't *hit* you? If he did, I'll—"

"No, no, no!" Beverly broke in. "Jonnie hasn't touched me. It's just that . . . Allan, I think he's gone to Elinor for good. He's been having an affair with her for some time. I guessed it but I wasn't sure. Today I went to see her. It was a stupid thing to do. She admitted everything. This evening, Jonnie and I had it out. He told me she had some kind of hold over him, that he couldn't promise to give her up. He said he didn't want a divorce, but still he wouldn't promise not to go on seeing her. Allan, how can a man expect his wife to *share* him with another woman? I couldn't. I know in books and magazines and things, they say the wife who wants to keep her husband should turn a blind eye, be that much nicer, even more understanding, make herself more attractive. But it isn't like that in real life . . . it isn't!"

Appalled, Allan listened to the rush of words, hearing them and believing them, yet still not understanding how any man could behave towards his wife in such a way and to Beverly of all people, who was so unsophisticated, so unworldly wise. What kind of a man must he be to ask his wife to *share* him with his mistress. No wonder she was so shocked, so hurt.

"And when you told him he had to choose, he chose *her*?" he asked quietly.

Beverly shook her head.

"No! He said he didn't want a divorce or to leave me and the children. He even said he didn't love her. He wanted time to fight against his own weakness for her, I suppose. But I had to know one way or another. I couldn't have gone on living in the same house, never knowing if he was going to give her up or leave me. I told him he must choose or I'd divorce him. Then he left the house and I know he went straight to her. I made him, Allan, that's the awful thing. Perhaps if I had given him time, he'd have stayed."

"Then you do still love him?"

"I hate him!" Beverly cried violently; then, more calmly, she said: "I don't know. I suppose I must still care to mind so desperately and to be so hurt. How could he, Allan? After all this time? I know I'm far from perfect; there's lots of ways I must have irritated him and failed him. But I've never looked at anyone else, and never once in my life considered anything or anyone but Jonnie and the children. They've *been* my life. I knew something was wrong between us a long time ago and that we'd grown apart some way. I just didn't know what was causing it. I thought if we could get away together alone for a bit, without the children, it would all come right. I never once imagined it was anything serious. Jonnie promised he'd come. I'd made all the arrangements, and then at the last moment he called off. Because of *her*. I see now, but I couldn't see it then. Allan, what am I to do? Should I let him go? Should I give him his divorce? What about the children?"

Allan Forbes remained silent. As she was speaking, the wild thought rushed through his mind. If she divorced her husband, she would be free to marry me. I'd make her happy and be a good father to those children. I could love them, too, since they are part of her. I'd never be lonely again. My life would have meaning and purpose . . .

But he couldn't say these things to her. He had no right to influence her to such a decision. He was sufficiently modern in his outlook to know that divorce was sometimes necessary, but when there were children it must always be the very last resort. Besides, he was far from certain that Beverly was out of love with her husband. Disillusioned she might be and deeply hurt, but that need not necessarily destroy love; not a real, deep-rooted love between a man and a woman.

"I think you should do nothing at all, at the moment," he said at last. "I realize that isn't easy. But from all you've said, my dear, it doesn't sound as if Jonnie really wants to bust up his home. I think if you can find some way to give him a little time, he'll give her up. There's no need to *share*. Just stay quietly for a week or two somewhere in the background."

"But I don't know if I *want* to be there!" Beverly cried passionately. "Why should I sit back and wait for Jonnie to come home? I don't know if I *want* him back."

"That's something else you have to think about, carefully," Allan said with deep sincerity. "You speak now from hurt pride. Do you really want to lose him? He's the father of your children. Have you a right to take them away from him?"

"He's forfeited all right to them," Beverly cried.

"Yes, but *they've* done nothing to deserve the loss of their father," Allan said with a calm he was far from feeling. "You have to decide for all of them as well as for yourself."

"I thought *you* might understand," Beverly said bitterly. "Apparently you think a man has a right to do this to a woman and get away with it. Suppose I had been unfaithful to Jonnie? Everyone would condemn me because I am a woman. It's different for a man. But why?"

"I think it's just that men and women are different and that probably most women are stronger than men and that they love more deeply. It makes it easier for them to be faithful."

"I think it's horrible!" Beverly burst out. "I couldn't ever trust him or respect him again. Yet I don't want my home broken up. I don't think I could bring up five children alone. I'm not strong enough. I know boys need a father – not that Jonnie's been much of a father lately. And there's the money side of it, too. We're not well off. If I divorced Jonnie, I suppose all that would be worse still."

"You might marry again," Allan said hesitantly. "You're young and very attractive."

Beverly gave a sardonic laugh. "Jonnie doesn't seem to have found me so. And, besides, who'd take on five children? No, Jonnie has it all his way. He must have known all along how dependent I am on him. It isn't fair, Allan. Even if I wanted to divorce him, you've shown me I couldn't afford it."

Allan looked at the flushed face before him, the hurt, bewildered, unhappy face of a little girl. She looked so incredibly young with her nose shining and the tears still wet on her cheeks. Inconsequently, he said:

"Most women look awful when they cry. You look about six years old, and very sweet!"

Suddenly she was crying again, this time in his arms.

"It isn't fair," she sobbed. "Life isn't fair."

With great tenderness, he turned her face upwards and touched her lips with his own.

"I used to say that," he said softly. "After Louise and my boy died. But life has its compensations. You and I at least have known love, even if we both have lost it. Do you know that poem, Beverly, called 'The Penalty of Love'?"

"No, say it to me." She chocked against another sob.

"All right. It goes like this:

"If love should count you worthy, and should deign
One day to seek your door and be your guest,
Pause! ere you draw the bolt and bid him rest,
If in your old content you would remain,

111

For not alone he enters; in his train
Are angels of the mist, the lonely quest,
Dreams of the unfulfilled and unpossessed,
And sorrow, and Life's immemorial pain.

He wakes desires you never may forget,
He shows you stars you never saw before,
He makes you share with him, for evermore,
The burden of the world's divine regret.
How wise you were to open not! and yet,
How poor if you should turn him from the door!"

Neither spoke for a moment as Allan's voice ceased. Then Beverly looked up, smiling through her tears, and said:

"It's said, and yet it's true, too. I wish I'd met you before – years ago. I feel somehow as if we have understood each other . . . been very close to each other. You said just now you loved me, yet we are strangers in fact. But I can understand, because somewhere inside me, I, too, have a strange feeling of belonging. Allan, would we have been happy? Would *you* have grown tired of me. Bored with me? Found someone else?"

"I can't answer that," Allan said with a smile. "I believed there was only one love for each person in this strange world of ours. When I met and married Louise, I knew I had found my love; that I could never want anyone else ever; that I could never love anyone else. Yet here I am, as much in love with you, my dear, as I ever was with her. Don't you remember the old song, 'It's when you think you're past love, then you meet your last love, and you love her as you never loved before'."

"Oh, Allan," Beverly said. "I know I ought not to be glad – in a way it only complicates everything still more . . . but I am glad you love me. I can't help it. It isn't just because . . . well, because it's flattering to my vanity after the kind of knock mine has had. It's more than that. I like you so much. When I'm with you, everything seems so right, so much what it should be. Does that sound crazy? It's a kind of peace you bring me. When I'm not with you, I feel like a bit of elastic stretched to breaking point. Now, like this, it's as if I have been released."

She lifted her head and looked into his face with sudden curiosity.

"This seems so strange, so unbelievable!" she said softly. "I don't understand anything any more. I don't know what made me come to you; I'd no real plan in mind. I had no idea when I rushed out of the house that you loved me."

Allan gave a half-smile. "Would it have made any difference if you had known? I hope not! I hope you'll always turn to me when you're in trouble."

"It seems so selfish to say 'of course, I will!' Allan, what is going to happen? It's all such a mess. You say I should go back and wait for Jonnie to come to his senses. But I don't want to do that. I'm not even sure I *care* whether Jonnie comes back at all."

He looked into the green uncertain depths of her eyes. He could see the pain, the bewilderment as clearly as he could read their beauty and innocence. What was this husband of hers *really* like? Would he be right to send her back to more humiliation? Or could he tell her to stay here, with him, to be looked after, protected, warmed back to life again.

"You must go back!" he said, his voice suddenly harsh. "You have to think of your children first, Beverly. Besides, the vows we make on our wedding day are for better *or for worse*. For worse, too, my dear. You must try to forgive, to start again. I'm sure it will come right and that you will find your love for your husband again."

"Will I?" Beverly asked doubtfully, her voice so like that of a small, frightened child, that for a moment Allan was desperately tempted to hold her to him in a passion of protective love. But he mustn't. Neither must he allow his own feelings for her to influence her against her duty. Perhaps already, by speaking of his love for her, he had done her marriage harm.

Abruptly, he walked away from her and stood with his back towards her, staring out of the uncurtained window into the darkness.

"I'm going to take you home," he said quietly. "You can't stay here, Beverly. I'm the respected local schoolmaster. I'd get the sack for harbouring a beautiful married woman in my house at this time of night."

His voice was casual, almost bantering, and Beverly looked at the strong, squared shoulders uncertainly.

Of course she could not stay here. She should not really have come at all. Poor Allan – inflicted with an hysterical woman at this time of night. She glanced at the clock over the mantelpiece. Ten fifteen. Annette would be wondering where she was. And for the first time in her life, she hadn't kissed the children good night.

"Yes, I'll go back now," she said. "I can go by myself, Allan. There's no need for you to come."

He turned towards her again, his face strangely twisted. "You don't think I'd let you go alone? Here's your coat. Would you like to tidy up a little first?"

Obediently, Beverly went to the bathroom and tidied her hair, washed her face. She felt calmer, certain at least that whatever tomorrow might hold for her, she *would* go back now, tonight. Maybe Jonnie had come home. And if he had? Her thoughts ended there. She did not want to think about Jonnie.

"Coming?" Allan's voice, quiet and matter of fact, steadied her. Together they went out of the house into the darkness. At once, she felt Allan's hand reach for her own and hold it tight. As her eyes became accustomed to the dark, she could see the firm, true lines of his profile. Quite suddenly, she felt a new rush of emotion assail her – a kind of electric current passing through their joined hands from one to the other.

What is happening to me? she thought. This is the first time in my life I've felt this way towards any man but Jonnie. What does Allan really mean to me? He has said he loves me. How can he know? We've only seen each other twice before this. Is my whole world going completely mad?

Of course, Allan must be terribly lonely. He'd lost the wife and child he loved and she reminded him of Louise. Was this bad for him? Was she inadvertently going to bring him a new loneliness, a fresh pain, just when he had learned to accept life as it was?

"Allan, are you happy?" she asked suddenly, breaking the silence between them.

She felt the pressure of his hand on hers and heard the quick intake of his breath.

"Like this, walking in the dark with you, yes! But I could not be completely happy unless I thought you were happy, too. It's all I want, my dear, your happiness. Do you believe that?"

"Yes, yes I do!" Beverly said. "But you mustn't be too unselfish, Allan. If we . . . if we're going to be friends, you must let me do some of the giving, too. I should be miserable if I thought that in any way you were unhappy because of me."

"I know. You don't have to say these things. I understand. And, Beverly, it isn't '*if*' we are going to be friends. We are – we were right from the start. That is true, isn't it?"

"Yes!"

They walked on, not hurrying their steps. To the girl, it was now as if she were in some kind of prolonged dream. It had begun as a nightmare – truly that wild rush along this same path had been a nightmare – but now all fear had gone and there was only peace. Nothing had been solved, yet her mind and heart were calmed and even happy. She knew this was because of Allan. Further, she would not question.

As they came to the end of the footpath where it joined the road, they both stopped as if by mutual consent. They turned towards one another and once more, as if in a dream, Beverly lifted her arms round Allan's neck and a moment later his lips were warm and hard against her own.

It had been a long time since any man had kissed her with love. Warm-hearted and passionate by nature, Beverly felt her whole body respond to this man with desperate need.

Why not? she thought wildly. Jonnie doesn't want me. He's found someone else. Allan needs me. We've both been alone.

For Allan, it was a brief moment of weakness, too. He'd never meant to kiss her. Beverly was another man's wife and could never belong to *him*. Perhaps it was this very knowledge that made him weak. As their steps had slowed at the end of the footpath, he'd known that he must soon lose her; that they might never be so close together again. When her arms went round him, he felt such a wild rush of longing for her, that his resistance was no more than momentary. But even as he felt her response, the demand of her mouth on his, her body soft and willing against his own, his conscience still told him that this was wrong. However right it might seem at this moment, he *knew* it was wrong.

"Beverly! Darling!" He drew away from her, trembling and deeply moved. "Not this way, my very dear, my darling. I love you too much. It could only be right if we were free."

The words hung between them, cold and factual. Slowly, Beverly's heart ceased its wild beating and she knew that Allan was right. She wasn't free. She had no more right to kiss Allan, be kissed by him, than Jonnie had to kiss Elinor. She had despised him for the same weakness and his wrong could not make the principle any different for her and Allan.

"Beverly?" She knew without words that he was asking for her understanding. He wasn't withdrawing his love for her, his need for her.

"It's all right, I know!" she whispered. "Dear Allan, I'm sorry."

She could just discern the half-smile on his face. His voice was like that of a naughty schoolboy as he said:

"I'm not – not really. I wanted it so much. But now you *must* go home, Beverly. Next time, I might not have the strength to leave you."

Reaching up, Beverly touched his lips very lightly with her own and then, before he had realized her intention, had run away from him into the darkness. He was about to follow her, afraid for her alone in the night at this late hour, but then remembered her house was only a few minutes' walk away. No harm would come to her and it was better this way. If he'd run into that husband of hers, he'd have surely done something wild and crazy.

Walking home, Allan tried to steady his thoughts. This whole evening had been so utterly unexpected. Had he been prepared, he could, perhaps, have controlled his emotions better. But with Beverly arriving as she had, shocked, hurt, unhappy and so much in need of him, how could he have denied his love for her?

And I do love her! he thought, without surprise, for now love had come to him a second time, it was almost as if he had never been without this deepest of all emotions. He tried to think of Louise but it was always Beverly's face that came into his mind. They were so alike. It had some strange effect on his mind and heart, as if the two were one. And because Louise was his – his love and his wife – it seemed as if Beverly must be, too, although he *knew* it was not so.

As he returned once more to his own sitting room; aware now of its emptiness, its quiet, yet filled with the memory of the girl who had been there, Allan fought with his heart. He knew he was hoping desperately that Beverly's marriage might crack completely. That was the only way he could have her. Yet he despised himself for the hope, the wish. He was as weak as that husband of hers. It was one thing to be strong and righteous when temptation wasn't there; another to be strong when one's whole mind, heart, body and soul, longed so deeply for what must not be.

It's madness to think this way! he told himself with an effort. She doesn't love me. She was just finding in my love a shadow of what she believed she had lost in Jonnie.

Despite her denials, she must still love her husband. Otherwise she would have been indifferent to his unfaithfulness. You can only be hurt by another human being, deeply hurt, when you care for them. Your pride can be hurt, but not you, not deep down.

Suddenly terribly alone and unhappy, he leant his arms on the mantelshelf and bowed his head.

"Oh, Louise!" he whispered the words aloud. "If you are somewhere now with God, pray for me, help me. Don't let me hope for what can never be mine."

But it was Beverly's faint, elusive presence that filled the cottage and seemed to follow him to his own room, her face which haunted the shadows round his bed and finally his dreams.

Nine

B everly opened the back door of her house and feeling her way across the kitchen switched on the light. The room was neat, tidy and warm from the boiler which Annette must have made up before going to bed. On the table top was a note.

> Madame,
>   I have retired to bed. The tea-tray for the morning is on the dresser ready for you. The children are asleep and all is well.
>
> Annette

All is well! Beverly sighed and went across to the electric kettle and filled it to make a cup of tea. Presently, she would put it on a second time for her hot-water bottle.

As she held the kettle under the tap, she heard the kitchen door open. Swinging round, she saw Jonnie standing in the doorway. His face looked twisted and – she sought for the right word and found it – crumpled. In his hand was a half-empty glass. She knew then why he looked so different. He was tight – or drunk.

"So you've decided to come home?" His voice was slurred and he shifted uneasily on his feet.

Beverly bit her lip and forced herself to continue with her job of making tea. "So have you, Jonnie. Now we're all here."

"Where've you been?"

"Out!" Beverly said crisply. "What about you?"

Her tone of voice checked him. She was different. This wasn't the tearful, strained Beverly he had left behind. This was a cool, collected young woman – someone strange. He wished he hadn't had so many whiskies and that he could think more clearly.

118

"Don't bother to answer that!" Beverly said quickly. "Obviously you've been with *her*. I hope you had a pleasant evening? I imagine she gave you a good dinner?"

Jonnie stared at her and shook his head. "No dinner!" he mumbled. "Thatsh the trouble."

"Oh, I see! Too much champagne on an empty stomach. You're drunk, Jonnie." As he came towards her, she backed away from him, some of her coolness and calm deserting her. "Don't come near me! Don't touch me!"

He gave her a stupid smile. "Thatsh no way to treat your husband. 'Sno way to keep him anyway. Your fault if I've drunk too much. Should have been home."

Beverly's face whitened. "Why? Sit back and wait for you to come back from *her*? No, thank you, Jonnie. I've better things to do."

"Where've you been?" Jonnie asked again, slumping into a kitchen chair and leaning over the table.

"It's no concern of yours, Jonnie."

"Afraid to tell me. With Forbes, I sh'pose. Not with Sue, anyway. Must have been lying. No need to lie if it was above board." He was almost talking to himself, but suddenly he looked up and said sharply, "Were you with Forbes?"

Beverly poured the now boiling water into the pot and spilled a little on the table as her hand shook.

"Yes, I was. He's one of the few friends I have. I needed a friend. You see, I didn't know what to do, Jonnie. I thought my life was finished. I was all in pieces and I thought Allan could help me. He did."

"Did he? Perhaps he can do the same for me."

Beverly poured out two cups of tea and pushed one across the table at Jonnie. She might be behaving strangely towards him, but his behaviour, his words, were just as strange-sounding to her.

"Surely *you* don't need help?" she said, unable to prevent the sarcasm from sharpening her voice. "It's really quite a simple decision for you, Jonnie. All you've got to do is make up your mind which of us you want: Elinor or me."

"Made up my mind. S'all over!" Jonnie said sadly. "Thas why I went to see her. To tell her s'all over."

Beverly sat down suddenly and stared at Jonnie aghast. "You mean you've finished with her? For always?"

"S'right!" He smiled again, stupidly.

Beverly stood up again, her mind whirling. It had happened. What she had wanted so much had happened. Jonnie had come back and it was all over. Now everything could be as it was before. *But could it?* Could it be the same? Did she still love him? Relief that now there was no longer any problem was there, uppermost in her mind. But what about her heart? Why couldn't she fling herself into Jonnie's arms and tell him how happy she was; how wonderful it was of him to come back!

"Is Elinor going away?" she asked.

Jonnie looked surprised. "Don't think so. Don't know. We didn't discush that."

"Jonnie, drink that tea, please. Perhaps it will sober you up. I want to get this straight. You say it's all over. Is it? Have you stopped wanting her or have you just done this because I asked you?"

"Don't want to bust up the home. Got to think of the kids!" Jonnie said. Suddenly he laughed. "My God, five of them, too. However did we have so many? Must have been mad."

"Jonnie!" Her voice pulled him up and he stopped laughing.

"Whatsa matter?"

"Please drink that tea!"

He did so, shook his head as if trying to clear it and then said suddenly: "Don't you want me back, Bev? What's happened? Don't you love me any more?"

Beverly felt a sudden desperate desire to cry. But she would not. This time she would not do so.

"I don't know, Jonnie," she said honestly. "I don't know. I want it all to be as if this hadn't ever happened. It all seems like some terrible dream from which I can't wake up. But I don't see how it can ever be the same as it was. Please don't think I'm not grateful that you want to keep the home together. I'm glad you feel it's worth it. But love . . . you don't love me, Jonnie, do you? It's her you want."

"I didn't want to – to want her. She's got something. I just can't

120

explain it, Bev. You wouldn't understand. I don't think I'm in love with her, it's just that, when I'm with her, I don't seem to be able to help myself. I know you're worth ten of her. She isn't half as nice a person as you. I know that, but all the same, I don't seem to be able to leave her alone."

Beverly listened white-faced. "I suppose you're talking about sex, Jonnie. Maybe it's different for men; perhaps they *can* make love to women they don't even like. It's different for women – at least for me it's different. I'd have to be deeply fond of and respect any man who wanted to love me that way."

"I said you couldn't understand!" Jonnie said helplessly.

"But what will happen?" Beverly asked. "If she doesn't go away, you'll meet her again and it'll all start up again. How can I trust you, Jonnie, when you don't even trust yourself?"

"I don't know!" Jonnie said, his voice suddenly sober and reasonable. "I don't suppose I've any right to ask you to have me back. You're fine, Beverly, and good and decent and strong. I'm not. I'm weak. But I mean to try."

Beverly looked into Jonnie's face, trying to feel love for him, pity for him, *something*. But she seemed to be unable to rouse any emotion in herself.

"I don't understand!" she said, more to herself than to him. "We don't seem the same people any more. I'm not strong, Jonnie. I found that out tonight. I don't know how to help you . . . help our marriage."

"Can't we pretend this hasn't happened? Maybe in time we will forget. If you like, Bev, we'll take that holiday?"

"No!" The cry was wrung from her. How could she bear a holiday like that now? It was to have been a second honeymoon. What kind of time would they have, Jonnie wishing all the time she were Elinor, and Beverly knowing it?

"Can't I do anything to put things right?"

"Oh, Jonnie!" Beverly cried, suddenly weakened despite herself. He sounded so like Nick or Philip or Julia – "I've said I'm sorry, now can I have a sweet?" – it was the same tone of voice, the same childish reasoning. One could forgive the children because they were children. But Jonnie was a man; a husband, a father. Hadn't he really grown up at all? Must she spend the rest of her life looking after another child? She wanted to be looked after by him, to be able to lean on him, trust in him, above all respect him.

"It's all right!" she said with difficulty. "Don't let's talk about it any more. We'll do as you say, Jonnie; pretend it never happened."

Jonnie nodded his head. "You're a good sport, Bev. Always thought so. Coming to bed?"

Oh no! Beverly cried in her heart. Not that! That's no way to do things, Jonnie.

Aloud she said: "Not just yet. I want to lay the breakfast things. Annette forgot. I'll be up presently."

After he had gone, she sat down again at the table, unbearably tired and feeling once again as if she were made of elastic, stretched to breaking point. She knew that Jonnie's way was wrong. How could he expect her to make love when he had been so recently in another woman's arms? Maybe he hoped to use her body to still his own need for Elinor? No, she couldn't, couldn't! Yet if she denied him this part of her married life, how could she expect him to remain faithful?

And Allan? she told herself cruelly. What about those moments in Allan's arms? His kisses? How much are they affecting your emotions. If you'd never gone to Allan tonight, might you not be in Jonnie's arms now?

No, no! It wasn't so. Her need for Allan now was merely a desire for the same peace, the same relaxing of tension, the same ability to be utterly dependent. Allan had nothing to do with this. It would be better not to see Allan again for a while; not until her relationship with Jonnie was on a firmer footing. Because that was what she must do – rebuild their marriage. She must learn to trust him again, to love him again, to *want* him again as her lover.

Jonnie is lying up there, waiting for me, she thought. I ought to go to him, let him feel my love for him, let him see how much more I need him than Elinor ever can do. He's given her up; he deserves something in return. He needs me to help him be strong against her.

But I can't, I can't! she tortured herself. I don't want him to touch me. I couldn't in any way respond.

It'll be your fault if he goes back to her, she told herself. If you want to keep your marriage intact, you've *got* to mean to him what she means. Go up. Go to him. Show him you care.

Slowly, she picked up the tea-tray and with trembling hands carried it up to their room.

"Bev? Wake up, darling. Here's a cup of tea!"

Slowly, she opened her eyes and became conscious of Jonnie's voice.

"Cup of tea, my sweet. You were dead to the world so I made it. God, I've got a hang-over. Think I'll cut the office and stay home."

Slowly, Beverly drank the tea, as she did so memories of last night flooded over her, bringing a hot blush to her cheeks. She could not look at Jonnie. Last night had been a wild, savage, unbelievable hour, at the end of which she had fallen swiftly and suddenly into a deep, almost drugged sleep. There had been no tenderness, no love, no gentleness, completely different from any other time they had been together. It had seemed impossible to her that under such circumstances, she could have responded to Jonnie's demands of her. Yet, in the end, she had been as wild and uncontrolled and savage as he, deriving the same purely physical enjoyment and satisfaction.

Only now, her cheeks flushed, her head and eyes averted from Jonnie, did she wonder: Was that how it was with Elinor? Was that what he wants from me? It isn't love. I felt no love . . .

"Think I'll take a couple of alka-seltzers!" Jonnie was saying brightly. "Shall I run you a bath, darling?"

His voice was affectionate, possessive, friendly. He was behaving as if there were nothing in the world that was wrong except his hang-over. Maybe that's how he felt. Maybe he believed that last night had put everything right. Was that really all Jonnie needed from her? Nothing of her heart? Only her body?

As if in direct reply to her thoughts, Jonnie suddenly leant forward and kissed her lightly on one bare shoulder.

"You look so tempting, lying there naked, only half awake. I've a good mind to get back into bed!"

"Jonnie!"

"Yes, darling?"

She couldn't after all talk to him and explain how she felt. He was so bright, so cheerful, so obviously content. How could she take that happiness from him by saying, 'We can't build a marriage on this!'

"I would like that bath!" she substituted quickly.

She locked the bathroom door as soon as she was in it, locked it against Jonnie, hoping he would not realize the reason for it. In the past he would sometimes come and sit on the edge of the bath, smoking a cigarette and talking to her. It had seemed perfectly natural. But now she did not want him to see her nakedness.

What's the matter with me? she asked herself desperately. I ought to be so happy. I've got my husband back. That's what I wanted. He's given her up. Last night proved to him I can be what she is! But I can't – not really. *That* isn't what I wanted. But what right have I to everything? I married him. That's what Allan told me; for better or for worse. This must be enough. It always used to be. Jonnie hasn't changed and I mustn't. But I have, I have! I feel as if I've grown twenty years since this time yesterday.

Somehow, the day wore on. After lunch, Annette took the twins for a walk with Julia. Philip and Nick were at school. Mercifully, none of the children seemed in the least aware of the upset between their parents yesterday. They took Jonnie's unexpected day at home with unconcern and since he was obviously in a very happy frame of mind, they were delighted to have him there. It was as if Jonnie were trying to make amends to them, too. Anything they asked, he did. At four o'clock, Nick and Philip returned. Nick handed Beverly a letter. She knew at once it was from Allan and was glad that at that moment, Jonnie was in the garden with Julia. Nick ran out to join them and she was able to take Allan's letter to the privacy of her bedroom to read.

My dear,

I have found it hard to concentrate on twice two this morning. Every time I look at young Nick's face across the room, I've thought of you and wondered if you are all right. The trouble with twice two is that it can so easily make five in the moonlight. Not that there was a moon last night, but I think you know what I mean.

I meant everything I said to you, but I want you to know and believe that in your case twice two was making five. You were upset and shocked and alone and your reactions were perfectly normal for someone in your state. I was there and offered comfort and you took it. It meant no more than that. I'm afraid, you see, that you might just possibly begin to think it did mean more.

I think your husband loves you, Beverly. Perhaps each of us loves in a different way according to our capabilities and our natures. A man can be unfaithful to his wife and still love her and need her. I hope very much you will both be able to find happiness again. I have great faith in you and I think you can be strong enough for both if you so choose.

If things go wrong, don't forget that you have one true friend who would do anything in the world to help you.

As always,
Allan

"Oh, Allan!" Beverly whispered to the empty room. "How well you seem to know me! I had wondered about myself last night. It would be so very easy to fall in love with you. But you are right, of course. There can never be a love between us and it's best not to think about it even as a possibility. I'll concentrate on Jonnie, on his need for me, his love for me."

Love! There again Allan was right. Each individual is capable of only so much loving. In his way, Jonnie *must* still care a lot or he would have left her for Elinor, of whom he'd said all along that her hold over him was purely physical; that he didn't love her.

She folded the letter and put it away in her writing case. Later, when she had read it again, she would burn it. Meanwhile, she must answer it, reassure Allan.

Dear Allan, she wrote, underlining the dear:

Thank you for your letter. It came at a moment when I was confused and you have helped, as usual, to straighten me out. I will never forget your kindness to me yesterday, nor will I forget that you helped me to grow up a little.

I suppose we must lose many of our ideals in life and that in doing so, we do grow up. I think I can face the future calmly. As you say, I believe Jonnie does love me in his way and he has given her up. Now it's up to me to build things up again.

I'm very happy to have your friendship. I hope you will feel we can meet and talk sometimes, as friends. Thank you again, dear Allan.

from
Beverly

Reading it through, it seemed somehow inadequate. It was complicated by his love for her. Knowing that he cared made it so hard to write without showing the depth of *her* affection for him. It wouldn't help either of them if she did so. Maybe it would be better not to meet again, for a long time. She didn't want to make things too hard for him. Yet he lived such a lonely life, and sometimes just to be together for a short while, with Nick, maybe . . .

I mustn't lean on him! Beverly thought as she hurriedly sealed the letter and stamped it. It would be wrong to become too dependent on their friendship, their understanding; to count too much on the strange bond between them.

The thought of his loneliness, the emptiness of his life, became suddenly unbearable to her. Impulsively, she leaned out of the window and called Nick in.

"Darling, I was going to post this, but if you like, you can run over to Mr Forbes with it. Maybe he'd like you to stay to tea. You can, if he asks you. Do you want to go?"

"Yes, I'll go, Mum. I say, Mum, he hasn't written about anything *bad* I've done at school, has he?"

"No!" Beverly smiled and ruffled Nick's hair. "He said last time I spoke to him that you were being very good. Run along then, darling. Be back by bedtime."

She felt happier when he had gone. Slowly, she walked downstairs and out into the garden. Philip and Julia were helping Jonnie build a vast bonfire. Not far away someone was mowing their lawn and the rhythmic sound drifted across the hedge. There was a sweet smell of honeysuckle from the plant which had spread itself through the clump of hazel trees. It was a beautiful afternoon, yet sad.

This day – this moment, is how I feel inside me, Beverly thought as she walked towards them. Before long, summer would be gone! she told herself, the smoke from the bonfire reminding her of November.

Jonnie's mind must have been running on similar lines.

"We must have some really good fireworks this year," he said as she came up to them. "Let's make a party of it, Bev. We'll ask Sue and Pete and anyone else we can think of. I'll get some decent rockets in town and we'll give the kids a real bang-up show."

He looked suddenly very young, very happy, very enthusiastic. There was no trace in his face of last night's drinking. It was almost as if all the lines of worry and tiredness had been wiped from him in one clean sweep. He looked young, clean, strong.

"Of course I'm still in love with him," Beverly told herself quickly. "It's just that it is a different kind of love now."

Quickly, she stooped and gathering a handful of hedge cuttings threw them on to the pile. The leaves curled in the heat, twisted, crackled and burst in to flame.

Ten

A month later, Jonnie was clearing up in the office, hoping to catch the early train home, when one of the typists came in.

"There's a lady to see you, Mr Colt," she said. "I told her you were just leaving, but she said she had to see you urgently."

"A lady?" Jonnie looked at the girl in annoyance. "Didn't you ask her name?"

"Yes, I did, sir, but she said just to tell you she was there."

Elinor! He knew it must be Elinor. There wasn't anyone else it could be. And the wretched girl had said he was still there. He didn't want to see her. She ought not to have come. Everything was all right at home and he couldn't risk another bust-up. Not even he could expect Beverly to forgive him a second time. He'd behaved pretty rottenly and he was damn sorry about it all. He'd just about convinced himself now that he didn't even *care* about losing Elinor. After all, it turned out so differently with Beverly; seemed she could attract him that same way, when she chose. *That*, he had convinced himself, was all that had been wrong with his marriage; all that had led him into Elinor's arms. They'd let that side of their life become humdrum and dull. Well, it was different now and he wanted to keep it that way.

"Can't you say I've gone?" he asked the girl desperately.

"You mustn't teach your staff to tell lies!"

Jonnie and the typist both flushed scarlet as Elinor walked into the room smiling. The girl ran out of the room making her escape, but Jonnie remained rooted to the floor.

Elinor gave a deep, throaty laugh. "You look so *guilty*, darling," she said easily, sitting down on the edge of his desk and toying with a paper knife. "Tell me, why don't you want to see me?"

He could smell her perfume now, heady and strong. It made him think of – but he wasn't going to think about her that way.

"You know why I don't want to see you," he said harshly. "It's all over, Elinor. You must have known I meant it."

Elinor nodded.

"But of course! All the same, I don't see why you have to avoid me as if I was the plague. You haven't been up to the club. I suppose in order not to see me. And now this. It's really rather *unkind* of you, darling."

"Elinor, please!"

She looked very smart. She was wearing a tight-fitting skirt that clung to her slim hips, over it a loose jacket that seemed in some odd way to accentuate her femininity although it hid the lines of waist and breast. On her dark head was a tiny fluffy white hat, piquante, coquettish, somehow French and naughty.

"You're not *afraid* of me, are you?" she asked, looking up at him from between long, blackened lashes.

"Damn it, you know I am!" Jonnie burst out. "It isn't playing fair, Elinor."

"Oh, I see. Not cricket and all that, what!" Her American drawl had become a parody of Oxford English. "But since when has love become a sport? I thought even you English agreed that all was fair in love and war."

"I'm not afraid. It's just that I've got to go home. It can't do any good, coming here, Elinor. It's all over."

"Well, I wasn't suggesting anything else, honey. I was passing by and I thought if I dropped in, you might stand me a drink for old time's sake, or something?"

"A drink?" Jonnie said stupidly. "You want me to take you out for a drink?"

"Why not? Six o'clock and opening time. Surely you can spare me ten minutes, Jonnie?"

He felt stupid. He'd been fighting against her trying to re-open their affair and, all the time, she'd only wanted a drink.

Suddenly he laughed. "It's really rather funny. Okay, we'll have a drink. Then I must get back. We've people coming to dinner tonight and I promised I wouldn't be late."

"Poor old Jonny-boy; tied to the apron strings again. Well, we can always drink to your funeral, I suppose."

"It isn't like that. They're my friends as well as Beverly's. I asked them, as a matter of fact."

Again Elinor laughed, her deep long laugh that seemed to come from somewhere right within her.

"You are touchy, darling. What's the matter with you? Surely your wife can't object to you having a drink with an ex-girlfriend. After all, I am an ex, aren't I? It's not as if she need be jealous any longer."

Jonnie was reassured. Clearly Elinor did not intend to reopen their affair.

"I could do with that drink myself," he said, reaching for his hat and brief-case. Elinor slipped gracefully off the edge of the desk and put her arm through Jonnie's. He could feel the warmth of her bare flesh between glove and cuff through the sleeve of his own jacket. His arm muscle jumped and pretending to need his arm for that purpose, he carefully and clumsily locked his office door.

Elinor preceded him downstairs, the eyes of both typists staring after them.

"Coo!" said the girl who had announced Elinor. "What a stunner!"

"I think she looks like a cat or something!" the other girl said. "I bet she purrs and scratches!"

"Go on! I think she's ever so smart. Wonder who she is?"

"*He* didn't want to see *her*, anyway," said her companion. "I would, if I were a man."

"Well, he's married, so shut up!" was the reply. "Come on, or we'll miss the bus."

At that moment, the telephone rang. "Oh, bother it!" said the younger girl, but she picked up the receiver all the same. "Who? Oh, Mrs Colt, I'm ever so sorry, he's just left. Is it important?"

"No, it doesn't matter, thank you," Beverly said. "I'd hoped to catch him because there were one or two things I wanted him to bring home, but I can manage."

"I think she's ever so nice!" the typist said to her friend as they made their way down to the bus stop. "Wonder what she'd have said if I'd told her *he'd* just left with a smashing American dame!"

"Don't be so nasty!" retorted the other. "You know he wasn't keen."

Neither realized how much they had already betrayed.

Jonnie sat beside Elinor in a quiet corner of the bar at the Fifty-One Club. Elinor's martini was nearly finished, but Jonnie's was untouched. She watched him toy with his glass, her eyes hard. "You're not being very sociable, darling! I'm beginning to feel sorry I looked you up."

Jonnie looked up at her anxiously. "Please try to understand, Elinor! It isn't that I'm not glad to see you . . . in a way, I am. It's just that it's easier to forget you when we don't see each other."

"I do believe you're afraid!" Elinor taunted him. "For a man of your age, it's really rather absurd, don't you think? Why, in the States a man can take another woman for a drink without his wife flying off the handle in a fit of jealousy. Perhaps she doesn't trust you, darling."

"Well, you can hardly blame her!" Jonnie was stung to reply on Beverly's behalf. "Besides, you're right. I don't even know if I can trust myself. You're so damned attractive, Elinor."

She smiled, a quick, secretive smile. "Have you thought about me this last month? Or had you forgotten all about me and our times together?"

"How could I forget!" Jonnie burst out. "I've tried. In a way, I've even settled down again. It's no good, Elinor. I know we can't ever be platonic friends. Maybe it's possible with some women, but not with you. I can't be with you more than a few minutes before I'm wanting you like hell!"

"Darling!" her voice was a soft caress. "Why torture ourselves this way? I've been miserable, too. It's not as if I ever wanted you to break up your home. I never expected you to do that. I never meant your wife to know and we must have been crazy to let her find out. We must just be more careful in future."

"There isn't going to be a future!" Jonnie said harshly. "It's over, Elinor, *it's got to be over*. I'm not the kind of man who can lead a double life and get away with it. Beverly would guess and I'm a rotten liar. I can't, Elinor, and you mustn't try to make me."

Elinor stubbed out her cigarette and lit another, blowing a cloud of smoke across the table. All around Jonnie was the strong heady smell of her perfume, undimmed by the cigarette smoke, reviving memories of Elinor's creamy white skin, of her smooth bare shoulders in the firelight, of her maddening, tantalizing laugh as she held him tightly and more tightly against her.

"I'm moving house!" Elinor said suddenly. "I'm selling the cottage and moving into an apartment in town. I thought I might try to find one somewhere in this district – not far from your office. Maybe you could drop in and see me sometimes, Jonnie? We might have lunch together or a quick drink before you catch your train home. I wouldn't ask for anything else, I promise. I'd never try to detain you if you *had* to get home. Beverly'd never find out. If I move away, she'll think it's all over and she'll stop being suspicious. It'll all be so easy."

The way she put it, it sounded easy, tempting, desirable; and yet in his heart, he didn't want to re-open the affair. Until this evening, he'd reconciled himself to the fact that it *was* all over. He hadn't even expected to see Elinor again. Now, damn her, he wanted to see her; wanted to take what she was offering him. If only he could reconcile his conscience and still the fears that if Beverly found out, she'd never forgive him a second time.

"She was only hurt because she *knew*," Elinor said, sensing with that extraordinary, witch-like sixth sense of hers Jonnie's hesitation. "What you don't know can't hurt you. This way, we can all be happy; you, me and your wife, too. And if you ever start to feel she's suspicious, or unhappy, well, we'll just have to stop seeing each other. But it's worth a try, surely?"

She reached out a gloveless hand and gently touched his knee. Jonnie looked up and stared at the face before him. It wasn't a pretty face – not by accepted standards anyway. What was it about this woman that was so devilishly attractive? Why should he still want her? His nights with Beverly had been just as satisfying as his love-making with Elinor, or at least, he'd believed so. What power did this woman possess that she could make him want her against his will? He didn't want to re-open the affair. He didn't want to cheat Beverly. The kind of life Elinor suggested was one he had condemned in other men. And it was dangerous. One slip and Beverly could and *would* divorce him.

"No!" he said wretchedly. "No, Elinor. Don't ask me. Please believe that if I were free . . . well, you know how it would be then. But I'm not free. I've never been free. We should never have given way in the first place."

"But we did, darling. What's between us is too strong for us both. I tried to put you out of my mind, really I did. You can't imagine this kind of thing is very satisfying for me? Besides, I could find someone else – there's plenty of other fish in the sea. But I don't want them, Jonnie, not the way I want you, *need* you. Night after night I lie awake thinking about us; of the things we did; the magic we made. There's never been anyone like you in my life before. That's why I'm prepared to take so little, Jonnie. Just a few odd hours. It's not even as if I'm asking for any of your time at home. Beverly would see as much of you as she would otherwise do. You can't throw all this away, Jonnie, life's too short."

Was Elinor right? Jonnie asked himself. Was there really something special between them that excused them from ordinary conventional behaviour? Elinor wasn't asking much. She didn't want him to bust up his home; she'd even been considering Beverly's side of the picture and making sure that she didn't suffer in any way. He could slip out of the office during the lunch hour; slip away a bit earlier in the evenings. Beverly would never guess – why should she? It was different for her; she was happy with the ordinary domestic life, the kids, and a husband to come home at night. And he would be home as usual. It would only be in office hours that he and Elinor . . .

"Jonnie, don't decide now. Think about it. I don't want to make you do anything you'll be sorry for. I wouldn't have suggested this if I didn't feel so very strongly that it's the solution for all of us. But you have to be sure, too. Otherwise, I could never let you come and see me. I'd rather find someone else – even if I don't, couldn't, love him – to help me forget you."

No! Jonnie thought with a rush of violent jealousy. No, not that, not another man. Why should another man take what was his? And she belonged to him. They belonged together. He'd been wrong to suppose he'd put her out of his mind; he'd only forced her out. That bond between them was as strong as ever.

"Ring me, tomorrow!" Elinor said. "From the office. I'll be home all day as I've people coming to see over the cottage. Think about it, honey, and ring me."

Going home in the train, Jonnie thought. He felt it was wonderful of Elinor to be asking so little, offering so much. There weren't many married men who had the advantage of such understanding, such unselfishness. He'd be mad to refuse, and yet what *would* Beverly think, feel, if she ever knew? She wouldn't know – couldn't know. He could say he'd taken up squash to replace the golf he'd finally given up. At least, he'd written his resignation to the club and hadn't been near the course since that night. He'd post the letter off and in a day or two, he'd tell Beverly he'd decided to play squash with one of the fellows in the office. They might play in the lunch hour or after work. Bev never came to town. She'd never doubt him. Or would she?

He drove home, silent and thoughtful, ill at ease. Their guests had not yet arrived but Beverly was ready dressed looking young and attractive in an olive-green dress that accentuated the colour of her eyes.

"Darling!" she greeted him with a light kiss. "Whatever happened to you? I thought you'd be on the early train. I rang the office to get you to bring home some cocktail biscuits but the girl said you'd just gone!"

There was no suspicion in her voice. That typist couldn't have mentioned Elinor, unless Beverly was trying to trap him. Maybe it would be better to tell the truth and say he'd run into Elinor, stopped to have a drink with her.

"As a matter of fact, I ran into Elinor. It was quite accidental. I mean, I had no idea . . . She's going, Bev, selling the cottage. She wanted to say goodbye."

"Going?" Beverly repeated stupidly. "Back to America?"

"No, I don't think so; she didn't say where. Just that she thought it best to leave here. It's what you wanted, isn't it? Now I can't run into her even accidentally."

Beverly gave her young husband a curious look. "Yet you ran into her *accidentally*, in town?"

Jonnie flushed. "No! Now, look, Beverly, don't start getting ideas. What actually happened was that she came to see me. I didn't invite her; she dropped by the office. It was only to tell me she was leaving and that it was all over. You ought to be glad, not so damned suspicious."

"I'm sorry!" Beverly said, her hands falling to her sides. Jonnie was right: she *must* trust him. Of course he was hesitant in telling her what had happened. He'd guessed she'd be unpleasant about it, and she had. And it wasn't his fault that woman had called to see him. To make amends, she said quickly:

"Now you won't feel you have to give up your golf, darling. I know what it means to you. You haven't posted your resignation, have you?"

"Well, as a matter of fact, I have. Anyway, I think I should give it up. After all, I don't see much of you and the kids. It means we can have all our weekends together. A fellow in the office was telling me today he plays squash in the lunch hour. I might take that up. I used to play, you know. Much better for me than eating too much in some restaurant. Look, I'd better go and get changed or Sue and Pete will be here before I'm ready."

He bent to kiss her on the forehead, but she reached up and pulled his face down so that their lips touched. Suddenly, she could detect the faint smell of perfume – not her perfume, but someone else's . . . Elinor's – and she pulled away from Jonnie sharply. He walked away up the stairs and she stood for a moment, watching him go, trying to overcome the inner, nagging suspicion that, despite her desire to trust him, was still torturing her.

Could she trust him? Could she? When was he lying, when telling the truth?

He'd never have told me he'd met Elinor this evening if it had been starting up again, she told herself sharply. He's being completely honest with me. She's going, and that will really be the end of it. I'm going to forget about her and let him forget.

The front-door bell rang suddenly, startling her out of her reverie. She hurried forward to open the door.

Eleven

It was nearly Christmas. Soon the term would be over and Nick and Philip home all day for the holidays. Already they were making calendars and colouring Christmas cards, and at this very moment, Julia was sitting on the floor surrounded by yards of paper chains she was making.

Annette was in the kitchen preparing tea and Beverly was playing with the twins in their play-pen in front of the fire.

It was a warm, domestic, happy atmosphere, and yet somehow, she wasn't happy. Her nerves were on edge and she did not know why. Something was wrong, but what? What? Outwardly, everything was so perfectly all right. It was Jonnie, of course, who worried her. But why?

I hate myself! Beverly thought. Jonnie's done everything possible to make amends and to be a good husband, a good father. He'd given up his golf, and true to his word, spent all his weekends at home. Nick and Phil were once more his adoring shadows and Jonnie had immense and quite unusual patience with them. Perhaps that was the trouble; he'd changed. He wasn't a cheerful young boy any more, he was quieter, more thoughtful, more considerate in every way – almost too considerate. It was as if he couldn't forget that he'd hurt her and had to go on proving to her and to himself that he *was* a good husband. Somehow, that in itself made it impossible for her to forget Elinor. If they'd only had a row sometimes, a cross word, a difference of opinion! It would be more natural; more normal. But they didn't. Whatever suggestion she made, Jonnie acquiesced. He was punctilious about little things, like bringing her early morning tea, helping her with the twins, opening doors, carrying trays. He never forgot to kiss her when he came back in the evenings, or when he left in the mornings. And there were presents, far too many – flowers, chocolates, a pair of gloves, something special for dinner.

Even Sue, who only came to the house occasionally, had noticed it and said, laughing: "I'd call it a guilty conscience, Beverly. Better watch out!"

Of course, Sue who didn't know about that brief affair with Elinor, couldn't have guessed how near the truth her remark had been. But Jonnie couldn't go on like this. Of course, she was happy to have him *want* to make amends in these small ways, but somehow she might have been easier in her mind if he'd chucked something at her one evening and then taken her into his arms and kissed her, shaken her, showed some small sign of passion.

There was that, too. Those brief moments when he had lost himself completely in their love-making, carried her away with him into some new, strange world . . . it was never like that now. He only occasionally made love to her; mostly when she had snuggled up closer to him, wanting affection, some physical sign of love. And then he had been gentle, considerate, kind, but never passionate, never beyond complete control.

If I only knew what was wrong? Beverly thought. Perhaps nothing at all. But I feel I'm always at arm's length; that he is just out of reach. *Why*?

She heard voices at the front door. Nick and Phil both chattering at once. They weren't supposed to come in that way with their muddy boots. She went to tell them when the door opened inwards and Nick, flushed and excited, said:

"Mum, we've brought Mr Forbes back to tea. He's got something for us. It's all right, isn't it? He can come!"

"Allan!" Beverly said, suddenly terribly glad to see him. They hadn't met since that night and it seemed a world away now. She had glimpsed him across the playing field at school or sometimes shopping in the village, but they hadn't done more than wave to each other and go their different ways.

"How nice. Come in, quickly. It's pouring with rain. But of

138

course, you know that! Boys, take off those boots and ask Annette to give you dry socks. Come in, Allan."

Julia ran out of the sitting-room to join the boys and for a moment, they were alone together in front of the blazing fire, only the two, chubby toddlers staring at them from round, blue eyes.

Allan took Beverly's hands in his and looked down at her, his face still wet with rain, but smiling. "Let me look at you! Are you well? I get snippets of news of you from the boys, but I had to find out for myself."

"I'm so glad you came, Allan!" Beverly said. "I get news of you, too, but it's much nicer to see you in person. Are you well? Are the boys behaving?"

In a moment, all trace of depression had left her and she felt happy, excited, warmed, comforted. It was so nice to see him.

"Sit here and get warm!" she said, pointing to a large wing-chair by the fire. "You'd better take your shoes off if they're wet. I'll get a pair of Jonnie's slippers for you."

"I'm not used to being spoilt!" Allan said with a smile. "And this is so nice and welcoming. What a charming room it is, Beverly, and how those babies have grown! *Look*, it's smiling at me!"

"Not *it*, Allan!" Beverly said, laughing. "She! That's Melanie, she's always very forward with strange men. This one is Suzanne. She's much shyer."

"They look alike to me, yet I can see the difference. I think Melanie is most like you. She has your expression, though not your eyes. Beverly, never mind the slippers. Tell me how you are. Happy? All well with your world?"

"Yes, yes, of course!" Beverly said hurriedly, too quickly. She walked away from him to the window and stared out across the rain-swept garden. "You know Elinor Wilmot left? Jonnie's working hard, of course, but he gave up his golf so we have more time together, really. Allan . . . I never really thanked you for being so good to me that night. You saved my marriage, I think."

He looked at the slim young back, seeing the slight droop of her shoulders, the delicate back of her neck, the shine of her hair. He knew that it would only be tormenting himself to come here, see her

139

again, yet he had *had* to come, to reassure himself that she was well and happy; that it had all turned out for the best.

Now he was suddenly painfully aware of something new about this girl he loved so dearly. A sadness . . . no, not quite that! A helplessness?

"I'm glad!" he said. "I'm afraid I didn't do much. Let's not talk about that. Tell me about yourself. What you've been doing. How is your husband? No, you've told me that. Tell me about *you*."

She turned to him, suddenly smiling. "There isn't much to tell. I lead a very quiet life, I suppose, though I'm always busy. It's these young horrors." She pointed to the rosy-checked, contented pair in the play-pen. "I suppose you can't take two more pupils of this age at your school?"

"Not quite yet!" Allan smiled back. "Besides, what would you do with yourself if they weren't here to keep you occupied?"

"That's just it!" Beverly said in a strange, taut voice. "I think about that at night, Allan. What will I do when they're all away at school?"

Allan drew out his pipe and slowly, methodically began to fill it. "I daresay most mothers feel that way," he said thoughtfully. "There'll be plenty to do, you'll see. You'll be able to get up to town occasionally, see a matinée, go shopping, get your hair done. I don't know what women do with their days. Get a job, perhaps? What do you want to do?"

Beverly went back to the fire and curled herself on her favourite pouffe, staring into the flames. "Nothing! I can't think of anything. I think the only ambition I ever had was to raise a family, have a home to care for. I've been so busy doing that ever since I was seventeen, I've never really had time to think about the future."

"It'll take care of itself!" Allan said comfortably. "Hullo!" he added as the boys came back into the room, carrying a cardboard shoe-box carefully between them.

"It's a model car but it's all in bits!" Nick said. "Phil and me thought you could help us put it together. Daddy brought it back last Sunday. It wasn't even our birthday, either. Dad's always bringing us things."

"You're lucky!" Allan said quietly. "Don't you think he'd like to help you put it together?"

"Oh, he won't mind if you help," Nick said. "Please, Mr Forbes."

Beverly laughed. "Unless Mr Forbes has any objection, I think 'Uncle Allan' might be more friendly when it is a social visit. Of course, it would still be Mr Forbes at school."

"That's a grand idea," said Allan, and although from force of habit, the boys forgot once or twice, they were soon calling him Uncle Allan as easily and naturally as if he had been a real relative.

"You know, you have a wonderful way with children," Beverly said later, when the boys had joined Julia and the twins in the kitchen for tea with Annette, while they had theirs in front of the fire. "You only have to be in the house ten minutes before they are all your adoring slaves. Julia positively makes me blush the way she flirts so obviously with you!"

Allan laughed contentedly.

"I think she's a dear little girl. I imagine she must be like you were when you were her age."

"I was perfectly horrible!" Beverly said, shaking her head. "My sister was the pretty one of our family and I was madly jealous of her. Mother used to try to make out I had the brains but it never consoled me. I suppose I knew it wasn't true, for one thing and for another, all I wanted was to be ravishingly beautiful!"

Allan looked across the room to where she sat, relaxed, flushed, contented, in front of the warm fire, her empty tea-cup held lightly between small, square, rather boyish hands.

"I suppose I should be gallant and say you are ravishingly beautiful now. But to me, you have something much more worth while than mere prettiness. I think you are one of the loveliest women I've ever known."

Allan's tone of voice was so impersonal, despite the intimacy of his words, that Beverly was not quite sure how best to reply to such a remark. Was this Allan's way of telling her he was still in love with her? No! It was just his way of speaking what he felt, without motive.

Without waiting for her to speak, he went on easily: "You're happy, aren't you, my dear? You are so much more relaxed than when we last met."

This time his voice did falter and, for a moment, uneasiness lay between them at the memory of their last meeting; of that last embrace.

"I'm afraid I behaved very badly, Allan. You must have thought me an hysterical little fool. Perhaps your ability to understand and deal with small children stood you in good stead with me! I was acting like a child."

Sensing her discomfort at being reminded of the past, believing that she truly was now reunited with Jonnie and happy with him once again, Allan quickly changed the subject.

"I believe that what you call 'dealing' with children successfully, is merely a matter of understanding them. It's so easy to forget how a child feels when it is young. Lots of people think it isn't important, but children do feel things and very deeply, too. Most of their behaviour is a direct result of how they feel – bad behaviour in particular. I don't think any child wants to be bad just for the sake of doing wrong. It's nearly always for one reason or another, to attract attention because they don't have enough love, or something of that sort. Of course, kids are full of mischief and I'm a firm believer in discipline!"

"Did you always want to be a teacher, Allan?"

Her companion nodded. "Yes, I think I did. It's a very rewarding occupation in so many ways. I know you must understand that. After all, a mother has the same kind of satisfaction in bringing up her children the way she wants them to be. It's a creative way to live. I should hate to deal, say, with accounts or statistics or anything like that. I'm one hundred per cent interested in human nature."

"It's a curious subject," Beverly said thoughtfully. "Human nature, I mean. You may think you know all there is to know about people; then suddenly you find out you don't know them at all. You have to begin all over again, trying to fathom out what is real. Allan, do you suppose men and women are really very different, fundamentally, I mean? Do you think that in some ways, life is more difficult for men? That a woman is more primitive at heart and that for this reason, it's easier for her to be sure of the essentials in her life?"

"Perhaps!" Allan replied quietly, wondering now what was behind Beverly's question. Wasn't she happy after all? Was it a generalization on life, or a question in her mind about that husband of hers? "Love, home, children; these are all essentials to any woman. But men need to be able to work, too. I think a man's job is very important to him. He must be able to do something and make something of his life beyond emotional satisfaction. Tell me, what does Jonnie actually do?"

"Oh, it's to do with steel exports!" Beverly said vaguely. "I don't really understand myself what he does. He's a very junior partner in this firm and I believe they are making quite a lot of money now the threat of nationalization seems to have eased off. Jonnie works terribly long hours now. It's often nine, sometimes ten before he gets home. Of course, it's partly his own fault. He doesn't really *have* to stay on at the office after six. But as he says, the work piles up and he daren't let it get ahead of him. He can't relax when he does get back if he hasn't completed everything there is to do. He's hoping for a rise soon, you see, and it'll make a big difference to us financially if they make him a full partner on equal terms."

"It seems a very long day for him," Allan said shortly.

"It is!" Beverly said. "Of course, the train journey doesn't help. It takes him an hour, even when he leaves the office on time, before he's back here. When he's very late leaving he has a bite of supper in town to save me having to cook a meal so late."

"Don't you ever get out together in the evenings?" Allan asked.

"Not very often!" Beverly said truthfully. "But we do have the weekends. Now Jonnie doesn't play golf, we have all Saturday and Sunday. I shouldn't complain."

No! Allan thought. On the strength of it, there is no cause for complaint. A man working hard to get the rise he needs for his family; giving up his golf to be with them weekends. It sounded as if Jonnie were the model husband. But was he? Or was he, Allan, being prejudiced in his mind when he felt rather than thought, that the old tale of "working late" somehow didn't ring true?

How can I be objective about the man when I'm in love with his wife? Allan thought dejectedly. He despised himself for the trend his thoughts had taken. Besides, he barely knew Jonnie and, had he taken the trouble to get to know him, he might have liked him a great deal better on closer acquaintance. What reason had he to distrust him? Lots of men made mistakes, regretted them, and turned out to be model husbands afterwards, even perhaps the better for that one slip. Why not believe Jonnie was one of them? Beverly trusted him. Or did she? Her voice had been so steady, so emphatic when she spoke of her husband's work. Was it over-emphasized? Was she trying to convince herself as well as him that Jonnie wasn't up to something else?

But what? Elinor Wilmot had left. Everyone knew she'd sold the cottage and disappeared. Back to the States? Gossip did not reveal her whereabouts and Allan certain had not been sufficiently interested in the woman to make any enquiries. Did Beverly know?

Suddenly hating himself for these thoughts, suspicions, Allan said: "I'm so happy to know it has all turned out so well for you, Beverly. I thought it would, you know."

"Yes, you did, Allan. I'm grateful that you made me see sense," Beverly said eagerly. "I was so hurt at the time that I just couldn't see Jonnie's good points for the bad ones. But I've grown up since then, Allan. I trust him now and I don't believe he'd ever betray that trust. He really loves us, you know. He spends so much more time with the children; everything's all right between them now. I know Jonnie would never risk losing them or me."

Yet even as she spoke those words with ringing conviction, some tiny voice, deep buried in her heart, spoke softly to her.

Wouldn't he? Does he really love you? Is everything exactly the same as it was before *her*? You want to trust him, but you don't. Why not? Is it because you feel rather than know that something is wrong, that something is missing?

But nothing was wrong. Jonnie was kind, affectionate, considerate. When they made love – even if it was very seldom these days – he was gentle, tender. What was it, then? Was it her fault? She who had changed? And not Jonnie? Could it be that Allan had somehow made a difference? Was there buried in her mind, a memory of

Allan's arms around her, his desperate need of her? Was that it? That Jonnie did not seem to need her now, not the real, essential woman beneath its outer shell. He needed her care of him, of his home, of his children. But did he ever make any demands on her mind, her thoughts, her longing to give of herself? Did he really want her *love*?

"Allan!" she said suddenly. "Tell me something. When you were married to Louise, what was the most important part of your relationship? What did you miss most when . . . when she died?"

Allan drew out his pipe and began slowly to fill it. "It's difficult to answer that without a bit of forethought. I missed her presence, of course. The house was suddenly completely empty. I missed all the little things she used to do for me – silly little things like sewing buttons on my shirt and finding my pipe when I'd lost it! But I think more than anything, I missed her company. You see, we used to talk over everything together, not deliberately debating everything that had happened in the day, but it was a kind of sharing of each other's lives. It was the same when we'd been out anywhere together. We always wanted to know what the other thought, felt, about a place, people, situations, life. I think I missed her mind as if I had suddenly lost half my own. Something would happen and I would turn to say "Louise, do you think—?" and then I would remember that she wasn't there. Each time it happened, it was like her dying all over again. I don't think I've really a very dependent nature. After all, I used to live alone before we were married and I've learned to do so since. But I needed her in so many ways when she was there; her mind, her love, her kindness, her sympathy, her encouragement. Even her criticism. Does that sound very silly?"

"No!" the word was almost a whisper. How could such a declaration of love sound silly? It was what every woman wanted from love – to be needed as a person as well as a woman . . . wife, mistress, friend. It had to be all three to be complete.

"We were very happy!" Allan said quietly. "I suppose some men might feel it would have been better never to have known that happiness than to have known and lost it. But I'm glad we had those years. Life can be a very long search. Some people never know love.

Louise and I thought we had found it in each other and we were happy."

Because in some odd way he felt so close to Beverly, it did not seem strange talking to her about Louise. It was many years now since he had spoken of his wife to anyone. He had grown so used to being without her until Beverly came into his life, reminding him of what he had lost, of what was good and warm and sweet in a man's life. He'd never thought to meet another woman who could mean to him what Louise had meant. Perhaps Beverly, had she been free, could not have meant exactly the same either. He and Louise were contemporaries, equals. With Beverly, he felt older, wiser, more protective. He wanted so much to be able to take care of her. Louise had never needed that; she was always complete in herself.

It is because there is something *lost* about Beverly, Allan thought. Even now that she is reunited with her husband, she is still somehow lost and alone. Her mouth might smile, but her eyes did not. Only when the children were in the room, noisy, demanding of her time, attention and love, did she become wholly herself. Then all that was warm and generous in her disposition flowed from her, making her a complete woman, wise, maternal, understanding. In those moments, she seemed to the man watching her to be older, wiser than himself.

Allan stayed on till the children's bedtime. When at last he rose to go, it was with reluctance. Outside, the rain fell in sheets and he knew that his fire would be out, that the cottage would seem contrastingly empty and horribly quiet.

Beverly must have thought the same as she helped him into his raincoat, for she said: "I wish you'd stay to supper, Allan. I hate to think of you having to go home now and cook a meal."

"Mrs Bates will have left me something prepared to 'pop in the oven' as she always says. I've overstayed my welcome as it is."

"No, no you haven't!" Beverly cried, suddenly unwilling to let him go. "You'll come again, won't you, Allan? It's so nice for me to have someone to talk to. Promise me you will come. The children love having you here, too."

"Yes, I'll come again," Allan said gently. "It's good of you to put up with me."

As he walked slowly homewards, he was unaware of the rain as he tried to sort out his impressions and emotions. He was honest enough with himself to admit that going to see Beverly and her children was not a good thing. He knew himself to be falling more and more deeply in love with her. He knew that such a love was bound to be fruitless. Beverly was married and therefore for ever beyond his reach. Even to love her silently and within himself was wrong. Yet he had not the power to keep away from her. He'd tried; these last few months he had thought a thousand times of going to see her, dropping in casually the way he had this afternoon. Each time, he had fought the temptation to see her face, hear her voice, share the same room with her. Now at last, he had weakened, telling himself that he had to know she was all right before he put her completely out of his mind.

What kind of lie was that? Her own letter had told him her marriage was patched up; that all was well. *She* would have come to him if there had been any fresh disaster. No! He had gone because he had wanted so much to see her. He was in need of a love he could never have.

And now he had promised to go back. Something wistful in the tone of her request that he should return, had again weakened him from what he knew to be the right thing to do. He ought to go far away, and forget about her. He ought to ask for a transfer where he would not see her children every day, seeing in Nick's or Philip's innocent young eyes, the reflection of *hers*. But how could he go when she had need of him?

I have no proof she needs me, Allan told himself sternly. I think that because I want it to be so. It would be wrong to let her depend on me, even as a friend. That way love might grow between us and if her marriage failed again, it would be my fault, just as surely as it was Elinor's fault that Jonnie was unfaithful to Beverly. I cannot be responsible for such a thing happening, however remote the chance. I *must* go away.

While this conviction was fresh in his mind and heart, Allan hurried homewards, and before he could change his mind, he sat down at his desk and drafted a letter to the local education authority, requesting a transfer.

Beverly would never know that he was going at his own demand. Better she should look on it as an unfortunate stroke of bad luck.

"I'll see her once more . . . only once more," he told himself, as he sealed the envelope and stamped it. "That can and must be our goodbye."

Twelve

J onnie lay on the large divan in Elinor's sitting-room, his jacket discarded, for, despite the near-freezing temperatures outside, Elinor's flat was centrally heated and always seemed to Jonnie like a greenhouse. The dry, airless atmosphere did not suit him and he always had a headache after he had been there a few hours.

It was the only criticism he had of Elinor's apartment. In a very expensive block of flats, it was in every way luxurious and Elinor herself had spared no expense in making it more so. Her own glittering cocktail cabinet stood in one corner of the large living-room; the latest television combined with radio and gramophone in another. There was, of course, a record cabinet and every disc by every new popular singer. Most of all, Elinor liked Eartha Kitt's records. Jonnie did, too, for in many ways, Elinor reminded him of the dusky American singer. Sometimes the two became confused in his mind and when he was making love to Elinor, Eartha's voice rasping yet sultry and provocative in the background, he would wonder just who it was he held in his arms.

Surprisingly, Elinor seemed to be a good cook. Right now she was in the small efficient kitchen "knocking something up" for their lunch. He was not sufficiently domesticated himself to realize that any exotic meal was easy enough to provide if you had the money. Elinor shopped at Fortnum's and did very little cooking herself.

She only had to open packages and tins and present them prettily on a plate. Her food always seemed so much more appetizing than Beverly's. Jonnie tried not to make comparisons because it always made him feel guilty towards Beverly, who struggled hard to make a tempting meal from the cheaper cuts of meat. Mostly, the food was well cooked, but the menu did not include avocado pears, prawns in aspic, cold partridge and such delicacies. Nor did any meal include the wines Elinor always provided in abundance.

"I wish you'd let me pay something towards all this!" Jonnie had once said. "I can't let you provide everything."

"But, honey, why not? I've so much pleasure doing it – for *you*. Besides, this way we don't either of us need to feel we're taking something that belongs to your family."

He'd thought at the time how decent it was of Elinor to think that way. She was right, too. He and Beverly had a hard enough time making-do without him drawing a lot more from the bank. All the same, he argued, Elinor should let him take her out sometimes.

"If we go to a restaurant, we lose so much of our time together," was her reply. He knew what she meant. These lunch hours in her flat meant half an hour to eat, and an hour or more to make love. And Elinor never seemed to have enough of him. It was flattering, Jonnie thought, as he waited for her to reappear with the lunch tray, that, after all these months, she still wanted him as much as ever. Of course, he felt the same way. But she was so exciting, so glamorous, so mysterious, whereas he was such a dull sort of fellow. He couldn't think why she still cared about him so deeply.

He couldn't know that it was his own behaviour that still kept Elinor interested. Never, even at their most intimate moments, could she believe that Jonnie was hers, *all* hers. It was as if he always had one eye to his watch face; was for ever hurrying away from her to the other, greater and more important part of his life in which she had no place.

"I must get back to the office, my sweet," or "I must rush or I'll miss my train!"

Once or twice she'd tried to persuade him to stay longer, trying every trick she knew to make him forget time, the office, his wife. But he'd only weakened once and then he had been so on edge, he might just as well not have been there for all the attention he paid her.

It maddened, exasperated and intrigued her, this woman who had never yet failed to bring a man to his knees. True, she had been able to establish this part-time relationship with him. He came now as a matter of course, nearly every day, either for lunch or before going home in the evening. But he was never completely, wholly hers, to the point of forgetting his wife. She knew he would unhesitatingly throw her over if he thought for one moment that Beverly might find out. That was behind everything he did or said.

In many ways, Jonnie was far from being her type. He was not really sophisticated at heart although he was fascinated, rather the way any very young man might be, with the sophisticated way of her life, her surroundings. He was not even particularly fun or amusing. But when he made love to her . . . Elinor wanted him and although now she was beginning to have her doubts as to whether she could ever make him leave that dull little wife of his, she was even more determined to have him, at all costs, waiting for her when she beckoned, and not just turning up when he could spare the time.

But she was too clever to make any new moves as yet. She wanted him to take all this, all these meetings, so much for granted that when she suddenly threatened to put an end to their affair, he couldn't face it. Then he'd choose her rather than his family. Meanwhile, he was still far too much on edge to be taking anything for granted. He still looked like a guilty schoolboy when he put his key in the lock; still jumped if the phone rang or the door bell went; still kept sufficient rein on himself to be forever watching that clock.

Later, lunch over and pushed into the kitchen out of sight, she lay in his arms and said tentatively: "No hope of you staying a whole night sometime, darling? These hours seem to go so quickly."

Jonnie's body stiffened. "Oh no, I don't think I could, Elinor. I've never done such a thing and Beverly would be sure to question me. I do so hate these lies I have to tell her."

"Does she cross-question you a lot?" Elinor asked carefully.

"No! That's just it! I think she trusts me. That's why it seems so awful sometimes – cheating her I mean. I think I'd almost rather she knew."

Elinor raised her pencilled eyebrows. "But then you say she'd surely divorce you?"

"Yes! That's why I can't tell her. But I want to, often. I know we ought to stop this, Elinor. We ought never to have started. Why am I so weak?"

For answer, she bent over and began to kiss him, knowing that for a little while at least, she could still even his conscience, certainly his doubts.

"I can't let you go, I can't!" Jonnie said at last when it was over and they were lying in each other's arms. "Life without you in it would be empty of all colour, all excitement, all magic. I think you must be a witch, my darling. You've cast a spell on me."

Elinor leaned across him and kissed him slowly. 'I love you, Jonnie!" she said.

"Do you? I wish I could be sure what love means!" Jonnie said, holding her closer. "Is it only a transient emotion, Elinor? Once I believed I was as much in love with Beverly as any man could be in love with a woman. There'd never been anyone else and I couldn't believe there ever would be. Now I'm lying here with you, wondering how I lived all those years without you. Is it love we feel? Real love? Or is it just a violent physical attraction?"

"You think too much, honey!" Elinor murmured. "No one knows what love is. I don't even know if I want that kind of love you read about in books. What we feel for each other is OK by me."

Jonnie raised himself on one elbow and looked down into those dark unfathomable eyes of the woman whose body he knew so well but whose mind was still a mystery to him.

"But, darling, don't you see that if we don't really love one another, we shouldn't be here together, like this? It's only if it is the real thing that this is excusable."

"This is real!" Elinor said, running her cool slender hands across his broad shoulders, smiling her enigmatic smile.

It isn't the same for her, Jonnie thought with a sudden despair in his heart. She doesn't have to lie and cheat and deceive anyone. She's free. She has no duty towards Beverly, the children. Naturally, it doesn't worry her as it worries me. If only I didn't hate myself so much every time I see her. Yet I can't live without her, we both know that. At least this way is better than breaking up my home, messing up Beverly's life, the kids . . .

152

He glanced at his watch. "I must go soon," he said sharply. "We've a board meeting at two-thirty and I daren't be late."

The usual acute depression at leaving her weighed down his thoughts. He knew he wouldn't be at his best for this meeting. And it was important, too. He had to pull himself together somehow, try to concentrate more on his job, less on Elinor. Old Barkington, the senior partner, had dropped a hint only yesterday about his work.

"Sure you're feeling well? I've been wondering about you these last few months. Nothing wrong at home?"

"No, nothing at all!" Jonnie had replied quickly.

"Well, in that case, I think I ought to warn you that you've made one or two rather bad mistakes lately and this kind of thing can lose us business we need. You know what I'm talking about of course; that contract you drew up and the way you replied to Jenkins' letter. Obviously your mind wasn't on your job in either case. If you want promotion, John, you'll have to learn to be more responsible. I haven't time to check on all you do, you know. And there's one other thing. I know it isn't easy to get lunch in an hour round here and I certainly don't expect you to clock in and out like the typists. But I do think you should start the afternoon before three, and stay after five if there's work to be done."

"I'm sorry, sir!"

There'd been no excuse; there was none. He knew these lapses had cost him the promotion he'd hoped for for at least another year or more. Old Barkington wasn't being unfair; he'd every right to tell him to pull himself together. You couldn't expect him to make allowances for Elinor.

I ought to stop seeing her! Jonnie told himself as he left the flat. Some men might be able to lead a double life and like it, but for me it's a kind of nightmare. Always wondering if Beverly has noticed something; lipstick on my handkerchief, Elinor's perfume, something! Maybe she did suspect. She was very quiet these days. There were no arguments, no scenes, no tears. It was as if everything had got a little too much for her, too. Poor Bev! And she tried so hard to make him happy. In a strange kind of way, he *was* happy with her. The hours they spent together with the children were always satisfying and often great fun. And she was a good mother as well as a good wife. None of this was her fault.

"I'll take her home some liqueur chocolates!" he thought with a lightening of his spirits. "She loves them and the thought will please her, too."

He bought a box at the confectioner's outside the office. It didn't occur to him that he might owe Elinor a box of chocolates, too.

"Jonnie! Thank you very much. You know, I haven't finished the last box you brought home yet! But it was nice of you to think of it. I'll put them away for Christmas."

Beverly picked up her knitting again and tried not to think of Sue.

The results of a guilty conscience. No, that was horrible. Think of something else quickly. Jonnie looked tired, and so much older. Maybe he was working too hard. But he'd said he hadn't a hope of getting a holiday before Christmas. Maybe they could go away at Easter. Where? With the children? Alone? What would they do alone together for two weeks? What would they talk about? What had they done with themselves before the children had been born? What aeons ago that seemed. They'd been married nearly ten years. Now she was almost twenty-seven and she felt old . . . old. Jonnie would be thirty next birthday.

"What are you making this time?" Jonnie's voice interrupted her thoughts.

"Oh, just a pullover for Phil. He needs another one for school. Jonnie, Nick said there was a rumour going around that Allan Forbes was leaving."

"Who's he when he's at home?"

"Allan? Darling, Nick's and Phil's teacher. You remember, you met him when—"

"Oh yes, your boy-friend!" Jonnie interrupted with a half-laugh.

Beverly flushed. "I don't think that's funny or fair," she said.

"Sorry, Bev! Still, you did like him, didn't you? Can't say I did much."

"Yes, I liked him. He came over to tea the week before last. He didn't say anything then about leaving."

"Well, I don't suppose it matters much one way or the other, does it? They'll get another teacher."

"Yes, but not like Allan. He's wonderful with the children. I hope he doesn't go."

Something in her voice really caught Jonnie's attention.

"You sound as if you really minded," he said.

Beverly let her hands fall idle in her lap.

"I do!" she said quietly. "I know we haven't seen much of him, yet he's been in a way a real friend. I'd be sorry to think of him going away somewhere where we can't ever meet."

Jonnie studied Beverly's face, his own puzzled.

"Bev, what really went on between you two? I never asked."

He was surprised by the colour that flooded Beverly's cheeks for an instant.

"Nothing, really! He told me not to be so silly and sent me off home – to you!"

"Did he?" Jonnie said, further surprised. "I think at the time I was a bit jealous. I had some idea he was in love with you."

"*You*, jealous *of me*?" Beverly said. "But, Jonnie, you were mad about Elinor at the time!"

Jonnie shrugged his shoulders. "All the same, I took a strong dislike to the fellow. Perhaps I was a bit unfair. After all, you say he sent you home. Does that mean you were really going to leave me, Bev?"

"I don't know, Jonnie!" she answered slowly. "I don't think I'd sorted anything out then. I just wanted someone to tell me what to do."

"And you haven't regretted it?" Jonnie asked curiously.

"Of course not!" Beverly said quickly. "Nor you, Jonnie?"

"No!" Jonnie said, glad that in this at least he could tell the truth.

Suddenly Beverly smiled. "You know, we haven't talked this way for ages – about ourselves, I mean. Jonnie, can you tell me now, about Elinor? You don't ever wish you could be with her?"

"No!" Jonnie lied quickly. "Let's not talk about her, Beverly. I'd rather not."

"So it still hurts?" Beverly said, as much to herself as to him. "Yet you weren't in love with her; you said so at the time. Jonnie, you've never been sorry you married me? That we had the children?"

"No, I haven't!" Jonnie said again. "You know how I feel about them, Bev. And you, too, of course. It's really you who should have regrets. I'm afraid I'm not all you hoped for in a husband. But, Bev, I swear I never mean and never meant to be anything less than perfect. I suppose I'm just weak, or something. I can't think why you don't hate me, really!"

Beverly looked up and met the strange look of appeal with an uneasiness in her heart. "Hate you! Jonnie, how can you think that? I'll admit I was terribly hurt at the time; any woman would have been. But I wouldn't have cared so much if I hadn't loved you so much. Besides, I don't really blame you, I blame her. She had so much with which to attract a man and she didn't hesitate to try. I think if she could, she'd have taken you away from us. I can understand how at the time she seemed new and exciting and different. But you chose us, Jonnie, and that's all that really matters."

He wanted then to tell her, to confess to these last months. It was so near the tip of his tongue to do so that silence hung like a thread in the room and but for the sudden whimper from one of the sleeping children, he might have done so, promising to finish with Elinor, this time for always.

But Beverly rose quickly to go upstairs and he was alone with his unspoken confession. In that moment, he hated Elinor, hated the power she had over him, hated her for his own basic weakness. It was Beverly he really loved and really admired, respected, liked. It was Elinor's body he wanted, needed, desired with a passion that seemed to know no abatement. She offered escape from all that was dull and humdrum and ordinary. She offered glamour instead of domesticity. She was the unknown, the quarry he must chase, the mystery, the temptation for a world only half experienced; a world he wanted, enjoyed. That which was evil and bad in her awakened all that was evil and bad in him. He knew it, yet he couldn't break away from it. He was like a man addicted to drugs. Beverly couldn't help him; no one could help him except himself. And he couldn't contemplate any more a life without that heady excitement, devoid of the passion, the colour, the sophistication she had taught him to appreciate.

Perhaps in the New Year, Jonnie thought helplessly. At the end of the year, I'll tell Elinor we've got to stop it. I'll really try to settle down without her. But the knowledge that soon he might have to do without her, only increased his desire.

Until Christmas, when he would be home for three days and a weekend, he visited the apartment even more often. Beverly understood that there would be several late nights before the holiday. He had every excuse to catch a late train. Christmas Eve he was in Elinor's arms at six o'clock, a time when Allan called to say goodbye to Beverly.

"Why, Allan! What a wonderful surprise!" Beverly greeted him with genuine warmth. She was tired from all the preparations for the next day and the children were so excited that, even with Annette to help her, it had been a difficult job getting them all settled down for the night.

She led him into the sitting-room, bright with paper chains the children had made, and holly over the pictures and the Christmas tree which stood in one corner.

"How nice it all looks!" Allan said, seeing not so much the detail as the resulting effect of a family's combined efforts to bring out the Christmas seasonal feelings. This was how a home should look at Christmas time. The home-made crib with the Baby in its cradle and the toy farm animals around, lit by a tiny candle, completed the scene.

His own cottage was undecorated, empty, without noise or light or fire. Ever since he had sent in his request for a transfer he had not been able to take any interest in it, knowing he must soon leave.

During a difficult interview with the school governors, he had tried to find adequate reasons for wishing to go, even inventing a sick aunt in Yorkshire. They'd been very unwilling to accede to his wishes and had told him outright that they wanted him to reconsider.

"The fact is, Forbes, we have been thinking of making you headmaster. Jackson retires at the end of the next year and we were all agreed that you'd be the ideal man for the post. I couldn't guarantee this step up if you leave. We'd have no control over you in Yorkshire although we would, of course, give you the best of references. But if you can find a way to sort out your family difficulties, then it would be well worth while staying on, Forbes. Think it over."

The man, meaning well, had refused to take Allan's on-the-spot denial that he would change his mind.

"We'll have another talk after the holidays. Your aunt may have taken a turn for the better by then. Or maybe you can see your way to moving her down to this part of the world. After all, Forbes, your financial position will soon be much improved. I know I ought not to say this, but I can pretty well guarantee you'll get the head-master's job when he goes."

Of course he'd been glad to think they *wanted* him as head and thought him capable and fit for the job. It was always satisfying to one's pride to have one's work and efforts appreciated. But the extra money? It wouldn't make much difference when he had only himself to think about. He had no big expenses, no hobbies demanding a lot of money. He'd managed pretty well, even saved a bit. All the same, he would have liked the job; liked to have run the school along his lines, and been in sole charge.

It made the going harder, for go he must. With every day, his thoughts turned more and more to Beverly, to her children, her home. He'd had to come this evening to wish her and the boys a happy Christmas, to bid her a silent farewell. He'd supposed that being Christmas Eve, Jonnie would be at home. He'd hoped the sight of her and Jonnie, close, linked with one another in their home and children, would make him realize how utterly useless such a love must be, now and always. Beverly did not need him and could not possibly do so. There was nothing to keep him here but everything to make him go if he valued peace of mind. Away from her and the boys, he would begin to forget, to find that peace of mind that he had attained with such difficulty after Louise's death.

But Jonnie was not here.

"He said he would almost certainly be late tonight," Beverly explained as she poured out drinks for them both. "Actually, I did think he might be on the train getting in at seven. But I suppose he missed it."

"It's very foggy out," Allan said, sitting down by the fire and stretching his long legs. "Maybe the train is held up."

"It must have come down suddenly," Beverly replied, going to the window to look out. "Yes, you're right, Allan. It is thick. I think I'll ring the station to find out if the train is in. You'll excuse me, won't you."

While she was away, Allan stared into the fire, knowing with a deep sense of pain that the girl he loved was still in love with the man she had married. He knew it was wrong to be jealous of her husband and that he should not allow himself to think of Beverly except as another man's wife. Yet he could not help the emotions she roused in him, even while he hid them firmly in the depths of his being.

"Allan, it seems there's been a hold-up. The stationmaster isn't quite sure what's wrong but he said there'd been an accident further up the line. He might know more in a little while, he said. I hope it wasn't Jonnie's train."

Her voice was full of anxiety.

"I'm sure it wasn't!" Allan replied in his slow calm voice. "It's easy enough on a night like this for a truck to get derailed. There's no reason to believe it is anything serious, is there?"

"No, I suppose not!" Beverly said. "All the same, I'd like to know what has happened. Whenever something is wrong, my mind always goes back to that dreadful Lewisham rail disaster! I suppose I'm morbid or something."

She laughed uncertainly.

"Well, ring again in fifteen minutes. Meanwhile, tell me what you've been doing since I last saw you."

"There's nothing to tell really," Beverly said, relaxing into the chair opposite him. "Why haven't you come before this, Allan? It's ages since you were last here."

Immediately she had spoken, she regretted her words. There was a look on Allan's face which betrayed all too easily his real feelings, as he struggled for some excuse.

"I just don't seem to have got around to it," he faltered. "Besides,

159

there's a possibility that I might be going away. I wanted to be sure before I told you."

"Going away? Where?" Beverly asked both questions in one breath.

"To another school. They may be sending me up to Yorkshire."

"Oh, Allan, no!" Beverly cried, despite herself. "Not all the way up there. Why, I'd never see you."

"I know!" Allan said quietly. "But these postings happen, you know, much the same way as in the Army. I've been here quite a few years, you know."

Beverly remained silent. Of course, he couldn't know what his words had done to her. Somehow she had never imagined such a thing happening. Allan was there, in the little school at the foot of the hill, or in his cottage. It wasn't that she had seen much of him, just that she'd *known* he was there and that he'd be there if ever she needed a friend.

How selfish I am! she thought suddenly, despising herself. Of course this wasn't much of a job for someone with Allan's gifts. Maybe he was being promoted; she hadn't even asked. He was probably glad to be going; and yet he wasn't. She knew he was not. She knew the real reason he was leaving just as surely as if he had told her. It was the best thing, really, yet she felt utterly miserable, all the joy of Christmas, all pleasure in this unexpected visit, wiped out in a terrible sense of impending loss.

As she could read him, so could he read her. Her face, always mobile, was to him quite transparent. For one brief moment, he was happy because of her sadness. Then he quickly controlled himself, saying: "You know, it won't make much difference to you, Beverly. Do you realize we've only met half a dozen times?"

"Yes, yes, I know!" Beverly said. "But it always seems as if we've known each other all our lives."

You, too, feel that! Allan thought but dared not say. It is the same for me. But I feel that way because I love you. You are not in love with me.

"I know!" he said as lightly as he could. "There are some people one feels that way about. I think it happens a lot between people who are basically rather alike. There's a familiarity about the way they think, the things they say. It makes you feel you've known them longer than you really have."

"The boys will be very upset!" Beverly said abruptly. "I don't know how I'm going to tell them."

"You mustn't say anything yet," Allan told her. "It's far from definite. Anyway, they've left it a bit late now. Term starts in another two weeks. But if I'm to make the move next holidays, well, I'll probably be pretty busy clearing up various odds and ends and there won't be much time for social calls. That's why I came tonight."

"I wish you hadn't!" Beverly cried impulsively. "I would rather not have known."

"Beverly!" The way he spoke her name was like a caress. She heard it and looked up, meeting his gaze and reading in those brown eyes love, compassion, appeal. "Don't let it bother you. It really won't make much difference. Besides, I'll write and tell you my news and I hope you will write and keep me in touch with the boys. I'd hate to think I'd never know what was happening to them. Little Julia, too. They've been a sort of substitute family, in a way."

There were tears in her eyes as she turned her head quickly away so that he should not see them. Tears she could not explain except that her own heart was echoing the loneliness, the longing in Allan's, and it hurt.

Why should it? she asked herself, attempting to regain her composure. He's quite right. It can't make any difference to me. I'm only feeling this way because I know *he* doesn't really want to go.

"It'll be a good thing for me," Allan was saying, trying not to see the bent head, the downward droop of her mouth. "One is apt to get in a rut in a small country place like this. I'll make new friends, see new places. In many ways, it'll be good."

"Yes, yes, of course. It was selfish of me to be thinking only of myself," Beverly said, attempting a smile.

Silence fell, not the gentle quiet silence that sometimes falls between two people who know each other well and have no need for words. But a difficult, strained period of time when the air was charged with all the words that remained unspoken. At last, Allan said:

"You were going to ring the station again. As soon as you've heard everything is all right, I must go."

Obediently, Beverly replaced her glass and hurried into the hall. Her mind was not fully occupied with Jonnie, half of it remaining in the room with Allan, when she repeated her request for information.

"You a relative?" the stationmaster was asking her.

"Yes, yes, I am!" Beverly said, suddenly becoming fully conscious of the situation. "Nothing's wrong, is it? My husband is on that train. At least, I think he might be."

"I'm very sorry, Madam, but there's been a nasty accident about fifteen miles outside London at the Junction. The six thirty-five ran into the back of a goods train. I'm afraid I can't give you any further information. If your husband was on the train it might be as well to phone the hospitals nearby. I doubt you'll get through to the station itself; they're jammed with callers."

White-faced, Beverly ran back into the sitting-room, too distraught with anxiety to feel thankful as yet that Allan was there to help and advise her. She stammered out the story.

"Suppose he's on it, Allan. What shall I do? I'm not even sure he caught that train. He may have missed it. Pray God he missed it."

"The first thing to do is to find out if he *was* on it," Allan said reasonably. "Will there be anyone at the office? Maybe someone can tell you what time he left. That would give you some idea."

"Yes, no . . . there won't be anyone there now, Allan. It's nearly eight o'clock. I don't know who to ring. There's the senior partner; I know his name but not his number."

"We can find that out!" Allan said calmly. "I'll ring directory enquiries. He lives in town?"

"Yes, Putney!" Beverly said, suddenly calm now that Allan was in charge. "He's sure to know when Jonnie left. They were having a conference at four. Jonnie said that might drag on and make him late."

Allan got through to directory enquiries and, without much difficulty, obtained the home address and telephone number of

162

James Barkington. Another few minutes and he handed the telephone to Beverly.

"He's on the line!" he whispered.

"Mr Barkington? Oh, this is Mrs Colt. I'm so sorry to disturb you but I'm rather worried about Jonnie. There's been a bad smash on our line and Jonnie isn't home. Can you possibly give me some idea when he left the office?"

"Why, yes, Mrs Colt. It was early, being Christmas Eve, you see. All the staff were away by five. We had a drink, just to toast the season, you know, and then we all left together. The typist locked up behind me. It wasn't later than five, I'm sure of that."

"I see. Thank you!" Beverly said, and after Mr Barkington had made a few reassuring remarks, which she did not really hear, she replaced the receiver, noticing as she did so that her hand was trembling.

"Beverly, what's wrong? What's happened?" Allan asked her, catching her arm to steady her as he led her back into the sitting-room.

"I don't know!" Beverly whispered. "It doesn't make sense, Allan. Jonnie left at five, certainly not after; Mr Barkington went at the same time, so he's sure of that. It means Jonnie could have caught the five-thirty. Easily. Even if he were held up in the rush hour, he could have caught the five-fifty. Allan, what shall I do now?"

Allan was shaken. Of course, there were a number of things which might have held Jonnie back from catching those two trains. He might have been doing some last-minute shopping. But then, if he said this to Beverly, it would reopen her fears that he was on the six thirty-five.

"He said he felt sure they'd be late. Yet Mr Barkington said he let the whole staff go early because it was Christmas Eve."

"Maybe they finished earlier than Jonnie anticipated. Beverly, there's no point in sitting here surmising all that might have gone wrong. We must ring the hospitals and try to find out some news."

"If Jonnie wasn't on the six thirty-five he'd have been home by now. If he was shopping, he'd surely have telephoned me."

"Only if he'd heard the news of the train smash. It would have been too late to catch the evening papers. He'd only know about it if he heard it on the radio and he wouldn't be likely to hear a radio in a shop. Besides, we don't even know if the accident has been announced officially."

"I'm going to ring the hospitals," Beverly said. And in the next breath: "But suppose Jonnie is trying to get through to me? No, I'll ring the hospitals. I'd rather do that than sit here waiting."

With Allan's help, they found the telephone numbers of the five hospitals in and around the locality of the accident. The first two reported numerous casualties received, but Jonnie's name was not among them.

"You mustn't worry," Allan said as firmly as he could. "We don't even know for sure he was on the train."

"But there are so many!" Beverly cried. "It must have been a terrible accident. Allan, put on the wireless. Something may come through on it. I'll try the next number."

Allan had barely tuned in to the Home Service before Beverly recalled him quickly to the phone.

"He's there!" she cried. "At least, they think so. They're checking the names again. Hullo? Yes?"

"We have a Mr Jonathan Colt in casualty now. Aged about thirty to thirty-five, fair hair, blue eyes. Height about six feet, clean shaven."

"Yes, that's my husband. I'm sure of it! Is he all right? Please tell me."

"I'm afraid I can't tell you the extent of his injuries at the moment. Can you ring again later?"

"But he's alive?" Beverly cried frantically to the cool measured tones on the other end of the wire.

"Yes, Mrs Colt. Will you call again? I will have more information for you then."

"Yes, yes, I'll ring again!" Beverly said, replacing the receiver.

"At least we know he's alive," Allan said. "Would you like to go to the hospital? Can you leave the children? If so, I'll take you up."

"Oh, Allan, would you?" Beverly cried gratefully. "Annette will be all right till the morning. The car's at the station, though."

"My car is outside your door!" Allan reminded her with a smile.

"Get a coat, Beverly, and if you haven't had anything to eat, then get some sandwiches to eat on the way."

"I don't want anything to eat," Beverly began but he interrupted her.

"I do! And whether you want it or not, you'll need it. Five minutes won't make any difference. We can be there in half an hour."

While she ran upstairs to tell Annette what was happening, Allan paced the sitting-room floor. His mind was deeply troubled, not just by the accident and the possible extent of Colt's injuries, but by the problem of his whereabouts after he'd left the office. With so much else to think about, it seemed to have slipped Beverly's mind for the moment, but at the time she had learned he'd left at five, she'd been shocked and deeply puzzled. Obviously she hadn't expected him to be shopping. Could he have stopped to have a drink with some friends? Hardly, on Christmas Eve, knowing his wife would be waiting for him; things to be done like hanging up the children's stockings, filling them. Where had he been during that hour and a half? With whom? Was it possible the man had been continuing his association with that American woman in town? Was that why he'd had to work so late so often?

It's no way to think of a man who might be dying, Allan told himself sharply. And the last thought in the world he wanted Beverly to have.

They'd both forgotten the fog. The drive was a nightmare crawl. Only Allan's slow, steady voice talking about nothing, everything, anything he could think of, kept Beverly from going out of her mind. It was nearly ten o'clock before they reached the hospital. Even as they arrived, ambulances were drawing up, lined up, waiting to disgorge their burdens.

"It's terrible!" Beverly whispered, holding hard to Allan's hand. "And it's Christmas Eve, too. Allan, I'm afraid."

He did not answer her, but led her to Reception where he made enquiries for her.

"He's all right, Beverly. Did you hear me? He's all right. They had to operate, but he's through that. They are ringing through to the ward to ask if you can see him."

Beverly felt the tears running down her cheeks. Tears of relief, of relief from the tension of this last few hours.

"Don't, darling, please don't!" She heard Allan's voice and felt the strength of his love for her, sustaining her. Somehow the knowledge did not seem important; it was something she had always known, never a burden, always a comfort when she needed him most.

"I always seem to cry when I'm with you!" she said, trying to wipe away the tears with the back of her hand. He did the job for her with a clean white handkerchief. "I'm so sorry."

"Don't be. That's what a friend's shoulder should be for – to cry on. Beverly, you can go up. Ward 8. I'll wait for you here. You probably won't be allowed to stay with him long."

She felt alone, anxious, afraid as she followed the young nurse down the long corridor, smelling of disinfectants and ether, a hospital smell she had always been afraid of. Outside the ward door she hesitated.

"There's nothing to worry about, Mrs Colt. Here, I'll take you in," the young nurse said, seeing Beverly's hesitation.

She took Beverly over to Jonnie's bed. At first, she thought he was asleep. He lay with his eyes closed, his face chalk-white; only the slight rise and fall of his chest showed he was breathing at all. Her eyes took in the bandages round both arms. Downstairs, she'd been told the injuries were internal. Perhaps they had meant only the serious injuries.

Suddenly, he opened his eyes and recognized her. "Hullo, Bev. Didn't expect to see you here. They told me you'd phoned. So sorry to drag you out on a night like this."

She knelt by the bed, regardless of the other patients and nurses in the ward, putting her arms round him gently. "Darling, of course I had to see you, to see for myself you were all right. What a horrible experience for you."

"Was pretty grim!" Jonnie said weakly. "Lucky to come out of it alive. Hundreds killed, I heard them saying so when they dragged me out. Don't let's talk about it."

"No! *You're* all right and that's all that matters. Darling, does it hurt? They say you had an operation."

"I'm okay. Hurts a bit when I breathe in too deeply. One of the nurses came along just now and said she'd give me something to help me sleep but I told them not till you'd been. Wanted to talk to you. Bev, I've messed up your Christmas, I'm afraid, and the kids'. So sorry. I always seem to be mucking up your life, don't I?"

"Jonnie, darling, don't. It doesn't matter. Everything is all right so long as you're going to be OK. I was so afraid . . ."

"That I'd die? So was I. Bev, it might have been better in lots of ways if I had."

"Jonnie!" she stared at him aghast. "You can't mean that. What would I do without you? And the children? Jonnie, say you didn't mean it!"

He looked at her for a long moment across the white coverlet of his bed. She looked so pretty. Even with her hair blown about and not much powder on her face, she still looked pretty. Funny how long it had been since he'd really looked at her. It was like seeing her for the first time all over again.

"You know, I do love you," he said. "I always have. Even if I haven't always seemed to do so, I still love you."

"Jonnie, I know. You're not to think about anything but getting well. There's nothing to worry about, nothing at all."

"There is!" Jonnie said the words almost as if he were speaking to himself. "You don't know, Bev, but there is. I've made such a mess of everything. I never meant it to turn out like this."

"Like what, Jonnie? What's happened? Tell me what it is that's worrying you."

"Should have told you," Jonnie said sleepily. "Ages ago. I wanted to. Tonight we had an awful scene. I told her it had to be all over because of you. Didn't want to lose you, you see. But she said she'd kill herself if I left her . . . nothing else to live for but me. Funny, I never thought she really loved me until this evening. She suddenly made me see what I'd been doing to her. Ruined her life, too. I'd only thought of you before. I knew then that I didn't love her and never had. She wanted me to leave you, marry her when the divorce came through. But I wouldn't do it. That's when she said she'd put an end to it all. Don't know if she would have done, but I didn't have the nerve to risk it. Had to stay a while longer. That's why I was on the six thirty-five, you see."

"Jonnie!" she grasped his hands in her own as his eyes closed. He mustn't go to sleep now; not until she was sure he wasn't delirious. But his eyes remained shut and he seemed quite unaware of her existence.

A nurse suddenly appeared at the bedside and seeing her patient asleep, his wife looking as if she might faint at any moment, she said briskly:

"Time you left, Mrs Colt. There's nothing to be upset about, you know. He's sleeping because he had an injection just before you came up."

"But he said—" Beverly began when the girl interrupted her.

"No, he didn't want it until after he'd seen you. Said he couldn't rest until he had. But we gave it to him all the same. He thought it was penicillin."

"Then he didn't know what he was saying just now?"

"Well, I can't be sure about that, but he would have been quite conscious until a moment or two before he dropped off. Come, Mrs Colt. Let me see if I can get you a cup of tea; you look all in."

"No, no, I'm all right!" Beverly said. "Besides, there's someone waiting for me downstairs. Thank you, Nurse."

"You can come in again in the morning," the nurse said. "Doctor or Matron will be able to see you then. As you can understand, they're frantically busy just now. Cases are still coming in all the time. You must be thankful your husband is going to be all right."

"Yes, yes, I am!" Beverly said with an effort. "Thank you, Nurse. Good night!"

Somehow, she found her way back along the corridors.

Allan was waiting where she had left him. As she approached him, he jumped up and went forward to meet her.

"Beverly, you look ghastly. He *is* all right?"

"Yes, he's asleep. Allan, take me away from here quickly. Let's go somewhere, have a drink or something. I want to think."

He knew then that something was terribly wrong. Mistakenly, he imagined it must be with Jonnie; that he might have lost a leg, an arm? Be injured about the face? Yet the hall porter had assured him that there were only internal injuries and a few cuts and bruises. Why was Beverly so shaken?

He waited until they were seated in a nearby restaurant, until Beverly had taken at least two sips of the large brandy he had ordered for her. Then he said quietly:

"You must tell me what is worrying you, Beverly. Unless you do, I can't help you."

"No one can help me!" Beverly said. And then: "I suppose you might as well know. It's Jonnie. He's been seeing Elinor again. I don't know how often but there must have been other times before this evening. That's why he was on that train. He'd been with her. It's probably been going on all along, ever since she left home. Oh, Allan, it's horrible, horrible."

Allan drew in his breath. With every nerve in his body, he wanted to say to her: "Leave him, come away with me. I love you . . . I love you so much. I'd die for you. Give me a chance; let me show you what love really is."

But he remained silent, trying to say only what was best for the woman he loved so dearly.

"What made him tell you, now?" he asked at last.

"I don't know, I just don't know. I think it was on his mind, on his conscience. It had all got too much for him. He hadn't meant it to be more than an affair. When he tried to break away – for good, he said – she threatened to kill herself."

"But she'd never do a thing like that," Allan said, astounded. "She isn't the type."

"No! But Jonnie believed her. He probably wanted to. I expect it appealed to his ego. No, that isn't true. I think he was badly shaken. He'd thought he could have his cake and eat it. Silly Jonnie! Surely he must have known that with a woman like that he couldn't come out the winner."

"I'm glad you can feel sorry for him!" Allan said quietly and truthfully. "I think it sounds as if he needs your help and understanding, Beverly. I'm sure he must love you and trust you. Otherwise he would never have told you, no matter how wrong things have gone."

"Trust me? Takes my love and my forgiveness for granted, you mean," Beverly said bitterly. "I forgave him once. Why not again? Oh yes, he loves me. If you can call what he feels love. It isn't my idea, Allan."

"Nor is it mine!" Allan agreed softly. "But it is wrong to judge other people by one's own standards. Obviously this woman had him under her thumb. He's weak, but that doesn't mean he loved her or that he had stopped caring about you."

"How can you be so damned righteous about him?" Beverly burst out, hysteria mounting in her. "I don't understand you, Allan. I don't understand anything any more."

"Darling!" The endearment calmed her instantly. "Darling," he said again. "Don't you see that it is because I love you so much that I have to think this way about him? It would be so terribly easy to say all kinds of things about him. That way would serve my ends, for then you might turn against him, divorce him, maybe even marry me. It's because of that, I have to make you see the best in him. I think you're still in love with him, and if you ever leave him, Beverly, it cannot be because of something I said to you."

She suddenly took both his hands in her own and clung to them tightly. "Allan, I'm sorry. Forgive me. I ought not to have made you talk this way. I knew you loved me, although I sometimes found it difficult to believe. I think I was afraid even to think about it because of what it might mean – to us. I needed you so badly, Allan. So I buried my head in the sand and pretended you were just a good friend. But deep down I knew. Now you are going away, and I can speak the truth to you. I'm Jonnie's wife; I hate him for what he has done to me, and yet I know I couldn't ever leave him. He is weak. He's like a small boy who can't resist the forbidden sweet, even though he knows he'll end up being punished for it. What would happen to him if I leave him? He'd get trapped by someone like Elinor Wilmot and go from bad to worse. I think I know now what my life with him will be like; this kind of betrayal over and over again. But he'd never leave me. I think he needs me, Allan, far more than you do. But if that isn't so—"

She broke off, uncertainly, but the man beside her finished it for her. "If ever it gets too much for you, Beverly, you *know* I'll be waiting for you."

"It's so unfair!" Beverly cried with a childish bitterness. "You deserve so much more, Allan. Life has treated you so badly."

"Don't pity me, darling!" Allan said gently. "Besides, it isn't true. Life gave me Louise to love and then you. I know I can never have you, but it means something to me that you are in the world, too, perhaps even thinking of me sometimes."

"Oh, Allan!" Beverly whispered, her heart so filled with pain and sadness that it was almost too much to bear. "I think I feel that way, too. Just to know you are there; that you love me. I suppose I should not feel this way but the thought is so wonderfully comforting. I know I ought to tell you to forget me, find someone else. You should be married, Allan, and have children. It isn't too late. I would hate myself so if I were responsible for keeping you from such happiness."

"Dearest Beverly, surely you know that no one else would do for me? Believe me, I don't want to get married, have children, just to ward off loneliness. I have lived and can live alone and be happy. That is true, you know. You see, my work is so much amongst others. I don't have a great deal of time to think about myself. I shan't be unhappy."

And I? Beverly asked herself. Can I ever be happy again? What kind of future can there be for Jonnie and me? I can't love him or respect him, ever again. Has it always been like this, only I unaware of the truth? Has Jonnie always been weak? Must he always want what is forbidden? Perhaps that is *why* he married me; because my mother was so set against it.

But she knew that wasn't altogether true. They had been deeply in love in the beginning. They had discovered love together. They'd been so very young, so full of ideals and confidence.

Beverly realized with a sense of shock that if she were willing to forgive a second time; to forbear from reproaching him; to give him affection and a happy home, then their marriage could still go on. Perhaps love could no longer exist, but she could never be indifferent to Jonnie's well-being. She had lived with him, cared for him, considered him too long. She could not put him out of her life as if he had never existed.

"I must stay with him!" She spoke her thoughts aloud. "I don't altogether understand why, Allan. I'd be justified this time in leaving him and going away with you. I think that is what I *want* to do. I could feel safe with you, certain about the future. This way there is no security."

"Marriage means more than a few words spoken in church and a piece of paper saying it is legally done. You make vows, promises before God. That is why you cannot cast off those promises, darling. I wouldn't ask you to. Jonnie's failure to keep his vows doesn't excuse you from breaking your own. You'll find happiness in deciding this way, I'm sure of it. If you came to me, you'd feel guilty all your life."

"You always understand!" Beverly said, with an immense gratitude in her heart for that understanding.

"That is because I love you!" Allan replied matter-of-factly. "I think that helps me to know you, perhaps better than you know yourself. Beverly, had you thought what you want to do about the immediate future? This is Christmas Eve. Tomorrow you will want to be with the children."

"Christmas!" Beverly echoed. "I'd forgotten. I told Jonnie I'd go in and see him in the morning. What shall I do? Will Jonnie understand, or will he think I've chosen to be with the children because of what he told me tonight?"

"Can't you write him a letter, explaining?"

"I'm not sure he would understand." She paused, uncertain where her duty lay.

"Why not come home, spend the morning with the children, have lunch and then come back up here?" Allan suggested. "I'm quite free tomorrow. If you like, I'd go in and spend the afternoon with them so they aren't disappointed. Annette could manage the twins."

"Yes, yes, she could!" Beverly cried gratefully. "Will you really do that, Allan? I'd be so grateful. And the children wouldn't mind my going if they knew you were going to stay with them. They all love you. You must come to lunch, too. I'm going to ring up the hospital now; ask the Ward Sister to tell Jonnie I won't be in until the afternoon."

As soon as she had done so, Allan drove her home, stopping at the station so that she could pick up her own car. It was dark and

172

deserted. No trains were running although the fog had cleared and the night was cold and starry. As Beverly stood by her own car to bid Allan good night, their breath was like smoke on the cold air.

"You'd better go, Beverly. You're shivering," Allan said considerately, opening the car door for her.

"Yes!" she agreed, but did not move. "But first I want to thank you, for so much, Allan. I don't know how I'd have got through this night without your help."

Impulsively, she stood on tip-toe and lightly kissed his cheek.

Every nerve in his body jerked with the swift rising desire to return her kiss; to hold her in his arms, show her with deeds, not words, how great was his love for her. She looked so young, so helpless, with her face turned in gratitude to his, her beautiful green eyes bewildered, as if life was proving too hard a task for her.

She couldn't know how provocative was that softly parted mouth, the gentle slope of her shoulders beneath the warm coat, the cloud of dark hair touched now with crystals of dew.

"I'm no better than Jonnie!" Allan told himself fiercely. "I love her, I want her, and she's another man's wife. I dare not touch her, or I'll never let her go."

"Good night!" he said harshly, abruptly, and turning on his heel, walked the few steps to his own car and hurriedly climbed in.

She stood a moment longer, staring after him, feeling already a sense of loss, loneliness at his going. Then, her heart beating in sudden knowledge, she guessed why he had gone so quickly from her.

Don't leave me! The words formed on her lips, an unbidden inarticulate cry from her heart. But they stayed unspoken, only half thought. And she, too, turned and climbed into her own car.

They drove off into the night, one behind the other until the road divided and each turned opposite ways. Only their thoughts remained together, each concerned with the other until, exhausted, they found release from torment in sleep.

Jonnie gave his wife a sheepish smile. He was sitting up in bed, more colour in his cheeks. He had seemed genuinely very pleased to see her.

"Jolly decent of you to come, Bev. Seeing it's Christmas and everything."

Beverly deliberately ignored the last words. "It's quite all right, Jonnie. I left Allan Forbes with the children and they didn't mind a bit. They sent their love and were, of course, thrilled to death to hear about the train accident."

"Ghoulish little horrors!" Jonnie said, grinning. "I suppose they were even glad I was in it! Were they pleased with their presents? What about you, Bev? Did you like my present to you?"

"I didn't open it!" Beverly said quietly. She hadn't wanted to. Any present from Jonnie would have seemed like a bartering; a bribe. But seeing the hurt disappointment on his face, she added: "I thought I'd wait till you were home to see me open it. I've brought these things up for you."

Jonnie took the parcels with enthusiasm and tore off the paper wrappings as eagerly as Nick or Phil or Julia had done that morning. He commented on everything.

"Super!" he said when he had opened Beverly's present to him – a set of carpenter's tools he had been coveting for some time in a local ironmonger's window. "Just what I wanted. You spoil me, Bev."

She didn't answer. She felt tired and on edge and this visit to Jonnie had been far more of an effort than he knew. But he seemed on top of the world. It was hard to believe that he'd had quite a serious operation only a few hours ago.

"Tough! That's me!" he told her. "The pretty little Irish night nurse said I was delirious last night and tried to kiss her—" He broke off, suddenly anxious in case Beverly should take this too seriously. But when she did not comment, he went on: "I wish you'd find out how long I've got to stay here, Bev. I'm fed up with it already and I can't get the Doc to tell me anything. He just says 'We'll see!' and that's that."

"I'll try and find out. I expect they will want to know at the office when to expect you back. Mr Barkington phoned this morning and I told him you were here. He asked me to send his best wishes."

"Oh, thanks!" Jonnie said. "By the way, Bev, I wonder if you'd be a real sport and do something for me. I don't really like asking this, but obviously they won't let me near a phone for a while. Could you make a phone call for me?"

Beverly felt the colour rush to her cheeks. From the hesitant way Jonnie was asking her, she was in little doubt that it was Elinor he wanted her to ring up. How could he ask such a thing?

Seeing the flushed face and downcast eyes, Jonnie went on quickly:

"I know it's a beastly thing to ask you, Bev, but I thought if you did, you could tell her then that I meant what I said, last night; that it was all over, I mean. I think she might believe it, coming from you. Then if she gets hysterical again, you'll know better than me how to deal with it."

He behaves as if I were his mother, helping him out of a scrape! Beverly thought with astonishment. He doesn't realize what he is asking me to do.

"All right!" she said weakly. "Give me the number and I'll ring on my way out."

"You are a good sport, Bev," Jonnie said thankfully. "I can always count on you. I know I don't deserve it. I've behaved rottenly to you and I wouldn't blame you a bit if you said you'd had enough of it. Believe me, darling, I despise myself. If she hadn't come to my office, I'd never have got in touch with her. You do believe that, don't you?"

"Yes! I believe she made the first move. But that doesn't exonerate you, Jonnie. You could have said 'no'."

Jonnie scowled. "It's all very well, Bev, but you don't know Elinor as well as I do. She just doesn't take 'no' for an answer. Oh, I know I'm weak. But I never meant you to be hurt, Bev. There were lots of times I *tried* to break away. But it's really finished now. You do believe me?"

"I want to believe you!" Beverly said truthfully. "I know you meant it to be the end, but you promised me it was all over before, when all the time—"

"No, it wasn't like that, Bev. I really did tell her it was all over. Then she came to see me at the office and it began again. Bev, you won't let it make any difference, will you? You don't want to divorce me?"

175

"No, I don't want a divorce!" It was all she could say with truth. It was bound, after all, to make a difference. It was Jonnie himself who had changed, at least in her eyes. He'd shown himself for exactly what he was, a Peter Pan, the little boy who would never grow up, on whom she could never depend. He was resilient, just as children are resilient. He'd forget about all this as soon as he knew she'd forgiven him. Things like unfaithfulness and lies and deceit were not important; his code was different from hers. He could even ask her to telephone Elinor for him. That more than anything showed her how incapable Jonnie was of understanding what Elinor had done with their lives. Any scheming woman could do as she pleased with Jonnie; he was weak, weak.

"Bev, you don't mind about ringing her. I can't help feeling responsible. Suppose she has done something awful. Last night was horrible; there was a ghastly scene. It was all so *unlike* her."

"I don't doubt it!" Beverly said wryly. "She put on a very good act, Jonnie, and you fell for it."

"You mean, you think she was pretending to be suicidal?" Jonnie asked, visibly brightening. "Gosh, I hope you're right, Bev. It isn't that I'd really care – at least, not much – about her, but I kept thinking of what the scandal would be like. It would be so awful for you and the children and at the office."

Even in love you are selfish, half-hearted, Beverly thought. I'd have respected you more, Jonnie, if you'd really loved her. Then there might have been some excuse. Aloud, she said: "Let's not talk about her any more, Jonnie. It's over and I want to – to forget. Tell me, how are you feeling? Does it hurt much? Did the doctor tell you what was wrong?"

"It isn't too bad," Jonnie said, cheerful again now he could forget about Elinor. "Bit of a mess inside, Doc said, but nothing he hasn't been able to put right. I was lucky. There were at least five other people in my carriage and three anyway were dead. I could see that before I was dragged out."

"It must have been horrible!" Beverly said shuddering. "The papers are full of it and the radio, too. It's ruined so many families' Christmas. Somehow it's all the worse because of that."

"I hate having to be away from you all too," Jonnie said

176

truthfully. "I did want to see Nick's and Phil's faces when they opened the Hornby. I wanted to help them set up the track, too. I suppose Forbes is doing it for them."

"Yes!" Beverly replied. After all, it wouldn't hurt Jonnie to be hurt just a little himself.

"Bev, I know you like the fellow. When I get home, would it make you happy if I try to make friends with him?"

Jonnie and Allan friends. No, it wasn't very possible even if Allan had been staying on. They were too unalike.

"Allan's going away; it's almost definite. I don't suppose we'll see much of him after these holidays are over."

Hearing the sadness in her voice when she spoke of Forbes' departure, Jonnie took a closer look at his young wife.

"Bev, you're not in love with him, are you? Oh, I know I couldn't blame you if you were, after the way I've behaved. But I'd hate to think that you and—"

"No!" Beverly broke in sharply. "There's nothing between us, Jonnie. We're just good friends. Now about tomorrow . . ." Quickly she changed the subject: "Mother can't get down immediately so I won't be up for a couple of days. Once she arrives, well, I'll be in every day to visit you. Anything you want when I next come?"

"I don't think so," Jonnie said. "A few decent books, that's all. And look, darling, if it's difficult for you to trail up here every day, well, I won't expect to see you. I don't deserve it. You've been absolutely topping about everything and I'd like to make amends. I'll be all right. I'll be home anyway in a week with any luck, you'll see."

But it was a month before Jonnie finally came home. He was very changed. Gone were the bright smile, the cheerful optimism. He was thin, irritable and very weak.

"I'm fed up with feeling lousy!" he said violently soon after his return. "Those damned doctors don't know half as much as they pretend. X-ray after X-ray until I felt like a half-cooked goose. And still they don't seem to have got me fit."

Beverly looked at him anxiously. "You're sure you *should* be home, Jonnie?"

"Darn right, I'm sure. If I'd stayed another day in that place, I'd have gone crazy. Oh, they didn't want to let me out. But I'd had enough. Old Doc Massie knows as much as the whole bunch of them, specialists included. He'll get me fit. I told them so, too."

"What is wrong with him?" Beverly asked their family doctor, the kindly man who had brought all her children into the world. "He seems to have got worse instead of better."

"I had a full report from the hospital, Beverly. I'm afraid much of it is Jonnie's own fault. He's a hopeless patient. Men of his temperament often are, you know. About ten days after the operation, he got out of bed and had a haemorrhage. He wouldn't let them tell you, but I think you ought to know what we're up against. Of course, that set him back another few weeks. Instead of learning his lesson, he fretted and champed at the bit, driving everyone silly with his requests to come home. Well, you must have heard him yourself on visiting days. Then finally, he discharged himself. Of course, he isn't right yet. You can't have your insides knocked about like that and not feel the consequences. He'll be OK if he'd only rest, take things easy. You've got to help me, Beverly. Find some occupation for him he can do sitting down; anything to keep him off his feet."

It wasn't easy. Jonnie seemed to a take a childish pleasure in getting up the moment her back was turned. When she caught him out, he would grin and tell her not to fuss. She had to restrain herself from a constant nagging to take care, take care. It became so that he regarded her in the same light as he had the hospital authorities.

"The trouble with you, Bev, is that you enjoy keeping me chained to the apron strings. I suppose so long as I can't get out of the house, you feel you can trust me!"

"Jonnie!" Such a thought had not crossed her mind. Deep down, she did not think Jonnie meant it. There were many other hurtful things he said which she did not think he meant. But they lay in the air between them.

He was irritable with the children, too, shouting at them to keep quiet because his head hurt; the next minute telling them not to look like a bunch of stuffed sheep and to wake up and *do* something. They didn't know where they were with him and it became Beverly's especial task to try and protect them from their father's bad moods.

178

She felt desperately alone and over-burdened. Sue came in when she could but there was another baby on the way and Beverly did not feel she could worry the girl with her problems. Allan was still at the school, but he had not come to see them since Christmas. Knowing why, Beverly could not turn to him for the comfort, advice, friendship she knew would be hers for the asking.

But for Jonnie's "good" days, she felt she might have been unable to bear it. But there were days when he was the old Jonnie, affectionate, grateful, understanding, apologetic. Then she would come close to loving him again. Pity for him was always uppermost in her feelings for him. He was often in pain and the days went by without any visible signs of his making any progress. Jonnie could never be patient and she knew how hard it was for him to sit still, day after day, week after week.

Mr Barkington had been extremely kind, keeping Jonnie on full pay so that they should not have any financial worries to add to their difficulties. Once he came to see Jonnie, making a special trip down from town. Jonnie had been surly and, afterwards, at his worst.

"Just wanted to make sure I wasn't faking!" he sneered at Beverly. "Don't give me that 'How kind of him!' any more. I know his sort."

Because he was so restless in bed at night, Beverly had moved their double bed into the spare room and replaced it with twin beds. It had, in fact, been Jonnie's suggestion. But he seemed to have forgotten that. One night when neither was asleep, he said:

"Don't think I don't know why you won't share my bed any more. It isn't because of Elinor . . . oh no! It's because you're in love with Forbes!"

"Jonnie!" Beverly sat up in bed, holding the sheet against her throat. "That's a lie and you know it. It was your idea, you know it was."

Jonnie ignored this. "Don't think I haven't noticed you mooning about the house with a face as long as a yard. You're thinking about him all the time, aren't you?"

"No!" The denial rose swiftly to her lips. "If I have been looking unhappy, it is only because I've been so worried about you. You're my husband, Jonnie. I want you to get well, to be fit and happy again."

"If I only knew what was wrong!" Jonnie burst out, suddenly despairing and wretched.

In a moment, Beverly was out of her own bed, sitting on the edge of Jonnie's, stroking the hair from his forehead. Appalled, she felt his shoulders shaking and knew that he was crying.

"Darling, don't, don't!" she begged. "You're going to be all right. Dr Massie said you could begin to walk around a bit next week. Be patient, darling. I know it isn't easy, but you're getting better. He promised me you were."

"It's been three months, Bev . . . a quarter of a year." Suddenly his arms were round her and she felt his cheek, wet against her own.

"You've been so wonderful to me. I wish I didn't hate myself so much. No, don't shake your head. Don't you think I've had a lot of time to think things over? Day after day I've had hours and hours to think about the mess I've made of your life and mine. Do you think Elinor would have cared for me the way you have? Nursed me, put up with my rotten temper and grumbling? No, she'd have left me to get on with it. No man ever had a better wife, Bev. I know that now."

Those few moments Beverly clung to long afterwards. They made it all worth while, the hurt, the humiliation, the loneliness, the bitterness, the tiredness. She was glad at last with her whole heart that she hadn't divorced him. Jonnie needed her and, for as long as he wanted her, she was his wife.

"Back to work next week," Jonnie said cheerfully as he walked through the french windows into the garden and stood for a moment, watching Phil bowl to Nicky at the far end of the lawn. Summer had come and there were delphiniums, lupins, pinks in full bloom all along the border. The birds were singing their usual mad chorus and there was real warmth in the sun for the first time this year.

"It'll be difficult sitting down at an office desk after so long," Beverly said, smiling.

"Oh well, do me good really. I'm getting fat and lazy," Jonnie said, his arm round Beverly's shoulders. "Besides, I do owe it to old Barkington, don't I? Six months on full pay. Pretty decent of him."

"Let's sit down for a bit!" Beverly said, pointing to the iron bench beneath the copper beech. "It's so nice and warm."

Obediently, Jonnie sat down beside her. He was watching the boys.

"Nick shows promise," he said contentedly. "I must give him some practice this summer; make a really good cricketer out of him. And you know, Bev, I've quite changed my opinion of Phil. I used to think he was growing up a bit of a sissy, but this morning, he was up the top of that apple tree like a cat – far higher than Nick went. Where are the girls?"

"Out for a walk with Annette," Beverly said, closing her eyes to the warm sunshine, feeling relaxed and happy.

Suddenly Jonnie bent and kissed her on the mouth – a lover's kiss which brought the colour into Beverly's cheeks.

"Pretty girl!" he said, smiling. "Prettiest and nicest girl in the world. I love you next best to Julia and those fat little scamps. We've been lucky, haven't we, Bev? With our kids, especially."

He leant back, reaching up his arms to stretch them above his head in lazy contentment. Quite suddenly, he gave a little gasp and his arms swung down to clasp his stomach.

"Oh, God!" he whispered. "Something snapped, I'm sure of it. Ring the doc, Bev!"

White-faced, Beverly tore indoors to the telephone. Within five minutes, she was racing back across the lawn, her heart beating with an appalling fear. Jonnie was slumped across the garden seat so that she could not see his face.

Kneeling beside him, she lifted his head and looked into his eyes.

"Jonnie! Jonnie!" Frantically, she slapped his cheek – anything to make him move, look at her properly, tell her where it hurt. Down at the far end of the lawn, the boys played on with their game of cricket, unaware.

"Jonnie!" But she knew then, quite suddenly, that it wasn't any good calling him. He wouldn't answer her, now or ever. He was dead.

"You're out!"

"I'm not!"

"You were. It was l.b.w."

"It wasn't . . . oh, all right. I quite like bowling anyway. I'll soon bowl you out."

"You won't!"

"Bet I will!"

"Beverly! Come, my dear. You must help me to get him indoors before the children notice."

"Doc! Doc, he's dead! Jonnie's dead. Why? Why?"

"Never mind now. Help me to get him in. Do you understand? You must help me get him to bed before Nick and Phil find out."

"Yes, yes, I'll help!" Beverly said.

They carried him to his room and Beverly slumped into the chair beside his bed, holding his hand. Doc was downstairs on the phone. Presently Annette came in with a cup of tea.

"The doctor says you must come down now, Madame."

"No, I must stay with him. He needs me. He's always hated being alone."

Presently there was another voice – Allan's.

"Beverly? Come away, darling. Please."

It was a kind, gentle voice.

"But, Allan, I can't. He needs me."

"No, not any more. Come with me."

"Why?" Beverly asked as she allowed him to lead her away. "I must know, Allan. He was so well, so happy, so pleased to be alive. Why? I have to know why?"

When she woke up from the stiff sleeping draught Dr Massie had given her, Allan was there beside the bed. For a moment, she could not understand what he was doing there or why she was in the spare room. She knew only that she was terribly glad to see him. Then slowly, sickeningly, memory returned. With it came tears of shock, unbelief, grief.

He held her tightly in his arms, rocking her to and fro like a child. He had been appalled at the change in her since he had last seen her at Christmas. She had lost at least a stone in weight and although she was not yet thirty, there were lines round her eyes, grooved into her forehead. These six months had taken their toll. Downstairs, while she slept, the doctor had told him something about her life these last months. Only in the last two weeks had Jonnie begun to behave like a rational human being. Up till then, he had made life pretty much of a hell for Beverly and the children. She'd never complained, but none knew better than Dr Massie what kind of patient Jonnie had been. Beverly was physically as well as mentally completed exhausted.

"I've been expecting a nervous breakdown any day," the doctor said. "How she kept going, I don't know. I'm afraid this shock will just about finish her. Try to make it easy for her when she comes round."

It was Annette, surprisingly, who had told Dr Massie to send for Allan. Returning from her walk, she had taken the news of Jonnie's death with her usual calm acceptance. She answered Dr Massie's questions quietly and told him that she thought Madame might prefer to have her good friend Mr Forbes to assist her in this difficult time.

"Very nice man!" Annette said in her halting English. "Madame tell me very good man, very kind."

"Yes, of course. He's the schoolmaster who teaches Nick and Phil, doesn't he?" agreed Dr Massie.

When Forbes arrived, the doctor had given him a brief account of what had transpired. "We must send for her mother, of course, but I know she lives in town and it will take a little while before she arrives. Meanwhile, I have a lot to see to. Can you stay with Mr Colt? She can't be left alone."

"Of course I'll stay," Allan said at once. He was deeply shocked by the news. It wasn't as if Jonnie had been ill. Only yesterday Nick had told him his father was returning to work after the weekend. Now he was dead.

"Allan, what can have happened? It's unbelievable. He was telling me how fond of us all he was, and then, suddenly, he gasped and by the time I came back from the telephone he was dead."

"We don't know why, Beverly. But they'll find out. Try to be happy about the way he went, suddenly, and when, as you say, he was so happy. That's a good way to die if die you must. He couldn't have suffered or known what was happening."

But he knew his words were of little comfort in this hour of shock and horror. He let her cry, holding her in his arms, feeling the deepest love and tenderness for her, thanking God that *he* had been called in to help when she most needed him.

Within an hour, she was asleep once more and he went quickly downstairs to telephone Beverly's mother. Having done this, he went into the sitting-room where Annette was reading a story to the children as if this was a quite ordinary day. They would have to be told soon. Jonnie's body would be taken to the hospital for a post mortem; the ambulance would call; the phone would be ringing. Already they had sensed something had happened for the boys jumped up and ran to him as he stood in the doorway.

"Where's Mum?" Nick asked. "Isn't she well?"

"Is something the matter with Daddy again?" Phil asked. "Why was Dr Massie here?"

Perhaps it would be best to wait and let Beverly's mother tell them, yet somehow he felt that he might be able to do it better, less emotionally.

He sat down and, taking Julia on his lap, he said, "I'm going to tell you a story."

"Oh good!" said Nick, curling up at Allan's feet. "Indians?"

"No! It's about a king and queen and their five children."

"Go on and begin!" ordered Julia from the safe circle of Allan's arms.

"Well, this king and queen lived very happily. They had five children, two princes and three princesses. They loved their children very much. One day, the king became ill. Of course, the queen was very worried about him because she loved him very much and she knew the king hated being ill. She nursed him herself and the five children were as good as they could possibly be to make things easier for the household."

"But the king got better, didn't he?" Nick broke in, somehow sensing something familiar about this tale although he could not recall Allan having told it before.

"Yes, Nick. The king got better and the queen and her children were very glad. But although the king looked better and felt better and everyone *thought* he was quite well, deep down inside he wasn't.

One day, he went into the garden with the queen and they sat down on a seat in the sunshine. The king was very happy, because he didn't know he wasn't really well after all. He could see the two little princes playing together and he thought proudly how big they had grown and what fine sensible boys they were. Then he fell asleep. When the queen tried to wake the king, she found she could not do so. She called the doctor and he told her that the king would never wake up again. You see, he'd gone to live in another Kingdom where people are always well and always happy, and he liked it so much, he decided to stay."

"But what about the queen and the five children?" Phil asked in a small querulous voice.

"Well, of course they were very sad. But the queen had the two brave princes and the oldest of the princesses to comfort her. The princes said they would take care of her and fight all her enemies. So she was not quite alone. And the five children had the beautiful queen to love them and take care of them, so they were not alone either. And as they all knew that the king would be very very happy in this new Kingdom, they tried not to be sad because he had gone away."

"I don't think I like that story!" Julia said, holding tight to Allan's neck with two chubby arms. "It's sad."

"I don't like you!" Nick said suddenly. "I think you're silly!" He turned, scowling, and ran out of the room.

Phil looked at Allan apprehensively. "Aren't you going to punish him, Mr Forbes, for being rude?"

"No!" said Allan. "You see, he didn't mean to be rude. He wanted to hurt me because I had had to hurt him. Nick guessed who the king and the queen really were."

"Well, I guessed *that*!" said Phil uneasily. "It's Mummy and Daddy. But it isn't true, is it? I mean, Daddy's not really gone away."

"Yes, yes, he has!" Allan said very gently.

"*You're* not going, too, are you?" Phil said, suddenly afraid.

"No, I'm not going, Phil. I'll be here whenever you or Nick or Julia or Mummy need me."

"Oh well, that's all right then," Phil said comforted.

"Do you love me, Uncle Allan?" Julia asked, half asleep.

"Yes!" said Allan. "I do."

"Will you marry me when I'm big enough?"

"No! You're a princess and you have to marry a nice young prince."

"All right!" agreed Julia. "But you've got to be the king."

"I hope so!" Allan barely breathed the words as he laid his cheek against the child's soft hair. "I hope so, Julia, with all my heart."